Chrissa Mills lives in No[...] the mother of three son[...] writer, and now she has started the stories are tumbling onto the page! *Relative Strangers* is her third novel. *Bonded* and *Love & Lies* are also published by Piatkus.

Relative Strangers

Chrissa Mills

PIATKUS

For more information on other books published by Piatkus,
visit our website at www.piatkus.co.uk

First published in Great Britain in 1999 by
Judy Piatkus (Publishers) Ltd
5 Windmill Street
London W1P 1HF
email: info@piatkus.co.uk

This edition published 2000

The moral right of the author has been asserted

A catalogue record for this book is available from the British Library

ISBN 0 7499 3192 9

Set in Times by
Phoenix Photosetting, Chatham, Kent

Printed and bound in Great Britain by
Mackays of Chatham plc, Chatham, Kent

For my mother
and to the
loving memory of my father

Part One

Chapter One

'Lily!' Sarah Hamilton called to her daughter across the crowded hall.

Her voice carried, even though Bill Hamilton's seventieth birthday party was in full swing and the hall throbbed with loud music. Tired from all her exertions, Sarah noticed her father-in-law trying to attract the attention of his granddaughter. Lily turned instantly, the excitement on her face plain for all to see. She pushed a long strand of reddish-brown hair away from her blue-green eyes and moved swiftly towards her mother.

'*Grandpa!*' Sarah indicated, pointing towards Bill who winced and shifted into a more comfortable standing position then beckoned Lily to him with outstretched hand, smiling at her fondly.

'Now, young lady, how would you like to earn yourself a few bob?' Lily giggled at the word *bob* and he lovingly tapped her on the nose. 'What with this painful hip o' mine, I'd like you to look after me tonight.' He looked across at Daisy, Lily's elder sister, diligently wrapping paper napkins around knives and forks then placing them in a tidy pile. 'It's no good me asking Daisy, she's too slow to catch a cold. But you, swecd'eart, can make me have a bloody good time.'

Lily's eyes widened. 'You don't need to pay me, Grandpa. Not on your birthday.' He grunted and put his arm gratefully around her, squeezing her, but the flimsy camisole top and brand new wrap-around skirt she wore unnerved him and he loosened his grip. Bill was only too aware of this ravishing young creature's curves. He felt something like an ache in his chest as he stifled his

3

overly protective instincts. It wouldn't do to tell Lily she looked too grown-up so instead he cupped her face in his hand. 'Now, young lady, the other thing is – don't you go doin' anything I wouldn't tonight, d'you hear?'

Her answering giggle changed into an intriguingly adult laugh. 'But that gives me plenty of scope!'

On impulse he smacked her bottom. 'Don't you be s'cheeky.' And when she slipped away from his grasp, stretching forward to pat a pink balloon with **70** stamped on it, he tutted, 'Pink balloons indeed. Whose bloody silly idea was that?'

Lily patted another pink balloon to Billy Hamilton, Jnr, eight-year-old grandson of Bill's brother Phil, and scolded her grandpa. 'Don't be sexist! This is the nineties and you're not allowed to be sexist.'

Bill frowned as Billy and Lily carried on patting balloons in front of him. 'Sexist! What's that when it's at 'ome?' He didn't wait for her reply. 'An' stop that silly patting, will you, and fetch me another o' these.' He snatched up his glass from the table and pushed it into Lily's hand.

'Whisky with a splash?'

'Hmm, but no splash. Not tonight. It's m'birthday.' He groaned stagily. 'Although maybe they should shoot us old buggers when we get to seventy. Mind you, it's not everyone who 'as a birthday party in the bloody Hayward Theatre, now is it?'

Bill felt a hand on his shoulder as Tom Hamilton remonstrated, 'What's all this then, Dad? Bloody this, bloody that? The place is filling up. Shouldn't you be minding your p's and q's? You're not in the fish 'n' chip shop now, y'know.'

Bill stared at his son, reminded of how sometimes he wasn't too keen on him. He loved him all right, as a son, but much preferred Stephen, Lily and Daisy's father. 'Since when have you cared about me minding my p's and q's?' A cunning look crossed his face. 'Unless this is about that son of yours *honouring* us with his presence?'

Tom withdrew his hand from his father's shoulder and shook his head. 'S'got nothing to do with it! I don't give a bloody monkey's about Guy.'

Bill poked Tom. 'You just said bloody. You did!' He laughed, turning back to watch Lily at the crowded bar. (And if she leaned any further across it, she'd be showing her knickers.) Reluctantly

4

he faced his son again. 'He is still comin' then?' Bill had a tender regard for his adopted grandson, even if he hadn't seen him in years.

Tom raised one eyebrow. 'Does it matter?'

Bill grimaced and Tom smiled, remembering it was the old man's birthday. Better be kind. 'Course he is. Wouldn't miss it. Said so to 'is mum this afternoon.'

Genuine relief washed over Bill. He wanted everyone to be there tonight. It was very important to him. He didn't expect to have another birthday party in the Hayward Theatre Hall of the Kings School, Ely. And *everyone* definitely included Guy Hamilton, even if he was getting too damned big for his no doubt finest leather shoes.

The very same Guy parked his bronze metallic Jaguar XJS in the Lamb Hotel car park and turned off the ignition. For a good few seconds he stared directly ahead of him.

'Guy?' said Naomi, moving closer and stroking his hair. 'You all right?'

He shuddered and stared at her, noting her cleverly made-up eyes and tousled blonde curls. She was pouting, prettily showing concern, and he stroked one knuckle down her cheek. Then he smiled. 'I'm all right, just not sure I'm up to all this.'

Shifting in her seat, she kissed him, running her tongue across his teeth. He tasted of toothpaste and cigarettes. 'Of course you are. You've got me with you. What more could you want?'

He sighed. 'Have you any idea what my family's like? Apart from my mother that is. You're used to your refined friends, but, I'm warning you, my family's about as different as you can get.'

'So?'

'So you've been warned, that's all.'

Naomi slumped back in her seat. 'Guy, I have met ordinary people before. And if I didn't know you better, I'd think you were one helluva snob!'

He laughed, a throaty sound, and gazed at the girl to whom he'd recently become engaged. With eyes gleaming he said, 'You guessed!'

She put both arms around his neck and kissed him hard. 'If you're so worried, why don't we just give it a miss?' She added seductively, 'We could go someplace and christen your car.' Her hand ran down to his crotch. 'In fact, why don't we do it here? Nobody's around. Have you ever done it in a hotel car park before?'

If only. Guy removed her hand, quickly bringing it to his mouth. 'I have to go to my grandfather's party and, what's more, I have to *enjoy* myself. And so do you. If we don't, they'll all say, "*See*, I told you he was an arrogant sod!"'

Naomi nuzzled closer again, her hands creeping up behind his neck. 'But what does it matter what they think? You're part of my family now and you know Daddy absolutely adores you.'

Daddy Jack Benson. Involuntarily Guy shuddered and pulled away, grabbing his cigarettes from the dashboard. Lighting one up, he savoured the smoke then rubbed his thumb across his forehead. He realised that Naomi didn't understand his dilemma. How could she? Hazily, he rolled the smoke round his tongue and reflected upon his own family as opposed to hers, feeling a moment's shame as he acknowledged his own burning ambition, his newly elevated position at Benson Motors, and that the trappings of Naomi's family appealed to him far more than fish 'n' chips ever had. Maybe he was a snob after all.

They left the car park, crossed the High Street and proceeded down Minster Place, past Ely's magnificent cathedral and into the Gallery where the King's School's ancient buildings jostled for space. Their surroundings were quite wonderful and truly historic; rambling medieval brick buildings with alleyways and arches and mullioned windows peeping out from under multi-levelled eaves. But in the twilight of this May evening Naomi tripped along beside Guy, high heels clicking on the pavement, and glanced neither to right nor left because old buildings simply didn't interest her. Culture played no part in her life. She looked very fetching in a pink linen suit with a short skirt and Guy felt proud of her, knowing full well how she turned heads. He smoked as he walked along, inhaling deeply. He knew the way well enough; Ely was where he'd been born and bred. When he was six his mother Lynda had married Tom Hamilton, and although she'd been relieved to find a husband, especially one with a bit of extra cash in his pocket to lavish on her, it had taken her son a long while to settle into the larger than life Hamilton family.

They turned right through the iron gates leading to the Hayward Theatre Hall. As they approached the double swing doors, Guy stamped out his cigarette and ran a finger round the neck of his charcoal-grey shirt. He straightened his Italian designer jacket and turned towards Naomi.

'Okay?'

She grinned, loving every minute of this. Naomi Benson had never seen the sharp, astute and fabulous-looking Guy Hamilton in a dither before. Even his hands were trembling now. What must this family of his be like? He pushed open the next set of double doors and she knew she was about to find out.

On the stage at the far end of the hall disco lights flashed psyche-delically and loud music belted out. The overhead lighting had been dimmed and as Guy and Naomi entered the first thing they noticed was a wealth of pink balloons hanging from the rafters and adorning every conceivable nook and cranny. On the ten or so trestle tables set back from the wood-strip floor, left free for dancing, candles created a warm glow. Which was about as subtle as it got.

To Guy's left two enormous trestle tables were laden with sliced baked ham, quiches, potato and assorted salads, and hunks of crusty bread. Folk were jostling each other in order to heap their paper plates and immediately Guy was reminded of his mother's wedding day. The whole scene had overawed him then. Instinctively he reached into his pocket for his cigarettes. He looked at Naomi's smiling face and noticed her foot tapping to the music. Guy was pleasantly surprised. Lighting his cigarette, he allowed his eyes to roam nervously round the room.

Although nobody appeared to have noticed his arrival, Guy saw his grandfather straight away, sitting with his father and Uncle Stephen, knocking back the whisky and looking red-faced. It was a very lively scene with outbursts of raucous laughter, womanly squeals of delight, and people knocking back beer and spirits as fast as they could because they were free. In fact they were all having a good time though Guy didn't see it that way. He turned to his fiancée who, in her sleek clothes, was definitely attracting attention, particularly from the males. At least Naomi had risen to the occasion. 'Would you like a drink?' he asked.

'Yes, please. A glass of dry white would be nice.'

His eyes scanned the bar. 'You'll be lucky. My family aren't into wine. It's beer or spirits?'

Naomi shrugged. 'Vodka then, please. With some ice and lime.'

Guy left her and walked over to the bar, which was jammed. He lowered his head, thankful for the subdued lighting, and waited his turn. It seemed to go on forever until he felt a pair of arms creeping round his waist. He turned and looked into the warm brown eyes of the woman he adored. Lynda, his mother, hugged him to her. 'It's great to see you, Mum,' he said lovingly.

She shifted back. 'Guy, you're so tall! I swear you've grown another couple of inches.'

'Not true. I stopped growing at seventeen.' He was more than happy with his height of just below six foot.

Lynda savoured her son's presence. He looked so smart and so handsome, those almond-shaped brown eyes enhancing his boyish looks. In a flash she was reminded of his natural father, who'd disappeared from her life at the mention of parenthood. Until then she'd thought him gorgeous too. She pulled on a lock of Guy's fair hair. 'What's all this then? You look like a girl, it's so long.'

He shook his head. 'It's fine, I like it like this.' He caught a glimpse of Naomi out of the corner of his eye, being chatted up by two burly-looking men and loving every minute of it. Her eyes danced from one man to the other. At least she was enjoying herself.

Lynda caught his arm. 'Thanks for coming, darling. It means a lot to your grandpa.'

Surprised, Guy looked across the room at the old man. 'Does it?'

Lynda nudged him. 'You know it does. Just because you never saw eye to eye about education and things, doesn't mean he's not proud of you. He asked me about five times what time you were coming.'

Guy almost smiled. 'Really?'

Lynda stood back. 'Yes, really.' She looked around her. 'Now, where's that wonderful girlfriend of yours? Whoops!' Her hand went to her mouth. '*Fiancée*, I mean. Did you bring her?'

Realising his turn at the bar had finally arrived, Guy ordered a beer and a large vodka and lime. Then, with a drink in either hand, he led his mother towards Naomi. His chest swelled with pride as they drew near her. She looked so lovely when she laughed, and she was certainly laughing tonight.

'Naomi,' Guy interrupted her, 'I'd like you to meet my mother.' He watched as his fiancée switched from flirting to the more serious business of meeting her future in-law. 'Mum, this is Naomi,' he added.

The two burly men nodded in Lynda's direction and immediately disappeared into the background. Guy noticed Naomi's eyes following them. Then she stepped forward and hugged his mother. 'It's nice to meet you. Guy's told me so much about you.'

'It's nice to meet you too, Naomi, and good of you to come. I know he's not too keen on these Hamilton parties.'

Naomi rolled her eyes. 'Oh, I know, he hasn't stopped going on about it. Still, never mind, he's here now.'

Lynda's eyes flashed to Guy who glared at Naomi. 'You know I'd never let you down, Mum.'

'Yes, I do. Now how about saying hallo to the birthday boy?' She didn't wait, just manoeuvred them through the merrymaking towards her husband and Bill. Guy handed Naomi her vodka and gave her a disapproving grimace. She looked back at him blankly as they followed Lynda.

Bill Hamilton's ruddy face puckered into a welcoming smile at the sight of Guy. His birthday party was now complete. All the people he really cared about had arrived. 'Well, well, well,' he chuntered, 'the wanderer returns! Come on, boy, sit down. Let's take a good look at you.'

Guy motioned to Naomi to take a seat opposite his grandfather. 'This is Naomi, Grandpa. Mum's probably told you all about her.'

With a nod, Bill peered across the table, taking careful note of Guy's choice of bride. He narrowed his eyes and came straight to the point. 'So you're the one with a rich daddy, are you?'

Guy gritted his teeth, as did Lynda. Naomi, however, loved it. She giggled and stretched her hand across the table. Bill, being amiable, grabbed it in his own. 'Is that what he's told you?'

'No, not Guy. Lynda mentioned it. Benson Motors, eh? So do you work there as well?'

Fleetingly Naomi looked at Guy. 'Some of the time, when I have to.'

Guy gulped back some beer and drew on his cigarette.

'Naomi's what you might call part-time.' He blew out the smoke. '*Very* part-time.'

Tom glared at him across the table. 'I'd have thought you'd have given that up by now? It's a disgusting habit and a complete waste of money.'

Guy inhaled again and stared at his father. 'I suppose that means you have?'

'Last year. Not that you'd know anything about that.'

'Tom,' soothed Lynda, 'you know he's busy with his job and everything.'

Her husband scoffed, 'It's only Cambridge. Not the other side of the bloody planet!'

'Well, why don't you visit *me* then?'

Tom bent across the table. 'If you can't be bothered to come here, why should I be bothered to go there?'

'Oh, for goodness' sake,' moaned Lynda, grabbing her husband's hand. 'Look, people are dancing. Come and have a dance with me, please?'

Tom hesitated for a second and then did as he was asked, much to Guy's relief.

'So all that education and university stuff paid off, did it?' asked Bill.

Guy nodded. 'Seems like it.'

'And what about you, young lady. 'Ave you got a university degree?'

Naomi hooted with laughter. ''Fraid not.' She also looked at the dancers on the floor. 'Shall we dance, Guy?'

'In a minute.'

'Well, do you mind if I do?'

He looked towards the floor where a handful of people were boldly displaying their dancing skills. 'No, go ahead.'

In a flash she was out of her seat and weaving her way on to the floor. Guy watched and within seconds she was joined by the same two burly admirers. He supposed he ought to be grateful and turned his attention back to the grandfather. 'You're looking well.'

Bill leaned back in his seat and downed the rest of his whisky. 'Appearances can be deceptive. Some days I feel proper poorly. It's m' leg, y'see. Need a new hip. Bin promised one for next year sometime, but you know what these hospital lists are like.'

'So you're not working anymore?'

'No. Retired a good while back. No point. Your dad and Stephen run the fish bar and the kids help out. Don't need me anymore.'

Guy picked up his grandfather's empty whisky glass. 'Would you like another drink?'

Bill craned his neck. 'Yes, but there's no need for you to get it. I'm supposed to 'ave my helper tonight.'

'Your helper?'

'Yes, Lily. Now where is the girl?'

Guy's eyes swept the room. 'Don't suppose I'd even recognise her or Daisy anymore.'

The old man snorted. 'Oh, you'd recognise Lily right enough.' He laughed, his face lighting up as he pointed to the middle of the dance floor. 'There she is, bless 'er. Did you ever see anythin' so pretty in all your life?'

Guy's eyes followed his grandfather's and rested on Lily. She was dancing with a small boy. Unbeknown to Guy it was Billy who hadn't even been born when he'd left home. At first Lily had her back to Guy. He recognised her by her distinctive glossy hair but she held his attention with her long shapely legs and the way she was dancing. Her timing was good, and her ingenuous manner and obvious pleasure in amusing her young friend appealing. Every now and again she gave a little jump and sashayed to the floor. Her small friend followed suit, laughing with delight. It was all very childlike and Guy was about to look away when, with one of her little jumps, she turned. At the same time the disco's flashing lights caught her face. From across the room it was as though her eyes met his and Guy was captivated. But it was more than that. Much more. She actually took his breath away. *'Is that Lily?'* he asked in a soft voice.

Bill laughed. 'See, I told you she was the prettiest thing.' He saw the astonishment on his grandson's face. 'She's quite took you by surprise, 'asn't she? Almost sixteen now, y'know. Gonna break some hearts, that one, I can tell you.'

Yes, mine, thought Guy. 'How old did you say?'

'Sixteen in June.' Bill straightened himself. 'About to start her A-levels next term. Just like you, a real bright kid.'

Guy tore his eyes away and looked at his grandfather, realising Lily was nearly ten years younger than him. 'And you don't mind?'

11

'No. Learned me lesson with you. Seems only Daisy'll be around to help in the business.'

Poor Daisy, thought Guy, compelled once more to look at Lily. But she'd gone. He twisted in his seat to see where.

'It's all right, she'll be here directly. She's a good girl.' It was as if the old man could read his mind.

Guy coughed in embarrassment. 'And Daisy? How's she?'

Bill shrugged. 'Well, as you know, she's never gonna be any great shakes, 'er being a sandwich short of a picnic an' all that, but she don't do s'bad.' He leaned closer to Guy. 'It's funny – give her some money to add up and she does it like lightnin'. We don't 'ave no trouble in the shop or on the vans. No one can put one over on Daisy.'

'Phew!' Naomi grabbed Guy's shoulders from behind as she came back to her seat. 'It's no good, I need a drink.'

He looked at her flushed face as she downed the rest of her vodka and lime. 'Who were your friends?'

Bill answered for her. 'Them's Shane and Pete. Good lads. They do the vans.'

Tom and Lynda also returned to the table, and Guy stood up in order to let his mother sit down.

'No, it's all right, love. I'll sit next to your dad.' She moved further down the trestle table to where Tom had chosen to sit. Guy's eyes followed her.

It was as he sat down again that he breathed in the sweet scent of the same red-brown hair he'd seen on the dance-floor. Now it tumbled over his grandfather's shoulder as Lily wrapped both arms around the old man's neck and kissed his cheek. He heard her whisper, 'Can I get you anything, Grandpa?'

The old man chuckled, not least because of the way Guy sat watching them. He felt proud and stroked Lily's hair before pointing to his glass. 'A refill wouldn't go amiss, and for that young lady over there. And how about some food for your cousin?'

Lily raised herself and smiled at Guy, her blue-green eyes focusing on his in an extraordinarily intent way. He said nothing, just gazed at her. Oblivious of his interest, Naomi came to the rescue. 'Yes, I'd love another vodka and lime, and some food. *I'm starving.*'

Bill laughed. 'I like a girl who likes 'er food. Lily here likes 'er food, don't you, sweed'eart?'

She nodded but didn't reply. She was thrown by Guy; struck by his good looks, but much too inexperienced in the art of flirting to let him know it. She was also in the throes of a mad crush on one of her teachers at school who was about as different from Guy as you could get.

He got to his feet. 'I'll help. You can't possibly look after us all.'

His grandfather's hand hit the table loudly. 'You sit down! This is my treat and we'll be doing the honours. Daisy's over there, she can 'elp, and Sarah's over by the food, she'll see you all right. Now . . .' Bill looked up at Lily. 'You fetch me another whisky and whatever Naomi wants, then bring Daisy over 'ere, all right?'

Lily nodded and reached over for Naomi's glass. 'Vodka and lime,' she said without looking up. Instead she was seeking out Shane and Pete on the other side of the room.

Guy watched Lily walk over to the bar. His eyes never left her until he felt the pressure of his grandfather's hand on his arm. 'Y'know, I always guessed you'd end up in motors. Right from the start you was car crazy. D'you remember that go-kart your dad bought you? Never seen anythin' like it in my life. Scared the bloody daylights outa me, I can tell you! Thought you was gonna break your scrawny neck, I did. Once you got on that thing there was no bloody stopping you.'

'It's still there,' piped up Tom with an unexpected smile. 'Still in pristine condition.' He nodded in Naomi's direction although she wasn't taking any notice. 'Keeping it nice for the grand-children we are.' Lynda nudged him but laughed.

Guy's eyes widened. 'That was my first real taste of speed. After that I was hooked!'

'You never fancied being a racin' driver then?' asked the old man.

'No. I like cars *per se*, not just race cars.' His face came alive as he started to elaborate. 'Sleazy bumpers, shrewd lines, distinctive alloys, slithering for the first time on to the soft leather of a spanking new car . . .' He suddenly realised he'd got an attentive audience, except for Naomi. He felt elated and continued. 'Turning the key for the first time and feeling her purr into action. Then rolling along the road, faster and faster, testing out the gadgets – *that's* my baby.'

'So, what sort of *baby* are you driving now?' asked his father.

13

'A Jag!' Naomi piped up. 'Thanks to Daddy. XJS – bronze metallic. Really cool.'

Guy suddenly felt irritated and looked over at his parents. 'And, as you've probably guessed, it's not exactly mine.'

'But near enough, if you behave yourself,' put in Tom sardonically.

Naomi threaded her hand through the crook of Guy's arm. 'And he always does that, don't you?'

Guy felt uncomfortable and drained the rest of his beer. He scraped back his chair and stood up. 'I think it's time I got myself a refill and said hallo to Aunt Sarah and Uncle Stephen.' Abruptly he left the table with everyone's eyes on him.

'Don't change,' chuckled Bill. 'Always was a prickly little bugger.'

'Not so little now,' said Lynda.

'You can say that again,' hooted Naomi, who was out of her seat in seconds and heading back on to the dance-floor and her beefy male admirers.

Bill Hamilton watched her go and thought, You're making a big mistake there, Guy, m'boy, for all your worldly ways and quick brain. If you marry that one, you'll be making one hell of a big mistake.

As part of his grandfatherly duties, albeit adoptive, he'd have to think of some way of telling his only grandson that before the night was out. He'd make sure of it. Struggling to turn in his seat, Bill saw Guy standing next to Lily at the bar. He also noticed his expression as he spoke to her. A huge smile slid over the old man's face before he turned away and sighed. Now there was a thing. Funny how beauty can override everything, and Lily had plenty of that. Wincing at the pain in his hip, Bill shifted again and looked down the table at Tom.

'And it wouldn't hurt for you to be a bit more friendly to that son o'yours, specially as you 'aven't seen him in ages.'

'Dad!' moaned Lynda, not wishing for a confrontation.

Tom stood up, holding out his hand. 'Come on, Lynda. Let's dance.'

She took her husband's hand and, smiling apologetically at Bill, made her way once more on to the dance-floor.

'Miserable buggers,' hissed Bill, shaking his head, not at all pleased to be left entirely on his own. 'Not allowed to say anythin'

14

these days. No good to man nor beast, me. *Nobody* 'cept Lily cares tuppence 'bout me.'

He looked around the hall at all his so-called friends and relatives, eating and drinking at his expense. Apart from a brief hallo when they'd arrived, hardly any of them had given him a second glance. Sadly he realised he was old. Old and unattractive and probably boring as well. Bill's mouth drooped as he comforted himself with thoughts of his dead wife. Now if she'd been here things would have been very different. He clenched his fists and wondered for the umpteenth time why she had to go and die like that, way before her time? Until then she'd barely left his side, not for a second. And she'd been a beauty, just like her namesake Lily whom she'd never seen.

Bill sucked in his breath, anxious for his refill of whisky. He muttered aloud, 'Might as well be kicking up the bloody daisies for all the use I am nowadays.' Then folded his arms, blew out his cheeks and, scowling, sank further back into his seat.

Chapter Two

Sarah and Stephen Hamilton's red-brick bungalow had been extended three times. Snugly situated behind Ely's golf course, it was a mere ten-minute walk from the busy town centre where Hamilton's Fish/Takeaway Bar thrived, especially on Thursday which was market day. Ely, a comfortable thirty-minute car journey from the university town of Cambridge and an equally easy distance from Newmarket's racecourses, was originally called the Isle of Ely because of its wealth of surrounding water, mainly the River Ouse. It was considered the heart of the Fens: its capital. Much ancient history had taken place within its quaint confines.

The Hamiltons had lived in either Soham, a nearby village, or Ely for many years. In the early fifties, Bill and his brother Phil, sons of a market stall holder, invested their hard-earned cash in a fish and chip shop. They worked side by side in it quite happily for years, both marrying and having children. They even bought a van which every day travelled miles out into the Fens selling exemplary fish and chips. Folk cut off in the uncompromisingly flat and watery area organised their family's weekly meals round Hamilton's Travelling Fish Bar, and to this day many still did. Eventually, because of ill health, Phil tired of the business and Bill, his own two sons rapidly growing up and able to help, offered his brother a sizeable sum for his share. This was readily accepted. After that Bill bought another van, then another, and extended the shop into a mini-restaurant. As times changed he introduced more lines, like pies, chicken and sausages, eventually pizzas and curry.

The red-brick bungalow was a happy home whose final extension had allowed Bill to move in. He had his own separate kitchen, bathroom, bedroom and mini-sitting room, but spent most of his time with the rest of the family. Sarah, who worked on Thursdays and Saturdays at the fish bar, was a meticulous housewife, always on the go, and consequently the whole place gleamed from regular assaults with spray polish and elbow grease. Even the front door was kept scrupulously clean.

From an early age Lily and Daisy had been taught to remove their shoes on entering and to clear up every speck of mess they made while inside. As she grew Lily found this hard to take, especially when she brought friends home, but because of her sunny nature she never complained. Daisy, on the other hand, slow at most things was probably a better and more organised person for her mother's constant nagging about tidiness, except that now she felt positively ill at ease in any sort of disarray. Bill, who'd been used to a far more happy-go-lucky attitude in the past, just went along with everything. He admired and respected his daughter-in-law far too much to give his point of view (which was unusual for Bill Hamilton) and was grateful she'd allowed him to share their home.

As the summer gave way to early autumn, Lily excitedly prepared to go back to school. She'd worked continuously for her parents during the holiday and now looked forward to Business Studies, French and Spanish, *and Mr Greene*, with only a modest amount of Saturday work in Hamilton's Fish Bar. She sat in her bedroom with Daisy and Cassie. Cassie Milbank was Lily's best friend and had already left school. She was fourteen months older and every day caught the train into Cambridge where she worked as a trainee florist.

Lily applied mauve eye-shadow and purple liner to Daisy's blue-green eyes then stood back, inspecting her handiwork. She licked her thumb and rubbed it gently along her sister's eyelid to remove a smudge.

'How's that, Daise?'

From a sitting position on the bed, Daisy stood up and peered at herself in the full-length gilt mirror. There was a lot of gilt in their home. 'Coo-ool.' She moved even closer to the mirror and stared hard at her own reflection. With make-up on her eyes, she was reminded of Lily. She turned, putting one hand on a well-rounded hip. 'I look like you now.' In fact Daisy did look like Lily, they could easily be identified as sisters, but it was as though Daisy was

17

Sarah and Stephen's first attempt – their trial run – and Lily, with her high cheekbones and perfectly rounded chin, their perfect specimen.

Lily smiled fondly and Cassie's violet eyes dilated at what she considered the impossible. But she liked Daisy. 'Gonna knock 'em dead,' she told her encouragingly.

'You already do, don't you, Daisy?' Lily pointed to the bed again and her sister returned to her former position, sitting down heavily. The bed creaked as she did so and Cassie, lolling against the pillows, curled up, laughing. Lily's sister always amused her.

Daisy watched as Lily searched through her make-up bag for a suitable mascara and lipstick. As she emptied its contents one by one, Daisy laid them carefully on the flat of one hand. 'Mustn't be untidy,' she muttered beneath her breath.

Finding what she wanted, Lily held open the bag for Daisy to put back the items she'd collected. 'Thanks.'

Her sister reached out one hand and zipped up the bag. 'Pays to be tidy,' she repeated.

Lily looked at Cassie who rolled her eyes. Swiftly, Lily looked away. Daisy wasn't retarded, she just laboured certain points. Deep down she was the kindest, most sensitive person imaginable. 'Right, look up,' Lily instructed. Daisy did as she was told and with a steady hand Lily stroked black mascara along her sister's long lashes. Daisy didn't blink, just kept her devoted eyes on Lily so fixedly that when she'd completed her task she dropped a kiss on Daisy's nose. 'Just the lipstick now,' she whispered. Immediately Daisy stretched wide her lips as previously instructed. Using a lip-brush, Lily applied the colour to her sister's mouth.

'Wow.' Cassie enthused.

'Oh, Daisy, you look amazing with make-up on!' Lily agreed.

Daisy shot off the bed and stared at her reflection. Her eyes then wandered over her stocky frame. 'The trouble is, I'm fat.'

'You and me both,' Cassie agreed, smoothing one hand over her own well-covered thigh.

Daisy looked at her sister's best friend. 'No, you're not. Mum said you're just plump.' She looked in the mirror. 'But I'm fat.'

Slightly miffed to hear that Mrs Hamilton had referred to her as plump, Cassie climbed off the bed and stood beside her. Together they stared in the mirror as Lily watched. Then they turned and both said, 'And Lily's perfect.'

Lily looked down at the make-up bag. She didn't consider herself perfect.

'Daisy, are you ready?'

Sarah Hamilton pushed open the bedroom door and stared at her elder daughter. 'Goodness, you look nice.'

'Except that I'm fat.'

Sarah sighed and beckoned to her. 'No, you're not, Daisy. Now come on. If we don't get a move on the film will 'ave started.' She cast Lily a glance. 'Are you sure you don't want to come?'

She shook her head. 'No, Cassie and I'll stay here, if you don't mind.'

Sarah looked fleetingly at Cassie who always made her slightly uneasy. She appeared so worldly in her American way. Then Sarah reminded herself that Lily was sixteen years old now. Not a baby anymore. 'We won't be late. Remember to lock the doors after we've gone, won't you?'

Lily didn't reply, just nodded and squeezed Daisy's arm. She winked at her and Daisy winked back in exaggerated fashion. It was their sisterly show of affection.

Daisy followed her mother out of the bedroom, excited to be going to the Maltings cinema in Ely especially as her father was coming too. Briefly she turned and with a serious expression on her face said, 'You won't forget to lock the doors, will you?'

Lily sighed and waved her hand. 'No, no. Off you go!' Daisy nodded thoughtfully and joined the rest of her family.

'Is your grandpa going with them?' asked Cassie.

''Course he is. He loves the cinema.' Lily beckoned her friend out of the bedroom as her mother, father, sister and grandpa were about to leave. Painfully, Bill Hamilton limped to Lily's side and kissed her cheek. 'Mind what you're up to while we're gone, young lady.'

'Oh, Grandpa, don't you start as well. Anybody would think I was ten, not sixteen.'

Smiling at Cassie, he wagged his finger. 'It's only your safety we're bothered about. Don't you go getting too big for your boots, else you'll regret it.'

Good-naturedly, Lily waved her family off then closed and bolted the front door. She turned, leaning her weight against it. 'Phew! Sometimes I think they'll never let me grow up.'

Cassie pulled a face. 'Could be worse. You could be like me

and have parents who're never there.' Cassie's parents ran a restaurant in Ely. It was an extremely popular place with live piano music and served the best steaks for miles around. Her American father, Mike Milbank, had originally met her mother Vicky while drafted to the USAF base at Lakenheath, not far away.

Lily's brow creased. She shifted forward, grabbing her friend's hand, and asked excitedly, 'Fancy a drink? How about a vodka and lime? My cousin's fiancée was drinking vodka and lime at Grandpa's party. It's really nice.' Lily's eyes widened. 'And so was she. You should have seen her, Cassie. Dressed to kill.'

'Are you allowed?'

Lily giggled. 'No. But that's never stopped us before, has it?'

'But they'll smell it on us.'

'No, they won't. Vodka has no smell. Come on, I'll top the bottle up with water. Nobody'll know.'

Following her friend into the family's cramped but pristine kitchen, Cassie laughed. 'Y'know, Lily, for such a goody two-shoes, you can be incredibly *bad*.'

She pouted. 'I'm not a goody two-shoes. Why'd you say that?'

Cassie leaned against the worktop and watched her friend pour liberal amounts of vodka into tall tumblers then add ice and lime juice. 'You just are.' She poked her friend. 'I've watched you, the dynamics. You're good but sort o' wicked.'

Ignoring all this, Lily handed her friend one of the glasses. 'Are you hungry? We've got some Haagen-Daz.'

'Lily! Didn't I just say, I'm too fat as it is?'

'No, you're not. I'm having some.'

Cassie shook her head and sipped her drink then choked. 'Hell's teeth! How much vodka did you put in this?'

'Lots. You saw me.' Lily put down her glass and moved swiftly to an upright freezer. She opened the door and withdrew a tub of chocolate chip icecream then proceeded to scoop two large spoon-fuls into a glass dish. To the onlooker, every action showed instinctive natural grace. Cassie studied her. Away from her friend, she made an effort to copy her.

'Are you sure you don't want some?' asked Lily.

Gritting her teeth, Cassie was about to say no then hesitated. 'I suppose I could cut down again tomorrow.'

Lily pointed the scoop at her. 'This is temptation and I'm responsible. You won't moan at me afterwards?'

'Yes. Definitely. But I'd still like some icecream.'

Lily laughed and scooped two more dollops into another glass dish. She passed it to her friend and returned the icecream to the freezer. 'Let's go back into my bedroom.'

'Okay.' Cassie followed.

They made themselves comfortable and ate their icecream, chatting away about this and that. As always Lily brought up the subject of her Business Studies teacher. Cassie shook her head in dismay. She'd never liked Adam Greene. In her eyes he was a creep.

'I just don't understand you, Lily. All those lovely young guys at school and you go for a weasel like Mr Greene? What on earth do you see in him?'

Immediately, Lily flushed. 'He's not a weasel. How can you say that?'

Cassie stared at her friend, realising that somehow or other Adam Greene had managed to crawl beneath her skin. Unfortunately, she'd seen it all before. Another girl in Cassie's final year (in fact her only year at an English school) had fallen for his unlikely charms and ended up thoroughly miserable. 'He's a shit. And don't forget he's got a wife and two children.'

Lily's eyes flared. 'I know that. But he's *not* a shit. He's helped me so much. I got an A in Business Studies because of him. But you needn't worry, I'm not going to have an affair with him or anything.'

Cassie weighed up her friend's defensive remark. 'I never thought you were. I mean, he could lose his job over something like that.'

Her eyes sweeping downwards, Lily swallowed the last of her icecream, put down the dish and picked up her vodka. She sipped it. 'Love's weird, isn't it?'

'What d'you mean?'

She shrugged. 'Well, one minute you feel perfectly normal when you're with someone, and the next they look at you in a particular way, or perhaps touch you, and before you know where you are, you're hooked.'

'That's not love.' Cassie too finished her icecream and picked up her drink. She looked at her friend. 'He's bound to look at you,

21

Lily. Everybody looks at you. But that doesn't explain why he's hooked you?'

Lily sighed. 'It really is just the way he looks at me. It sends shivers down my spine.' She hesitated then as someone from the not too distant past returned to mind. Cousin Guy too had sent shivers down her spine. She shrugged and pushed the thought of him away. Mr Greene was going to be part of her life for the next two years and surely a little flirtation couldn't do any harm? It would just make the day-to-day grind of sixth form more bearable and there was no way it could be other than harmless. All the same, she often imagined how she'd feel if he did actually kiss her ... She stole a look at Cassie who was staring back at her. Both girls smiled and Cassie grabbed Lily's hand.

'Don't ever do it, d'you hear?'

'Do what?'

'*It!* You know what I mean. *It*, with *stupid* Mr Greene.'

'Do you really think I would?'

Cassie squeezed her friend's hand. 'Sometimes, Lily, you can be so *wonderfully* wicked and certain people might take advantage of that.'

She laughed at her friend and reached forward to hug her. This was the side of Cassie she could never explain about to her mother, the caring side. Sarah Hamilton only saw the slick, knowing side.

'So, when's school start?'

A shiver of delight ran through Lily. 'Two days' time.'

'Well, let's just hope someone else takes his fancy this term, shall we? Then perhaps he'll leave you alone to get on with your work.'

Lily jumped up and grabbed her friend's glass. 'Refill?'

'Lily! I haven't finished this one yet!' She looked at her friend's empty glass. 'You'll be drunk.'

Lily considered this and realised that she already was half-drunk. 'Coffee then?'

Cassie laughed and stood up beside her friend. 'Yeah, coffee would be great.'

Together they left the bedroom for the kitchen and the subject of Adam Greene was temporarily dropped.

Chapter Three

The showroom and forecourt of Benson Motors, off the Hills Road in Cambridge, was not a place for the less well-heeled motorist to wander around. He or she could glance in its direction if they desired but to be taken seriously at this particular garage they needed either a large bank balance or a healthy salary. All types of Jaguars, Range-Rovers, an Aston Martin or two, and even the odd Rolls-Royce adorned the showroom, albeit fleetingly, and it seemed a ridiculous fact that many customers were prepared to wait months and months for a particular vehicle. It was in fact considered *de rigueur* in certain circles to be on Benson Motors' waiting list.

It went without saying that the Hills Road garage was Jack Benson's absolute pride and joy. His other two rather less prestigious outlets on the outskirts of Cambridge didn't have quite the same pull for him. He felt at home at Hills Road. Totally at peace with himself there.

Even though he came from a middle-class family and had been taught at a minor public school, Jack Benson was a self-made man. Any wealth he now had (which was in fact considerable) was due entirely to his own wheeling and dealing and so he felt entirely justified in sneering at lesser mortals who came unstuck along the way. He'd made it, so anybody could if they really tried. Humility was not part of his nature.

When he first laid eyes on Guy Hamilton, he saw something of himself in the young man and liked him instantly. Guy was a go-getter and promised to be a shrewd businessman. The fact that his adored daughter and only child fell madly in love with Guy, and he returned her affections, was the cherry on the cake for

Jack. Hence he had elevated his future son-in-law to a very senior position in Benson Motors within a short space of time and, indeed, Guy proved himself a worthy choice. Only one man held a position above Guy, and that was Keir Doughty, but this fact would soon change. It was Jack's intention to semi-retire and who better to hand over the precious reins of his empire to than his future son-in-law? Jack's mind was made up. He knew Keir was several years older than Guy, more experienced, a loyal employee and quite capable of doing the job. He would most probably be miffed (to put it mildly), but it wasn't as if he was being ousted. On the contrary, his position would remain the same. It was merely that Guy, now his junior, would become his boss. Jack couldn't be bothered to foresee any problems with that.

Guy parked his Jaguar in the staff car park at the rear of the garage and stubbed out his cigarette in the car's freshly cleaned ashtray. He climbed out and locked the door, stuffing the keys in his pocket. He looked smart, extremely so in fact. Guy always looked smart for work. Meticulously clean shirt, trendy silk tie and designer suit, and on his feet polished leather shoes. This wasn't entirely natural to him, more acquired. As a student he'd been typically scruffy, wearing the same Levis for weeks on end, but as soon as he'd graduated and decided on the course of his career, he'd made a conscientious effort to smarten himself up. And gradually he'd grown to like the results. Guy no longer enjoyed being scruffy. Casual, yes; unkempt, no. The only tell-tale sign of his often misspent university years was his longish hair. But even that looked interesting and gave his good looks an edge. His straight fair hair, cleverly cut to just below his chin, was kept scrupulously clean and he was lucky – it was the sort that fell back into position whatever the weather.

He entered the building from the staff entrance and walked towards the office he shared with Keir. They were good friends, having hit it off straight away. They'd even considered sharing a flat together, as Keir was single, but then along came Naomi and she'd put paid to Guy's bachelor days. He'd soon found himself ensconced in her sprawling apartment overlooking the river and his life was never the same again. Nonetheless, Keir gradually became his closest friend and they regularly hit the town together and helped each other out business-wise. There was no rivalry on the showroom floor; each had his own strong points when it came to selling and together they were dynamite.

As Guy passed the enormous flower display in the middle of the showroom he turned to stare at it, not for the first time noting its wilting blooms and in some cases dead flowers. He passed his briefcase from one hand to the other, touched one of the flowers, and immediately the delicate petals collapsed into his hand. Guy hissed through his teeth, closing his hand around the petals. He carried on to his office and after saying good morning to Keir, opened his hand over a waste-bin and watched the bruised petals float into it.

'Who does the flowers in this place?'

Keir looked up from his desk which faced the door. Guy's was tucked away in the corner. 'Some florist. Can't remember which. Kelly'll know. Ask her.'

'I will.' Placing his briefcase on the floor beside his chair, Guy left the office and walked over to reception. Kelly, largish, forty, but spruce and good-looking, beamed at him.

'Morning, Guy.'

He returned her smile. 'Morning.' Then he waved towards the display. 'Who does the flowers, Kelly?'

'Let me think ... Quality Blooms? Yes, I'm sure it is. They do all three showrooms. Have done for years.'

'And how often are they supposed to come?'

'It's funny you should say that, I noticed half the flowers were past their best.'

'Past their best? They're approaching *death*.'

Kelly looked defensive. 'It must be once a week although she asks me to water them between visits. And I do.'

Guy patted her hand. 'It's not your fault, Kelly. Do you know how much we pay them?'

She frowned. 'Can I get back to you on that? I need the file.'

'Yes, of course. When you're ready.' He strode back to his office.

Almost immediately Kelly bustled in after him, carrying a file. 'There's no set pattern as to how often they come, Guy, and their invoices vary according to the time of the year, certain blooms being more difficult to get hold of and all that, but the flowers are definitely supposed to be either completely replaced or weeded out on a Friday morning, so they look nice over the weekend.'

'Did they come last Friday?'

Kelly shrugged. 'They must have done, but I really can't remember seeing them.'

'Well, it's only Tuesday now. By this Friday the flowers'll look clapped out! Get on to them. Explain the situation. Tell them we're not happy about it.'

Kelly's eyes flicked to Keir who just laughed. 'Don't look at me! I'm not into flowers. I only notice the cars in the showroom. Do as the wise man says.'

Guy held out his hand. 'Can I have a quick look at that file, please?'

Kelly handed it over. 'It doesn't make very interesting reading.'

A smile crept round Guy's mouth. 'What we actually pay them probably does.'

Kelly wandered off and he propped himself against his desk and scanned the file. He whistled. 'You ought to look at this, Keir. Considering we're only just into September, Quality Blooms' costs have been steadily rising over the whole of the summer. In fact, for the last three years. This is ridiculous. You could run a Range Rover on what we pay them.'

Keir held out his hand for the file. Guy passed it to him. His friend glanced idly at it before saying. 'Well, if I were you, I'd tread carefully because if my memory serves me well Quality Blooms is run by friends of Jack's. He might not like you upsetting them.'

'To hell with that! This is supposed to be a top-class showroom. Some friends.'

Momentarily Keir bristled. Then he chuckled. 'Don't say I didn't warn you.'

'No, I won't. And I won't let Quality Blooms treat us like this either.' Guy slid off his desk and went back to the showroom and Kelly. Keir watched him go.

Guy walked round the second-hand Jaguar sports, running his hand along its ice-blue metallic bodywork. His would-be customer watched his movements, just as interested in him as the car itself. She smiled. 'Do you touch all the cars like that?'

Guy turned, staring into the smiling face of Jane Richardson, sports editor of the *Cambridge Chronicle*. 'How's that?'

She shifted towards him and ran her own hand along the

26

bodywork. 'Like this. As though you're making love to it; as though you know your touch is pleasurable to both you and this little monster.' She smiled and drew a packet of cigarettes from her jacket pocket. 'Do you mind if I smoke? Am I allowed?'

'Of course.' Guy declined when she offered him one. He never smoked in the showroom. 'Feel free.' He opened the car door, exposing the lavish cream leather seats and ornate walnut-trimmed facia. He slipped the key into the ignition and turned it, at the same time flicking a switch with his other hand. Immediately the hood began to glide away from the windscreen, upwards and backwards, gradually folding and nestling neatly behind the tiny back seats.

Jane Richardson's eyes twinkled as she watched, continually drawing on her cigarette. 'Wow. Can I sit in it?'

Guy stepped back. 'Please do.'

She slipped gracefully into the driving seat and, with her cigarette still between the first two fingers of her right hand, gripped the leather-trimmed steering wheel. 'Nought to sixty in six minutes, did you say?'

'Seconds. Look, why don't you let me show you? We could take it for a spin, it's quite easy to get out of the showroom.' Guy took the cigarette from Jane's fingers and hastily knocked the ash on to the showroom floor. He returned it within seconds and she gazed at him breathlessly. He smiled down at her. 'Can't mess up the interior, can we?'

Just briefly she was lost for words. 'No, of course not.' She wriggled in her seat. 'But, hey, tell me more about this little monster's engine, will you?'

'V12. Twin cam, fuel injection, 5.3-litre engine. A tiger really. Come for a ride. I can tell you, this monster is as smooth and silent as the night. It creeps up on its closest competitor like silk. Then – *vroom*! Overtakes and is gone within the blink of an eye. It'll make you dizzy with desire.'

Mouth open, Jane gazed into Guy's mischievous eyes, after which she looked at her watch and pouted in disappointment. 'Sadly I haven't the time. But I am very interested. What if I take your card and come back later? Perhaps I could even persuade you to buy me a drink afterwards? I mean, you do want to sell her, don't you?'

Guy smiled. 'If you buy this car, I'll buy you several drinks.'

Jane looked across at the coffee machine installed within the sumptuous lounge area of the showroom. 'Now why do I get the feeling you might be talking about cups of coffee and not something more heady?'

Leaning towards her, Guy murmured, 'I'm definitely talking about something more heady.' Then he caught a glimpse of Naomi across the showroom and his expression changed dramatically.

Jane craned her neck in the same direction, noting Naomi's icy glare. 'I believe that's the boss's daughter. Pity, you're absolutely wasted on her.'

Guy winced then stroked the car door. 'So, you'd like a test drive?'

'Yes. You, me, and this little monster. Can't wait.' Briefly Jane's eyes held his before she started to ease herself out of the seat. Guy watched as she unfurled her body to its full height, deliberately brushing against him. He wasn't sure whether this was for Naomi's benefit or his.

Jane looked him in the eye. 'I'll be back tomorrow then. Around lunchtime. Is that all right?'

He handed her his card. 'Absolutely.'

'See you tomorrow then, *Guy*.' Jane Richardson slung her handbag over her shoulder and walked out of the showroom. Guy turned back to Naomi but she was gone.

Jack Benson's office was at the far end of the showroom; large, airy and well equipped with easy chairs, sofa and a coffee table. Guy was summoned there after lunch. He hadn't a clue what it was about. Jack waved him into the seat opposite his enormous desk. Gruffly, he said, 'What's all this about flowers then? I hear you've been complaining about our display?'

Sliding into his seat, Guy suppressed a smile. It hadn't taken Jack long to get to the point. Guy supposed he was going to be ticked off and shrugged. 'I've noticed for some time that the flowers in the showroom aren't very special. Haven't you?'

Jack frowned. 'No. Not particularly.'

'Well, they seem to use a lot of dried flowers in the arrangement which is rather a cop-out, don't you think? And the florist doesn't come every Friday as they're supposed to. Have you seen what you're paying for this poor service, Jack? It's staggering.'

Colour started to rise in his face. Guy knew exactly how to handle his future father-in-law. Any mention of being fleeced and he went ballistic. 'What do you mean? How much do we pay them?'

Guy got out of his seat. 'I'll get the file.'

Jack stalled him. 'No need. Just tell me.'

Guy threw a figure at him, the last invoice figure to be precise. Jack looked very surprised. 'Well, why hasn't this been brought to my attention before? How am I supposed to know? This is Kelly's responsibility, she should have said something before.'

'You can't blame her. She doesn't deal with accounts. Anyway, Quality Blooms have promised us a better service in the future.'

Jack raised himself from his seat and walked over to the glass partition looking out over the showroom. He stared at the flower display. 'But it's still dead.'

'They're coming tomorrow. Apparently they couldn't make it today.'

Seething, Jack turned and shoved his hands in his trouser pockets. 'Well, that's settled then. Get rid of them. Straight away. *Just get rid of them.* And don't pay their last invoice. Whatever you do, make sure we don't pay their last invoice.'

Mildly surprised, Guy stared at his boss. 'Are you sure? I thought they were friends of yours?'

'They are. Or were. But friends don't treat you like that.'

Guy agreed but thought it best not to say so. He got up from his seat. 'I'll see to it then.'

Jack waved to him to sit down again. 'I haven't finished yet. That's not why I wanted to see you, Guy. I've something much more important to discuss with you. Sit down.'

Making himself comfortable again, he wondered what he'd done wrong. Nothing, so far as he could remember, apart from flirting with the customers which Naomi hated. But flirting sold cars. Guy folded his arms and gave Jack his full attention.

'As you probably know, Felicity hasn't been feeling too well of late and I promised her a long holiday somewhere really warm. Anyway, that got us both thinking and, to cut a long story short, I've decided to take a sabbatical.'

Guy's eyebrows shot up and he stared at Jack. 'Sounds good to me.'

The older man laid both hands flat on the desk. 'But what we'd both like to know, before we take off to Australia or the like, is when you and my daughter are getting married? These bloody long engagements! You either want to marry her or you don't. The trouble with you young people is you wind up living together then there's no damned need to tie the knot!'

With a casual shrug, Guy shifted in his seat. But before he could think of anything to say, Jack carried on.

'We thought about next spring? That way we'll be home from our holiday, having missed England's lousy winter, and if you and Naomi are prepared to wait until then we can go away quite happily.'

'Next spring?'

'Don't look so worried, Guy. This can't be coming as too much of a surprise to you?'

'No, of course it isn't. It's just, well, Naomi and I hadn't actually discussed a date.'

'Which brings me to my second point. As I intend to be away a lot in the future, I'm going to need someone to look after things here. Oversee the three garages. Be responsible for everything. I think it goes without saying that I'd like to keep it in the family. You've proved yourself to me, Guy, in more ways than one.'

Once more his eyebrows shot up. This he had not expected. 'But what about Keir?'

'What about him?'

'Well, don't you think he ought to be offered the job?'

Jack Benson sat back in his seat and chuckled until he started to cough. He leaned one elbow on his desk. 'You never cease to amaze me, d'you know that? You're so damned self-assured, so bloody cock-sure of my daughter and everything. Then, wham. You behave as though butter wouldn't melt in your mouth.'

Guy frowned, not at all liking this analogy. 'That's hardly the point. As I see the situation, Keir's been groomed to take over from you, family ties or no, so it's hardly fair to promote me over him. Is it?'

'Don't be an idiot, Guy. Do you really think I'm going to hand over my empire to Keir bloody Doughty to do with as he likes? No way. That was never my intention.' Jack reached into his inside jacket pocket and withdrew two Havana cigars. He handed one to Guy, removed the cellophane from his own and ran it slowly beneath his nostrils. Guy copied him exactly, enjoying the cigar's fine aroma. Jack withdrew some matches from another pocket and, after snipping off the end, lit his cigar. He threw both clipper and matches across to Guy who did the same. 'Family ties, that's what we need round here. You won't go far wrong casting your lot in with me. I'll see you all right. More than all right. Before you hit thirty, you'll be rich, just you wait and see.'

Guy pulled on the enormous cigar, allowing the smoke to curl from his mouth. He hesitated before speaking, not at all comfortable with his future being organised for him. He hadn't planned on staying at Benson Motors forever. 'I'm flattered, Jack, of course I am. Highly flattered.'

'Don't be flattered, accept the offer and start the ball rolling.'

'The ball?'

Jack held his hand above his head, as though it was a bell, and swung it from side to side. 'Wedding bells and all that.'

'And does Naomi know about this?'

Jack shifted rather uncomfortably in his seat, chuckling and puffing on his cigar. He held out one hand. 'We're a family, Guy, we discuss everything. Come on now, what's all this contemplation? You look exactly like you do when you've just lost a sale. I thought you'd be delighted?'

Guy raised his eyes. 'Oh I am. Of course I am. And I accept your offer.'

Jack was out of his seat in a flash and round the desk to Guy's side, slapping him on the back and chortling away as though he was both relieved and grateful. Which was odd, thought Guy. Shouldn't he be the delighted party?

'You won't regret this, Guy. She'll make you a damned good wife. Mind you, you'd better take bloody good care of her because she's very precious to Fliss and me. And I shall expect the utmost loyalty from you in the future. That's my only proviso. The utmost loyalty.'

Guy smiled, aware his life was now sewn up for good. His eyes flicked to the showroom and he wondered what changes he'd be able to make with Jack out of the way. A shiver of excitement ran through him. And as far as his loyalty to both the garage and Naomi went, he had no fear. Loyalty was one of his best traits.

Chapter Four

'What time? What time are you taking her for a test run?' Naomi's mouth turned down at the corners and twisted unattractively.

'For Christ's sake, Naomi, this is my job! Just because I'm *engaged* to you doesn't mean I can't do my job anymore.'

'Why did you say engaged like that?' She pulled another face. '*Engaged.*'

'I didn't say it like anything. We are engaged and you've got to trust me because in the future I'm bound to be taking a lot of young ladies for test drives.'

'Well, I don't see why. Can't Keir or someone else do it? You're the overall manager now or very soon will be. Daddy never goes on test runs.'

Something tightened then within Guy's chest and he straightened his back, determined not to give in on this one. Naomi had a way of manipulating every single thing he did. He looked at her, suddenly recognising her failings, and then smiled understandingly. She obviously didn't have a very high opinion of herself and couldn't believe he'd be loyal to her. Guy took a deep breath and squeezed her shoulder as she stood at the reception desk. She flinched and jerked away.

He appealed to the sweeter side of her nature. 'I have to go on the test run, Naomi, and deep down you know that.' Before she could object he turned and started to walk towards his office.

She shouted after him, 'If you do, we're through! Through, do you hear? And I'll never speak to you again.'

He sighed, knowing her fury would pass. It always did. She'd be contrite then and spend hours showering him with love and affection. It was a pattern he was coming to recognise and even look forward to. It was exciting when they made love again after an argument. So without responding to her threat, he returned to the office he shared with Keir.

Jane arrived at a quarter to two, which meant Guy had been obliged to hang around all lunch-time waiting for her. It crossed his mind that she might not turn up and then Naomi really would have something to be smug about. As it was she had gone out to lunch with her father and had not yet returned. Perhaps she was going to complain to him and Guy's promotion would be snatched away before he'd had time to try out his new chair. After scanning the showroom to make sure Naomi hadn't returned, he allowed his eyes to wander appreciatively over Ms Richardson's attire. She'd obviously made an effort today with her black city suit, sheer tights (or stockings?) and high-heeled shoes. He ushered her outside to where the secondhand Jaguar sports awaited them. It was spitting with rain and so they kept the hood up and were already seated with Jane steering her way off the forecourt when Guy caught sight of Jack Benson's Bentley. He raised his hand and smiled. Jack returned the smile, but all Guy got from Naomi was an icy stare.

'Phew! If looks could kill,' commented Jane crisply. She looked at Guy who was concentrating on the safe manoeuvring of this expensive piece of machinery on to busy Hills Road. 'What's bugging her?'

He strained to look one way, then the other, trying his best to ignore her remarks. 'You can move out now, Jane,' he said and licked his lips, aware that he'd used her first name, something he didn't usually do with clients.

She joined the road but was obviously determined not to let the subject drop. She asked mockingly, 'Does she go with the job or something?' Jane took her eyes off the road to look at him. 'Do you really have to put up with that? The girl has a serious attitude problem.'

'I think you should keep your eyes on the road, Jane.' He used her Christian name again and immediately corrected himself. 'I'm sorry, Ms Richardson.'

'Oh, for God's sake, call me Jane. It's my name.'

'Okay, Jane it is. Now, if you carry on along here, I thought we'd head south out of Cambridge towards the M11. You can really put your foot down there.'

With both hands clutching the steering wheel, she wriggled gleefully in her seat. 'S'really comfy. Great vision.' She laughed. 'Especially when I look to my left.'

He laughed as well, noting the enchanting rustle as she rubbed her legs together. 'I think I'm in enough trouble as it is, don't you?'

'Yeah, I think you are. But, hell, you're only doing your job.'

'Ah, well, that's not always the way Naomi sees it.'

'Hmm, well, Naomi Benson has tunnel vision. She was like that at school too.'

Surprised, Guy looked at her. 'You went to school with Naomi?'

'Some of the time. Different years, of course.' Jane laughed softly. 'I'm slightly older than her.'

'You don't look it.'

'Charmer! Actually it was a couple of years' difference but for some reason she stuck in my memory. Maybe it was Daddy's Rolls!' Jane turned to Guy. 'I always loved cars, even in those days.'

'Yes, well, you could do a lot worse than this baby.' He reached forward and ran his finger along the walnut facia.

Jane rested her eyes on his long slim fingers. 'So, tell me, how come Naomi's got her claws into you?'

He was defensive. 'She hasn't got her claws into me.'

'Huh! The signals she sends out say that *you belong to her*.'

'She just doesn't like me doing test runs, that's all.'

'Yeah. Thinks she owns you.'

'No, she doesn't.' He faced Jane. 'Nobody owns me.'

She looked at him closely. 'So you're not going to marry her or anything stupid like that?'

Guy took a deep breath, rather surprised by this woman's directness. 'Well as a matter of fact, I am.'

'Are you kidding?' Jane sagged back in her seat but her eyes remained fixed on the road ahead and Guy relaxed a little. She drove well and he was relieved. 'Poor you!' she sympathised, completely unembarrassed.

This conversation was getting out of hand. Guy didn't like it. He cleared his throat and folded his arms. 'So, what do you think of the car?'

Jane shuffled in her seat and grinned. 'I love it! Smooth, great traction. A really cool machine, I'd say.'

By this time they were heading past Duxford on the A505 and as they joined the M11 Jane really put her foot down. She handled the car well and Guy only momentarily looked at the speedometer. She was pushing a hundred when he glanced around for any police cars.

'Remember, this little monster will take control if you're not careful.'

She ignored him completely and pushed her foot down even further, whooping as the speedometer went past a hundred and ten. 'This is *great*! Phew, I must say, it's a crazy machine!'

Guy smiled, well used to such eulogising by customers. They continued along the motorway, zipping past everything in sight. Fortunately the road was comparatively clear. 'Do you realise we're almost at Bishop's Stortford? You'll need to come off at the next junction and head back towards Cambridge.'

'Oooh, spoil-sport. I'm enjoying myself. Why can't we just carry on?'

'Because if we do, I'll most probably get the sack.'

'Oh, no, you won't.' Briefly she took her eyes off the road and looked at him. 'You're all-powerful, Guy Hamilton. You can do exactly as you like. Don't be pushed into a corner by that whining cow.'

He was shocked. 'Naomi is *not* a whining cow.'

'Okay, sorry. Just don't get bogged down by a woman with zero personality.'

'Start indicating now, Jane, we need to come off at the next exit.'

She did as she was told and slowed down to take the slip road off the M11. The car's throttle made all the right noises and Jane drove carefully off the motorway. And then she giggled delightedly. 'I just love this car.'

He looked at her then, noting her flushed cheeks and sparkling eyes. He grinned. 'So have I made a sale?'

Turning right, she laughed out loud and slapped her hands on the steering wheel. 'You most certainly have. This car is *sexy*.'

He laughed. 'You know, Jane, I think you're seriously wicked.'

She took one hand off the steering wheel and patted his. 'I am. *And so is this machine*.' She sighed and pulled into the side of the

35

road, crawling to a standstill. 'So, is it straight back to Cambridge or do we find somewhere cosy for a while?' Her eyes rested on his, glowing with interest – and something else. Desire.

He looked at her in astonishment and stumbled over his words. 'You must know I can't . . .'

'*Coward.*'

His eyes wandered down to her legs and he was sorely tempted. He smiled. 'Maybe I am.'

She looked ahead, disappointed, then turned off the ignition, removed the keys and opened the door. She climbed out and came round to his side. Guy looked out at her. 'You drive now,' she said, 'At least give me that thrill.'

He shifted out of his seat and stood beside her, gazing into her eyes. She passed him the keys, her fingers wrapping round his. She was hard to resist. 'I must be mad,' he said, shaking his head and swallowing hard.

She parted his arm. 'No, you're not mad. Nor are you a coward. Believe it or not, I admire you for not taking advantage. Even wicked old I might regret my behaviour in the morning – as they say. So, in case you're wondering, you just made yourself a friend.' She stood on tiptoe and brushed her lips over his then shifted round him into the passenger seat. Clutching the keys, Guy watched as she made herself comfortable. He closed her door and nipped round to the driver's side. Quickly he started up the car and steered competently back on to the motorway. And then, with a crafty smile in her direction, he gave her the ride of her life.

It was as Guy was sitting in his office with Jane opposite him, sorting out all the necessary paperwork for the purchase of the car, that Jack strode casually in. He looked around, taking careful note of Jane, then asked where Keir was. Guy pointed across the showroom. Jack nodded and left, walking straight over to Keir. Guy watched through the glass partition of his office and knew Keir was about to be told of the decision to promote Jack's future son-in-law. Guy thrust his pen into his mouth and bit down on it, hard. How would Keir take it? He couldn't be sure. He might even leave. Guy's eyes met Jane's and she smiled.

'Trouble?'

It was as though she could read his mind. He looked at her, almost losing himself in her eyes. She was a bewitching woman, not beautiful but prepossessing, and sharp as a razor. She'd be good for him, if he were free.

He shrugged. 'Not really.' He wasn't about to involve Jane Richardson in the politics of Benson Motors. Enough had already been said about Naomi. He watched as Jack gestured for Keir to go through to his office. Keir smiled disarmingly, as was his nature, and Jack, looking unusually nervous, followed him. Of course Guy could have got it all wrong. Perhaps, after speaking to his daughter, Jack had changed his mind. Perhaps he was going to give the coveted job of overall manager to Keir after all. Again Guy's eyes rested on Jane, maybe for a fraction too long. He swallowed hard and looked down at the form in front of him.

'In case you don't realise it,' she said softly, 'Jack Benson is in awe of you.'

Guy's eyes went to her. 'Sorry?'

She sat back in her seat, chuckling. 'You really don't get it, do you?' She pointed at him. 'You know, you should be in the movies. You are one incredible-looking guy.'

He blushed then, feeling stupid. 'Why do I get the feeling you're taking the piss?'

She reached across the desk and touched his hand. 'What I'm trying to say is, you can have it *all* without the price tag.'

He frowned. 'I don't know what you mean?'

Jane put her forefinger to her chin and smiled. 'I think you do.'

And then Naomi appeared, framed in the doorway, only this time without the scowl. In fact she smiled at Guy with adoring eyes. 'When you've got a minute, can I have a word?'

He half-raised himself from his seat. 'Of course.' He looked at Jane, with a tinge of embarrassment, and then at the form on his desk. 'This shouldn't take too long. We've nearly finished.'

Naomi smiled at him once more. 'Yes. *Do* finish what you're doing.' She glanced at Jane, allowing her eyes to sweep carelessly over her. It was done to imply disdain. But Naomi had met her match.

Jane just ignored her and said, 'Where were we, Guy?'

Naomi's eyes blazed as she left the office. He watched her go uneasily before glancing across at Jane. She was busy lighting a cigarette and he watched before reaching over and snatching it from her hands, bringing it to his own mouth and drawing on it

37

greedily. She smiled at his audacity. Guy grinned. Together they finished the paperwork.

Keir left Jack's office in a daze. After all Jack's promises, all his hard work *and* his conscientious efforts to do exactly as the older man wanted, he'd been passed over for a younger and far less experienced man. Then he reflected, somewhat reluctantly, that they weren't exactly promises, more carrots dangled beneath his nose; but this was still a kick in the teeth. Keir made a beeline for the staff exit. Once outside he took a deep breath and leaned against the wall. He lit up a cigarette, contemplating his untenable position. In future he'd be answerable to Guy. Keir shook his head and drew on his cigarette as hatred trickled through his veins. But who was really to blame? Jack or Guy? He shook his head again. No, not Guy, and not the old man either. Keir knew who was really responsible for this turn of events. It was Naomi. That little cow simply couldn't keep her nose out. And he knew her so well. Hadn't he worked at Benson's a good five years before Guy came along. During that time she'd made umpteen passes at him but because she was the boss's daughter he'd flirted but kept a decent distance. And then Guy came along and Naomi was chafing at the bit – couldn't drop her knickers quick enough! Keir nodded. Of course, he should have seen it coming. What a fool he'd been.

He reflected some more. This was monstrously unfair. He'd behaved like a gentleman and been treated shabbily. Well, he'd have to do something about that. From now on he'd still be the same amiable Keir but if he couldn't have the job, he might as well have the fucking reason for that.

Chapter Five

Lily opened her wardrobe door and glanced at the clothes hanging there. She wanted to wear something a little out of the ordinary, something she wouldn't normally wear for school, but not too dressy. That would never do. Adam Greene's wife would think it odd if one of her husband's sixth-form students turned up at their house for coaching looking as though she was ready for a party. But Lily didn't have that much choice in her wardrobe and so pulled out her best pair of jeans and a soft V-necked cream jumper. She'd already showered and lightly sprayed herself with perfume. Now she quickly slipped into her clothes and as quickly flicked a brush through her hair. Normally, for school, Lily wore her hair tied back, but tonight she'd decided to wear it loose. She looked at her appearance in the bedroom mirror and then grabbed a lipstick, delicately outlining her lips. A thin coating of mascara had already been applied to her long lashes, she even did that for school, but nothing else, no other adornment.

Lily grabbed her school bag and left her bedroom, walking towards the kitchen where she could hear her parents' raised voices. Her father, Stephen, was in full flow, angrily saying, 'I think it's ridiculous, Sarah. She's at school all day long then has to go for coaching! For God's sake, we're not made of money. How much did you say?'

Quietly, she replied, 'Fifteen pounds an hour. It's A-level now, Stephen, but it's money well spent, you know it is. You saw the good result she got in her GCSE.'

'But the girl doesn't even know what she wants to do! Have you asked her recently? Every time I do she looks blank. What's the point of all this? She could work for me. We could expand, open another restaurant. Lily's a brilliant little cook. Why's she having coaching for business studies? Bloody ridiculous. I agree with Dad, it's a complete waste of money.'

'Oh, I see. I wondered how long it'd be before you brought your father into it.'

'Sshhh! He'll hear you.'

'I don't care if he does, Stephen. This is my daughter we're talking about. And, anyway, you've got Daisy. She can work for you. She'll more than likely work for you *forever*.'

'Yes, and look at her!' he snorted, then continued, 'I haven't got a son and I'd like Lily to keep the business going.'

'For goodness sake, she doesn't want to work for you anymore than Guy wanted to work for his father. Can't you see, these young people want lives of their own? What difference does it make? You've made your bit. When you retire we can sell up and enjoy the proceeds.'

Lily stood outside the kitchen and sighed. She looked at her watch; soon she'd be late for her lesson. Tentatively she went inside the kitchen and smiled at her mother. Sarah nodded in her direction and left to fetch her handbag. She returned and handed Lily the necessary fifteen pounds. 'Don't lose it,' she muttered.

'*Mum*, of course I won't lose it.'

Stephen looked across at his beautiful daughter and felt a stab of fatherly pride mixed with anxiety. 'You're all tarted up, aren't you?'

'She looks lovely,' put in Sarah, scowling at him.

Lily half-turned to leave the kitchen. 'I won't be late.'

'Do you want a lift?' asked her father, feeling guilty because deep down he was scared stiff of losing her. Daisy, his first-born, had been a disappointment, but when Lily came along, so beautiful and full of beans, his life changed; so much so he felt she belonged to him.

Lily shook her head and smiled sweetly. 'No, it's not far. I'd rather walk.' She knew if her father gave her a lift, he'd lecture her all the way there. Very quickly she left the kitchen and called a cheerful goodbye to everyone before opening the front door. Stepping outside she noticed a nip in the late September air and clutched her leather jacket to herself. Then she set off at a brisk pace. It only took about ten minutes to get to Adam Greene's post-war semi. She made it in seven. Breathlessly she rang the doorbell.

Mrs Greene opened the door and smiled at her. 'Lily, come in.' She rubbed one hand against her arm. ' 'S chilly tonight.'

Lily nodded and entered the Greenes' house, noting the familiar smell of dogs mixed with joss sticks. It wasn't exactly unpleasant, more strange. The Greenes had three dogs of assorted breeds and although Lily loved animals she felt sorry for them because it was obvious they were hardly exercised. 'My wife doesn't get time,' admitted Adam, 'she can hardly cope with the two children, let alone the dogs.' Lily thought about her own mother who'd always managed several jobs with the greatest of ease.

She was shown into a study at the far end of the narrow hallway. In the background squealing children could be heard and Adam's controlled but raised voice. Mrs Greene made no comment, just clicked on the light and beckoned Lily towards a tired-looking chair opposite a scuffed mahogany desk. On the floor was a threadbare carpet. 'He won't be long,' she said and left. Lily smiled, noticing that Mrs Greene never referred to her husband by his Christian name or at least not in her presence. She'd also noticed that Adam did likewise; he referred to *my wife*. Lily lolled her head against the high-backed chair and took a deep breath, glancing around at the untidy bookshelves and dour Cambridgeshire landscapes dotted around. The room was obviously well used but lacked personality. Not that she'd anything to compare it with. On the contrary, her own parents' home didn't have a study and all the rooms were kept so clean and tidy they looked clinical. Deep in thought, Lily's eyes swept round the room once more. There were no little extras here. Perhaps the Greenes weren't interested in such mundane things.

After about five minutes she emptied her bag of the necessary school books, taking out an A4-size pad and a couple of pens. She put all of these on to the desk and started to flick through one of the textbooks. Eventually Adam rushed into the room, full of apologies, his glasses askew across his nose and hair flopping into his eyes. In Lily's opinion it made him look endearing. He stood before her in tight-fitting jeans, one hand raised to his temple. He adjusted his glasses and for a good few seconds allowed his eyes to rest on her lovely face. He grinned then and moved behind his desk. 'I see you've got started. Well done.'

41

Lily reached into her pocket and withdrew the fifteen pounds. She stretched across the desk and Adam held out his hand. 'I'd better give you this now, in case I forget.'

His fingers gripped hers for a second. 'Thanks, Lily. I'm sorry it's gone up.' He shrugged. 'Needs must, I'm afraid.'

He cleared his throat and shifted in his seat, tucking the money into his pocket. 'Right, let's get started, shall we? I thought we'd run through absorption costing this evening – defining cost centres.' Lily nodded as the coaching began.

During the following hour nothing untoward took place. The onlooker would see a teacher imparting knowledge to a keen student on a one-to-one basis. But perhaps even an onlooker wouldn't miss the lingering glances, the too-often brushed fingers and continual footplay beneath the desk. All cleverly done so as to appear accidental, but by the end of the lesson Lily's young body was fizzing with lust. Something she blamed entirely on herself. Hadn't Adam behaved in the most gentlemanly manner? Any questionable behaviour was purely in her head.

She collected her books together and put them back into her school bag. She stood up and Adam raced round the desk to her side. Almost in a whisper, he said, 'Next week, if you like, we could make the lesson a little longer?'

Lily stared into his face, his closeness making her nervous. 'Why?' she croaked.

Averting his eyes, he continued, 'My wife is away for a few days. Visiting her mother.' He smiled, fixing Lily with his gaze. 'So, if you like, we could really go to town on the marketing side?'

Her heart raced and she lowered her eyes, remembering the conversation between her parents before she left. 'I really don't know . . . I'm not sure my parents can afford anymore than an hour.'

He grabbed her arm and squeezed it. 'Oh, no. I certainly don't want anymore money. Not at all. I just thought, as I'd be free, it would be an ideal time for me to really help you. If you think it'll be too much for you, please don't worry. It's only a suggestion. I'm certainly not trying to make more money out of you.'

Lily shook her head. 'I never thought that.'

He laughed. 'Good. I'm just interested in you getting the best possible grade in your A-level.'

'So how long exactly were you thinking of? I mean, I'd have to let my parents know.'

He shrugged. 'A couple of hours, I suppose. And then I might get some other students to come along later and we could have a coffee and a few sandwiches perhaps. It's not often I get the chance to really relax. There always seem to be screaming kids in the background.'

Lily blanched. It was his own children he was talking about. But she ignored the warning sign and smiled. 'Okay, I'll look forward to it.'

He touched her again, fingers lingering too long on the back of her hand. 'Don't look forward to it too much, Lily. I intend to work you really hard next week.'

Nervously she gazed back at him then slung her bag over her shoulder and walked out of the Greenes' dreary study. Adam followed her to the front door and gently pushed past her to open it. 'See you tomorrow at school. Hurry home.' He chuckled. 'Don't go talking to any strangers on the way.'

She looked into his eyes and shook her head then said goodnight. She walked home slowly, mind and body in turmoil.

43

Chapter Six

Lily alighted from the bus in Cambridge and set off at a brisk pace towards St Andrew's Street. Wearing the same clothes she'd worn to Adam Greene's, she turned heads as she strode along with her vibrant hair tumbling over the back of her leather jacket. Lily noticed none of this. She was buzzing with thoughts of her Business Studies teacher and the fact that she'd be alone with him for the first time the following week. Part of her wanted to stop this roller-coaster now; she should tell her mother everything, perhaps even leave the school. The other more positive and forceful side of her nature yearned for next Thursday. And anyway, she might just have misread the signs. After all, hadn't he said he intended to invite some other students along? Lily's head was a jumble, but not so much that she couldn't recognise her own craving for Adam.

Hence the trip to Cambridge. Cassie usually managed an hour off for lunch and Lily was desperate to talk to someone. She knew her friend would tell her to stay away from Adam at all costs, but still she needed a confidante, someone to share the burden. Even her school work was suffering. Lily simply couldn't concentrate anymore.

She approached the florist's where Cassie worked and as she stepped inside the heavy scent of autumnal blooms enveloped her. Cassie was busy serving a customer but her face lit up at the sight of her friend. Lily stood back and waited until the customer left the shop.

'Any chance of an early lunch?'

Cassie looked at her watch then walked through to the rear of the shop. Lily heard her ask the owner, a Mrs Sniffnel, if she could take an early lunch. After much discussion she was granted her wish and Cassie grabbed her coat before her employer could change her mind. Tucking her hand through the crook of Lily's arm, she practically bundled her friend out of the shop as another customer arrived.

'Phew!' she exhaled when they were outside. 'What a morning. I swear that old bag enjoys watching me sweat.'

Lily giggled. 'I didn't know you could sweat over flowers.'

'Honey,' emphasised Cassie, 'believe me, you can.'

'But you're happy, aren't you? You do like your job?'

'Oh, yes, I like it well enough. But she sure works me hard.' Cassie squeezed her friend's arm as they hesitated before crossing the busy road. 'It's like, the other day we landed this job for some garage – well, three garages actually.' Dodging between two cars, she pulled Lily over with her. 'Benson Motors, have you heard of them? Well, anyway, old Snifter's urging me to take driving lessons now so I can use the van and be responsible for the whole job. It's a great opportunity, arranging their displays, but I'm hardly experienced enough to do it.'

'Hmm, I bet you are.' Lily knew how artistic her friend was. 'And you must have learned a lot at Cambridge Regional College?'

'Sure I have, but it's only one day a week and I'm just into my second term. I've still got a helluva lot to learn.'

The two girls entered Burger King and stood in line to be served. 'So, are you?' Lily asked.

'Am I what?'

'Taking driving lessons?'

'*Lily*, there's no way I can afford driving lessons on my salary,' Cassie laughed. 'But I have to admit old Snifter's weighing up the pros and cons of paying for them herself!'

'Well, that would be good.'

'Sure, if it comes off, but I'd still be scared stiff. And Snifter is such a tight-fisted old witch. The quote she put in was humungous! But I'll be expected to provide the magnificent displays for a mere pittance.'

'Perhaps you should think of moving, Cassie? She doesn't sound very nice to work for.'

'She isn't, but there's nothing she doesn't know about flowers and plants so I'm learning all the time.' Cassie looked resigned.

45

'And I like the shop, its position and everything. I guess I'm not ready to move on just yet.'

Lily considered her friend. 'You know, I think you're going to be really successful one day. You've got loads of common sense.'

Cassie guffawed. 'And if you'd lived my life, Lily Hamilton, so would you have.'

Lily finished her chicken burger and wiped her mouth with a paper napkin. She sucked the straw of her milkshake and looked across at her friend. Tentatively, she started to speak. 'Cassie, the reason I came today, apart from wanting to see you, was to ask your advice.'

She rolled her eyes. 'Oh, no, not Greene-ache again?'

'Don't be like that! At least, not before you've heard what I have to say.'

Cassie leaned forward over the table. 'Sorry, I'm all ears.'

Lily pushed away her milkshake. 'I'm just so confused.' She clutched her stomach. 'And I have these really strong feelings that are absolutely driving me crazy.'

Cassie's eyes widened. 'Stomach cramps?'

'Not stomach cramps, silly. You know, other feelings.'

'Lust? Is that what you mean?'

Lily lowered her eyes as her cheeks coloured. She studied her friend through her lashes. 'You've never told me anything about yourself, have you, Cassie?' She leaned closer. 'About how far you've gone with a bloke, I mean.'

'Forget about me, Lily, let's talk about you!' Cassie summoned a smile. 'If you're fool enough to get too close to that smooth-talking bastard, you'll regret it, I know you will.' In earnest now, she continued, 'You're a sweet and beautiful kid, Lily. Can't you see how that pervert is using his position to try and seduce you?'

'Oh, Cassie, he isn't!'

'Isn't he?'

Lily implored her friend with her eyes. 'I promise you, he always behaves properly. It's me, Cassie. I just can't stop this craving for him.' She hesitated and then at last blurted it all out. 'The trouble is, he's asked me along for a double lesson next week when his wife is away.' Lily hurried on when she saw the expression on her friend's face. 'And he's inviting other people along as well afterwards.'

'Afterwards?'

'Yes. After the lesson.'

'Oh. That's cool, I *don't* think!'

'Cassie! Why are you so down on him?'

'Because he's not behaving properly. And you know it.'

'But what if . . . ? Well, what if he really cares about me? What if I really mean something to him?'

'I'm sure you do, Lily. I don't doubt it.'

'What's that supposed to mean?'

'It's that thing, Lily. That thing between his legs. It grows when you get close. *That's* what you mean to him.'

Swallowing hard, Lily's face coloured even more deeply and she averted her eyes. Cassie knew then she was wasting her time trying to deter her from Adam Greene's advances. She just hoped Lily was right about him and she was wrong. Then she bundled the remains of their lunch on to a tray and tweaked her friend's arm. 'Lesson over. Come on, if we hurry I can show you this *wonderful* dress in Jigsaw.'

Relief washed over Lily's face. She too was pleased to drop the subject of Adam. At least for the time being.

Chapter Seven

How quickly one week spins into another. It was Thursday already and during school-time Adam had reminded Lily to come earlier that evening. She'd struggled to find sensible words with which to reply. 'Lily?' he'd asked. 'Anything wrong?'

'No.' She'd shrugged then summoned up her courage, 'But won't your wife mind?' That courage evaporated as she saw the look of genuine surprise in her teacher's eyes.

'Mind? She's not there. Why should she mind?'

Feeling thoroughly silly, Lily blurted out, 'It's just, well, me being alone with you, I suppose.'

Adam Greene laughed out loud and squeezed her arm. 'You silly goose, what on earth do you think's going to happen?' He frowned. 'Concentrate, Lily, *concentrate*.' He looked almost stern. 'It's your A-levels I'm interested in, nothing else.'

Her face coloured to the roots of her hair and she felt uncomfortably hot. What a fool she was! All this angst and apparently she was imagining the whole damned situation. And then disappointment washed over her as she looked her tutor in the eye. 'Of course,' she muttered and shifted away.

As though sensing her embarrassment, he caught her arm again. 'Lily, I didn't mean to upset you. I haven't, have I?'

'Of course not.' She was saved by the bell and managed a smile. 'I'll see you this evening.'

He grinned.' That's my girl. As soon as you like.' He started to walk away then turned back. 'The earlier the better!'

Lily hugged her books to her churning stomach, nodded, then continued on her way to the next class.

*

In her bedroom she stood before the gilt mirror looking at her long shapely legs beneath a short denim skirt. This was teamed with opaque tights, boots and a chunky jumper. Lily looked adorable. She stood back, turning slightly. Since her conversation with Adam she no longer anticipated any close contact with him so it seemed all right to wear a skirt. But now, standing before the mirror, she thought perhaps it wasn't suitable after all. She sighed, whipped off the skirt and replaced it with her jeans then thrust her hands in her pockets. Scowling at her reflection, she turned to leave the room.

'What's all this then?' asked her father as she entered the sitting room. He looked at his watch. 'We haven't eaten yet and your mother says you're off out?'

'Yes, Dad, I'm having a longer lesson tonight with Mr Greene.' She added, 'Although he's not charging me anymore.'

Stephen smiled. 'Giving it you for free, is he?'

The words struck a chord. 'Something like that.'

Her father stood up and walked towards her. 'You look lovely, Lily.' He put his arm around her, squeezing her tightly. 'You know, I only want you to be happy. I don't begrudge you these coaching sessions, not in the least. I know you're a bright girl and extra coaching like this'll get you through your exams better than anything. If sometimes I seem crotchety about it, it's only because I can't believe my lovely little girl has grown up into such a gorgeous young lady who's going to leave me one day.'

Disconcerted, her eyes flicked to her sister who was sitting in front of the television with their grandpa. Both Bill and Daisy turned to look at Lily. Bill, in his usual John Blunt manner, said, ' 'E's trying to apologise, Lily, for being such a miserable bugger, that's what 'e's trying t'do.'

Lily giggled and her eyes rested on her father once more. 'It's all right, Dad. You don't need to explain. I know it's a lot of money.'

'I just wish I knew what your plans were. You do realise there'll always be a place for you with me? The business could do with a bright spark like you.'

'Of course I realise and I'm really grateful.' She fidgeted, very aware that Daisy was listening to every word being said. It was as though her parents forgot Daisy had feelings. If anything, her feelings were more acute than Lily's as she knew only too well.

49

'It's just that I'd like to try something on my own first. Something different.'

Her father appeared miffed. 'Like what?'

'I'm not sure yet.'

'Well, dithering won't do any good, nor will wasting good money on bloody coaching you won't be needing in the future.'

'But I will be needing it, Dad, because whatever I do will be business-oriented.'

Stephen grimaced. 'All sounds very grand to me.'

'Not grand, not grand at all, and don't forget *you're* in business.' Lily looked at her sister and winked. In her exaggerated way, Daisy winked back. Stephen turned towards his other daughter.

'Stop messing about, Daisy! I'm trying to have a serious conversation with your sister.'

'Oh, Dad, that's not fair,' argued Lily.

'Yes, well, certain things in life aren't fair.' He tossed his thumb backwards at Daisy, 'And she should know that better'an anyone.'

'*Dad!*' winced Lily, hating it when her father spoke about Daisy in such a way.

Stephen looked at his elder child once more. 'You know what I mean, don't you, Daise? You and me call a spade a spade, don't we?'

She looked from her father to Lily and then back again at her father, confusion clouding her sad eyes. But she did understand what her father was saying; that she was different; slightly stupid. Bill saved the moment by slapping her on the back. 'There's never been a finer waitress than you, Daise, and that's a fact.'

She beamed and nodded in agreement, then noticed a biscuit crumb on the carpet next to her grandpa's chair. He always had tea and biscuits in the afternoon. She picked the speck off the carpet and put it on his plate.

Bill nudged her and laughed. 'Chip off the ol' block, you.'

Daisy had never understood what that phrase meant, although she'd heard it often enough. She didn't ask; Daisy never asked about anything she didn't understand, unless she was on her own with Lily, because it only brought attention to her lack of understanding. She shrugged and turned back to the television screen.

50

'I'd better be going or I'll be late.' Lily glanced towards the kitchen. 'Is Mum in there?'

Stephen snorted. 'Yeah, more than likely.' He shoved his hand in his pocket and withdrew a twenty-pound note. 'Here, take this, give it to your teacher. We don't want 'im thinking we want extra time for free.'

'Oh, Dad, he doesn't think that. I'll get you the change.'

Stephen put his hand on top of his daughter's open palm. 'No, I don't want any change. Like I said, Lily, I do want what's best for you.'

She hugged her father then. 'I know you do, and I love you very much.' She kissed his cheek and her closeness took his breath away. She was so lovely Stephen feared for her safety. What man wouldn't try to take advantage of her, given the chance? But he had to let her go. She had to live her own life the way she wanted. Hadn't his wife said so time and time again? He fleetingly glanced across at Daisy who was staring at them both, and felt a twinge of guilt. No matter how hard Stephen tried he couldn't feel the same way about his elder daughter. Daisy just didn't tug at his heartstrings.

He put his hands on Lily's arms. 'Get along then. Would you like a lift?'

'No, I'd rather walk. Thanks, Dad.' She looked across at her sister and grandpa. 'Bye, Daise, see you soon. 'Bye, Grandpa.'

They all said goodbye and Lily walked quickly back into her bedroom to pick up her books. She caught sight of herself in the mirror and in a flash unzipped her jeans and stepped into her skirt once more. Without a backward glance she left the bedroom, called another goodbye to her mother in the kitchen and started on her way to Adam Greene's.

She could hear laughter inside the house. Lily stiffened and waited after ringing the doorbell. It seemed an age before it was answered but eventually her tutor pulled back the door and waved her inside. 'Go through,' he said, indicating the kitchen, an area of the house Lily had never entered before; the side that had intrigued her for months and months. Tentatively she did as she was told and was met by two schoolgirls, not in her class but roughly the same age as her. They wore jeans and sweaters and Lily noticed they both looked at her short skirt. She smiled

51

sheepishly and Adam moved in close behind her, almost breathing in her ear, 'Can I offer you a glass of wine, Lily?'

She looked at the glasses in both girls' hands and would have felt silly to refuse. Anyway, she didn't want to. 'Yes, please.' As Adam set about opening another bottle of wine and pouring her a glass she allowed her eyes to wander around the kitchen-cum-dining area of his home. It was obviously the nucleus of the household and rather shabby with a battered-looking television wedged on a corner shelf and a couple of easy chairs shoved before it. Behind these stood a table and four chairs, the table covered with dreary-looking books and household detritus. Nothing seemed cared for and Lily realised that the Greene household probably concentrated wholly on academia. As a glass was placed in her hand she felt her tutor's fingers brush lightly against hers. Quickly she looked at her peers who stared coldly back. Little did she know but they too harboured designs on Adam Greene and her arrival had shattered any hopes they might have had. She sipped her wine.

'Susie and Hannah called to pick up some books. They're leaving soon.' Adam's eyes held Lily's and she was aware that he was hinting for them to leave. The two girls shuffled around for a bit longer before putting their empty glasses on a draining board already cluttered with dirty cooking utensils. The sink too was full of unwashed mugs and plates. Lily mused to herself that her mother would have a field day in this kitchen. Adam followed the two girls out of the house and Lily could hear him joking with them. Both girls squealed with laughter and Lily cringed, thinking that this whole set-up was not quite right. But as he re-entered the kitchen she forgot all her misgivings and took an enormous gulp of wine. Immediately it went to her head. He touched her arm. 'Can I take your jacket?' Lily allowed him to remove it. 'I haven't eaten actually . I thought I might order a pizza. What do you think?'

Lily bit her lip and stumbled over her words. 'Yes, fine, if you like.'

He clutched her shoulder, just briefly allowing his eyes to rest on her well-developed breasts beneath her jumper. 'Don't look so worried, Lily. Anybody would think I'd asked you to take acid with me or something.' He chuckled. 'Although perhaps that wouldn't be a bad idea! Have you ever taken it?' She looked shocked and vigorously shook her head. Adam burst out laughing.

'Lighten up, will you? It's after school. You're a big girl now.' He moved in, glasses sliding slightly down his nose. 'And I'm not going to *eat* you!'

She flinched and looked into his blue eyes, noting the depth of their colour, the penetrating quality they had. She was mesmerised yet slightly put off; her stomach churned. Adam tipped her chin up with his forefinger. 'What do you say then? Pepperoni, mushrooms, extra cheese – the works?'

'Great, whatever,' she feebly answered and sipped some more wine. He turned and grabbed the bottle, refilling both their glasses. 'Careful,' she spluttered, 'I shan't be able to concentrate if I'm drunk.'

He smiled and walked past her to the phone on the wall near the door. He picked it up and dialled automatically. Obviously he was used to ordering in food. Lily supposed correctly that his wife was no cook. She looked down at the filthy tiled floor where her school bag sat neatly by her feet. Her books poked out and she remembered the twenty-pound note her father had given her. Guilt started to niggle at her. She bent down and rummaged around in her bag. Perhaps by offering the money she would get things back to normality? As Adam wound up his phone call and walked back to her she proffered the money. Lily smiled. 'Dad insisted you take a bit more for the extra time. I know it's not much, but he's very particular about paying for things.'

Adam looked down at the money in her hand and pushed his glasses higher on his nose. He grimaced as though weighing up whether or not to take it. Finally he plucked it from her fingers and stuffed it into his own pocket. 'That'll pay for the pizza,' he said, then picked up his wineglass once more, knocking back the contents and refilling it.

Lily frowned and wrapped her arms around herself. Adam looked at her out of the corner of his eye, recognising that she was no push-over. 'Come on then,' he said, gesturing towards the table. 'We can work here tonight.' He cleared a space and beckoned her to sit down. Lily picked up her bag and did as she was told, emptying her books on to the space made available. Adam sat close beside to her.

They worked solidly for about half an hour, during which time Adam finished the bottle of wine. Over and over again he covered points Lily had already grasped. She sat and listened and soon realised the evening had been a terrible mistake. But then he astonished her by slumping back in his seat and focusing his attention entirely on her face. As his eyes studied every detail of her she felt more and more breathless. It was a deliberate ploy but to Lily appeared artless. After a while his expression changed, became pained. In exasperated fashion he threw down his pen. Then he whispered, 'You were right all along, Lily. You should go now. I'm drunk and thoroughly ashamed of myself.'

She gazed at him, allowing his words to sink in. 'I'm sorry. Why?'

He left his seat, walking towards the kitchen area with the palm of his hand on his forehead. 'This is dreadful. You stir such feelings within me.' He turned slightly, hand still aloft, and smiled. 'It's like being a teenager again.' He put his hands to either side of the sink and shook his head. 'I mean, I've always enjoyed the odd bit of flirting. But *nothing* like this.' He shifted round and looked at her as though his heart would break. 'Lily, I can't get you out of my mind. You're driving me crazy.'

Helplessly, she sat listening, totally taken in by what he said. And then the doorbell rang and Adam struggled to smile. 'Oh, yes. The pizza.' He went to collect and pay for it, returning with it in his hands. 'Can I tempt you before you go?'

She swallowed hard, still mulling over his declaration. Adam put the pizza on the table and lifted back the lid. It looked delicious but Lily couldn't have eaten a bite. 'I'm just not hungry,' she said.

He fixed his gaze on her face once more. 'No, of course you're not. How stupid of me to suppose you were.'

He looked forlorn and younger somehow and Lily's heart ached for him. She stood up and reached across the table although she withdrew her hand before touching him. 'I think you're a wonderful teacher, Mr Greene.'

'Oh, please don't call me that. You make me feel so bloody ancient.'

'I'm sorry.'

'Don't be sorry. You're the sweetest, most beautiful creature I've ever laid eyes on.' His gaze swept the room. 'Do you realise what a miserable life I have here? Can you possibly comprehend what a lazy cow I'm married to? Believe me when I tell you

you're like a beacon in my dreary future. Something pure to aspire to.' He put his hand on his forehead again. 'Do you read poetry, Lily?' She frowned and he didn't wait for her reply. 'Well, you should. Read Blake. 'Love seeketh not itself to please . . .' And I know I shouldn't say this, but I'd leave my wife tomorrow if only I could.' He grabbed her hand and held it in both of his. 'I know I have no right, I know you're a young woman on the brink of life, but it's only a little bit of you I want. Just to hold you in my arms, kiss you maybe. Is that so wrong? I mean, can we really help our feelings? You do feel it too, don't you, Lily? Go on, admit it. You do feel it too, I know you do.'

How could she deny it? He was overpowering and she was enveloped in his misery, wishing she could do anything to make his life a little better. He pulled her round the table and into his arms immediately, kissing her lips, gently at first, but soon his tongue was whipping round her mouth in a tantalising way. Adam Greene was a master of the art of kissing and Lily soon succumbed to his charms.

He led her towards one of the easy chairs and pushed her gently into it while kneeling on the floor before her. To Lily, seeing Adam on his knees was like the answer to a prayer. Then he planted delicate kisses around her mouth and neck. He bit the lobe of one ear, sending shivers through her body, and all the while eased his own legs between hers, allowing her skirt to creep further and further up her thighs. Like lightning his hands moved from her shoulders to beneath her skirt. Still being smothered with tender kisses, she felt his hands fumbling about until with one swift movement he wrenched down her tights. Lily caught her breath and shot back in her seat as he tugged them to her boots. 'No!' she heard herself say. 'Please, no!' Adam continued until he'd removed both her boots and her tights.

And then he looked at her, noting the horror on her face, and his own crumpled completely. Still with her tights in his hands, he covered his face. Lily quickly sat forward. 'Adam, please. What are you doing?'

He dropped the tights and flung himself into her arms, rocking her backwards and forwards. 'Oh, Christ, I'm sorry. I'm so, so sorry!'

And then he was kissing her again and his hand moved back to her crotch, fingers easing their way inside her knickers. Lily caught her breath again, only this time she began to relish the feeling as his fingers delved inside her. It was all so wickedly wrong. Within seconds Adam had removed her knickers and was unzipping his own jeans, pulling them down with his underpants, exposing himself completely. She looked at him, for the first time seeing a naked man, and gasped. And then he was pulling her away from the seat and easing himself closer and closer until he slightly penetrated her. He made no further move to enter her, just carried on with his kisses and fondling; stimulating her. When she was totally within his control, with one swift movement he entered her completely, thrusting again and again and again until he reached his own urgent climax. The whole experience was a painful awakening for Lily; she felt torn apart. As Adam withdrew she watched helplessly and before she finally started to blame herself it crossed her mind that he'd lied about his feelings. There wasn't a shred of truth in anything he'd said.

Adam was zipping himself up and standing before Lily had time to gather her wits. Ashamed and sick-feeling, she stretched forward for her knickers and tights, wincing at the sharp pain between her legs and noticing blood on her thighs as she shakily dressed herself. She pushed her feet into her boots, zipped them up and straightened herself. 'Adam?' she croaked.

He looked at her, adjusting his glasses, livid blotches on his cheeks. Then he gathered her in his arms, almost hurting her. 'I'm so sorry, Lily. I truly never meant it to go that far.' He looked down at her and gave a wry smile. 'Girls like you ought to be locked up. You drive us men wild.' He let go of her and stood back a bit. Lily's face puckered as if she was about to cry. 'Don't,' he said immediately. 'Please, don't cry.'

She swallowed hard and pinched her lips together. 'I'm not going to—'

He turned away and walked over to the pizza. Pulling off a chunk, he started to eat it, still with his back to Lily. She was appalled. Was that it? Was that the depth of his feelings for her? She walked towards her leather jacket slung on the back of a chair. She picked it up and put it on. All the time Adam continued to pull pieces off the pizza and eat it. Lily reached beside the box to collect her books together, putting them into her bag. She slid it on to her shoulder and looked at her tutor. 'I'll be off then.'

He peered at her, still munching away, grease shimmering

around his mouth. 'Am I forgiven?' he muttered. Never, she thought. Lily just stared at him and made to leave. 'Lily!' he called after her. She stopped. 'Don't go like this. Not after – well, after what we've just done.'

She gathered her senses. 'How should I go then? Would you prefer me to help you eat the pizza?'

He laughed then, still with his mouth full. 'Well, I'll never finish it on my own.'

'Save it for the next lesson.'

He glared at her. 'What's that supposed to mean?'

His eyes frightened her. She wanted to leave. She shrugged. 'Nothing.'

He walked towards her and took her arm. 'I don't much like your tone. It was with your consent, Lily. Don't go getting all virginal on me now.'

Pain swept across her young face and she wrenched her arm away from him. 'I thought you cared!'

'I did! I do! But I'm married! You know I am.' He was repri-manding her now, like the school master he was. Humiliation engulfed her and she turned to leave, not trusting herself to say anything else. Adam followed her to the door and stopped her from opening it. 'Promise you won't cause a fuss, Lily. *Promise me?*'

She felt his breath on her cheek and struggled to open the door. He pushed her then, angrily, and Lily looked up into his face. 'I won't cause a fuss, I promise.'

He summoned a smile and opened the door. 'Goodnight then. See you tomorrow.'

She was out of the house like lightning, running down the street without a backward glance. Even though she was sore and uncomfortable she didn't stop running until she was safely home.

Chapter Eight

Her parents were only just finishing the washing up from their evening meal when Lily arrived home. She went straight to her room, threw down her bag and jacket then rushed off to the bathroom. After locking the door she started to run hot and cold water into the bath then looked in the mirror, noting the expression of horror on her face and clutching her cheeks, almost dragging her fingernails down them in fury and disgust. She removed all her clothes but rolled her knickers and tights into a tight ball, ready to be destroyed at the earliest opportunity. She swished the water around before turning off the taps, climbing into the tub and submerging herself completely to drown her shame.

'Lily! Lily, is that you?' demanded her mother, tapping on the door.

With an almighty effort she raised herself slightly in the bath and struggled to sound bright and cheerful. 'Yes, Mum, I'm . . . just having a bath.'

'You're home early, aren't you? I thought you were having a double lesson?'

'Oh, I was, but . . . er, Mr Greene had some other people there as well.'

The was a pause and a rather disgruntled noise from Sarah. Lily covered her mouth with her hand, stifling a sob. How she would have loved to clamber out of the bath, unlock the door and throw herself into her mother's arms, tell her everything, but she couldn't. Instantly she was reminded of her own part in tonight's drama. She'd got what she'd asked for, there was absolutely no doubt of that in her mind whatsoever. Lily had been raised to accept punishment when it was due, and her pain and humiliation

this evening were her just deserts. Nothing more. Adam Greene
was her tutor and a married man; even thinking about messing
with him was a sin. And she had thought and thought and thought
about messing with him before she'd met her nemesis.

'Have you eaten?'

'I'm really not hungry, Mum.'

'Lily! You must eat. This studying is all very well, but you are
what you eat. You know that.'

'*I can't eat.*' Her hand covered her mouth again at the
involuntary pitch of her own voice.

'Lily, are you sure you're all right? Nothing's happened, has
it?'

She shoved her fist into her mouth to stifle another sob – then
struggled to swallow. 'I'm all right, Mum. Just a bit tired. I think
I'll have an early night.'

'Well, you don't sound all right.' Another pause. 'Anyway, I'd
best go and make some coffee. Would you like some?'

'No, thank you.'

Sarah shrugged and walked away from the bathroom. Lily
breathed a sigh of relief and set about vigorously washing away
any trace of Adam Greene.

Lily crawled beneath the duvet, burying her face in the pillow.
She'd been there for about half an hour before her mother
reappeared. After a quick tap on the door, Sarah entered and
walked over to her daughter's bed. Lily had her back to her so
Sarah stretched out a hand and jogged her shoulder. 'Are you all
right?' There was real concern in her voice this time.

'You didn't come through and say goodnight. That's not like
you. You always come and say goodnight.'

Without turning, she whispered, 'Sorry, Mum. I forgot.'

'I don't think you forgot, Lily. There's something wrong, isn't
there?' Sarah sat on the bed, her weight rolling Lily over slightly.
She pulled her daughter the rest of the way until she was lying on
her back. 'He didn't do anything to you, did he? Mr Greene?'

Laughter was forced from Lily's throat. Not real laughter. 'No,
Mum. Of course he didn't.'

'Well, what's wrong then? Something obviously is.'

Lily squeezed her eyes shut then forced them open again to
look at her mother. She blurted out, 'I don't want to do Business

59

Studies anymore, Mum. In fact, I don't want to go back to school ever again.' Even in her state of mind, Lily was shaken by the look of horror on her mother's face. 'It's all getting too much for me. Really it is.'

'But I don't understand? You've never said anything like this before. What on earth do you mean?'

Lily struggled to sit up. 'I just don't want to do it anymore. Please, Mum, don't make me do Business Studies.'

'Lily! What's happened? Have you had an argument with Mr Greene or something? I mean, something pretty disastrous must have happened to bring about this change of heart. You practically begged me for these coaching lessons.'

'I know I did, but tonight everything came to a head and I realised I just can't cope with it all. Long days at school then coaching in the evening.' Lily started to whimper, 'I just can't cope with it.'

Sarah wrapped one arm round her daughter. 'Oh, Lily, don't go upsetting yourself like this, sweetheart. Did he tell you your work's not up to scratch or something? Is that what it is?'

'No! No, he didn't. I just don't like Business Studies! I hate it now. Really, really hate it.'

Sarah looked at her daughter's wretched face. 'Is it the subject or the teacher you hate?'

Lily slumped back on her pillow and struggled to suppress tears. 'Both. Don't make me go back to school.' She brightened slightly, imploring her mother. 'I could go and work for Dad. He keeps saying he wants me to. Don't you think, Mum? That's an excellent idea. I'd really like to go and work for Dad.'

Sarah laughed. 'Well, that certainly is a change of heart. Your dad was only saying at suppertime that you wanted to go into business of some other kind, try something entirely new.'

Lily snapped her eyes shut and willed the whole world to go away. She turned her face from her mother. 'I don't want to go back to school. Please don't make me go back there.'

Sarah stroked her daughter's cheek. 'I'm not going to make you do anything. You're obviously very distressed and I'm pretty sure it's got something to do with this Mr Greene. Would you like me to go and see him?'

'*No!*'

'All right! There's no need to snap my head off.'

'I'm sorry, but please promise me you won't go and see him?'

'Oh, Lily, all right. I promise. But calm yourself, sweetheart. Right now I think you must be coming down with flu or something. Or is it your period? Is that what's the matter?'

Lily thought about the blood she'd seen on the soft inner flesh of her thighs. She shuddered and forced her thoughts back to her mother. 'It's not my period, but I really don't feel very well.'

'Would you like a Paracetamol?' Lily nodded and was relieved when her mother got up off the bed and briefly left the room. Within no time she returned and Lily dutifully took two pills with some water. She lay back on the bed. 'Try and get some sleep.' Sarah bent across her and kissed her forehead. 'And don't forget,' she said, 'if there's anything else bothering you, whatever it is, you can talk to me.'

A sob caught in Lily's throat. 'I know. But there isn't anything bothering me, only too much work. I mean it, I really don't want to go back to school. I really, really don't.'

'Get some sleep, Lily, and we'll talk about it in the morning.'

But Lily didn't get any sleep. She heard the usual sounds of her family in the house until at long last they retired for the night. It was only then, when everything around her was still, that she allowed herself to cry. And once she started she couldn't stop. Stifling her sobs in her pillow, she wept and wept, banging her fists against the bed, cursing Adam Greene and cursing herself even more.

'Lily?'

She started guiltily, expecting to see her mother, but it wasn't Sarah, it was Daisy. Clad in her pink satin pyjamas, face a picture of concern, she stared down at her sister. Lily looked up then reached out for the comfort she knew her big sister would give. Daisy automatically climbed beneath the duvet and wrapped her arms around the person she loved most in the world. Gratefully, Lily sobbed against her soft breasts until there were no more tears left to be shed.

Eventually the girls lay quietly side by side, with only the occasional little sob catching in the back of Lily's throat. Daisy, on her side, never taking her eyes off her sister's face, lay thinking. Finally she asked, 'He did it to you, didn't he?'

Flabbergasted, Lily gasped, '*What* did you say?'

Innocently, or seemingly so, Daisy smiled. 'I heard you moaning and crying about him, just now. I heard you saying that you'd never *ever* let him hurt you again . . . and anyway, Mum said she was worried in case Mr Greene had done something to you.' There was silence as Daisy continued to look into her sister's face. 'It's all right, Lily, there's no need to cry. It doesn't hurt so much the next time.'

She blinked at her sister's words. 'What did you say? Daisy . . . what do you mean, it doesn't hurt so much the next time?'

There was a gurgle of laughter in Daisy's throat. 'Well, it doesn't.' She rolled her eyes. 'The first time is awful, I didn't enjoy it at all, but after that it's much better. Then it gets really nice.'

'What are you talking about, Daisy? I don't understand what you're talking about.'

'You know. Sex.'

'And you've done it? You've actually had sex, Daisy?'

She nodded proudly. 'Yes. Loads of times. With Paul. You remember Paul on the vans? We used to do it all the time when I went out on them with him.'

'*Daisy!* Are you telling me the truth? You actually had sex with Paul Carrington on our vans?'

In a panicky voice she quickly replied, 'I'm not lying. Honest I'm not.'

Seeing her confusion, Lily reached out and stroked her face. 'Oh, Daisy, I know you're not lying. But you could have got pregnant. He could have made you pregnant.'

Another gurgle. 'No, he couldn't. He always wore a mac on his willy.'

Lily's eyes widened and her mouth dropped open. 'He what?'

'Wore a mac, you know, on his thingy . . . his willy.'

'A mac?'

Daisy nodded. 'A rubber thing. I forget what they're called.'

'Condoms. They're called condoms.'

Daisy's face lit up. 'Yes! That's right. They were condoms.'

Lily swallowed hard. 'And did you care about Paul?'

Her sister lowered her eyes. 'I was very sad when he left. I was sad for a long time. You won't be sad like that, will you? I mean, if Mr Greene goes away? I couldn't bear it if you were sad. I like you being happy. When you're happy you make me happy.'

Tears sprang into Lily's eyes. 'The trouble is, Mr Greene's not going away.'

'Will you do it again then? It won't hurt so much next time. It won't make you cry next time.'

'No, Daisy. I definitely won't be doing it again . . . Did it make you cry the first time?'

'Oh, yes. But that's because I'm thick. I didn't know what he was doing. 'Til he explained.'

Lily stared at her sister. 'What did he explain?'

'That if I didn't let him do it he'd be angry with me. I'm frightened when people get angry, you know that. Don't you be angry anymore, Lily. I like it when you're happy. You will be happy again tomorrow, won't you?'

Lily struggled to smile, filled with a host of different feelings about the molestation of her dear sister. Then she remembered it had all happened long ago. Paul Carrington had left years before. 'I'll try,' she said, snuggling closer, much calmer now. For a while both girls remained silent. Lily spoke first. 'You won't tell Mum about me and Mr Greene, will you, Daisy?'

She sucked in her breath in horror. '*No way!*'

Again, Lily smiled and hugged her. 'Good. I knew I could trust you.' She snuggled into her sister's arms. 'Don't leave me tonight, Daise, stay with me all night.'

'Just like when we were little?'

'Yes . . . Just like when we were little.'

Lily didn't go to school the next day. Her mother looked in on her, bringing tea and toast, and with a worried expression insisted that if she was no better by mid-morning she must go to the doctor's. Lily assured her it was nothing serious and was relieved when everybody except her grandpa left for work. Bill always stayed in his own part of the bungalow during the morning, so Lily knew she wouldn't be bothered by him. As soon as everywhere was quiet, she climbed out of bed and, still feeling sore between her legs, made for the phone in the kitchen. She dialled Cassie's number at the flower shop in Cambridge. Mrs Sniffnel answered and was none too pleased for Cassie to be taking a personal call. However, even she noted the distress in the caller's voice and eventually fetched Cassie to the phone.

'Hi there?'

'Cassie! Oh, Cassie, I *really* need to see you. Can you get off for an early lunch? Can I come to Cambridge and see you?'

'Lily? What's happened? You sound awful.'

'I need to see you. I can't talk about it on the phone.'

'Sure. Come to the shop about twelve. I'll be waiting for you.'

'Thank you, Cassie. I'll see you then.'

Lily breathed a sigh of relief as she replaced the receiver. Cassie would tell her what to do.

Burger King wasn't quite the place to talk so the two girls opted to buy sandwiches and eat them in Christ's Pieces, a small park merely a few minutes' walk from the town centre. Hungrily tucking into a prawn mayonnaise sandwich, Cassie looked at the pale, drawn face of her friend. 'I don't need to ask what all this is about,' she said matter-of-factly. 'It's crisis time, isn't it? You wish you'd never laid eyes on the evil bastard.'

Lily's eyes swung guiltily to her friend's. She toyed with the sandwich in her left hand, breaking tiny pieces off the granary bread and nibbling them. It crossed Cassie's mind that Lily had natural poise, whether she was starving hungry or unable to swallow a morsel, like now. 'I wish I'd listened to you,' she muttered.

'If I remember rightly, you did listen to me. I think, though, your mind was already made up. Some lessons in life are only learned through mistakes.'

Laughter caught in the back of Lily's throat. 'Is that what it was, a lesson?'

Cassie stopped chomping on her sandwich and faced her friend. 'He fucked you then, is that it?'

Shock flashed across Lily's face and her perfectly shaped chin quivered as it had done the night before. First Daisy hitting the bull's-eye and now her best friend. Momentarily she closed her eyes before allowing tears to spill down her face.

'Ah, Lily, why'd you do it, you silly sod? Why'd you do it?'

'It wasn't like you think, Cassie. I honestly don't think I had much choice.'

'What! You mean the geek forced you?'

Lily shook her head. 'No, he didn't force me but he was . . . Oh, I don't know, very persuasive. *Very*.'

Cassie's face was now consumed with hatred for the teacher

she'd despised from day one. 'Even if he was only persuasive, as you say, that's still taking advantage. You're a schoolgirl, Lily, and he's your teacher. It's an abuse of your trust.'

'But you know I was crazy about him.'

'So you went along with it, did you? His persuasion, I mean?'

Lily shifted uncomfortably, shuffling her feet beneath the bench. 'I sort of did.' She faced her friend. 'But you're absolutely right about him, Cassie. And, do you know, the miserable pig took my twenty quid for a measly half-hour lesson!'

Cassie squeezed her friend's arm. 'You really ought to report him, Lily. He'll keep doing this if you don't. Think of the next poor creature who gets caught in his rotten web.'

'*I can't!* Just think what it'd mean – my parents would find out, and the whole damned school, and when all's said and done . . .' Lily's eyes filled with shame '. . . I arrived at Mr Greene's house in a very short skirt. At first there were two other girls there and you should have seen the way they looked at me. They knew I fancied him.'

Cassie snorted and pursed her lips. 'I see.' She mumbled something incoherent, followed by, 'But how are you going to face him in the future?'

'I'm not! That's what I wanted to talk to you about. I'm leaving school. I just wanted you to know.'

'Like hell you are! Ah, come on, Lily, use your brain. That's exactly what the pervert'll want you to do.' Cassie stared at her friend. 'If you're not going to report him, forget him! And then get on with your work.'

A small smile crept around the corners of Lily's mouth. 'You sound just like my mother.'

'I don't care what I sound like, it's what you must do.'

Lily's thoughts flew to Daisy. She'd managed to get over Paul Carrington. Lily put her sandwich on the bench beside her. 'I'm not the only one in our family who's suffered like this. In fact, I worked it out on the bus coming here today – Daisy would have been about fourteen at the time.' She saw the confusion on Cassie's face. 'Oh, sorry, another bombshell from last night. Daisy told me she'd been seduced by this guy called Paul Carrington. I remember him really well because he had such a lovely wife and two young children. I was only twelve at the time and adored them. He drove one of the fish and chip vans and Daisy

65

used to go out with him to help. She did it all one summer. Anyway, it turns out that frying fish wasn't all they did that summer.'

Cassie looked genuinely horrified. 'Daisy?'

'Yes . . . Are you all right, Cassie?'

'I'm fine. Go on.'

'Well, he told her he'd be angry if she didn't do what he wanted. Daisy doesn't like it if people get angry with her.'

'Poor kid.'

Kicking her feet, Lily added, 'She comforted me last night. I don't think I could have got through it without her.'

'Are you going to tell your parents? I mean, Daisy being Daisy, it could happen again.'

'*No*. She'd hate that.' And then Lily chuckled. 'Anyway, it turns out she used to enjoy it as time went by.'

Cassie's face reddened as though she was angry, then she threw back her head and laughed. 'No kidding?'

Lily laughed too. 'Absolutely no kidding.' She looked at her watch. 'Gosh, is that the time? We're both going to be late. I must be home before Mum is, and old Mrs Sniffnel'll have your guts for garters.'

Cassie giggled. 'You and your quaint English sayings.'

Both girls rose from their seat, Lily stuffing her sandwich into her bag, thinking she'd probably eat it on the bus going home. 'So,' said Cassie, 'back to school next week, promise?'

Narrowing her eyes, Lily jutted out her chin. 'I suppose.' As quickly she looked less confident. 'It'll be difficult though. I'm not looking forward to facing him, especially during Business Studies.'

'Honey, don't give it a second thought. You're in a position of power now; that miserable bastard'll be worried sick you're going to nail him. My advice is, ignore him and *work!*'

Lily laughed. 'Like you?'

'Sure like me. And, to prove it, guess what? Mrs Sniffnel's paying for an intensive driving course. In a couple of weeks I'm having a whole week's driving tuition then I take my test at the end of it. She's so determined for me to do Benson Motors' flowers.'

'But that's wonderful, Cassie! Well done!'

'It sure is and I aim to pass my test first time, just you wait and see.' She poked her friend in the chest. 'And you, Lily Hamilton, will pass your A-levels, so no more talk about quitting school.'

Lily sucked in her breath, refreshed by her friend's counselling. She put her hand through the crook of Cassie's arm and, linked, the two girls walked back into the town centre.

Chapter Nine

Cassie did pass her test and breathed a sigh of relief. She knew only too well that Mrs Sniffnel would not pay for a second round of lessons. Another sigh of relief was heaved when Lily started her period. For all Cassie's counselling, if she'd been pregnant her life would have taken another cruel twist. Much to her mother's relief she'd gone back to school and never mentioned Business Studies or Adam Greene again. Sarah worried about her daughter's outburst, but also knew that Lily would only reveal what she wanted to.

Lily's ability to continue at school came from burying her feelings and completely ignoring Adam, except in class, when she concentrated totally on her work. In that way she proved her strength. At first he was bemused by her behaviour and greatly relieved, but before long he had the nerve to ask if she'd like to continue with coaching. She said no and fled. From then on he stayed away, at first as though she'd cut him to the quick (after all he'd done for her!) and later because he realised he was wasting his time and would be better off looking elsewhere for his sordid little thrills. But the wound was deep. Lily made up her mind she'd never be so stupid again.

Pensively, Cassie stood before the flowers she'd carefully arranged at Benson's Hills Road garage. This was her first visit; it was important to make the right impression. She was using Starburst lilies, globe thistles, twisted hazel and variegated grasses, nothing more. Simply done yet already looking sensational.

Cassie had always loved flowers and the countryside, which didn't exactly go hand in hand with someone reared within the concrete jungle of New York's Manhattan. Maybe it was inbred in her. Cassie's maternal grandparents, during their lifetime, had hardly left the confines of quaint old Ely. It was her mother, Vicky, who'd changed all that; she'd been very different. With a mind of her own, she'd ventured much further afield and at the age of eighteen, much to her parents' horror, took up with American serviceman Mike Milbank, a musician who just happened to be drafted to Lakenheath, not far from Ely. This wasn't at all what they wanted for their precious only child, but within no time she was madly in love and only too happy to return with him to New York where her life changed dramatically. It was only a few short weeks before she started to pine for the flat open spaces of once-despised Ely.

But returning wasn't an option. With her new husband she was obliged to run a piano bar off Broadway, West 46th to be precise, and they lived over the premises in a cramped apartment where Cassie was conceived and raised. Life jogged on for the next fifteen or so years and would perhaps have stayed like that except Vicky's parents both died within a year of each other and left her their picturesque Victorian terraced house overlooking the river in Ely and hard-earned savings. £60,000 to be precise. This was Vicky's means of escape. She told her husband in no uncertain terms that she intended to return to Ely, with Cassie if she wanted to go, and by this time Vicky didn't much care if Mike stayed or not. But he surprised her. He agreed and overnight jacked in the piano bar. Within a short space of time all three of them moved to England. Life changed for the better then. With their newfound wealth they bought a basement restaurant in Ely's Market Street which they turned into a successful business. They also bought a baby grand piano, going for a song, and Mike played it most nights at the restaurant which, with Vicky's help, he organised and ran. It worked well. There was no hectic pace of life in Ely and their sixteen-year-old daughter seemed to flower and change character overnight. Cassie went from being a reserved and moody teenager to the chirpy happy person she was today. She also joined the local comprehensive school sixth form but hated it and after a year left to find work in Cambridge. But she made one very special friend during that year, a girl in the fifth form. Her name, of course, was Lily Hamilton.

*

69

From his office off the showroom Keir Doughty watched, unusually interested in this new girl. Keir was always on the lookout for *the female* – the one who was going to change and enhance his life forever. So far she'd eluded him. Being the product of a public school education but an uncaring and loveless homelife, Keir craved adoration. He'd found solace in sex and had become an adept and clever lover. Once he'd hooked his prey, they *always* came back for more. But the problem for Keir was hooking the ones he really fancied. And life was very unfair at times because Guy Hamilton, Keir had observed, was a past master at hooking beautiful and seemingly unobtainable women. They just fell at his feet. Yes, Keir really felt that life was unfair.

He narrowed his eyes and raised his chin as he studied the young blonde bombshell arranging the flowers. Over the last couple of months he'd become used to Mrs Sniffnel and had assumed her assistant would be similar. This gorgeous thing set his heart alight. Keir particularly liked blondes and she had the most amazing blue eyes and a truly lovely smile and was pleasantly plump, the way he liked his women. He took a step forward, then as quickly a step back as he saw Guy approach. It was nine-fifteen in the morning and Guy, wearing a dark grey suit, white shirt and chequered tie, looked dashing. Keir swallowed his envy and stopped in his tracks. Then he watched. He spent a lot of time watching Guy.

'Hallo. You're new.'

Cassie turned and for the first time looked into the face of the man she would idolise. His dark brown eyes skimmed her face as he passed his briefcase from one hand to the other and extended his hand. 'Guy Hamilton.'

Cassie allowed her own hand to linger, aware of his firm yet gentle touch. She muttered, 'Cassie Milbank. Pleased to meet you.'

Guy looked at the flowers. 'I like that. Very classy.'

'You do?' She became aware of the heightened colour in her cheeks and waved her hand towards the showroom. 'They've got to be classy to compete with this lot. Pretty grand, isn't it? I mean, you do work here?'

Guy raised an eyebrow. 'Yeah. You could say that.' He laughed, moving closer to Cassie. So close in fact that she caught a whiff of his tangy after-shave. 'For my sins,' he added. Then he did something that would remain in her memory forever and each time she remembered send the same familiar message to her brain. He reached out and plucked a tiny leaf from her hair. In doing so he tugged a little, making the follicles stand to attention and her whole body shudder with delight. He rubbed his fingers, dropping the leaf, and Cassie watched it float to the floor. As she raised her eyes she followed the line of his body. He noticed and smiled. 'You're American?'

She looked surprised. 'Yes. You noticed?'

He nodded. 'Where are you from?'

He was interested in her. Actually interested in her. 'New York, although I've lived here for nearly three years now.'

'So d'you like Cambridge or do you prefer New York?'

She pulled a face. 'I guess I prefer Cambridge.'

He moved back a few paces. 'Good. Nice to meet you, Cassie, you're doing a great job.'

Feeling brave now, and not wanting him to go, she asked, 'Who do I speak to about plants and things?'

He frowned. 'Plants and things?'

'Yes.' She swept her hand around. 'This place would look great with a couple of bay trees or maybe photinias either side. Don't you think?'

He looked thoughtful. 'Okay, get them.'

She blinked. 'On your say-so?'

Guy smiled then raised his eyes. 'Yes, although I'm not the boss. She's over there and her name is Naomi Benson.' Cassie swivelled round and saw a glamorous female rush past, wafting a trail of expensive perfume. Naomi sort of smiled at Guy but didn't spare a glance in Cassie's direction. After she'd gone he laughed softly and started to walk away, saying, 'I'm only joking. You don't really need to ask her.' Cassie's eyes followed him as he added, 'It's all right. She's my fiancée. Naomi Benson. Recognise the name?'

Of course Cassie recognised it. She took a deep breath and continued to watch him until he entered an office at the far end of the showroom. It was a particularly grand-looking office. Within seconds she summed up the situation. He *was* the boss. Her eyes moved down the showroom a little and she caught a glimpse of another man, a tall, dark-haired and very arrogant-looking man who had obviously been staring at her but now turned and went

71

back to his desk. She sighed and turned her attention once more to the flowers.

It wasn't long before Naomi floated past Cassie again. Interested, she watched her make a bee-line for the middle office and continued to watch as the dark-haired man raised his head and beamed at Guy Hamilton's fiancée. She, in turn, wiggled her bottom and sat on his desk, her skirt riding up to her thighs, then slid right round so that she was perched as close to him as could be. Cassie caught her breath, thinking it rather an overt thing to do. She decided to concentrate on her flowers but looked over again as laughter came from the office. This time Cassie definitely saw the man's hand glide over Naomi's legs. As quickly she slid off the desk and disappeared from view. The man did too. Cassie shook her head, deciding it couldn't possibly be how it looked, not if Naomi had a fiancé like Guy Hamilton. She continued with her flowers and was almost finished, gathering everything together, when there was a tap on her shoulder. She turned and came face to face with the dark-haired man.

'Hallo, I'm Keir Doughty. I just wanted to say that you've done a great job.' He touched one of the lilies and some of the rich pollen marked his finger.

'Careful!' said Cassie. 'Here, use this.' She passed him a wipe. 'Lily pollen stains like fury.'

Keir used the wipe. 'Does it? Thank you. So . . . are you the permanent replacement?'

'It looks like it.' Cassie noticed he looked pleased and was intrigued. She didn't fancy him, perhaps because he seemed considerably older than she was and perhaps because she'd been put off by his behaviour with Naomi, but he definitely had a way with him. She raised her eyebrows. 'Who do I ask about watering?'

Keir smiled. 'It's probably best if you speak to Kelly over there.'

'Okay, I'll do that.' She left him, walked over to the reception desk and very pleasantly asked Kelly to check each day that the flowers had enough water. She then returned. Keir was still in the same position. Cassie smiled. 'I'll be back in a few days to check they're still alive.'

'That's good, I shall look forward to seeing you then. What did you say your name was?'

She held out her hand. 'Cassie Milbank.' His handshake was just a little too firm.

She gathered the rest of her things into a hold-all and started to walk towards the door. Keir followed her, pushing the door open and even waiting as she walked towards the van she was driving. He watched as she unlocked it and put her hold-all into the back. She raised her hand in a small wave and climbed in. As she drove away, Cassie looked into her rear-view mirror and Keir Doughty was still standing watching her. She smiled and wondered why.

Chapter Ten

The weeks rolled by and Christmas passed uneventfully. Lily did not attend the end-of-term school disco, she knew Adam would be there, and her mother began to worry more and more about her daughter. She'd noticed a complete change in her personality. Although she was still sweet-tempered and amiable, Lily no longer wanted to go out and no longer brought schoolfriends home. She threw herself more and more into her work, so much so that even Cassie had to badger her to go anywhere. Sarah did ask Cassie if she could throw some light on the situation, but her daughter's faithful friend just pointed out that Lily was intent on passing her A-levels.

In fact, Lily was afraid to go out and meet other males and Cassie understood this only too well. Over the months, their friendship had deepened through long conversations and stolen vodka and limes in Lily's mother's kitchen.

And then, as spring hovered invitingly, one Saturday morning an invitation arrived on the Hamiltons' door-mat. An invitation which sent all the women into a flurry of excitement, particularly Lily. She couldn't wait to speak to Cassie about it, and fortunately didn't have to because she'd reluctantly agreed to accompany her to De Niro's nightclub in Newmarket. Cassie had managed to keep the van all weekend.

'Look at this!' Lily proudly said as Cassie stepped over the threshold.

She looked down at the gilt-edged and embossed card inviting Lily's family to the wedding of Naomi Benson to Guy Hamilton. Her eyes widened. 'Lily! You *know* Guy Hamilton?' Even the mention of his name sent her into a spin.

Lily was surprised at her friend's reaction. 'Of course I do, silly, he's my cousin.'

Cassie stared at her. 'Of course. *Hamilton*. But how come you've never mentioned this before?'

Lily shrugged. 'I don't know. How do *you* know him?'

'Through work. Remember? I told you I do Benson Motors' flowers and Guy is overall manager there.'

'Is he?' Lily looked once more at the invitation. How strange she knew so little about her own cousin. Perhaps she'd been too wrapped up in her own life. The beginnings of a smile crossed her face as she remembered Grandpa's party and the way Guy had looked at her then. Familiar feelings, dead for months, stirred. 'He used to live in Ely but went off to university and then moved to Cambridge. I don't *really* know him at all.'

Cassie seemed surprised. 'He went to university?'

'Oh, yes. Guy's very clever.'

Hungry for any information about Guy Hamilton, Cassie moved in the direction of her friend's bedroom. 'Tell me about him then?'

Lily followed, saying, 'Nothing to tell . . . Except his mother Lynda married my Uncle Tom when Guy was a small boy, so he's my cousin by adoption. But that happened before I was born.' She grinned at Cassie. 'I've always known him as my *smarty-pants* cousin, at least that's how Grandpa refers to him. Apart from that, he's mad keen on cars . . . And his fiancée's rather gorgeous, and that really is all I know.'

'His fiancée is a cow.'

'*What?*' Lily protested. 'That's not a very nice thing to say.'

'Lily, Naomi Benson is definitely a stuck-up cow.' But Cassie decided not to reveal how many times she'd watched Naomi spread her legs on Keir Doughty's desk and how once, when Guy wasn't there, she'd seen them drive off together.

And Lily decided not to pry. Instead she looked once more at the invitation. 'The reception's at the Viking Hotel in Cambridge. It'll be so grand.'

'They're loaded, the Bensons. Absolutely loaded.'

Lily lowered herself on to the bed and lay sideways, propping her head on her hand. 'Mum said I can have something new for the wedding. Will you help me choose?'

'Of course I will. Are you going to wear a hat?'

'*No*. I'd feel silly in a hat.'

'Of course you wouldn't. I bet everybody'll be wearing a hat.'

'Hmm, I suppose Mum will.'

Cassie sat down on the bed. 'Are we going out tonight? I'm really looking forward to it.'

Lily sighed and said reluctantly, 'I suppose so. We won't stay too long though, will we?'

Nudging her friend with her fist, Cassie appeased her. 'No, we won't stay too long. Now come on, get dressed.'

Lily looked down at her jeans. 'I'm wearing these.'

'Lily! You can't wear your jeans. It's a nightclub!'

'Why ever not?' She lowered her eyes. 'Besides, I feel safe in my jeans.'

Cassie moved her face close to her friend's. 'You *are* safe, Lily. Nothing's going to happen to you. Now get up and get changed, I insist. Phew, if I had legs like yours I'd never stop showing them off!'

Lily grinned and slid off the bed, walking over to her wardrobe. She opened the door and faced her friend. 'You choose then. I really don't care.'

Standing up, Cassie pulled out a simple white dress. 'Wear this, Lily, you'll look fabulous.'

She studied it then slipped out of her jeans and top and into the dress, transforming her appearance instantly. 'Okay?' she asked.

'*Okay*,' Cassie heartily agreed, and wondered for a moment what Guy Hamilton would think when next he laid eyes on his beautiful cousin. For the first time in their friendship the tiniest trickle of jealousy seeped into Cassie's warm heart.

Chapter Eleven

Wearing a yellow suit and a wide-brimmed yellow hat Lily undoubtedly stole the show at Guy Hamilton's wedding to Naomi Benson. The hat had been a very late addition to her outfit. Cassie had spied it in Robert Sayle's in Cambridge and tried it on herself. Not *too* expensive, it was made of the silkiest straw and the brim lipped inwards in the most flattering way. It was a typical *Four Weddings and a Funeral* hat and Cassie was determined that her friend was going to wear it and look stunning. By this time she actually wanted Lily to steal the limelight from awful Naomi Benson, hence her forking out half a week's wages for a hat to be worn at a wedding she wasn't even invited to. But that was Cassie for you.

The sun shone and the church was packed. Lily sat near the rear in the middle. It was as Guy walked back down the aisle after the ceremony that his eyes sought hers. He looked magnificent in his tails and she smiled, as if to hold his attention, and Guy had actually to struggle to tear his eyes away from her because the bewitching girl at his grandfather's seventieth birthday party had now turned into a ravishing young woman.

Daisy, Bill, Stephen and Sarah all noticed the way he looked at Lily. They too turned towards her, noting her flushed cheeks and the fact that she'd responded to his admiration. Sarah and Stephen looked at each other and in unison breathed a sigh of relief. They'd been so worried about her hermit-like existence and total lack of interest in the opposite sex. Sarah felt quite sure Mr Greene had somehow or other disturbed her daughter's peace of mind although she'd given up trying to get to the bottom of it. But now, looking at the glow on Lily's face because her cousin Guy had looked at her, she felt reassured that her daughter might be on the mend.

The privately owned Viking Hotel, a beautiful rambling early-Victorian building in the most perfect setting overlooking the River Cam, enthralled Lily. As if the compact but palatial surroundings weren't enough, the food was superb: stoned baked peaches with Roquefort sauce, tiny crab cakes, melt-in-your-mouth medallions of lamb, all followed by frothy zabaglione and cheeses. The service was without fault. Lily looked around her from her family's table, not too far from the bride and groom, totally entranced, sizing everything up, becoming more and more inspired by the minute. First Guy's attention which was ongoing – every time she glanced in his direction he seemed to be looking at her – and now all this. During that fine spring day Lily turned a corner. She also boldly decided on her future. This was where she wanted to be, at the sharp end of elegant parties. And hadn't she been brought up within the business of catering? Albeit humble fish and chips. But it wasn't cooking she wanted to do, it was management. Like fashion, food tastes change and somebody has to stay ahead of the game. Lily liked the idea of catering to the latest whim. It was exciting.

After all the speeches, and when the guests had started to leave their tables and mingle, Guy's best man, Keir Doughty, turned to Naomi and asked, 'Who's the girl sitting over there?' He pointed to Lily.

Naomi, looking radiant in *decollétée* cream taffeta silk, glanced in the direction in which Keir pointed. Her again, she thought, and scowled. She'd noticed her new husband's eyes continually wandering in that direction. She turned to Keir and pulled a face. 'I'm not sure. A cousin or something.'

He sat back in his seat, enjoying a cigarette, allowing the smoke to escape from his nostrils. He rubbed his chin thoughtfully. 'I don't think I've ever seen such a beautiful girl in the whole of my life.'

Naomi instantly glowered, hating the silly tart he was referring to. 'Thanks very much. In case you've forgotten, this is *my* wedding day.'

Keir's left hand sought her knee beneath the table and he squeezed it. 'You know I only have eyes for you, Naomi, but if you will go and marry somebody else, what do you expect?'

She pushed his hand away and her eyes sought out Guy who was talking in animated fashion to his mother. Fresh jealousy overwhelmed Naomi. She didn't like Lynda either. She pushed back her seat and walked towards her husband, determined to have him to herself for a while. Why couldn't he be like her father, who alway showered her with love and attention? Why couldn't Guy be attentive like that? She would feel so much more secure if he continually showed the world he adored her.

Keir watched her go, noting her well-covered backside in her tight-fitting dress. He remembered the same backside, naked and squirming on the rear seat of his car. He smiled and returned his attention to the girl. Now *she* sparkled, he noticed; was animated but totally without artifice. Stubbing out his cigarette, he rose from his seat, deciding to go over and introduce himself. He left the table and started to weave his way through the guests then stopped, noticing Guy heading in the same direction. With a pinched mouth, Keir hissed through his teeth, deciding not to butt in; it wasn't his style. Instead, he retraced his steps and sat down again. Once more he lit up and watched through narrowed eyes.

Lily scraped back her chair and turned to Daisy. 'This is it, Daise, this is what I want to do.'

Daisy, who'd taken her hat off and was unaware of the indentation it had left on her hair, smiled lovingly at her sister. 'Get married?'

'No, not get married. Go into catering.' She grabbed Daisy's arm and ran her fingers through her sister's hair, breaking up the line left by her hat. 'I could go to catering college, and then perhaps get a job in a hotel, but eventually I could have my own business.' Lily's thoughts rambled on and she was unaware that Daisy was no longer listening. Instead she was watching Guy move towards them. Daisy caught her breath because, like Lily and Cassie, she found him extremely attractive.

He pulled up a chair and sat down next to her, almost facing Lily. His eyes automatically stayed on her face, it was as though he couldn't drag them away. For a few seconds no one spoke. Then he put one arm round the back of Daisy's chair and as his coat tails fell away they revealed the tension on the buttons of his patterned waistcoat. Lily's eyes locked on to his torso in fascination and then further down to his legs, set slightly apart, feet flat on the floor. She swallowed as certain feelings were rekindled in her body; until she remembered Mr Greene, and quickly averted her eyes.

'Lily?' Guy's eyes were questioning, as if he'd noticed her discomfort.

She looked at him again and smiled, and Guy was so elated that he was tempted to lean across Daisy and kiss her on the mouth. But instead he turned as though remembering why he was in this reception hall and saw Naomi's jealous stare across the room. He smiled weakly in her direction then gave his attention once more to Lily.

'You both look beautiful,' he finally managed to say.

Daisy went into fits of giggles and covered her mouth. 'Lily does! I'm not beautiful!'

Immediately Guy looked at her. 'Yes, you are, Daisy.' In an endearing way he touched her hair, which was almost the same colour as Lily's but shorter, and his simple gesture sent shivers down her spine. Lily noticed and it crossed her mind that her cousin didn't quite realise the effect he had on women. 'So,' he said, 'what are you two doing with yourselves these days?'

'The business,' Daisy said matter-of-factly. Guy smiled and raised his eyebrows at Lily.

Her eyes swept round the room as excitedly she said, 'I've decided this is what I want to do.' He frowned and followed her gaze. 'I thought about catering college. What do you think?'

His hand moved to his forehead as he stroked away a lock of hair then slid down into his jacket pocket. He felt the comforting cardboard of his cigarette packet but decided against lighting up. Was this gorgeous creature really asking him if he thought she should go away to catering college? Perhaps follow in the Hamilton family footsteps and head up Ely's fish and chip business? He cleared his throat. 'Cooking?'

Lily's eyes flashed. 'No! Not cooking. Management. That sort of thing.'

He didn't hesitate. 'Sounds good. If that's what you want to do.'

'It is. Definitely.'

Daisy touched Guy's leg. 'Lily's brilliant. She can do anything.' Daisy was proud of her sister.

He looked down at his cousin's hand on his knee and was aware that Daisy was totally unaware you just don't touch men like that. Then he looked at Lily, noticing she too was looking at Daisy's hand on his knee. Their eyes locked in mutual understanding and he shifted so that Daisy's hand fell away naturally. 'I hear you're a friend of Cassie Milbank's?'

Lily's eyes lit up. 'Yes. She's my best friend.'

Guy nodded appreciatively. 'She's special. Very artistic.'

Daisy put her hand on Guy's knee again and leaned forward in her chair. 'Cassie's not fat like me, but she is plump.' She looked at her sister then back at Guy, tightening her grip on his knee. 'And neither of us is beautiful like Lily.'

Guy laughed and Lily nudged her sister. 'Stop saying I'm beautiful, Daisy. People will think I'm paying you to do it.'

Daisy's hand flew from Guy's knee to her mouth as she gasped. Then she looked at him. 'Lily's *not* paying me to say she's beautiful.'

Shifting closer in his seat, he wrapped one arm around Daisy. 'I know that. And you're not fat.'

Daisy's face was a picture of happiness. She looked at Lily. 'Did you hear that? Guy said I'm not fat.'

Lily smiled and looked at his hand dangling round her sister, just a few inches away. His fingers were long and slim, his fingernails scrupulously clean. When her eyes returned to his face she noticed he was looking at her with interest and warmth. And then they were rudely interrupted.

'Are you going to stay here all day? We do have other guests to talk to!'

Guy looked up at his bride then back again at Lily and Daisy. He withdrew his arm from around Daisy and said, 'Naomi, I'd like you to meet my cousins.' He inclined his hand towards Lily. 'This is Lily.' Then he squeezed Daisy's shoulder. 'And this is Daisy.' Naomi nodded brusquely but said nothing. Her eyes smouldered in annoyance and Guy reluctantly stood up. 'Duty calls. Talk to you both later.' Then he winked at Daisy, smiled at Lily and waved his hand for his bride to lead the way. With a tight smile, Naomi shifted forward. Guy followed.

'He doesn't love her,' said Daisy bluntly.

Her eyes feasting on his retreating figure, Lily quickly disagreed. 'Of course he does. He wouldn't marry her if he didn't love her.'

Not about to argue, Daisy shrugged. But in this instance she knew her sister couldn't possibly be right.

Lily stood up and smoothed down the skirt of her suit. She looked around. 'Fancy a walk outside, Daisy?'

'A walk? What for?'

Lily held out her hands. 'To get some fresh air. It's smoky in here. Come on, the gardens are lovely.'

Daisy pulled a face. 'Do we have to?'

Lily tugged at her sister's arm. 'Yes, lazy bones, we do.'

Daisy allowed herself to be pulled into a standing position then looked around the room. 'I'd much rather stay here and watch everyone. It's much better than going for a walk.'

Lily pushed her arm through Daisy's and started to guide her out of the reception room. Once again she noticed Guy glancing in her direction and wished he wouldn't. It was so obvious his new wife did not like it. And who could blame her? She turned her attention to her sister. 'What did you mean just now, Daisy, when you said Guy didn't love Naomi?'

'I know he doesn't.'

'How?'

'Because he doesn't look at her right.'

'What do you mean?'

Daisy chuckled and squeezed Lily's arm. 'If you ask me, it's *you* he loves.'

'Oh, Daisy! That's ridiculous! Whatever makes you think that?'

'His eyes. He's got very expressive eyes.' Daisy was thoughtful for a second. 'And so have you, Lily, but I'm not sure yet whether you love him.'

'Of course I don't love him! He's just got married to someone else.'

'But it won't last, will it?'

'Daisy! What makes you say that?'

She frowned. 'I don't know. I never know what makes me say anything, 'cept a feeling I get inside.' Then she smiled smugly. 'But I know I'm right. Just wait and see. Shall we have a bet on it?'

Lily smiled and shook her head. Not likely. Whenever she bet with Daisy, she always, *always* lost.

82

Part Two

Chapter Twelve

Guy woke fitfully and rolled over in bed, peering at the clock. The figures glinted back at him. *Two-thirty a.m.* He turned on to his back and put his hand to his forehead in dismay then looked at the vacant space in the marital bed. This was unforgivable; it was humiliating. What had happened? How could it be a mere two and a half years down the line from his glorious wedding day and his wife coming and going as she pleased? This wasn't a marriage, it was a joke.

Guy reached for his cigarettes on the bedside table and nervously lit up, drawing almost hungrily on the weed before contemplating his own misery. This situation was sapping his confidence. If he'd had so much as a suspicion how she'd mess him about he'd never have married Naomi. Was the woman he now knew – hard-bitten, mouthy and without an ounce of compassion – the same one who'd gazed up at him with loving eyes on their wedding day? Okay, so maybe he hadn't always been able to give her the adoration she craved, but he'd been faithful and loyal as his father-in-law had insisted. Naomi by contrast didn't cook, she didn't clean, she didn't even respond to his love-making anymore. And she was a disaster to live with and he was growing to despise her. The trouble was, he despised himself more for failing to make her happy.

His ears pricked at the now familiar sound of her car tyres on their gravelled drive. As the headlights briefly lit up their bedroom, he flung back the duvet and, with his cigarette in his mouth, grabbed a robe, tying it tightly round himself. He pulled on the cigarette and left the cobalt blue and white split-level bedroom of their luxurious *Norman Golding* five-bedroomed house near the river in Chesterton. On the landing he leaned over the handrail of the stainless steel tubular balustrade looking on to the spacious entrance hall below.

Her key twisted and clunked and Naomi entered, closing the door with care. She slipped off her high-heeled shoes so as not to make a noise as she crossed the maple floor. She tiptoed up the stairs and only when she reached the very top saw Guy standing there, one hand clutching the banister rail and the other holding his cigarette.

'Guy.'

'Naomi.'

She giggled. 'Got held up with the girls.' She was well oiled and tottered to the left as she passed him, making her way into their bedroom. Watching carefully, he followed as she threw her shoes in one corner, her jacket in another, then flung herself on to the bed and started to peel away the rest of her clothing. In times gone by Guy would have helped her, maybe even laughed with her, relieved she wasn't so clingy anymore. After all, he'd never liked not being allowed out of her sight. But their situation now filled him with loathing and compounded his own sense of guilt.

Her stockings and panties were the last items to be flung across the room. Laughing, she burrowed beneath the duvet. Guy had noticed that Naomi never bothered to remove her make-up at night. By the morning she looked like a panda. During this short interlude no words had been spoken. He had continued to watch, leaning against the white fitted wardrobes and smoking his cigarette to the very last.

Then he took a step forward and caught his toe on his wife's panties. He bent forward and picked them up, with her stockings, intending to toss them to one side. He noticed they were damp: tacky damp. Guy looked at Naomi happily sleeping in their bed and raised her panties to his nose. The unmistakable smell of semen hit his nostrils and his heartbeat rapidly increased.

'Naomi!' He walked towards her, still clutching the offending item in his hand. He pulled back the duvet. '*Who is he?*' He practically shoved the panties in her face.

She roused herself and grabbed her knickers, pushing them down the side of the bed. Then she glared at him. 'What are you talking about?'

'The man who's been *fucking* you! Who is he?'

She rolled on to her back, drawing one arm across her forehead. 'It's late, Guy. I'm tired.'

He grabbed her arm and yanked her into a sitting position. 'You're tired! *You're bloody tired?* How do you think it is for me?'

Sleepily, she said, 'For you?'

'Yes! Wondering where you are all the time. Or has that thought never crossed your tiny mind?'

Her face twisted as she noticed his creased brow, drawn face and dishevelled hair. 'Yes, often actually.'

'Oh, really? And should I be grateful for that?'

'Perhaps.'

'And?'

'*And what?*'

Angrily, he pushed her backwards and walked away, seething inside. 'Who is he, Naomi? Just tell me who he is?'

She yelled at him, making him reel, 'He's nobody! He's fucking nobody!'

Guy spun round. 'Well, if he's Mr *fucking* Nobody, at least tell me why?'

'Because of you, you shit! Why d'you think.'

Confused, he moved back to his wife. 'But what have I ever done?'

She laughed out loud. 'Tell me what you *haven't* done?'

He sat on the bed and in a controlled voice asked, 'I haven't a clue what you're talking about so you'd better tell me?'

She hitched herself backwards, plumping the pillows behind her as though ready for battle. 'Well, for starters, you've humiliated me more times than I can mention.'

'What the hell are you talking about? How have I humiliated you?'

Naomi's nostrils flared as she remembered Guy's former supremacy over her. Well, she'd soon sorted that out. He was all hers now. She'd well and truly put him in his place. In fact, it had been easy, he'd been a puppy-dog, not smacked her in the face once. That alone had given her an enormous kick. Things had somehow or other gathered momentum since then and she'd grown dizzy with the delicious thrill of it all. Now she knew it was only a matter of time before he was absolutely on his knees. 'It started on our wedding day, if you must know.'

Guy's memory rather reluctantly took him back to their wedding day. 'Our wedding day?'

'Yes! It could have been wonderful but you spoiled it! You bloody spoiled it!'

'For Christ's sake, Naomi, what are you talking about?'

She lowered her eyes and appeared to be blinking back tears. He watched her face, recognising the signs as she prepared to whine. 'That girl! *That bitch!*' she eventually hissed.

His face creased as he tried to recollect who on earth Naomi was talking about. 'What girl?'

Naomi shook her head. 'I forget her bloody name. But she wore a hat! She had ghastly hair. Ghastly red hair.'

Ghastly red hair . . . who on earth did he know with red hair? Lily? Could she be talking about Lily? But Lily didn't have ghastly hair. It was a burnished red-brown, like silk. 'My cousin, you mean? Lily?'

Narrowing her eyes, Naomi drew a quick intake of breath. 'Yes, that's right. She was your cousin, I remember now.'

'But what's she got to do with anything? I hardly spoke to her.'

Naomi shouted at him, leaning forward with her face flushed and petulant, 'You humiliated me! You sat there making eyes at that little tart and then when I got upset – after all, it was my *wedding day* – you behaved as though it was me who was at fault! How do you think that made me feel? You just can't treat me like that and get away with it.'

'I didn't treat you like anything, Naomi, other than my newly married wife. And if I remember rightly it was you who humiliated me. You showed no friendliness whatsoever to Lily and Daisy.'

'Well, why should I?'

'Because they're members of my family'

'Oh, yes. And it wasn't so long ago *you* looked down your nose at members of your bloody family!'

'I never looked down my nose at them, that's absolute rubbish! I just didn't like their parties. There's a big difference, Naomi.'

'Is there? Well, you could have fooled me.'

Guy gathered his thoughts, recognising the unbridgeable gulf between himself and his wife. 'It seems to me there isn't very much about me you do like.'

'Spot on! So now you know why I seek my pleasures elsewhere.'

'Why you fuck around, you mean?'

'And what if I do? Don't tell me you don't when you get the chance?'

Guy grabbed her arm again. 'I don't! Ever!'

'Oh, yeah, and you expect me to believe that?'

'I don't give a damn if you believe it or not, but it's the truth.' He ran his hand across his parched mouth then looked at his wife's pinched and bitter face. He wanted to hurt her. 'You really are a cow, aren't you, Naomi?'

She swiped at him then, hitting him clean across the face. 'Don't you ever call me a cow, do you hear?'

Grabbing her hand, he twisted it away. 'So who is it, Naomi? Tell me?

She sneered at him. 'Oh, wouldn't you like to know?'

'I think I have a right to know.'

'You have no rights! None whatsoever.'

Guy let go of her, appalled by her behaviour, and got up off the bed. 'Well, if that's the case, I may as well pack my bags and leave.'

She surprised him then, even in this dreadful hour of reckoning. 'Feel free. I certainly won't try to stop you.'

Guy halted in his tracks and put one hand to his forehead, rubbing two fingers across his brow in agitated fashion. Did she mean it? Was this how his marriage was going to end? As the tension mounted within his temples, he tried to stay calm. 'In that case, *I will go.*'

'Good!' Naomi hurled at him, flinging herself down in the bed and almost covering her face with the duvet. She spat out from beneath it, '*Good riddance.*'

Guy grabbed his clothes, cigarettes and wallet and left the bedroom. Outside he pulled on his trousers and buttoned up the shirt he'd worn all day. He pushed his bare feet into his shoes and started down the stairs. At the bottom he took a blazer from the coatstand and grabbed his car-keys. During this time he quite expected, and hoped, Naomi would jump out of bed and try to stop him, but she didn't so much as make a peep. Guy unlocked the front door and slammed it shut behind him. Then he walked over to his car and drove to Keir's.

*

89

Almost lovingly Keir guided him to a comfortable seat in his flat overlooking Midsummer Common, plied him with malt whisky and listened to his tale of woe. He hardly spoke, just heeded his friend's ramblings with the odd comforting grunt during natural pauses. In this particular instance Keir was not guilty. He'd deliberately steered clear of Naomi since her marriage to Guy; had in fact acquired a couple of totally different girlfriends, and was still trying in vain to persuade the elusive Cassie Milbank to agree to a date. So far she'd always come up with an excuse not to go out with him.

But Keir was shocked by Guy's haggard appearance and bloodshot eyes, and more to the point his crumbling confidence. Was this really the man he'd continually watched and admired? The one he'd striven to emulate, held in such high esteem? Even the garages were suffering. Guy had made a few blunders lately including misreading one particular client's genuine desire to buy a brand new Jaguar XJS 4-litre V8 – so much so that the client purchased the vehicle elsewhere and then wrote a two-page letter of complaint to Jack Benson.

Guy ran a hand through his hair and slumped back in Keir's black leather settee. He stifled a yawn. 'I'm so bloody tired.'

'Go to bed. Things won't seem half so bad in the morning.'

'Won't they? I think they will. My life suddenly seems pointless.'

Keir studied his friend. 'How can you say that? You've made a mistake; married the wrong girl. You can rectify it and get on with things again. To look at you, anyone would think it was the end of the fucking world. If you'd told me three years ago that Naomi Benson was going to screw you up like this, Guy, I'd never have believed it. This whole episode is grounds for divorce. She stinks! Sue the bitch!'

Guy grimaced as his head spun with the logic of Keir's words and the likely consequences if he did as advised. Without Naomi his position at the garages would change. He sat forward, putting his elbows on his knees, and cradled his head in his hands. 'But where did I go wrong? I've done something terribly wrong and I don't know what.' He raised his face. 'I wanted it to work, Keir, I really did.'

'Because you loved her?'

With tired eyes, Guy reflected on his question. 'I must have done, once.'

Changing the subject completely, Keir waved his hand. 'That girl at your wedding, the beautiful one, do you ever get to see her these days?'

Guy was surprised at the abrupt change of subject. Lily. First Naomi and now Kier. 'Are you talking about my cousin Lily?'

'Yes, that's the one. Lovely Lily.'

'But why should I see her?'

'Well, isn't she family or something?'

A smile touched Guy's cracked lips. 'Yes. But how often do you see your cousins?'

'Never. I thought you knew, my family don't even like me.' Guy frowned then dismissed Keir's words. He'd got enough worries of his own. 'She'd be good for you, Guy. You should get in touch.'

Guy's eyes kindled. 'What are you talking about? Aren't you forgetting I'm already married? And besides, Lily's far too young for me.'

Keir laughed and patted his hand. 'Oh, what a tortured soul you are. Don't become a martyr, Guy, it doesn't suit you at all.'

'*Keir, this isn't a fucking game I'm playing!*'

He sat back in his seat, grinning. 'I never said it was. And I'm pleased to see the old fire's not entirely out.'

Slowly, Guy grinned and reached over to the small table for one of Keir's cigarettes. He offered the packet to his friend, who took one, then lit both cigarettes with a lighter. He sucked in the palliative smoke. 'Thanks, Keir. For listening.'

'A pleasure. Another whisky before we retire?'

Half-drunk, Guy nodded. 'Why not?'

Keir stood up, wobbling slightly. 'Why not indeed?'

Chapter Thirteen

Dressed in Keir's shirt, tie, socks, underpants, and smelling of his aftershave, Guy boldly walked into Benson's Hills Road garage. Shifting his briefcase from one hand to the other, he proffered a weak hallo to Cassie and continued to his office at the far end of the showroom. He wasn't expecting to find Jack Benson sitting in his seat, wasn't expecting to see such a scowl on his face.

'Jack.' Guy placed his briefcase on the floor beside his desk. 'You're up and about early.'

He looked at his wristwatch and replied crisply, 'Which is more than can be said for you.'

Still hung over from Keir's malt whisky, Guy managed a smile. Feigning confidence, he perched on the desk and folded his arms. 'What can I do for you?'

Grunting, Jack pointed to the desk and then the chair opposite. 'I can't stand folk who sit on desks. Never could.'

Guy slid off the desk and sat down, all the time aware of the clumsy beat of his heart and the cotton wool in his brain. He folded his arms again and turned as Kelly walked in with a cup of coffee for Jack. She put it on the desk. 'I didn't realise you were in, Guy. Coffee?' He nodded and she went off to fetch it.

Jack Benson picked up the letter sitting in the middle of the desk, browsed through it for the umpteenth time, then threw it across to Guy. 'Perhaps you'd like to read *that*.'

He picked it up and started to read the contents. It was from the client who had taken his business elsewhere. Guy coughed into his hand. 'I do know all about this, Jack, and I am sorry.' He could hear the sound of his own feeble voice, almost like Naomi's when she whined. 'It was a genuine error. He came in on a Sunday morning and I was helping out because we had a rush of people. I showed him the XJS but he gave no real signs of interest.'

Jack reached over and grabbed the letter, stabbing at one paragraph with his forefinger. 'He says he asked you for a test run. You were supposed to get one of our salesmen to organise it and get back to him. Or are you too high and mighty now to remember such things?'

'Of course not. Because of his lack of enthusiasm ... it completely slipped my mind.'

'Incompetence! Bloody incompetence! We don't make that much money you can afford to pass up on a bloody good sale, Guy.'

'I know, Jack. I know.'

The older man slumped back in his seat, opening his mouth to speak. Then he closed it again as Kelly arrived with Guy's coffee. She put it on the desk and hurried out, aware that trouble was brewing. After she'd gone Jack continued, 'What's happening to you, son?' He flung out his hands. 'You used to turn heads with your good looks ... and now look at you! For God's sake, when was the last time you had a decent haircut? Straggly long hair doesn't suit men your age. You look bloody stupid, if you ask me.' Jack leaned over the desk and jabbed his finger in his son-in-law's direction. 'You represent *me* and at the moment I wish you *fucking* didn't!'

Narrowing his eyes, Guy knew he'd reached rock-bottom. Insults about his appearance and, worse, about his work; all from the man who supposedly trusted him. He'd sunk about as far as he could go. And with this knowledge something shifted inside him. He got up off the chair and walked over to the glass partition separating his office from the showroom. Cassie was arranging her magnificent blooms there and immediately he was soothed by the sight. Along with Keir, she was the only decent thing in this place. Jack watched his daughter's husband, intrigued by the sudden change in his stance. This was more like the old Guy. Jack waited as he turned, almost fiercely. 'I'm sorry, Jack, but things aren't going too well for me at the moment. My life is a mess!'

There was a pause. 'What do you mean? Things not good at home?'

Guy's mouth twitched as he struggled against his better nature. He really ought not to drag his wife into business worries but simply couldn't help himself. 'Understatement. Things are decidedly shitty at home . . . hence my balls up.'

Jack bristled and slammed his fist on the desk, spilling coffee everywhere. 'Don't bring my daughter into this, Guy! They're two separate issues!'

He glared at his father-in-law. 'No, they're bloody not!' At the sound of his own anger something snapped and he went on, anxious at last to spill it all out. Guy pointed his finger at Jack. 'Your one condition when you offered me this job was to be loyal to your daughter. Well, I've stuck to my side of the bargain. So I think if you've got any complaints about me you should go and see your daughter and ask about *her* side of things!'

For a few seconds Jack sat with his mouth open. This was something completely new to him. Not a murmur had he heard of any trouble between Naomi and Guy. He scratched his head. 'What are you talking about?' Genuinely horrified, he asked, 'Are you saying my daughter is messing about?'

Briefly, Guy hesitated then rushed on, 'Yes, and . . . *it's doing my head in!*'

There was a deathly silence in the whole of the showroom. Everybody heard Guy's strangled appeal to his father-in-law that morning. Cassie flinched, genuinely sorry. Then she raised her eyes and stuffed a single white carnation into the middle of the display as a shiver ran through her. He was going to leave, she knew it, and then she'd most probably never see him again. For three years now Cassie had lived for the next time she'd see Guy Hamilton. Fear mingled with sorrow made her want to cry.

'You should bloody sort her out then!' boomed Jack. 'Don't you know the first thing about women? You should sort the little tart out!'

Hardly able to believe his ears, Guy stared at his father-in-law. Pitifully, he asked, 'How? In God's name, how?'

'Smack her round the face for a start! Give her a good hiding. I don't stand for any of that, never have done. She's always been a flighty little thing, but if she ever tries to come the high-handed bit with me, I just knock her straight off her pedestal.'

Swallowing hard, Guy was completely taken aback. 'You're actually saying I should hit her?'

Jack stood up and walked round the desk, flicking his hand as he did so. 'Don't make it sound so brutal, son. I'm not talking heavy stuff here, but a quick smack never did a woman any harm.'

'Are you serious? You'd condone me smacking your daughter?'

Jack braced himself. 'Certainly.' Then he poked Guy in the shoulder. 'I'm telling you now, if you smacked her a few times she wouldn't step out of line so much as an inch.'

'But I don't want to smack her. Don't you think I loathe myself enough as it is?'

Jack stared at Guy then raised his hand to squeeze the young man's shoulder. 'What on earth do you loathe yourself for?'

Exasperated, he sighed and looked around the room. Finally he said, 'For failing, I suppose.'

Jack swept his hand towards the showroom. 'But you haven't failed. Just because I blast you out once, doesn't mean you've failed.' He stuck out his chin and moved his face closer to Guy's. 'Get your hair cut. Tidy yourself up a bit. Sort this daughter of mine out for good and all, then things'll get back on an even keel.'

'And you'd be happy with that, would you?'

Jack straightened and reached into his pocket for a cigar. He thrust one at Guy who had no alternative but to take it. 'What's happy got to do with it? It's business we're really talking about, Guy. Business.'

He shook his head and threw the cigar on the desk. It rolled on to the floor. 'No, Jack, actually it's not business. It's my private life and happiness we're talking about, and your daughter's. Your business just happens to have got messed up in it all . . . for which I'm sorry.'

Jack laughed then. He slapped Guy on the back. 'I know you are, so forget it. The best thing you can do is get behind that desk and start concentrating on cars. Like I say, forget about Naomi. I'll sort her out. Just you leave her to me.'

Guy opened his mouth to object when Kelly bustled into the room once more. 'I'm really sorry to interrupt, Guy, but your mother's on the phone. I think it's important.'

For a few seconds, he stared at her. 'Sorry?'

'Your mum! She needs to talk to you, urgently.'

Guy rubbed his forehead and turned to the phone, snatching it up. He looked at his father-in-law. 'Sorry, Jack. I won't be a minute.' Jack just nodded.

Taking a deep breath, Guy said, 'Mum?'

'Oh, Guy!' Lynda Hamilton's voice was anguished. 'I'm really sorry to ring you like this but you must get here! To Addenbrooke's! It's your grandpa. He's not well. He's not well at all.'

'Grandpa? But what's the matter with him?'

She took a sharp breath, more like a sob. Then, in a pitiful voice she said, 'They say he's dying . . . and he's been asking for you, Guy.'

Already shattered by the last twenty-four hours, his brain seemed unable to grasp the meaning of this conversation. Guy slumped into a seat in total shock. 'Dying? What do you mean, *dying?*'

'I'm sorry, I should have warned you before this. I just kept thinking he'd get better. Grandpa never really got over his hip operation, some infection or other, and the doctors said they couldn't re-operate until it had cleared up. And now he's got pneumonia, darling, and he's most terribly ill and keeps asking to see you and Lily. She's on her way from Sheffield.'

Clutching at the telephone, Guy stared at the coffee spills on his desk, his mind spinning. Grandpa was dying, Lily was coming down from university in Sheffield. He looked at Jack who stood staring back at him. 'I'll be there, Mum. Which ward?' Lynda Hamilton explained to her son how to get there. Guy replaced the receiver and stood up. 'I have to go to Addenbrooke's. My grandfather's terribly ill . . . dying. I'm sorry, Jack, to run out like this, but he's asking for me.'

Jack frowned and sucked on his cigar. 'But I thought you were adopted?'

Guy glared at him. 'Yes, I am.'

Jack shrugged. 'It's just that Naomi always said you weren't too keen on your adoptive family.'

Guy just stared at him, his true feelings for this awful man suddenly slotting into place. He decided not to explain himself. Instead he turned on his heel and walked away.

Bill Hamilton was a shadow of his former self. Sitting on a chair beside his bed, Guy lifted the old man's arthritic hand and brought it to his lips. He caught Daisy's eye. She sat opposite, next to his Aunt Sarah. Pressing his lips against the blue-veined, mottled skin, Guy winked and smiled at her. In exaggerated fashion she winked back. Lynda sat beside him. Stephen and Tom had gone down to the foyer for a much-needed break. Aunt Sarah leaned forward in her seat and whispered, 'He'll wake in a bit, Guy. He did so want to see you. You and Lily. He speaks of nothing else.'

Trying to swallow an enormous lump in his throat, and struggling to keep his tears at bay, Guy looked once more at his grandfather. On a drip, skin tinged grey, he looked pathetic. In all Guy's life, Bill Hamilton had never looked pathetic. He'd dominated a room with his presence, commanded everyone's attention with his wicked tongue. And now all that was about to be snuffed out. Guy remembered someone saying, *You're a long time dead*, and realised that although some periods in life may seem an eternity, in reality they are just a blip. Like life itself. Suddenly it seemed so important for him to get it right. If he couldn't, he must move on before it was too late.

He sighed as the old man stirred, finally opening his eyes. Immediately the atmosphere in the room changed. Bill Hamilton's wide open eyes rested on Guy and in a strained whisper, he said, 'You got here then?' Then he searched the tiny hospital room. 'No Lily yet?'

Sarah touched her father-in-law's shoulder. 'She's on her way, Dad. She won't be long.'

Bill turned to look at her and smiled. 'Good. I need to see 'er afore I go.'

Sarah nudged him. 'Don't talk so silly. You're not going anywhere.'

Bill looked at Guy, sizing up his only grandson. This young man had always bowled him over, right from the start; since arriving in his life at the tender age of six with enough passion in his young body to light up Ely Cathedral until now, his dying hour. Except – Guy didn't look too well at the moment. Bill searched his face, noting his sunken cheeks and bloodshot eyes, immediately recognising his unhappiness. Gruffly he murmured, ''S not working out then, boy?'

Momentarily Guy closed his eyes, lowering them slightly before resting them once more on his grandfather. He squeezed his hand. 'Seems you were right, Grandpa. All those years ago when you told me to steer clear of her. D'you remember?'

Bill chuckled. ' 'Course I remember, and 'course I were right.' He shifted slightly, but it was as though each tiny movement sapped his energy. 'Chuck 'er! Don't mess with the likes of 'er, boy. Chuck 'er!'

Lynda tugged slightly on Guy's arm, shaking her head. 'Don't distress him, Guy. Now's not the time.'

'You leave 'im be!' Scolded the old man. 'Me and 'im's always bin straight with each other.' Lynda sat back in her seat, resigned to Bill's bloody-mindedness.

He scanned the room anxiously. 'When'd you say Lily'd get 'ere?'

Sarah looked at her watch. 'Soon, Dad. In a couple of hours.'

'Huh,' he muttered. 'Not sure I can last 'til then.'

Guy squeezed his hand. 'Oh, I think you can. The one thing you taught me was how to be stubborn.' Softly, he laughed. 'And it's not such a bad thing. A bit of stubbornness can really sort the men from the boys, can't it?' A sob then caught in his throat but he continued, 'Lily needs to see you, Grandpa. The same as me.'

A crafty smile lit the old man's face as he closed his eyes again. He whispered, 'Best rest then . . . 'til she gets 'ere.'

With a pained expression, Guy watched his grandfather drift off once more. Then, sorrowfully, he lowered his own head as tears welled into his eyes and dripped on to the bedclothes. This really was about as much as he could bear. Lynda wrapped her arm around her son, aware from the few words he'd just exchanged with his grandfather that all was not well in his life. She hugged him and kissed his hair and Daisy and Sarah just sat and watched in sadness and fascination.

Chapter Fourteen

Bill Hamilton died at twelve-thirty-nine in the early afternoon, about thirteen minutes after Lily arrived. During the two and a half hours before his grandfather's death, Guy didn't move from his seat. At about eleven o'clock he lowered his head on to his arms on the bed and slept. Nobody disturbed him, not even when his father and Stephen returned to the hospital room. Moving from her seat next to Guy, Lynda pulled Tom aside, whispering softly to her husband, warning him of Guy's unhappiness. Watching her son cry had been a first for her. Even as a child Guy never cried. Tom, already heartbroken at what he considered the untimely death of his father, looked across at the sleeping form of his adoptive son and was filled with pity. Deep down, he'd always cared for Guy.

He woke with a start as a nurse fussed around his grandfather. He raised himself from the bed, stretched slightly and ran his hands through his dishevelled hair. Then he saw her, sitting opposite, where Daisy had been, looking radiant and calm: Lily. Their eyes met, locking for a few seconds, but no words or smiles were exchanged. To Guy she was as always a vision of beauty.

Bill opened his eyes and feasted upon the vision too. Lily shifted closer to him, placing both hands around his neck and putting her head on his chest. 'Lily,' he groaned. 'Knew you wouldn't let me down.' Then he closed his eyes again and she moved back a little, fleetingly casting her eyes in Guy's direction. He noticed they were full of tears. A short while later Bill died.

Guy decided not to go back to the garage. He was incapable of doing any work, his powers of concentration dulled even further by the death of his grandfather. Briefly, he toyed with the idea of travelling to Ely with his mother and father, but that didn't appeal either. He knew his mother would ask questions and fuss over him. He wanted neither. What he wanted was peace and solitude in order to decide his future. He could think of nowhere to get that peace.

In the end he went home to Chesterton and as he pulled into his drive saw Naomi's red BMW cabriolet sitting there. In vain he'd hoped she'd be out, as was so often the case, shopping perhaps. All Guy wanted was a quiet place to think; even this was to be denied him. In despair he turned off the ignition and released his seat-belt but made no attempt to get out. He sat there for a full five minutes before coming to the only conclusion possible. He'd take a shower, pack a few things and leave Naomi for good. He knew this meant no job, but maybe he didn't like his job anymore. He braced himself, unsure he was up to facing his wife, but he had no choice. In his present state of mind she'd most probably annihilate him with her waspish tongue.

He unlocked the front door and, from habit, threw his keys on to a table situated nearby. He continued across the hall floor, shoes clicking on the polished maple, towards the kitchen where he intended to make himself a cup of tea. Bright November sunshine streamed in through the south-facing window as he ran fresh water into the kettle and plugged it in. Then Guy took a mug from a sink full of dirty pots and rinsed it under the hot tap. Looking for a tea-towel, he found none so shook the mug partially dry then dropped a Lapsang tea-bag into it. As he waited for the kettle to boil he raised his face, catching sight of himself in a mirror, one of many strategically placed so that at all times Naomi could check on her appearance. Guy often wondered if she was in love with herself. Peering closer he didn't at all like what he saw; was appalled in fact. His mind flicked back to Lily, a picture of health and loveliness. What must she have thought of him? Guy ran a hand through his clean but lank hair and wondered how he could have let his appearance deteriorate so. He racked his brain to remember the last time he'd eaten and genuinely couldn't. Was it two or three days ago? His eyes wandered down to the blazer and trousers he was wearing and he realised for the first time that his clothes hung on him baggily and were sorely in need of dry-cleaning.

'Guy.' Naomi's weak voice came from behind and he turned nervously as though caught doing something wrong. But all thoughts of himself disappeared immediately as he looked into the face of his wife.

'My God . . . *Naomi!*' Guy took a few paces forward, shocked and appalled. The left side of her face was so bruised and swollen that her eye was almost closed. She'd brushed her hair forward in an attempt to conceal it, but hadn't. She stood in a hunched fashion, as though her shoulder ached as well. 'Did your father do this? My God . . . Naomi, did he do this?'

Spitefully she hissed at him, 'As if you didn't know.'

'What do you mean? For Christ's sake, Naomi, you don't think I've got anything to do with this, do you?'

Her eyes filled and he was reminded of how in the beginning she'd always resorted to tears. But she hadn't cried in a long time and he was actually moved by her doing so now. 'You complained to him about me, Guy. You used me as your excuse for doing a lousy job at the garage. I think that's despicable, don't you?' Her words sounded thick, as though her tongue was swollen too.

In that instance he knew she was right. But all the sadness and disappointment in his marriage and his work were bound together, blurred like a fog too thick to see through, and as long as he continued along this road, Naomi would always manipulate him and he would always be consumed with self-loathing. 'I'm sorry,' he muttered.

'So am I.'

This was useless. Guy turned, took the tea-bag out of his mug then walked over to the fridge for some milk. He added a splash to the smoky tea, returned the milk and picked up the mug. Then he moved to one side of Naomi to leave the kitchen.

In a surprised voice she asked, 'Where are you going?'

He hesitated, noticing a trace of wildness in her eyes. 'To shower . . . then pack. I think you'll agree it's for the best?'

Her eyes were fierce now and in a flash she raised her hand and swiped him clean round the side of his head. For such a tiny person, she certainly packed a punch. It was as though all her pent-up anger against her father was taken out on Guy. His scalding tea was sent flying across the kitchen, splashing everywhere. The mug shattered on the floor. Guy's left ear stung from the force of her blow and he stared at her in disbelief.

'Go on then, hit me back . . . if you dare.'

He continued to stare at her, recognising her innate weakness and feeling sick to the pit of his stomach. How could he have allowed himself to be sucked in by this family? He sneered, 'You'd like that, wouldn't you, Naomi? Then maybe we could fuck like wild animals, huh?'

Her eyes flashed and he knew he'd scored a bull's-eye. Guy continued out of the kitchen and that was when she really let rip with her verbal abuse. She called him everything under the sun, using swear words he'd forgotten existed. He carried on up the perforated stainless steel stairs to their bedroom and grabbed as many clothes as he could lay his hands on. She followed him everywhere, screaming at him and pushing and thumping him with her fists. He left the bedroom, without a bag, his clothes bundled in his arms, and stumbled down the stairs. She was two steps behind him all the way.

Guy had difficulty picking up his keys and for a few brief seconds her insults stopped. He struggled to open the front door then venomously she continued, 'You're going nowhere, Guy. You've had your moment of glory. Daddy won't want you at the garage and you'll never get another decent job for as long as you live. You're useless! Fucking useless!' She grabbed his arm as he made to step outside. 'And would you like to know why I fucked around? Would you? You may as well know the truth . . . everybody else does. It's common knowledge among our friends.' Gleefully she caught the interest mixed with hurt in his eyes and savagely hurled her next words at him. 'Yes, the *truth*! It's because I had to fake every sodding orgasm with you! *Every sodding one!* Because when it comes to *fucking* you're just the same as you are at the garage . . . *useless!*'

If he hadn't been so worn out and bitterly wounded, he'd have laughed. The final insult. As it was he did manage a smile then shook his head and turned to leave. 'It's true!' she yelled after him. Naomi drew breath and screamed again, '*It's fucking true!*'

Guy struggled to open his car door, slung his clothes on to the passenger seat, got in and drove off without a backward glance.

Temporarily, he moved in with Keir. For the second night running they talked into the early hours and it was Keir who straightened out Guy's thoughts on how to handle the demise of his marriage and the abrupt termination of his position at Benson Motors.

'Get as much as you can from it. Fleece the old bugger! You deserve it. Haven't you given them the best part of five years? Don't walk away empty-handed. Only an idiot would do that.'

Keir insisted that Jack Benson would offer Guy nothing and had a suspicion his friend would accept this without objecting, such was his low opinion of himself, but what good would that do his future? With his car and a pay-off Guy could buy a few more cars, do a bit of trading, maybe even set up his own business. If things worked out, Keir could join him in the future. By the end of their long night's discussion, Guy's spirits had risen slightly.

He parked his brand new racing green XJS 4-litre V8 down a side-street off Hills Road and walked the short distance to Benson Motors. He entered the garage for what he knew would be the last time and strode through to his office. Nobody was about, not a soul. Perhaps this was a deliberate ploy on Jack's behalf; create the right atmosphere for a showdown. Guy shook his head, recognising his own imagination working overtime.

But perhaps he was right after all for as he entered his office he saw immediately that his father-in-law had wasted no time. All Guy's belongings had been cleared and put in a large box which stood by the side of the desk. Five years and it ended like this. Swiftly, he moved round the desk and tried to open a couple of the drawers. All locked. He hurried to the filing cabinet; it had been his intention to grab a few client names and telephone numbers. Locked. He turned, cursing himself for not carrying spare keys, then saw the man himself framed in the doorway, looking threatening.

'Hallo and goodbye, Guy.' Jack held out his hand. 'The car keys, please.'

Anger welled within him. Keir had been spot on. Thank goodness he'd been warned. He cleared his throat. 'The car stays with me, Jack. It's the least I deserve.'

'Oh, no, it doesn't! That car belongs to this garage and there's nothing you can do about it.'

'Nothing I can do, no, but something *you* can do. You owe it to me.'

Jack's face was going puce. 'You must be joking! No chance,' he spluttered. 'You walked out on my daughter! No chance at all.'

Guy held up his hands. 'I'm going quietly, Jack, without a fuss. I could take you to the cleaners over this, industrial tribunal and all that, and I'm certainly in a position to sue your daughter for divorce. Drag her name through the dirt and get half the house, half the contents.'

Jack bellowed, 'You little shit! *I* paid for that house. It was *my* wedding present to *my* daughter!' He drew breath. 'Out of decency, because you were marrying her, I put you in a job you're bloody incapable of doing! You don't deserve a penny!'

Something registered in Guy's brain then and he actually started to see the funny side of this ridiculous scene. Maybe he would eventually walk away with nothing, have his car towed away in the middle of the night but, hell, he might as well try for as much as he could get in the meantime. Sordid reality had turned into a game and, thanks to Keir, he was picking up the threads quite nicely. Spurred on, he glared at his father-in-law. 'Fifty thousand, cash, plus the car and I walk away quietly.'

Almost choking, Jack had to steady himself against the door. 'You must be joking! Get *fucking* lost.'

Guy moved a few paces forward. He actually looked intimidating. 'I'm not joking, Jack. I think that's fair. Don't underestimate me, please, because if you do I shall kick up such a stink among your high-flown associates your name will be a laughing stock. After all, don't forget, I have been party to all your little scams! And I shall drag your precious daughter's name through every conceivable dung-heap I can think of. If you don't believe me . . . try me?'

Jack blanched and started to look physically sick. In a flash Guy knew he'd won. And it had been so easy. Jack feebly flicked his wrist. 'And if I agree – to these terms – you walk away quietly? Get an amicable divorce, no mud-slinging?'

Guy nodded. 'I won't bother you in the future, if you don't bother me.'

Jack dipped his hand into his inside pocket and withdrew his cheque book. He mumbled, 'Forty – no more. That's all your getting.'

'Oh, no! Fifty – *cash*. And my car.'

Jack balked. 'I haven't got that sort of money in cash. Who d'you think I am? A Rothschild?'

'You can get it. I'll give you till tomorrow.' Guy bent down and with a struggle picked up the box. Then he pushed past Jack. 'I'm staying with Keir for the time being, so give it to him.' He raised an eyebrow and did his best to look menacing. 'I'm trusting you so don't shaft me on this. For your own sake.'

Eyes bulging, Jack caught his breath then reluctantly nodded. Guy walked out of the showroom via the visitors' entrance and hurried, as best as he could carrying five years' belongings in a cardboard box, to his car.

Jack walked straight through to Keir's office. He sat himself down and plunged one hand into his inside pocket, withdrawing two cigars. He offered one to Keir, who accepted gratefully.

Jack drew a deep breath. 'I suppose you heard all that palaver just now?' Keir nodded, making himself more comfortable in his seat. 'Well, how would you feel about standing in for Guy ... until I've had time to sort things out in my own head, that is?'

A sly smile crept round Keir's mouth. He turned it into a genuine smile. 'Fine. If you think I'm capable?'

'No thinking about it, I know you are. A darn' sight more able than he was. Can't promise anything permanent, though, but there will be a salary increase while you're running the show.'

'Thanks, Jack. I'm much obliged.'

His face creased, Jack said in a reproachful voice, 'Why'd you take him in, Keir? I'd have thought a bloke like you would have had enough of the likes of Guy Hamilton. I mean, he did steal your thunder here, didn't he?'

'We're friends,' Keir said simply.

'Oh, I realise that, but he's not to be trusted, you do realise that?'

Keir chuckled. 'There's not much I don't know about Guy.' After all, he'd spent a very long time watching and copying him.

Jack clipped the end off his cigar and threw the clippers over to Keir. 'Well, don't let him spoil things for you now. He's bad news. *Bad news.*'

Keir shrugged and studied Jack Benson's face, wondering why he couldn't appreciate the vital flame he'd just snuffed out through his own bull-headedness and stupidity. He and his bitch of a daughter had suffocated Guy with their appalling behaviour. If they'd just let him flourish and grow in his own way, Benson Motors would have grown with him. If there was a choice, Keir knew only too well which star he would follow. The one that would undoubtedly rise in the future.

Chapter Fifteen

The early November sun glimmered weakly throughout the afternoon of Bill Hamilton's funeral in Ely. As he was laid to rest next to his beloved wife, both Tom and Stephen couldn't help thinking that at last their father was at peace. He'd never been quite the same without her.

There was a gathering at Stephen and Sarah's afterwards. With the help of Lily and Daisy, she had prepared a tasty feast of open sandwiches, slices of mouth-watering quiche, hot sausage rolls and an assortment of cakes. Guy, with his hair cut shorter and wearing a navy-blue suit, a whole size smaller than anything he'd previously owned, looked more like his old self. Since he could remember, he'd never weighed himself, not once, but didn't much like his new skinny frame and fully intended to eat wisely and visit the gym regularly in the future.

He was surprised by the turnout of people. Inside his aunt and uncle's bungalow there was standing room only. He still couldn't believe his cantankerous old grandfather was gone and not about to pop up at any second, cussing. Nor could he understand his own feeling of pain when he realised this was not going to happen. It seemed such a short while ago he'd fled the Hamilton family with alacrity. And now, well, it was as though a part of him had died alongside his grandfather. It was weird; in a short while he'd lost his wife, his job and his grandfather, but he only grieved for one of them.

He bit into the butterfly cake in his hand, thinking it'd been years since he'd eaten anything so light and delicious, then licked his lips. He felt a jolt in the small of his back. As he turned a smile crossed his face. 'Cassie! I didn't expect to see you here.'

Tilting her head slightly, she scrutinised him. 'You've cut your hair.'

He touched his ears. 'Yes. Thought I'd better smarten myself up a bit.'

A little too enthusiastically, she agreed. 'It's good. Like the suit.'

Guy looked down at himself. 'Thanks. So do I. Don't suppose it'll fit me for too long, but I thought it was the least I could do for the old man.' He frowned. 'Ah, I get it now – you and Lily. That's how you know my grandfather.'

'Correct, and he certainly was a character. Lily adored him.'

Guy's eyes darted round the room. 'Where is she?'

Cassie caught his interest. 'In the kitchen, beavering away. It seems more people turned up than expected.'

'Yes, so I noticed.' He looked once more into Cassie's impressive violet eyes. 'So, how's things at Benson's?'

She laughed and shrugged. 'It's only been a week, Guy, but already you're missed. At least, I miss you.'

'Do you? That's nice to know.'

It's the truth, she thought. 'Well, you always said such nice things about my flowers, how could I not miss you? Nobody else comments on them. *Ever!*'

'I find that hard to believe. Although it hasn't escaped my notice that half the staff do look bored stiff.' He smiled. 'You and me aren't the type to be bored, are we?'

Cassie's throat tightened and she sighed, grateful to have been paired with this man, albeit in such a casual way. 'Well, I'm certainly bored with Benson Motors.'

Guy squeezed her arm, just below the curve of her shoulder, and his touch sent shivers through her. 'Branch out on your own. You're very artistic, Cassie, extraordinarily so.'

She stifled a guffaw. 'Hey, we're really having a gloat here, aren't we?'

He smiled at her American accent, liking it. 'We're speaking the truth. I'm branching out on my own, although perhaps I haven't had much choice, and already it feels right.'

'Yeah, but you're in cars and the mark-up on flowers isn't *quite* as high.'

'But your talent is. You have to look for openings, consider all opportunities.'

108

'What opportunities? You make it all sound so easy.'

He studied her a moment and she lowered her eyes, flattered by the way he was looking at her, as though she was the only person in the room. Then the moment was lost because Lily, flushed from her labours in the kitchen, appeared. She beamed first at Cassie then at Guy. Cassie's eyes darted from her friend to the man of her dreams who stood looking at Lily with such heat in his eyes no onlooker could miss it. Cassie's eyes switched to Lily then and in a flash she knew they were capable of loving each other to the exclusion of everyone else, including her. Cassie braced herself. 'You're doing a great job, Lily.'

'Oh, thanks.' Lily pointed to the kitchen. 'It's bedlam in there. What would Grandpa have said? As soon as I finish one load of sandwiches they're gone. I don't know about grieving, we have some very hungry people here today.'

'It's the weather. Makes people hungry,' said Guy, noting the fullness of Lily's mouth and the perfect symmetry of her teeth.

Her eyes ranged around the room. 'It's funny, but I keep expecting him to appear – start swearing at everyone.'

Guy nodded in agreement. 'That's exactly what I've been thinking.'

For a few seconds, Lily hesitated. 'I just wish—'

Searching her face, he prompted, 'Yes? What do you wish?'

'That he *would* reappear so that I could tell him I miss him. I never really told him how much I loved him.'

Cassie shifted back a few steps, feeling very much in the way. Thankfully she spied Daisy across the room. She nudged her friend. 'He knew, Lily. It showed in your eyes.'

She turned to Cassie who was already making her way to Daisy. Both she and Guy watched her go. 'What a lovely thing to say,' commented Lily.

'Well, you do have . . . incredible eyes.'

She looked at Guy. 'And so do you.'

Embarrassed and flattered, he laughed. 'Tell me, is there anything to drink around here?'

'Tea?'

'I was thinking of something maybe stronger?'

Lily moved forward slightly, actually brushing against him. He caught the scent of her hair and was transported back to his grandpa's party; she'd kissed the old man then, her hair falling forward, and Guy had wanted to touch it, run his fingers through it.

'Follow me,' she said.

'I'm right behind you.'

Cassie watched as Lily and Guy made their way out of the room. She noted the way they spoke to each other continually, pausing to look into each other's eyes.

'Makes you jealous, doesn't it?'

Blinking with surprise, Cassie looked at Daisy. 'Is that how you feel?'

She reddened slightly. 'A bit, although he wouldn't want me, so I s'pose there's no point.'

Raising her eyebrows, Cassie sighed. 'And he wouldn't want me either.'

Fiercely, Daisy shook her head. 'You're wrong there. He would . . . except he wouldn't because of Lily.'

Aware of this young woman's grasp on the important things in life, Cassie asked, 'And d'you suppose he really cares for Lily? I mean, *really cares?*'

Without hesitation, Daisy nodded. 'Oh, yes. You should have seen the way he looked at her at Grandpa's party. I watched him from across the room. And even at his wedding and every time since.' Earnestly now, she continued, 'Do you ever wonder what he'd be like?' Sheepishly she lowered her eyes. 'You know . . .'

'What d'you mean?'

'Oh, you know . . . with his thing.'

Amused and titillated, Cassie tried to keep a straight face. 'His thing? What's his thing, Daisy?'

She leaned forward and cupped one hand round Cassie's ear. 'His willy.'

Cassie nodded. 'Oh, that thing. Well, I expect he's quite adept with that thing, but no, I haven't wondered about it, Daisy, not until you just mentioned it.' Liar, she added in her head.

'Don't tell Lily I said that, will you, Cassie?'

'No way. It's totally between you and me.'

'Oh, good. I like secrets.'

Cassie looked at her. 'Yeah, and so do I. Perhaps in time you and me'll share a few more.'

'Cool. I'm good at secrets. Not much good at anything else, apart from betting. I always win when we go to Newmarket races.'

'You underestimate yourself, Daisy. You're as good as the next person at everything.'

Daisy looked very pleased but said, 'Just a bit slow, though.'

Cassie frowned then shrugged. 'What the hell? Not every gal needs to be speedy.'

Daisy's eyes moved to the hall where she could see Guy drinking beer. Beside him, engrossed in conversation, was Lily. She sipped at her glass of white wine. 'Would you like a drink?' she asked.

Cassie's eyes followed hers and she watched in fascination as Guy stroked something off Lily's hair. It was history repeating itself. Hadn't he once picked a leaf off her hair? She could still remember her body's reaction. But this time it was done in such a loving way Cassie was jealous. She swallowed hard and forced herself to sound cheerful. 'What a good idea.'

Daisy walked out of the room towards her sister and cousin. Diffidently Cassie followed.

Guy was still there long after most people had left. After a long discussion with his mother, during which Lynda was at last put in the picture about Naomi and Jack Benson, he made an effort to sound a lot more cheerful than he actually felt. Lynda was obviously reassured because she looked across the room at Tom, indicating she'd like to go home. It had been a long day. 'You're welcome to come back with us and stay the night, Guy? It's so good to talk like this. I have missed our chats.'

He declined the offer but stood up with his mother and together they walked over to Tom. Guy stretched out his hand to his father who gratefully clutched it, drawing his son closer. Guy whispered, 'Dad . . . thanks for making today bearable.'

Tom shrugged. 'Don't thank me. Thank you uncle and aunt. They did all the hard work. Along with Lily and Daisy, of course.'

Guy looked across at his cousins and Cassie and didn't feel like going back to Cambridge just yet. After saying goodbye to his parents he approached the girls, looking at his watch. 'Do you fancy coming to the pub for an hour or so?'

All three looked keen but Guy's eyes were on Lily. Cassie grabbed Daisy's arm as she was about to agree. 'You go with Lily, Guy. Daisy and I are done in.'

Immediately Lily faced her friend. 'What do you mean? We must all go.'

Cassie rested back in her seat. 'I really am tired.'

'Well, can I give you a lift home then? You live in Ely, don't you?'

Disappointed at his lack of persuasion, Cassie stood up. 'Okay. You can drop me off on your way to the pub with Lily.'

She too stood up and turned to her sister. 'Are you sure you wouldn't like to come?'

Daisy frowned. She did want to go to the pub, but she also understood it would be polite to refuse, more's the pity. And then the whole thing was taken out of her hands. Guy stretched out and pulled her into a standing position. 'I insist.' He looked sideways at Cassie. 'You must all come. Just for a little while. We can have our own private little wake. Grandpa would have approved, I'm sure.'

Cassie said nothing but of course she wanted to go.

They all squeezed into Guy's car and drove the short distance to the Fountain in Barton Square where they enjoyed themselves tremendously. Cassie relaxed and made everyone laugh with her lazy humour, and Daisy relaxed and made everyone laugh with her blatant honesty. They all drank far too much and Guy realised he was well over the limit, but to hell with it. He could leave his car until morning, it would be safe in Barton Square. He'd walk the girls home then take his parents up on their offer. And this he did, except Cassie lived closer to his parents and so walked with him back to Lily and Daisy's where she watched as he kissed both girls chastely on the cheek. Then, chattering easily, the two of them made their way to her parents' house near the river in Ely.

As they approached her home, she turned to Guy. 'I know it's late but would you like a coffee? I have my own room at the top of the house.' Cassie looked up at her window under the eaves of the early Victorian house, adding hopefully, 'It's very private.'

Guy's eyes went from the window to her face then to the river as he fumbled in his pocket for his cigarettes. He wasn't stupid, he recognised the signs, but he liked Cassie far too much to take advantage of such an offer. 'I ought to get back.' He left his cigarettes in his pocket and looked at his watch. 'It's late as it is and I don't want to have to knock my parents up.'

For a few seconds Cassie was speechless. She stepped forward and touched his arm. 'I did just mean coffee, Guy. I wasn't trying to proposition you or anything.'

He was embarrassed, not least because he thought she was. 'Of course. Another time, perhaps.'

Words were tumbling through her brain but she couldn't get them out. Deciding it was best to walk away she took a deep breath and turned, at least with some dignity intact. And that was when he recognised her humility and grabbed her, pulling her into his arms. Now his face was so close she stopped breathing. Guy brought down his mouth and kissed her with some force. Was she dreaming? Was this actually happening? She barely had time to respond before it was over, but still he held her tightly in his arms. 'You're special. Don't ever forget that.'

'But not special enough, huh?'

'You're certainly special enough.' Then he kissed her again and this time she did have time to respond.

He pulled away and stepped back; either that or drag her inside. To Cassie it was like losing everything, the feeling of separation was so intense. 'Guy,' she whispered.

Retreating further from her, he blew her a kiss. 'See you, Cassie. Take care.'

She copied him in an effort to sound carefree. 'You too . . . See you.'

Cassie Milbank watched Guy Hamilton until he was completely out of sight and wondered how she could possibly live the rest of her life without him.

Chapter Sixteen

Eighteen months down the line Guy had a comfortable business going, if you could ever call living by your wits comfortable. His real love was for nearly new specialist cars and over a short period of time he built up a reliable network of contacts. This enabled him to supply any customer with a Maserati, Lamborghini, Ferrari, Porsche, Aston Martin, Caterham, Morgan – even the odd Corvette or Dodge Viper. Such would-be buyers could do a lot worse than deal with Guy Hamilton who had a reputation for being scrupulously fair. The cars he sold came with no warranty, unless they still held the manufacturer's, but each carried Guy's own personal guarantee of good quality. He also dealt with BMWs, Mercedes, Jaguars, etc., which he bought privately, at auction or from garages. His buying was done mostly with the guidance of a mechanic friend, Robert Unwin, who also provided garaging space and an excellent valet service at his premises in Chesterton. Often Guy's mobile phone was red-hot and he travelled miles to deliver a car, after which he'd make his own way home. Very soon he got used to trains, buses, even hitching a lift. The affluent days of sitting behind a desk with a fat cigar were truly over, but at least all earnings were his to do with as he pleased. Of course, most of it went straight back into buying more cars and gradually his reputation preceded him.

Keir was fascinated and avidly chronicled Guy's progress. They still shared a flat although they'd moved to a much larger one in Newnham. Keir particularly noticed that Guy was never still; he seemed constantly to have his ear to the ground, knowing exactly what was for sale in Cambridgeshire, Suffolk, and even further afield. He also knew which garage salesmen to trust. In one way or another he'd dealt with most of them, and even Benson's helped him out a few times. With Keir's crafty intervention that is. As Jack was never there anymore, he often put enquiries for up-market secondhand vehicles Guy's way. With his confidence restored, he felt the world was there to do business with; there was no door he wouldn't knock on to that end.

But so far as his love-life was concerned it was a blank. The truth was Naomi had hurt him far too deeply.

Although still a couple of months short of her twenty-first birthday, Lily was now winding up her degree course in Hotel and Catering Management at Sheffield Hallam University. With just a few more weeks to go, she sat with Cassie in a bar in Cambridge Station, drinking white wine and mulling over her future.

'But I like my job at Henri's and I'm seriously considering taking up his offer of full-time employment. I mean, the food they serve and the functions they arrange are excellent and he has offered me good money and quite flexible hours to co-manage it. I could do a lot worse . . . couldn't I?'

Disappointment washed over Cassie. She was very keen for Lily to return to Cambridgeshire. She missed her, all the time she missed her. Although both girls had many other friends, there was nobody like each other. It was special, their relationship, a once in a lifetime thing. 'It's miles away, Lily. Sheffield's miles away! Something's bound to crop up here. Don't commit yourself just yet.'

She sighed. 'Yes, well, my biggest fear is I'll end up working for my father.'

'But you won't! Surely he wouldn't expect you to work for him?'

'Oh, wouldn't he? Even though I've got my part-time job, they've still supported me through university and Dad never lets me forget it. He'd be only too pleased for me to join the family business. He keeps dropping hints all the time.'

'But that's ridiculous. You haven't spent three years gaining a degree to serve fish and chips! What does your mum say?'

Lily sipped her wine. 'Actually Mum misses me very much, and so does Daisy. And Dad says I wouldn't be serving fish and chips, I'd be running the business, thinking up expansion ideas.' She pulled a face.

115

Cassie squeezed her friend's hand. 'Don't, Lily. You'd die of boredom. You're meant for finer things, I know you are. I tell you what, I'll keep my eyes open, shall I? As soon as a job comes up I'll let you know.' She looked at her watch. 'What time does your train go?'

Lily also looked at her watch. 'Oh, not for another ten minutes. Thanks, Cassie, for driving me here.' She looked out of the window towards the car park. 'And I love your new car.'

Cassie raised her fists in the air. 'Yes! My little Fripon! I did it! I bought my own car, my little French marvel. It's been hell, I can tell you, never going out, saving, saving, saving and working all these years for that cow, Sniffnel, but I bloody did it!'

'What do you mean, never going out? I don't believe that for a second.'

'It's true. Believe me.' Cassie fixed her eyes on her drink. 'Besides, I miss you. Stupid, isn't it? Three years and I still miss you.' She implored her friend, 'Please come home, Lily? Please?'

'I will if I can find a job.' She chuckled. 'If only Grandpa was still alive. He always used to fight my corner.'

'But I thought your grandpa wanted you to join the business?'

Lily laughed. 'Grandpa just liked a good fight. He switched sides to antagonise.'

Cassie laughed. 'And I bet you miss him like crazy?'

'Yes, I do.'

Narrowing her eyes, Cassie saw her way clear to enquiring into Lily's family affairs. 'Do you ever hear from Guy these days?'

There was a flicker in Lily's eyes and Cassie didn't miss it. 'He seems to be doing okay. I don't see Aunt Lynda very often and I haven't seen Guy since Grandpa's funeral.' She frowned. 'But doesn't that Keir bloke keep you informed? Didn't you say they share a flat?'

Doing her best to look nonchalant, Cassie took a long sip of her wine. 'Sometimes, when I think to mention it. But I don't get to see Mr Doughty so often these days. He's flashing about all over the place being Mr Important.'

Lily laughed. 'You really don't like him, do you?'

'Understatement.'

'Why?'

Cassie shrugged her shoulders, remembering the countless times she'd seen Keir Doughty with his hand up Naomi Benson's skirt. Although not since he'd been promoted. 'Just the way he is, I suppose. And he looks at me kinda funny.'

'He fancies you. You could do worse.'

'Oh, for pity's sake, Lily! He's gross!'

Lily looked out of the window again. 'Well, it's nice to be able to be choosy. Chance would be a fine thing so far as I'm concerned.'

'What's that supposed to mean?'

Taking a deep breath, Lily twiddled with the stem of her glass. 'You probably won't believe this, but since Adam Greene there's been nobody.' She laughed and shifted forward in her seat, saying softly, 'Three whole years at *fucking* university, and I mean that literally, and I didn't get fucked once!'

'Only because you didn't want to be.'

'Well, maybe I did. It just didn't happen. Perhaps I send out all the wrong signals.'

'Oh, Lily, don't be a clown. You send out the right signals.' Cassie levelled her hand like a gun. 'Keep off – keep away – don't tamper – no fucking allowed!'

As bystanders overheard the two girls' ribald conversation and stared at them, Lily covered her face with her hands. 'My God, am I really like that?'

'Yeah, too true you are. And, for that matter, so am I.'

Eyes agog, Lily asked, 'But have you?' Then she lowered her voice to a whisper. 'Fucked, I mean?' Considering the two girls' closeness, Lily had never managed to get her friend to open up on this one. 'You've never mentioned it.'

'You're never here!'

'Well, in that case, answer the question now that I am.'

Cassie downed the rest of her drink and slammed the glass back on the table. 'Nope. And I don't want to either.'

Incredulously, Lily looked at her friend. 'You really don't want to?'

Putting her elbow on the table, Cassie cupped her face in her hand. 'Well, I guess I could be tempted if he had the right credentials.'

Lily copied her friend's actions and asked, 'And what are they?'

'Well, for starters, he has to look like . . .' Cassie swallowed quickly '. . . Brad Pitt.'

Lily sat back in her chair, giggling. 'In that case you'd better get back to the States.'

'I will one day, but just for a vacation. I tell you what, you come with me. Just the two of us?'

'Oh, Cassie, I'd love to. Yes, definitely. That's a wonderful idea.'

'I'll keep you to it.'

Looking at her watch, Lily gulped back the rest of her wine. 'I must dash. Mustn't miss my train.' She touched her friend's hand. 'Ring me, Cassie. Often.'

'I will.' She scraped back her chair and followed her friend out of the bar. They embraced each other and there was a lump in Cassie's throat as she watched Lily go through the gate to catch her train. Then she turned, plunging her hand into her pocket and withdrawing the keys of her brand new car. She threw them up in the air and caught them again then, with a smile on her face, left the station for the car park.

Chapter Seventeen

As Lily's train left the station for Sheffield, Guy's arrived from King's Cross. He was feeling particularly pleased with himself, having just sold a Lamborghini Diablo to a customer who'd promised him more business. As he considered whether to walk or take a taxi to Newnham he spotted a zazzy black 2-litre Fripon coupé coming towards the tiny roundabout outside Cambridge station. He gazed at the design, studiously taking in every detail, and remembered an article recently written in the *Cambridge Chronicle* about this latest French car. It had been well and truly slagged off; the writer had said it was pretentious, a low-budget car trying unsuccessfully to compete with the bigger boys!

To his surprise the car drew to a halt in front of him, much to the annoyance of the drivers behind, and the electric window slid down. 'Need a lift?' asked the driver.

Looking extremely smart in a dark grey Armani suit and matching grey tie, Guy peered inside. It was a good few seconds before he recognised Cassie. Her sleek blonde hair now rested on her shoulders and she looked stunning. The sweet chubby kid from the garage had become a svelte classy lady. Before he knew it, he'd opened the door and was seated beside her. 'Dig the car!' was all he said.

'Thanks. So do I.'

He looked around. Not much room in the back but he liked the dash and also the way Cassie sped off to counteract the annoyance of the people behind her. Immediately he relaxed and sat back into the comfort of the passenger seat. 'I'm starving!' he said. 'Fancy a Chinese?'

By this time she was at the traffic lights at the end of Station

Road and dithering about whether to turn left or right. 'Sure. Where?'

'Turn left. Let's head out to Duxford. There's a great Chinese restaurant there.'

Hardly able to believe her good fortune, Cassie did as she was told and Guy just enjoyed watching her drive. 'You certainly don't hang about.'

She spared him a glance. 'Do you?'

He laughed. 'No, I don't suppose I do. But it's not often women drive like men.'

'And do I?'

He grinned, pleased with her handling of the car. 'Yes, I think you do.' He turned towards her, enjoying the view. 'Is it yours?'

'Of course it's mine. At least it will be when I've finished paying for it.'

'It's cool, Cassie. Really cool.'

'Thanks, Guy. I'm glad you approve.'

Guy ordered beer and Cassie allowed herself one more glass of wine. By the time they'd finished eating their hot and sour soup, crispy duck and prawns in yellow bean sauce, both had been entirely filled in on each other's lives over the previous eighteen months, although Lily's name had not cropped up once during the conversation. Until, that is, Guy asked, 'How's Lily?'

'She's absolutely fine. You just missed her, actually. I dropped her off to catch her train back to Sheffield. Another couple of weeks and she'll have finished her degree.'

Guy shifted in his seat and toyed with the cigarette packet in his pocket; he'd been trying desperately hard to cut down. He succumbed and withdrew the packet, offering it to Cassie. She declined. 'Do you mind if I do?' She shook her head. Guy had to ask, 'So what is Lily going to do?'

'She's talking about staying up in Sheffield, working in a restaurant there, but I'm doing my utmost to persuade her to come back home. I miss her so much.'

'Do you?'

'Yes. Why so surprised?'

He drew on his cigarette and sighed before blowing the smoke away from the table. Almost too casually, he said, 'I'm not really surprised. She's a great kid.' Cassie was tempted to pump him about his true feelings but something stopped her. Maybe she didn't really want to know, at least not tonight. Many of Guy's tomorrows might belong to Lily but tonight was hers. 'Where are you living now, Cassie?'

'Still in Ely although I'm looking to move into Cambridge. If I could find a suitable flatmate I'd take the plunge tomorrow. But I just can't afford the rent on my own.'

'So you still live with your parents near the river?'

Blushing slightly, Cassie lowered her eyes. 'Yes. It's convenient.'

'Are you close to them?'

Why was he asking her all these questions? 'Sort of.'

Guy pondered, aware that Cassie didn't want to talk about her parents. 'Would you like coffee here or shall we go back to my place?'

She stopped breathing and stared at him. 'Sure. But won't Keir be there?'

Guy shrugged. 'He might be. Is that a problem?'

Rapidly she shook her head. 'No. No, of course not.'

'Great. I'll pay the bill.' Guy slid out of his seat. Cassie stalled him.

'I'll go halves, Guy.

He frowned. 'No, you won't. This is on me.'

'But you really don't have to.'

He touched her arm. 'Yes, I do. I want to.'

They left the restaurant and were speeding towards Cambridge. 'Wooh! This baby almost throbs when you put your foot down!'

Cassie snatched a look at Guy. 'It sounds good, doesn't it.'

'I'm almost tempted to write to the *Cambridge Chronicle* and voice my opinion on this little number.'

'Oh don't! Everyone'll want a Fripon if you do.'

'Fripon. I wonder what it means?'

'Rascal. I looked it up.'

'Does it really? Hey, I like it.' Guy smiled as his thoughts drifted to a certain Jane Richardson to whom he'd sold a Jaguar sports years before. She was now Senior Sports Editor of the *Cambridge Chronicle* and he decided to try and exert a little influence; send her his appraisal of Le Fripon . . . or *Le Throb!* If he worded it correctly he might even see his name in print. Idly,

Guy grinned, and tapped the leather facia. 'I think the critics are going to be proved wrong on this one.' He suddenly felt light-headed, giddy even, and Cassie's presence was certainly heightening that.

There was ample parking at the rear of Guy's apartment block and Cassie easily slid into a space not far from his Jaguar. She pointed to it as she stepped out of her car. 'You've still got your Jag then?'

He nodded. 'For the time being. I'll run it a while longer then think about a change.'

'What sort of change?' She was really interested. He could tell by the way her eyes glowed in the May twilight and because of this was tempted to pull her into his arms and kiss her.

'Maybe a Porsche. You really like cars, don't you, Cassie?'

'Of course I do. Most women like cars.'

'So tell me, why'd you choose yours?'

Without hesitation she replied, 'Easy. Looks and price.'

'Looks and price. In that order?'

'Yep – except if the price hadn't been right then it would have negated the looks.'

'So what particularly appealed looks-wise?'

They were entering the apartment block now and waiting for the lift. 'The backend particularly, the alloys, and of course the sexy bonnet.'

'Sexy bonnet?' Guy chuckled.

They stepped into the lift and he pressed the button for the top floor. Within seconds they'd arrived and stepped out again. He guided Cassie to his flat at the front of the building and unlocked the door. Once inside he called out, 'Keir?'

No reply. Guy looked at his watch. It was nearly ten o'clock. 'Must be out.' He touched Cassie's chin with the tip of his finger. 'Coffee? Or something stronger?'

As his finger slid away she was really tempted to ask for a brandy and bit her lip. Reading her mind, he smiled. 'You can stay the night if you're worried about driving?'

Cassie blinked. This was a change from the last time. 'I'm not sure.'

'It's okay, Cassie. I'm not trying to proposition you.' He remembered a similar situation by the river in Ely. 'We do have a spare room.'

122

Nervously she smiled then shrugged. 'Sure. Great idea. Why not? In that case I'll have an unadulterated triple brandy.'

Guy laughed at this. 'If we've got some.'

'Well, it won't be a problem if you haven't. I'll drink anything. Anything at all.'

Guy found some Armagnac in the back of a long narrow cupboard against one wall lined with bookshelves but hardly any books. It was an unopened bottle, obviously belonging to Keir. He looked at it for a few seconds, sussing out that it was special, then ripped off the seal, pouring a healthy measure into a goblet. Keir wouldn't mind. He sniffed the contents and decided to go for it himself, so poured another healthy measure. Walking over to the settee, he sat down next to Cassie and handed her the drink.

She sipped the Armagnac and glanced around the spacious open-plan flat with its pale oak stripped floor and cream paintwork. There were no rugs in the sitting room, just the sheen of the wooden floor, and off to the right the black granite surfaces of an ultra-modern kitchen. To the left a small hallway led to three bedrooms, each with its own bathroom. Cassie soon found this out because she asked to use the cloakroom and somehow or other tried each door before she found it.

For two men the flat was luxuriously furnished although there was no dining table and chairs, just a bar and stools in the kitchen area. A couple of sprawling and rather sumptuous cream settees were the focal point of the sitting room and an enormous and quite beautiful perspex table sat between them, scattered with car magazines and local and national newspapers. Strategically dotted around the walls were several modern water-colours; three exquisite wrought iron lamps graced the available space. Guy put all of them on. They seemed to glow rather than shed light. When Cassie returned from the bathroom she slipped off her shoes and tucked her feet beneath her on the settee, snuggling deeper into its welcoming softness.

Making himself equally comfortable, Guy's body actually touched hers. He had removed his jacket and tie. Cassie felt the warmth of his skin. It was both comforting and alluring, and she knew then that at some stage in the evening this wonderful man was going to make a pass at her. Rather smugly, and with some trepidation, she continued to sip her Armagnac.

It was cleverly done. One minute he was looking at her as she spoke, focusing his eyes on her mouth. The next his lips were on hers. Then he shifted and pulled her down on to the settee, and all the time he kissed her lips, face, neck, and slipped his fingers through her hair. Lying side by side, Cassie could distinctly feel his hardness against her belly but he just continued to kiss her, only very gently touching her breasts, and certainly making no move to take things a stage further. Almost unwittingly her hand crept around him, pulling him closer, urging him on. Then he asked, 'Is this what you want?'

She was surprised. Why ask? Wasn't it obvious? Cassie nodded rather weakly. Immediately Guy got up off the settee and pulled her with him. 'Keir'll be back any minute. Let's go to my room.' Still holding her hand, he led her into his bedroom and said, 'Be back in a minute.'

Cassie looked around at the sparse but classy surroundings then at the double bed and wondered how many women he'd had in it. Probably dozens. She gulped and tentatively walked towards it. Meanwhile, Guy was searching through Keir's bedside table drawers for condoms. Since his divorce from the promiscuous Naomi he'd had an Aids test (negative) and intended to take no risks, even if Cassie was on the pill as he assumed she might well be. He found what he was looking for and walked back into his bedroom, closing the door behind him.

He smiled at Cassie who was now sitting on the bed looking a little lost. Confidently he moved towards her and sat down. Discreetly Guy put the condoms on the bedside table and, cupping her face in his hands, kissed her lips then her neck while guiding her back on to the bed. Cassie noticed a complete change in him now as urgently her cotton sweater was removed and he began tugging at her jeans. She helped him willingly and within minutes was lying beside him in just bra and pants. His eyes wandered greedily over her delightful body as he unbuttoned his shirt and tossed it across the room, quickly followed by his trousers and socks. He kissed her again and removed her bra then her panties. Cassie panicked slightly, as his fingers lingered between her legs, but he soon moved them back to her breasts before removing his underpants. She stared at him. His size startled her. Things started to go a little haywire in her head. Memories resurged.

The caressing continued and she calmed down. It was going well. Why shouldn't it? She was crazy about him. Wasn't it time to bury the past and enjoy her sexuality? Then he uttered the words that turned everything askew. She froze. Four simple little words that totally confounded her. Cassie just wanted him to get on with it, hopefully in a frenzy of blind passion, instilling the same in her. Instead he asked rather anxiously, 'What do you like?' He noticed her stiffen and tilted her chin with his forefinger. 'Cassie, it's okay. Just tell me. What do you like?'

What the hell did he mean? He was supposed to take charge – not ask her what she liked. How did she know what she liked? *She only knew what she didn't like.* Cassie caught her breath and buried her head beneath his chin so that he couldn't see her face. And that was when she noticed his erection dwindle. Christ, she thought. This is all going wrong.

'It's okay,' he whispered and began caressing her again, gradually moving his hand over her belly. Cassie fought the tension in her body and Guy shifted so she rolled on to her back. Then he separated her legs with his hand and stroked her. She was unresponsive but he continued, his fingers delving deeper. Then he withdrew his hand and rolled on to his back and just stared at the ceiling. Cassie burst into tears. Turning quickly, Guy was dismayed to see her so distraught and allowed Naomi's parting words to drift into his mind. Useless. Fucking useless.

He waited for her sobs to subside before, taking a deep breath, he stroked her face. 'What's the matter, Cassie? I'm not that repulsive, am I?'

She clung to him, saying between sobs, 'You're not repulsive at all, Guy. It's me who's repulsive.'

He frowned. 'What on earth do you mean?'

Struggling not to cry anymore, she uttered, 'I'm a freak . . . aren't I?'

He leaned back slightly, trying to look into her face which she struggled to turn away from him. 'Look at me, Cassie. Look at me.' Timidly she did so. 'What do you mean? How are you a freak?'

She lowered her eyes and with embarrassment inclined her head. 'Down there.'

Nervously he laughed and shook his head. 'What do you mean, *down there?*'

A sob stuck in the back of her throat and it was a while before she spoke. Patiently, Guy waited, never taking his eyes off her

125

tortured face. 'If I tell you, you'll find me even more repulsive.'

In confusion, he kissed her forehead, cuddling her closer. 'I could never find you repulsive, Cassie, and that's the truth.'

'But I am! I'm despicable.'

'How? What on earth makes you think that?'

'Because I'm deformed!'

'For Christ's sake, what are you talking about?'

Then she raised her face to his and looked at him until he thought his heart would break, such was the sorrow in her eyes. 'It was when I was a little girl. And now I'm deformed. . . . I must be!'

He struggled against nervous laughter even though he saw how real her misery was. 'What are you saying?'

She shook her head. 'It was a long time ago. It doesn't matter anymore.'

'It obviously does matter. Tell me?'

'I want to, Guy, but I can't. I haven't told anybody. Ever.'

Taking a deep breath, he decided to guess. He started with the obvious. 'Were you abused or something?' She shuddered and stuck her fist in her mouth. He took this as a yes and licked his dry lips, weighing up his next words. 'Your father?'

Rapidly she shook her head. '*Not* my father.'

'Somebody else in the family. Male or female?'

'*Not female.*'

'A brother? . . . Or an uncle?' That was enough. He saw her flinch. 'It was an uncle, wasn't it? Tell me, Cassie. I need to know.'

He needed to know. And for some reason she needed to tell him. But the words wouldn't come out because that part of her life had been so well and truly buried. But this was her chance of a small measure of release. She blurted out, 'I was only five . . .'

This was like nothing Guy had ever heard before. 'Christ! *He abused you when you were five?*'

Shame overwhelmed her. 'Not the whole way . . . at least, not then. But gradually. When I was eight or nine.'

Guy felt sick. He wanted to pull away, not because he was repelled but because of her suffering. Somehow, it made her feel like a spectacle to study from a distance. But instead he drew her into his arms and knew she was about to spill everything out and all he could do was listen.

Shakily, she began, 'At first, he just used to get his thing out and play with it in front of me. Then after a while he got to sticking it in my ear, under my arm, anywhere really. But not down there. I suppose he felt he wasn't abusing me if he didn't stick it down there. But then he started and it was *horrible*.' Cassie shuddered. 'It went on for years and I was *so* frightened.' She raised her face. 'Can you imagine how frightened I was? He told me I was a wicked kid because I made him do it. He said they'd send me away, that I'd be locked up.

'We lived off Broadway. My folks ran a pretty second-rate piano bar although they didn't own it, just managed it, and we lived upstairs on the premises. Most evenings they were busy and when my uncle came to stay he'd offer to look after me. I was scared of him, Guy, and he knew exactly how to control me because he was a bright guy, a medic of some sort, but old, so bloody old. His thing was the most awful grey colour.'

She looked up at him and said innocently, 'Not pink like yours . . . but, thank God, his was only teeny, really teeny. Perhaps that was his problem? Maybe he thought that entitled him to have little kids! Anyway, I couldn't figure it out, because he was so much older than my mom, even though he was supposed to be her brother. Then it turned out he wasn't her brother at all, she'd just said that when I was little. She felt sorry for me because I didn't have any real aunts and uncles. How stupid can you get! Anyway, the miserable bastard stopped abusing me when I reached puberty, but it was too late, the damage had been done.'

Guy took a deep breath. 'Have you seen anyone about this, Cassie? I mean, have you had any counselling?'

She looked at him as though he was quite stupid. 'Are you kidding? What would I want with counselling?'

'To help you, of course. This is awful, Cassie, and not a burden you should be bearing alone.'

'Well, I'm not anymore, am I? I'm sharing it with you.'

'But I can't advise you. Other than to say, shoot the bastard!'

'Huh! I would if he ever came near me again!'

'Is that likely?'

'God knows. Well, I don't suppose he'd ever come near me like that, but my mom often talks about him, mentions the fact that he might come over to England on vacation.'

'Why don't you tell her?'

'Are you joking? She'd never believe me! Oh, Guy, not all families are like yours.'

He sighed. 'No, I don't suppose they are.' Then he squeezed her tightly. 'But all this doesn't make you a freak. You're definitely not a freak. You're a whole woman, and don't let that bastard take that away from you. Don't let him ruin your womanhood, Cassie. That would be a gross travesty.'

'But he already has, don't you see? He's ruined me. You know he has.'

Guy frowned and grimaced all at the same time then cupped her chin with his hand. 'What do you mean? How are you ruined?'

'Well, you felt it, don't say you didn't.'

'Felt what?'

She cowered. 'Don't make me say it, Guy. Not when it turned you off like that.'

'Cassie, I genuinely don't know what you're talking about. You were dry, that's all. I wasn't turned off. In fact it was the other way round. I thought you were. When women want it they're *wet*.'

Cassie implored him, 'But I'm ruined!'

Bemused, he chuckled. 'What do you mean, ruined?'

She stared at him and then put her hand between her legs. 'I've looked at myself in the mirror. I'm not normal.'

Scrutinising her face now, very carefully he said, 'You know, Cassie, you really ought to see a doctor. Perhaps a woman doctor. I'm sure she'd put your mind at rest.'

Cassie hit back, 'You see, you do think I'm ruined. And then you wonder why I can't do anything about it! Don't you understand, I'm scared stiff of seeing anyone!'

'*Okay*. I understand.' Guy bit his lip considering her plight. Finally he said, 'Look, if you won't see a doctor, perhaps I can help?'

She peered at him defensively. 'In what way?'

Trying to keep the embarrassment out of his eyes, he suggested, 'I could take a proper look?' She panicked and he placated her with several light kisses on her forehead. 'When I touched you just now, nothing felt abnormal. I'm not a doctor,' he smiled, 'but I do know what a woman looks like.'

Narrowing her eyes, Cassie thrust her head against the pillows. 'This is so embarrassing, Guy.'

He kissed her mouth. 'It needn't be. I'm not embarrassed. I just want to help you.'

'But what if . . . ?'

'Cassie, think about it. If I thought you were deformed would I offer to look?'

She pondered a while. 'I suppose not. But you won't repeat any of this to anyone . . . do you promise?'

'Cassie! Never.'

'Promise?'

'On my honour, I promise.'

'Okay, I believe you. Do it.'

Cautiously he shifted down the bed. Then, very quickly, shuffled back up again, smiling. He kissed her 'All looks pretty normal to me.' He took her hand and placed it on himself. 'Does that?'

With relief practically consuming her, she felt him grow in her hand. 'But what about inside?' Guy saw the worry drain from Cassie's face and recognised her unspoken invitation. He turned and snatched up a condom. She stopped him. 'You don't need that. I've just finished my period. I'm as regular as clockwork. You won't feel me properly if you wear that.'

He frowned and decided to trust her, tossing the condom back on to the bedside table. Then he took Cassie into his arms and caressed and kissed her. When she was quite relaxed he began to make love to her. For Guy, it had been a long time and making love to Cassie was like being a teenager again. For her, it was over much too quickly. But afterwards he was able to reassure her that she felt as normal on the inside as she had on the out.

Unable to sleep, Cassie watched him drift off into a deep slumber and realised he must be totally exhausted, first from his travels and then from her tale of woe. For a long time she studied him, anxious about what she'd told him, relieved by his assurances and further consumed with love for his gentle and sympathetic behaviour. Finally, she slipped off the bed, knowing she'd never sleep, and tugged at the duvet in order to cover him completely. Then she found her handbag and withdrew a pen. Finding a piece of notepaper on the bedside table she scribbled, *Our secret, okay?* and put this on top of her pillow. She tiptoed into the bathroom with her clothes, dressed, and finally, after one last lingering look at Guy, left the bedroom.

Cassie crept along the short hallway into the spacious sitting room where the lamps still burned and immediately stiffened because sprawled across one of the settees lay Keir. He wore a towelling robe which barely covered him and clutched a whisky tumbler. Lazily he raised his eyes and fixed them for a good few seconds on Cassie as his face formed a knowing smile. Anybody who understood Keir's nature would have known this was a front. In truth he was sick to the pit of his stomach because the girl of his dreams had just climbed out of Guy Hamilton's bed. Why did all the best females fall into Guy's lap? Tersely he remarked, 'Ah! I wondered who his bedmate was.'

Embarrassed, Cassie acknowledged him then made for the door. Keir quipped, 'Before you rush off, I'm dying to know – is he up to it at long last?' Noting the bewilderment on her face, he started to enjoy himself. Finally, he was getting a reaction from her. 'What I mean is, *did the earth move for you?*' As undoubtedly it would have done if you'd given me the chance, he thought.

She turned away. 'Keir . . . get lost.'

He pursed his mouth, loving the way she said Keir. He was roused by her anger. 'Oh, I see. Like that, eh? Better luck next time. Or should I say, better fuck next time?'

She rounded on him then. 'You really are gross, do you know that?'

His eyes panned to between his legs. God, this girl was really turning him on. It briefly crossed his mind that he should stop now – he knew he was drunk – but some spark was driving him on. Jealousy perhaps? A need to prove he was a better lover? 'Yes, down there I really am gross.' Then he ambled off the settee and moved swiftly towards her, his dressing gown gaping open as he did so. When he was as close as could be he began running his fingers through her hair. She squirmed; even so he would have kissed her but indignantly she pulled away from him. He leered. 'But, Cassie – you and I could have such fun.'

What with the rest of the evening's events and now this, humiliation got the better of her and hot tears pricked the backs of her eyes. She practically stumbled to the front door. He called after her, angry and resentful that in the past she'd never responded to his countless more pleasant overtures and now was repelled by his forthright one. He felt a desperate need to hurt her. 'Don't pretend to be so innocent, Cassie. I've met your type before.'

She glared at him. 'You've never met my type before, Keir, because if you had, you'd never have behaved as you just did!' And with that she slammed out, knowing in her heart she'd most probably never be invited back. It was a sad note on which to end an evening which could only be described as a watershed in her life.

Chapter Eighteen

'Daisy! What are you doing here?' Lily felt the colour rise in her cheeks as she approached her sister. Henri's restaurant in Sheffield was quiet with just a few business people eating a late lunch and Lily was anxious to get off duty as soon as possible. It had been her intention to return to the house she shared with four other students, have a long bath then try and catch up on some sleep. Since she'd finished her finals there'd been many celebrations, especially amongst friends on her course, and although she'd missed most of them because of working here she'd made it to last night's which had been particularly wild.

With a newspaper rolled under one arm and an overnight bag in the other, Daisy hugged and kissed her sister. 'I've got a couple of days off so I thought I'd surprise you.' She stepped back, looking anxious. 'It was all my idea. Mum and Dad didn't trust me to get here in one piece. In fact I need to ring them to say I've made it. You don't mind me being here, do you?'

Feeling tired, Lily cast her eyes around the room, shaking her head. 'Of course not, Daisy, it's great to see you.' This wasn't strictly true and she was quite relieved to see that nobody in the restaurant seemed to be taking any notice of them. Then Leonard, who co-owned the restaurant with Henri, came through from the kitchens, walked over and beamed at the two sisters. Lily turned rather defensively. 'Leonard, would it be all right if I got off now? I've done my three hours.'

He waved his hand. 'Sure, sure.' He ran his eyes over Daisy. 'Let me guess, Lily's mum?'

There was a stony silence as Daisy's face dropped. She was speechless. Lily flashed a look at Leonard. 'Sister!'

His mouth gaped at his dreadful error and he babbled on, 'Of course, I can see now. Oh, yes!' He touched her arm. 'It was the light! It plays tricks on my eyes. All the time it plays tricks. I can see clearly now you're so young! Very, very young. And beautiful . . . like Lily.'

Frowning, Daisy assured him, 'It's okay. I'm not angry or anything. Anyway, how old are you?'

Lily nudged her. 'You don't ask people their ages, Daisy. It's rude.'

She pointed at Leonard. 'But he was rude to me.'

With widening eyes, Lily glared at her sister. 'Not intentionally, Daisy.'

'Well, I'm not being intentionally rude to him.' She stared at Leonard. 'It's just that old people often think young people are much older than they are.'

Touché, thought Lily as her hand flew to her mouth. How to get your own back in one easy lesson. She grinned at Leonard who peered at Daisy. 'I can see, Lily's sister, you are one of those who studies other people very, very carefully.'

Her face lit up and transformed her into a beauty. 'I do! I love studying people. I'm getting better and better at it all the time.' She waved one hand saying loudly, 'I could tell you so much about the people in this restaurant.' Leonard raised his eyebrows and Lily cringed. Then Daisy felt the pressure of her sister's hand on her arm and realised she'd said enough. Lily looked apologetically at Leonard and said a quick goodbye before pulling her sister away. She hurried off to fetch her jacket and bag, returning very quickly. The two sisters left the restaurant.

'I'm sorry if I embarrassed you,' mumbled Daisy rather glumly when they were outside. 'These days I always seem to embarrass everybody.'

While wishing Daisy was safely back in Ely, Lily squeezed her arm. 'You didn't embarrass me, Daise. You're you, and I love you for it.'

Daisy hesitated and stared at her sister. 'Well, you're the only one who does. Since Grandpa died, nobody wants to be with me anymore. Mum and Dad like to go out on their own and . . .' She bit her lip. 'I get lonely sometimes because I miss you so much.'

Lily gulped and tugged at her sister's arm, moving her along. 'I

133

miss you too, Daisy, and I'm sure you're wrong about Mum and Dad. I bet they do like you to be with them.'

'They don't, Lily. Really, they don't. I go to work in the fish bar and I come home and watch the telly. For three years that's all I've done. When you're not there I don't get to talk to anyone my age. There just isn't anybody anymore who wants to be my friend. I miss you so much, and I miss Cassie too.'

Lily frowned and quickened her pace. Daisy had a tendency to walk very slowly and Lily liked to walk swiftly. She urged her sister along. 'Come on, I need a bath. You can fix us something to eat then we'll have a really long chat.'

Daisy panicked. 'But I don't know where the things are in your place, and I might drop something, and you've got gas and I'm used to electricity.'

'Okay! I'll fix us something to eat. It's not a problem, Daisy. Don't make it into one.'

She stopped in her tracks. 'And now you're angry with me.'

Taking a deep breath, Lily stared at Daisy, then, consumed with a mixture of guilt and fury, allowed her eyes to wander over her sister's attire. Dressed in a hideous red polyester suit and equally hideous shoes it became obvious why Leonard had mistaken her for her mother. The colour alone was ghastly and it crossed Lily's mind that Daisy was right. Since she'd left Ely, her sister had changed; she'd become decidedly frumpy. 'Who chose that suit?' Lily asked with an edge in her voice.

Daisy looked down at it, immediately noticing a tiny mark on the skirt. 'Oh, no!' she cried, pushing the newspaper into Lily's hand and dropping her bag to a precise position between her feet on the path. With a frenzied rubbing action, she tried to remove the mark. 'Oh, no!' she repeated. 'It won't come off.'

'It doesn't matter, Daisy. We can get it off when we get home. Leave it now.'

'But Mum'll be furious!'

'Why? It's not Mum's suit, is it?'

Tears appeared in Daisy's eyes and she looked up at her sister pitifully. 'No. But she told me not to buy anything on my own. Said I'd get it all wrong. And then when she saw it she said it'd show every speck of dirt! Mum said so and she was right! Now she'll really moan at me.'

'But Mum doesn't normally moan at you for such things, does she?'

'She does! All the time. And I can't help being stupid. In fact, it's horrible being stupid.'

Lily was indignant. 'You're *not* stupid! Don't say that. I hate it when you say that.'

Sadly, Daisy peered at her sister. 'But Mum says I am, and so does Dad, so I must be.'

Shaking her head, Lily was adamant. 'I don't believe you. I'm sure they don't.'

Rather comically, Daisy sighed and put her hands on her hips. 'So now you think I'm lying as well as stupid?' Lily turned and noticed passers-by watching them. She scooped up Daisy's bag and started to walk on briskly. Her sister rushed to catch up with her. 'Don't be angry with me, Lily. I can't bear it when you're angry with me.'

'I'm not angry with you, Daisy. If you must know, I'm angry with Mum and Dad.'

Daisy stopped in front of her sister and grabbed her arm. 'But you mustn't be angry with them because, remember, they have to put up with me all the time!' She lowered her eyes. 'That's why I came to see you. To get out of their hair.'

Lily's face crumpled. 'Out of their hair?'

Daisy looked sheepish. 'Well, they didn't say it to my face, but I overheard them saying it to each other.'

All the things in Lily's hands found their way to the ground as she gathered her sister into her arms. She didn't care about passers-by anymore. 'Well, I'm glad you're out of their hair, Daisy. You're certainly welcome in mine.'

Very pleased, Daisy drew back, wanting to impress her sister further. 'It's only a saying, y'know. I wasn't *really* in their hair.' Then she picked up the things Lily had dropped. 'You shouldn't make the street look untidy like this, Lily. Somebody might trip up.'

Lily sighed, and smiled, and at a gentler pace led the way back to her Sheffield home.

After having a less leisurely bath than she'd have liked, Lily pulled on her jeans and a comfortable sweater then set about making a large onion and herb pan-omelette. None of her house-mates were home which was a relief, because Lily nearly always ended up having to share her food with them. Whatever she threw together in a pan bore little resemblance to other people's efforts. It not only looked wonderful, it tasted divine. She didn't mind being the cook but soon realised she was out of pocket. Lily started off university with a warm, generous heart and ended up being rather careful of her private food store which she now kept locked in a cupboard in her room. Her parents paid for her room, heating bills and her books, but everything else was Lily's responsibility. They'd insisted from the beginning she get herself a part-time job and she'd had several until, a year previously, she'd started work at Henri's.

Daisy had set the small round table as best she could in the untidy cramped kitchen. All around were unwashed plates, pans and cutlery, and near the back door a couple of bin-liners stuffed with trash. Daisy tutted and turned up her nose, enquiring who was responsible for clearing it up.

'We each clear up our own rubbish,' retorted Lily, 'and most of that stuff is the responsibility of Rod and Chris. I used to wash up for them and help out but I soon found that the more I did the worse they became, so I gave up. You get used to it after a while, Daise, it's called university life.'

'But it smells.'

Lily smiled. 'Only if you breathe in.'

Daisy's face showed her alarm. 'But you have to breathe in.'

Lily placed half the omelette, sliced and fanned out, on a plate in front of her sister. 'Not through your nose, you don't.'

'But that's bad for you. You could get a sore throat.'

'Oh, I've got that all right, along with a runny nose. Sore throat, bad head, no clean underwear because when I leave it to dry in the bathroom it gets nicked by Sally or Chaznia.' She grinned. 'So, you see, my tale of woe is endless.'

Daisy was hungry. As her sister served herself and sat down, she tucked in. 'It's changed you, all this, hasn't it?' She said wisely.

Raising her eyebrows, Lily weighed up her sister's comment. 'Yes, I suppose it has. Made me loosen up. You have to go with the flow, Daise, otherwise you have a very bumpy ride.'

'Well, I wouldn't like it! I'd hate it!' Daisy looked around. 'It's disgusting!'

Lily laughed between mouthfuls of omelette. 'Only if you're used to our mother's pristine surroundings. It's not that disgusting, but maybe I would like it a bit in between.'

Daisy looked at the rolled up newspaper lying next to her on the table. 'I brought the *Cambridge Chronicle* with me. I thought you might like to see the bit that Guy wrote.'

Something hammered in Lily's heart. Only lightly, but she felt it. She reached over to grab the paper but Daisy got to it first and turned to the sports page. Then she passed it over to her sister. 'Aunt Lynda told Mum about it. We don't normally buy the *Cambridge Chronicle*. Apparently he's going to write a regular spot from now on. This one's several weeks old but Aunt Lynda said they liked what he wrote so much they want him to write about lots of different cars.' As Daisy spoke her face was animated. Lily's eyes met hers over the top of the newspaper and she realised how fond of Guy Daisy was.

Then her eyes feasted on her cousin's words as she read the short piece from beginning to end, loving it. It was witty and clever and, more importantly, very easy to read. 'But that's what Cassie's got, a Fripon. And she loves it too!'

'I know. I should think she's the owner he's talking about?'

Startled, Lily darted a look across the table at her sister. 'Well, she never said. I speak to her regularly on the phone.' Lily looked shamefaced. 'Or, at least, I did before we got cut off. Which reminds me, I owe her a call.'

Daisy's hand flew to her mouth. 'Oh, dear! I'm supposed to have rung home!'

'Don't worry. There's a call box down the road. There's plenty of time, Daise. Don't bust a gut.'

'Well, I should do it now. They might be worried.'

Lily watched. Her sister was already making for the front door. She called after her, 'Have you got the code and everything? And the right money? You do know what to do?'

Daisy turned and glared at her. 'Of course I have, and of course I know what to do. I can read, Lily. I'm not *that* stupid!'

Good old Daisy. Lily saluted her sister before returning to the newspaper article. It had been printed in letter form but presented, with a picture of a Fripon, to catch the eye. She read it again, noting how he'd described the little French car as *Le Throb*. Lily was tempted to rush out and ring Cassie at work, ask her if she knew anything about the piece. Perhaps Daisy was right, perhaps it was Cassie's car. Lily pondered a while, wondering how she felt about that. She wasn't sure so shrugged and quickly turned the page, deciding not to think about it anymore.

And that was when she saw the advertisement that changed her life.

Chapter Nineteen

Using the phonebox after Daisy, Lily rang the Viking Hotel straight away. It was important to waste no time, the advertisment had been placed three weeks previously. Assistant Catering Manager. She knew she was much too inexperienced to even to think of applying for such a position but also knew she could do the job if given the chance. The receptionist at the hotel assured her the position was still open, although they'd been inundated with enquiries. But if Lily was quick with her CV, she would be considered. Lily knew this was no good. There was very little on her CV. But if she could present herself and convince the manager she was the person for the job, she just might stand a chance. Lily was ever the optimist.

'When are you going back?' she asked Daisy.

Her sister, busy clearing up the kitchen, looked surprised. 'Why?'

'Because I'm coming with you.' Lily held out the *Cambridge Chronicle* and pointed to the advertisement. 'I want this job, Daisy. I want it *so much*. I need to go there. Present myself. Beg. Do anything in my power to get it!'

It took a few seconds for Lily's delivery to sink in, then Daisy's face broke into a smile. 'Does that mean you're coming home?'

Not wishing to raise her sister's hopes, Lily said, 'Sort of.'

'What do you mean, sort of?'

'I've got to get the job first, then I'm not sure where I'll live. Most probably in Cambridge.'

'In that case, can I live with you?'

Lily stared at her sister, not knowing what to say. As much as she loved and respected her, this was her future and she'd somehow never imagined Daisy *in it*. At least, not living *in it*. 'I'm not sure. I mean, it wouldn't be very convenient for the fish bar in Ely, would it? All that travelling.'

Daisy pulled a face. 'Oh, Lily, *really*. I don't want to spend the rest of my life working in a fish bar.'

A smile whipped across Lily's lovely face. Fortunately, Daisy's way of looking at life had always amused her. How could anybody say her sister wasn't normal? She shared the same aspirations and desires as anyone else and was capable of carrying them out – albeit at a slower pace. 'What do you want to do then, Daise?'

She took her hands out of the hot soapy water, turned and leaned her weight against the sink, which she'd wiped thoroughly before using it. 'I want to help you. I'd love to help you. One day you'll go into business with Cassie, I know you will, and I'd like to be there and help you both.' Daisy's eyes were entreating, 'I won't get in the way. I know you think I will but I promise I won't.'

Lily walked towards her. 'Of course you won't get in the way, but I never said I was going into business with Cassie. Whatever makes you think that?'

'You did! You said so at Guy's wedding. I heard you say it, about how you'd love to work in a hotel like the Viking then go into business.' Daisy pointed to the *Chronicle*. 'And see, it's all coming true like I knew it would.'

Lily perched herself on the kitchen table and folded her arms. 'Well, maybe I did say something like that, but even if it does happen, it'll be absolutely ages away. And I haven't even got the job in the Viking yet! And I don't understand where Cassie comes into all this?'

Daisy frowned as though contemplating the question. How could she begin to explain the thoughts that sprang into her head? She turned back to her washing up and shrugged, running her hand around the inside of a mug, trying to budge the coffee stains there. 'She could do the flowers or something. Everybody likes flowers.'

Lily laughed and shifted forward, hugging her sister. 'You've got it all worked out, haven't you?'

Daisy turned and grinned. 'Well, can I then?'

'Can you what?'

140

'Live with you if you move to Cambridge?'

Lily squeezed her eyes shut then opened them again, anxious never to hurt her sister. 'If I get a job in Cambridge, and *you* get a job in Cambridge, then yes of course you can. But you do realise you'll have to pay your share of the rent?'

'Yes, I know all that.'

'It's a big step.'

'Lily, I'm not stupid.'

She crossed her heart. 'Daisy, I have never, ever thought you were.'

A smug look crossed her elder sister's face. 'It's a good job I came then, isn't it? You'd never have known about that job if I hadn't.'

Lily laughed. 'You're priceless, Daisy. And, as always, you're right.'

They went to Meadowhall shopping centre in Sheffield where Lily bought a beautifully cut city suit in slate grey. This she combined with a white silk top, black high-heeled shoes and a matching handbag. The following day, with her hair in a shiny twisted knot at the back of her head, she looked stunning and as the two sisters caught the train to Cambridge, heads turned after them. Lily had persuaded Daisy to buy a pair of blue jeans, some smart black trousers and several assorted tops together with a cream fitted jacket from M&S. A simple combination of any of these items took years off her.

Rather nervously Lily entered the Viking Hotel, remembering the last time she'd done so at Guy's wedding. It was a lovely June day and Daisy had chosen to wander around the hotel's well-tended grounds. She made herself comfortable on a bench beneath an ancient oak overhanging the snaking River Cam. All the time she kept her fingers crossed because the last thing her sister had said was, 'Keep your fingers crossed!'

'I was wondering,' said Lily to the receptionist on duty, 'if I could possibly speak to Mr Bates?' The advertisement had said all applications should be sent to the Hotel Manager, Nigel Bates.

'Do you have an appointment?'

She shook her head matter-of-factly. 'Not exactly. But if you could say my name is Lily Hamilton.'

The girl didn't argue, just buzzed his office. Fortunately he was there and picked up the phone. 'A Ms Lily Hamilton in reception for you, Nigel.' The girl peered at her. 'Business or personal?'

Lily cleared her throat. 'Business.'

The receptionist repeated, 'Business.'

Mr Bates, on the other end of the line, asked what it was about. Lily smiled and said she'd rather discuss it with him. The receptionist said, 'Business but private, Nigel.' And knowing the hotel manager's weakness for a pretty face, added in a low voice, 'I think you should see her.'

Thank you, thank you, thought Lily, holding her breath.

The receptionist put down the phone. 'He'll be out in a minute. Take a seat over there.' She pointed to a sofa and Lily walked towards it, doing her best to look elegant. All she needed now was to win over Nigel Bates; convince him she was the one for the job. She sat down and crossed her legs.

Within minutes, Nigel Bates – divorced, mid-thirties, average height, average-looking and wearing glasses – approached reception, but his eyes latched on to the stunning redhead straight away. The receptionist nodded and Nigel's face lit up. Thank God he hadn't passed on this one. He held out his hand then sat down next to her. 'I'm Nigel Bates. And you must be Ms Hamilton? How can I help you?'

'Simple really,' Lily said, smiling warmly, aware of Nigel's eyes fixed on her mouth. 'I've been working in Sheffield at Henri's. Have you heard of it?' The manager looked blank as she knew he would. 'Anyway, it was only yesterday that I saw your advertisement for an Assistant Catering Manager.' She leaned forward and picked up her handbag, withdrawing her CV. 'I've loved this place since a cousin of mine had his wedding reception here. In fact, it was the excellent service and superb food here that persuaded me to go into catering. I rang yesterday. Your receptionist assured me I wasn't too late.' Lily paused, slightly unnerved by Nigel's eyes still fixed on her mouth. She licked her lips. 'So here I am. I've brought my CV and my degree is in Hotel and Catering Management.'

Nigel Bates was bowled over. He'd interviewed thirty-two applicants for this job and none had looked like Lily Hamilton; more to the point, none had approached him in such a forthright, confident way. Added to this few had degrees so what more could he want? The job was hers for the taking. But he curbed his enthusiasm and adjusted his glasses fussily. Lily was instantly reminded of Adam Greene and shifted away slightly. 'The competition has been hot.' He tapped her CV. 'This had better be good.'

She gathered her wits. 'But can I tell you a little about myself first? Why I think I'd be very suitable for the position?' He looked surprised but allowed her to continue. 'My family's in the food business, although I confess nothing like this. But it's an established business with a restaurant and . . . a mobile service. So, you see, I've been involved with catering and food since I was tiny. And I adore looking after people.' She smiled, her face radiant.

'Fine, but you understand this is a managerial post? The waiters are here to look after people. Your job is organising the nitty-gritty of functions. Weddings, banquets, large parties, that sort of thing. We're only a small hotel but our reputation is the best for miles around. At all costs we must keep our customers happy. Strings of enquiries will be thrown your way and if you're not up to it you'll be out on your ear! Plus you'll be required to liaise with Chef, and believe me he needs kid-glove handling. You'll also be responsible for hiring in extra catering equipment if needed and placing orders for unusual foodstuffs. It can get hair-raising at times, I can tell you. The last Catering Manager definitely wasn't up to it and left after a very short time.'

Lily frowned. 'So I won't be specifically under anyone?'

Nigel liked that. Yes, darling, you can be under me any time you like. 'I'm the Manager here. All Assistants answer to me!' He noticed that so far Ms Hamilton seemed unfazed by his brusque manner and decided to ease up a little, just in case he had frightened her off and she was too proud to show it. 'As I said, we're a small hotel so any real problems I'm only too happy to help out with. Are you still interested?'

Without hesitation she replied, 'Yes, I am.'

He looked into her fabulous eyes, then at her left hand. No wedding ring. Good. 'You live in Cambridge?'

'Not at the moment. As I said, I'm working in Sheffield. But if you offered me the position I could stay with friends locally until I found a place of my own.'

'That's important. The hours are long and changeable. It's no good if you have difficulty getting in and out, and we don't have

143

room for staff to live in.' He coughed. 'Of course, I live in. I have my own suite on the top floor.'

Lily gave him her best smile. 'How wonderful, living here.'

Then he touched her, on the shoulder. 'It is,' he said, applying a little more pressure. He removed his hand and looked at his watch. 'Unfortunately I'm going to have to wind this up. I have another appointment in a few minutes. I'd like to show you round, introduce you to a few people, but needs must . . . So, you're definitely interested?'

'I am most definitely interested.'

He beamed at her, showing irregular teeth. 'When could you start?'

'In a couple of weeks, if you like?'

'Splendid. And what sort of salary are you looking for?'

'If you make me a reasonable offer, I shall accept.'

He liked her style. 'Well, can I say it's looking very hopeful?' He tapped her CV. 'You have a contact number?'

Then she remembered they'd been cut off in Sheffield. 'Can I ring you? It's just that with my present job I never know when I'll be home.'

'So you're used to working tricky hours?'

'Of course.'

'Good. Okay, Lily, you ring me. We may as well get the show on the road so how about tomorrow morning, say about ten?'

She nodded gratefully then shifted and stood up, smoothing down her skirt. Still in his seated position, Nigel allowed his eyes to wander over her long shapely legs. Eventually he stood up. He held out his hand and shook hers as though he didn't want to let go. 'I think I can safely say I shall look forward to working with you in the future.'

She withdrew her hand and restrained herself from wiping it on her jacket. 'You won't regret it, Mr Bates, I promise you.'

He squeezed her shoulder. 'Call me Nigel. Everybody else does.'

'Nigel. I'll ring you tomorrow.'

As she walked away, high heels clicking across the stone-flagged foyer, he called after her, 'Don't forget now! Ten a.m.' Lily just smiled and continued her journey, resigned to the fact that when something comes easily there's always a drawback.

144

Chapter Twenty

As luck would have it it was Cassie's afternoon off so immediately after leaving the Viking Hotel, Daisy and Lily walked back into town and the three young women met in Trinity Street's Blue Boar. Cassie had waited, sipping a glass of wine and munching on a bag of smoky bacon crisps. When she saw how businesslike and elegant Lily looked her mouth dropped open and her perfectly arched brows rose in approval.

'Wow! So, did you get the job?'

Lily couldn't wait to talk about her interview with slimy Nigel Bates, but first she went to the bar for two more glasses of wine. She returned to the table and found Cassie engrossed in conversation with Daisy. Lily sat down and listened for a few seconds while Cassie's eyes switched from one sister to the other. Finally she asked, 'So, tell me, do you think you've got the job?'

Lily held up a hand with two crossed fingers. 'I shall know tomorrow. I have to ring at ten.'

'But does it sound hopeful?'

Trying not to appear over-confident, she hunched her shoulders. 'I think so. The Manager, Nigel Bates, appeared to really like me. The trouble is, he hasn't read my CV yet, and when he does, he'll realise I'm not very experienced and, more to the point, I've only just sat my finals.'

'But you've passed, haven't you?'

'Oh, I'm reasonably confident that I've passed, but I won't know how good my degree is until the results come out.' She shrugged. 'It's not just that . . . it's my age. I'm sure he thinks I'm a lot older than I am and the job sounds incredibly high-powered

– dealing with influential people, working on your own initiative, that sort of thing.'

Cassie leaned across the table and tapped her friend's hand. 'I bet he's already in love with you, Lily, and he'll offer you the job for that reason alone.'

Daisy sipped her wine, listening, quite happy just to be there and not really caring if she was included in the conversation or not. It was like old times, when she'd sat close by as the two of them chattered on about this and that. It was all Daisy ever wanted, just to be a small part of her sister's and Cassie's life.

Lily screwed up her face. 'He's a bit unctuous. A bit full of himself.'

Cassie smiled. 'There's a lot of 'em about.' Daisy frowned, wondering whether to ask what unctuous meant. She decided against it. Cassie continued, 'But you do look stunning, Lily. I should think the poor guy didn't know what hit him!'

And then it was as though time stood still for Cassie because Guy Hamilton, wearing blue jeans, white tee-shirt and a beige linen jacket, walked into the Blue Boar. She hadn't seen or heard from him since she'd climbed out of his bed and her face turned pink. He really did create an aura. She noticed both men and women turn to stare after him and her desire escalated. As she faced the door she saw him first but Lily soon turned to see what the attraction was. To begin with Guy didn't see them, just carried on talking in animated fashion to the very attractive female he accompanied. All Cassie could do was look. Lily too had difficulty dragging her eyes away.

Then he saw them and immediately felt ashamed because he hadn't contacted Cassie since their night together although he'd fully intended to. Things had happened so fast since then and already his life was moving in another direction. But all thoughts of Cassie melted into nothingness as his eyes rested on Lily. Guy even forgot about Jane Richardson standing beside him, he forgot about everything – just walked towards his cousin.

'Lily,' he said softly then flashed a look at Cassie. 'Cassie . . . how nice to see you.' He ran a hand over Daisy's hair. 'You too, Daisy.'

Jane was on his heels. 'Er, Jane, I'd like you to meet my two cousins, Lily and Daisy, and over here's . . . Cassie.' There was a slight pause before he said her name and she wondered why.

146

Warmly, Jane greeted the three young women then looked at Guy. 'I'll get the drinks. Your usual?'

He agreed and she walked towards the bar. Cassie was consumed with jealousy. His usual. She wondered what that was? And how long he'd been with this particular female? Was he seeing Jane when he'd made love to her? Guy's eyes were now on her and embarrassment crept over her like a rash. 'I've been meaning to get in touch, Cassie. I wanted to thank you for the ride in your car.' He grinned rather sheepishly. 'They printed my letter in the *Chronicle* . . . they've even given me a regular spot!'

Daisy turned in her seat and looked up at her cousin. 'We know! At least, Lily and I do. Aunt Lynda told Mum and she bought the *Chronicle*, although we don't normally buy the *Chronicle*. I even took it to Sheffield and showed it to Lily.' Then she frowned. 'But we didn't know for sure it was Cassie's car you wrote about.' Daisy's eyes panned to her. 'Because she never told us.'

Cassie's face was now a deep red. Guy's eyes held hers but were filled with something she interpreted as pity. 'Hey, I'm glad I could be of service, Guy. Anytime you need a driver, I'll do my best to make myself available – for a fee, of course.'

He laughed then turned his attention back to Lily. 'You look very businesslike?'

'Do I? I've just been for an interview.'

'Oh. Where?'

'The Viking Hotel. Assistant Catering Manager.'

Guy pulled a face. The Viking held nothing but bad memories for him. 'Have you got the job?'

Again, Lily held up a hand with crossed fingers. To Guy, her lovely tapered fingers seemed to be suspended in mid-air just for him. He reached out and grabbed them, holding them tightly for a second or so. All three women stared at his hand enfolding Lily's. Then he let go and turned towards Jane. 'I'd better get back to my friend.' He shifted away a few paces, as though reluctant to leave but embarrassed to stay. 'See you soon.' He walked away, rubbing the palm of his hand with his thumb. It really tingled.

Lily tucked her own hand into her lap and peered at Cassie with questioning eyes. Her friend was quick. 'It was the night I gave you a lift to the station, remember? As I was driving away, Guy appeared so I gave him a lift. He really liked my car and asked me lots of questions. I would have told you, Lily, but as I can't get through on the phone these days and you're never here, it's been difficult.'

For a good few seconds Lily didn't speak. She was weighing up how much of the story Cassie had left out. Something had happened between the pair of them and it wasn't an innocent drive in a Fripon. Lily twisted in her seat, eyes seeking out Guy. At exactly the same moment he looked at her. They both smiled then looked away. Lily considered her feelings. Each time she saw her cousin he made her feel she was the single most important person in the room, a feeling she liked. It was both seductive and addictive. Her eyes flicked back to Cassie. Perhaps he made her feel the same. Perhaps Guy made every female feel like that.

Boldly she asked, 'You don't fancy him then?'

Daisy went into guffaws of laughter, snorting into her hand as though her sister had said something quite wicked. She tapped Lily's hand. 'That's private!'

Again, Cassie was quick, 'Of course I fancy him. Don't we all?'

Lily frowned and sipped her wine. 'You know, Cassie, you never tell me anything. In the past I've poured out my soul to you, and when I come to think of it, you tell me zilch.'

Panicking, Cassie stretched her hand across the table. 'That's because there's nothing to tell. My life *is* zilch. I lead the most boring life and, believe me, the only things I ever get to make love to are flowers!'

Daisy stole a look at Guy then asked her friend, 'Did Guy make love to you?'

Cassie spluttered, '*Daisy!*'

'Sorry! I didn't mean it like that, I just meant, well, you know, did he kiss you or anything?'

'Oh, Daisy, Guy stroked your hair just now and he held Lily's hand. He does things like that all the time. He's very tactile.'

Daisy frowned, 'So is tactile like kissing?'

Lily sensed her friend's panic and decided to change the subject. 'Cassie, if I do get this job, would you be prepared to share a flat with me?' She saw Daisy's eyes widen in anticipation of being included, 'And perhaps Daisy?'

Cassie's face glowed. '*I'd love to.*' Playfully, she punched Daisy's arm, 'And you too? You're thinking of moving to Cambridge as well?'

Daisy rolled her eyes, 'Only if I can get a job.'

'Oh, I'm sure you'll be able to find something. Perhaps Lily'll be able to find you a little job in the kitchens at the Viking.'

Daisy turned to her sister. 'That would be wonderful! Do you think you could, Lily?'

Lily held up her hands, 'Hang on! Let me get the job first!'

Daisy grabbed her sister's arm, 'But if you do, will you try . . . please, Lily?'

'I'll see. I'm not promising anything, so please don't raise your hopes.'

Cassie looked across at Lily and winked, thinking what a huge responsibility her friend carried for her simple sister. Then she finished her wine and asked if anyone would like another. Lily and Daisy both declined. 'Can I give you a lift back to Ely?'

'I'm sure Daisy'd like a lift, but I'm getting the train to Sheffield.' Lily looked at her watch, 'And I'd better get going. It leaves at three-thirty.'

Cassie stood up. 'I'll drop you off at the station.'

Lily agreed and all three women prepared to leave the Blue Boar. Each cast her eyes towards Guy, who acknowledged them by raising his hand. Jane did too.

As Lily reached the doors, she turned and sure enough his eyes were still on them, or was it just her? She sighed, not at all sure, and walked out into the street.

Chapter Twenty-One

Jane Richardson watched Guy's face as his cousins left the Blue Boar. 'The girl in the suit's a bit *pulchritudinous*, isn't she?'

Guy raised his brows. 'Lily? Yes. I suppose you could say that.'

Jane nudged him and laughed, 'Trying to be cool, are you? I saw the way you looked at her. Is she single?'

'Of course she's single. She's only twenty!' Guy frowned, 'Well, nearly twenty-one actually. But still too young.'

'Too young for what? For you, Guy? Is that what you mean? Lots of women are married with babies at twenty-one.'

Guy shook his head, 'Not Lily.'

'Why?'

He smiled, 'Because she's destined for better things, that's why?'

'Jesus, Guy! What could be better than marriage and babies? Even old hacks like me quite aspire to the idea.'

'I didn't mean it like that. I'm sure in time Lily'll settle down and have babies, but not just yet.'

'You don't fancy it with her yourself then?'

Guy opened his mouth to speak then closed it again. What business was this of Jane's? 'She's my cousin, Jane, I've known her since she was a baby.'

'So? Lots of cousins get it together.' Jane saw the stern look on Guy's face. 'Anyway, what's with the other one? I thought she looked a bit vacant.'

Guy's hackles rose. 'She's not vacant! That's Daisy! Daisy's not vacant!'

'Oh! Sorry I spoke!'

'So you bloody should be! Daisy's the sweetest girl in the

150

world. She might not be sharp, but she's certainly not vacant.'

Jane reached out and stroked Guy's hair. 'Calm down, sweetie pie, ditch your Kalashnikov and I shall remember never to insult your family again.'

Guy raised a smile, 'Good. I'll keep you to that.'

Jane touched Guy's chin with her forefinger, turning his face to hers; she felt a strong desire to kiss him. So far their relationship had remained on a business footing, she'd played it extremely cool this time, but she was working up to the kill. And he really did have the most delectable mouth. It crossed Jane's mind that Guy was the sort of bloke a girl could eat. 'I think you'd better be nice to me, Guy. That is, if you want to hear my good news.'

He sipped his beer. 'I wondered what the cryptic note in your voice was this morning.'

She nudged him, 'I got a phone call yesterday, from one of the big boys.'

He wiped his mouth on the back of his hand. 'And who might the big boys be?'

She grinned, 'Those guys round and about Fleet Street. Although, come to think of it, they're not round Fleet Street anymore, are they? Isn't it Canary Wharf for most of 'em? No matter, this particular agent obviously read your piece in the *Chronicle* and he'd now like to meet you. He asked me loads of questions and when I explained about your business and how absolutely gorgeous you are, he got quite excited!' Guy's eyes widened in embarrassment and Jane tweaked his cheek. 'Anyway, he says he'd like you to write something similar, still on the Fripon, and still calling it *Le Throb* of course, for him. Says that with a few subtle changes he could get it into one of the tabloid weekend magazines.'

Guy's hand reached into his jacket pocket for his cigarettes. He withdrew the packet and offered one to Jane. She accepted and Guy lit them both. Almost hungrily he drew on his and looked at Jane. 'So what am I supposed to do?'

From her handbag she withdrew a slip of paper. 'There you are. Peter Kent. His phone number's underneath. Just give him a ring. Put on your best clobber and go and see him. You've got nothing to lose, Guy, and everything to gain.'

A sheepish smile curved Guy's mouth. 'But isn't this supposed to be your scene? I'm not the journalist. You are. I almost feel as though I'm stealing your thunder, and I'm not even sure I want to write. I was useless at writing at school.'

'Oh, shame on you, Guy Hamilton. Stop this self-effacing crap, will you, because you were never useless at writing, I just don't believe it. I'm sure the words flow off your pen in the same way your sexuality—'

'Yes?'

She let out her breath. 'Becomes you.'

'Jane, I have it on good authority that my sexuality dried up ages ago.'

'Oh dearie me. Poor, poor Guy.' In a patronising manner she began stroking his hair and he shifted away, sitting back in his seat. She leaned forward and peered at him. 'Hey, ducky, come on now, why so heavy?'

'I'm not being heavy! You just passed on some incredible news and then you take the piss!' He grabbed her hand and held it so tightly it took her breath away. 'Why do you always take the piss!'

She snatched her hand away. 'I'm not taking the piss! I haven't said anything to you that I don't mean.' She poked him in the shoulder with her forefinger. 'D'you know something? Since you split from your *fucking* wife you're one hellishly prickly person.' She tapped his arm. 'She screwed you up, didn't she? That Naomi Benson.'

Guy shook his head noncommittally and looked towards the bar. 'Do you fancy another drink?'

'Don't change the subject!' Jane checked her watch. 'Tell you what – come back to my place instead?' She smiled and Guy was secretly shocked by such an invitation in the middle of a heated discussion. She quickly added, 'Why are you looking like that? I only meant for a cup of tea.'

But his memory drifted back to an occasion years ago when he was trying to sell her a Jaguar sports. Then he'd rejected her advances because of his attachment to Naomi. He could only imagine the sort of cup of tea she was talking about now. 'Is it Lapsang?'

She stood up and gathered her things together. 'It's whatever you'd like to call it.' Raising one eyebrow, she said invitingly, 'Coming?'

Years ago he'd have been excited at the prospect. Now he quaked in his shoes. Jane could make mincemeat of him – if he let her. Guy stood up and extended his hand towards the door. 'I'm all yours.'

Her enchanting yellow-brick house was in the middle of a Victorian terrace close to the north side of the river, off Chesterton Road where no cars were allowed. The area was typically Cambridge with a winding path leading past Jane's front door to a well-trodden footpath alongside the Cam. As the eye followed the path the vista was softened by a profusion of trailing plants covering arches and porticoes left from former buildings. The whole area was ancient but well cared for and only ten minutes from the centre of town.

Guy parked his car behind Jane's in the next street and together they approached her house. There were three stone steps to her front door and while waiting for her to unlock it Guy glanced below to the basement. It looked like an untidy storeroom of some kind. He soon realised that Jane liked living amidst clutter. As he walked through the door all around were books and newspapers and stacks of this and that, precariously spilling on to attractive antique furniture which looked as though it hadn't been polished in months. The house itself was a mixture of wonderful high ceilings, ornate plasterwork, wood block floors, sash windows and a pair of elegant French doors opening out on to a patio which overlooked a tiny overgrown garden.

'Don't mind the mess,' she said, waving her hand about. 'It's always like this. I can't function properly if everything's tidy. I have tried and it doesn't work.'

Briefly, Guy studied Jane and recognised the differences between them. He didn't mind clutter, but a mess on this scale would drive him up the wall. Not that it mattered because he was only downstairs for a fleeting moment. She took his hand and led him up the stairs with their worn carpet. Her bedroom was surprising. Although still heaped with this and that, the bedding was freshly laundered appliquéd linen in the purest shade of white and the plain and simple blinds at the window matched. There was a soft beige carpet on the floor and fitted cupboards all round. The whole effect was very pleasing.

She pointed to a door opposite. 'The bathroom's over there and if you don't mind I'll use it first.' Jane walked past him, brushing against him as she did so. Guy sank his hands in his pockets and walked over to the window. Then he removed his jacket and wondered what to do with it. In the end he draped it round a chair. There were already about six items of clothing thrown over it. He waited for Jane to return and when she did so, still fully clothed, took his turn in the bathroom. He closed the door and smiled at all the girly things everywhere, including a black lacy bra and matching panties hanging over the showerhead to dry. Guy shook his head, remembering Naomi, but was determined to rid himself of such thoughts. Instead he filled the sink with hot water and proceeded to wash his face and hands, he didn't know why. Then he cleaned his teeth with her toothbrush, feeling sure she wouldn't mind.

On his return Jane was in bed and he was pretty sure by the heap of clothes on the floor next to the bed that she was naked. He didn't look at her face, just moved round to the other side of the bed and sat down, removing his shoes and socks. He stood up and undid his belt, pulling down his jeans. He stripped off his tee-shirt, threw it to the floor, turned and climbed into bed. He did everything as though it was expected of him. She'd done him a favour and now it was his turn.

'You forgot something,' she whispered, snuggling closer.

Smiling, Guy removed his underpants and tossed them out of bed. Her hand was on him immediately and adeptly she set to work. 'You don't waste any time, do you?'

She reached over to her bedside table and picked up a condom. 'You'll be needing this – but not just yet. Put it under your pillow.' He frowned and did as he was told. She whispered, 'We don't want to rush things. After all, we've got all afternoon.'

He sighed. 'What if I can't wait that long?'

She threw back the duvet, raising herself, and slid astride his belly. Softly, she cupped his face and kissed his nose and mouth, then ran her fingers through his hair. 'I want you to stroke me, Guy. I love to be stroked. I'm a cat, you know – at least I was in a previous life. Just keep stroking me, will you . . . like this.'

She slipped off him again and lay on her back and like a child he did as he was told. As his fingers slid over her flesh she shivered and writhed. With his forefinger he traced her mouth then kissed her. Gently, then more passionately. She pulled away. 'Slow down . . . easy.'

154

Immediately he backed off. 'I'm in danger of falling asleep, Jane.'

She grinned and stroked his face. 'Dear heart, I just want to enjoy you.'

His hand slid beneath the pillow and he withdrew the condom. 'I think you'd better put me down as the normal male retard, Jane. I want to enjoy you too.'

'Philistine!'

'But you won't be saying that when we leave this bedroom.' He kissed her nose. 'I promise.'

She watched his manly actions as he rolled on the sheath. 'Your fucking rhythm had better be good!'

He moved in, putting his hand between her legs, anxious to have her. 'It's fucking brilliant. How's yours?'

She didn't answer, just writhed as he entered her. And later, at a more leisurely pace, he stroked her until she purred.

Chapter Twenty-Two

Two months later the intense July sun was wilting its most ardent worshipper. As Lily had feared, there was indeed a price to pay for achieving her ambition. In her case the price for her job at the Viking Hotel was the slimy manager, Nigel Bates, the nasty Chef, Wally Reddington, and the navy suit and white blouse Nigel insisted she wore at all times. And if she was meeting clients, it didn't matter how hot the weather was, he insisted she wore the jacket. Lily, who'd always adored sunshine and willingly stripped off to the barest essentials to be comfortable, started to feel smothered by layers of clothing. She detested the polyester navy suit and prissy buttoned blouse. Why couldn't she wear a smart dress? And her sunny nature was further irked by the fact that Nigel wore whatever he liked, including a short-sleeved shirt.

But she wasn't going to be beaten; she saw the whole set-up as a challenge. Lily knew she could do this job and thought of it as her testing ground for the future. She also knew that, normally, she could handle the trickiest of people. Mind you, Chef, as he insisted on being called, was proving to be extremely difficult. For some reason he'd taken a dislike to Lily and made this abundantly clear at every opportunity. About two weeks into the job she'd tentatively asked him if there was any chance that her sister Daisy could help out, washing up or something, and this request had been flatly refused. He'd scowled at Lily and said, 'I select my kitchen staff. You do your job and I'll do mine!'

Will Cummings, his sous-chef, and as Lily soon found out the real cook and brains behind the scenes, made things more bearable. He would stand behind Chef and grin, even pull faces sometimes. Will had worked at the Viking, doing various jobs, since leaving school and had no formal training whatsoever but an enormous flair with food and a quick and easy attitude. This meant he was now irreplaceable. Lily surmised that Chef prized Will like a trusty slave. The young man was his brilliant crutch and kept under Wally's wing so that nobody would ever realise Chef wasn't doing it all by himself. As luck would have it Will was an unambitious sort of chap and at twenty-eight quite content just to jog along with things the way they were.

Within a month it amazed Lily how the Viking kept its fine reputation. Nigel Bates continually made petty mistakes for which he blamed the nearest person – it was never his fault – and she was also surprised to learn he hadn't even looked at her CV. As she was flicking through some files in his office one day, she found it still in the sealed envelope she'd put it in. He'd obviously offered her the job on the strength of their informal interview and still assumed she was much older than she was and had been in the business for some time. What sort of efficiency was that? And Lily soon learned why the previous Catering Manager had left. You needed a special talent to fit into this place. Although she wasn't sure she'd got it or even wanted it, for the time being she'd make damned sure she fooled those around into thinking she had.

Despite Lily's strait-jacket attire, Nigel's hands were constantly wandering. The previous Catering Manager had used the communal office behind Reception but Nigel plucked Lily away from there. She had a desk in his office, neatly tucked behind the door, because he wanted her to himself as much as possible. Consequently, she made sure she used it as little as possible. His cloying after-shave was enough to put her off, but also his habit of touching her backside or stroking her hair incited her almost to rage. Instead of showing this she disarmed him by saying something like, 'Nigel, would you be so kind as to pass me that file over there?'

He'd turn and look around then glance back at her, saying, 'Which file?'

'Silly me,' she'd say, having taken several paces away from him and now holding up a file. 'It was here all the time.'

He was never quite sure if she was giving him the brush-off or not. He chose to assume not and after only a couple of weeks asked her up to his rooms for a nightcap. Lily did her best to look suitably coy. 'I couldn't possibly,' she said.

'Why?'

'Because I want to keep this job.'

Again Nigel assumed she meant he might tire of her and throw her out, which was totally unfeasible. Wasn't she the most gorgeous creature he'd ever laid eyes on? So rather smugly he'd said, 'I can separate business from pleasure, y'know.'

She touched him lightly on his arm and said, 'All the same I won't, thank you.'

He'd frowned and grabbed her hand. 'Are you for real, Lily? I don't like being used.'

Panicking slightly and recognising his quick temper, she'd said, 'I don't know what you mean?' She ran her finger round the uncomfortably high neckline of her blouse, mumbling, 'Gosh, it's hot in here.'

He'd pulled her closer. 'Well, if you came upstairs with me, you could take that off.'

Old memories stirred within Lily. She was appalled and wanted to run out of the hotel and never come back. But what good would that do? Her parents would only say, I told you so, and where would she find another job like this one? Instead she laughed, rising to the occasion, and as confidently as she was able, said, 'Another time, Nigel, *it's late.*'

'You'd better get yourself off home, then.'

'Thank you, Nigel. I'll see you tomorrow.' Lily's feet flew across the floor to the staff door.

'Straight to sleep now,' he'd called after her.

She hadn't even bothered to reply.

Lily, Cassie and Daisy found a flat in Grantchester Road, not far from the hotel. It wasn't self-contained, more shared space in an oldish house with three other females. The large and draughty 1930s dour-looking stuccoed house was on a busy main road and rather noisy but at least the rent wasn't too high. Fortunately the other three sharers were busy working girls and all easy-going. The space was allocated on a shared kitchen and bathroom basis, last one out had to clean up, but each girl had her own bedroom and Cassie, Lily and Daisy their own sitting room. Often the six females breezed in and out of each other's space, particularly the bathroom which was enormous with a separate shower, bath, washhand basin and loo. It worked, which was just as well, because if it hadn't things could have been tricky. Lily was particularly pleased because the other girls took to Daisy and she to them. They laughed with her when she made gaffes, not at her. They also loved the way she continually tidied up the kitchen, sweeping every single crumb from the floor and thoroughly washing even slightly grubby utensils and the shelves they stood on; and the way she scrubbed and polished the bathroom and the downstairs cloakroom until they shone. Never had the house been so clean and tidy. Daisy was worth her weight in gold.

But, try as she might, Daisy could not find a job. She kept a meticulous list of all the positions she'd applied for, stating why they'd turned her down. Had she not saved her money in the past, she would have been unable to share with the girls but eventually it would run out. She needed work and soon. Lily couldn't support her and it wasn't fair to expect Cassie to. As it was, her parents were not at all pleased that she'd left them in the lurch in Ely. Daisy worried about this, but not enough to deter her from living in Cambridge. She had the same determined streak running through her as her sister did and was absolutely loving her freedom, particularly the lively conversations that went on when her flatmates returned home to the supper she'd painstakingly prepared for them.

Then Cassie came up trumps. Mrs Sniffnel was preparing to go into hospital for an hysterectomy and intended to take six months off at least to recuperate. It had all happened very quickly and the poor woman was in a terrible state and turned to Cassie for support. She promoted her young assistant, with a salary increase, and instructed her to find a temporary assistant. Cassie knew just the person. Which was how Daisy found herself selling and arranging flowers, a job she soon came to love.

The heat of the summer continued, as did the glut of weddings and parties at the Viking Hotel. Most of these had been booked way before Lily's time which made things doubly difficult for her. There tended to be at least one large function each week and she was continually checking details. Chef was totally unco-operative, in fact just plain awkward, and she soon realised that even Nigel was scared stiff of him, as were the remaining four assistants in his kitchen. Only Will Cummings knew how to handle Chef. Lily wanted no mistakes so she tended to double-check food selections, quantities, wines, etc. The maître d' and most of the waiting staff fell over themselves to assist Lily and by late summer she was on first name terms with everyone else in the hotel, including the room-service maids. But the kitchen was the nucleus of her job and she found herself reluctant to visit it when Chef was there. Instead she chose to deal with Will and it wasn't long before a firm friendship developed between them.

'You won't be 'ere long!' he joked as they stood alone in the kitchen in the lull of the afternoon. 'I've met your sort before. The Viking might be the bee's knees round these parts but it certainly can't 'old on to folk like you.' In his white coat and apron, checked trousers, and with his chef's hat slightly askew, he'd leaned closer. 'You're too thorough and dedicated for the likes of us, Lily.'

She'd deliberated over his words. 'But what I don't understand is how this place maintains its reputation? I mean, have you seen the complaints file?' She whistled through her teeth. 'And Nigel seems to spend most of his time apologising to customers!'

'I know, sweed'eart, I know.' Will shook his dark curls beneath his hat and then, with a flourish, adopted a lofty pose, raising his right hand and flicking his fingers. 'But, y'see, they come for the exquisite *cuisine* lovingly created by *moi* and the wonderful ambience exuded from this fine ol' building! There 'ent nowhere quite like it in the whole of Cambridgeshire and East Anglia!'

Lily frowned. 'But surely its reputation was intact before you came along, Will?'

'Yes, well, that was in the days of Max. Maximilian Lavender, no less. He left about six years ago for bigger and better things. He's now in Park Lane! Wally, of course, was his sous-chef and took over from 'im. Things deteriorated pretty rapidly after that, I can tell you, at least for a while.' He grinned, crinkling his saucy eyes. 'But we don't talk about that partic'lar era!'

'So how long have you worked in the kitchen?'

'I've been in the 'otel for eight years and five of those in the kitchen.'

'So you remember Max . . . whatever-his-name-was?'

'Indeed I do. He was the finest *chef de cuisine* you could 'ope to meet and he inspired me to wanna cook.'

Lily smiled. 'And I suppose it's your ambition to take over from Wally?'

160

Will shrugged. 'Who knows? I can't really see him leaving.'

'But Max was offered another job. Wally might be. After all, people think he's the inspiration behind the food.'

Will shook his head. 'No, Max left of 'is own accord. He actually sought other employment. I told you, Lily, people like you and Max don't 'ang around the likes of 'ere for too long. But Wally will. Things are nice and safe for 'im 'ere.'

'Huh! And he gets you to do all the work!'

Will placed his large hands on Lily's shoulders. 'I really don't mind. At least he allows me to use my ideas. Some Chefs wouldn't.'

'But he's lazy and you're worth far more than this.'

'Ah, you're just saying that because he doesn't like you, Lily. Nigel's lazy too but I don't 'ear you complaining about 'im.'

She pouted. 'Well, there's plenty of time. Hang about and you might . . . Anyway, *why* doesn't Wally like me?'

Will laughed. 'Easy! He feels threatened by you! You're very much in control. He can't stand people who're in control, apart from me that is. You might expose 'im.' He guffawed, 'Whereas Nigel likes people to take control. He's such a dickhead he don't question his own supremacy.'

Lily went into peals of laughter at this explanation just as Chef arrived back in the kitchen after his afternoon nap. He scowled at her. 'Haven't you anything better to do than waylay my staff?' He flapped his hand at Will. 'Come on, come on, don't stand about fraternising, boy, there's food to prepare. I don't pay you to stand about fraternising!'

Will raised his eyebrows then amiably set about his preparations for the evening. Fuming, Lily turned on her heel and started to leave the kitchen. She hesitated and then retraced her steps, standing defiantly before Wally who just glared at her. Quite calmly she said, 'Chef, as you know, liaising with the kitchen is part of my job and I think it would make things rather more pleasant if you remembered that.' She noticed Will's eyes widen and Chef's mouth drop open.

He spluttered, 'I don't have to be polite to you if I don't want to be! Nobody speaks to me like that, and certainly not the likes of you!'

Lily stepped backwards, quite shocked by his vehemence.

161

What a thoroughly nasty man he was. She had no choice but to turn and leave.

Still spluttering, Wally looked at Will. 'Who on earth does she think she is? The Queen of fucking Sheba! Huh! I'll soon sort her out, just see if I don't!'

Impressed with Lily's nerve, Will knew better than to say anything. Instead he got on with his work.

Chapter Twenty-Three

'Have you seen this?' Cassie held up a Sunday supplement magazine.

Half way through a bowl of muesli, Lily raised her eyes. It was late on a Monday evening and she'd only just finished work. Cassie tended not to retire until the early hours and Lily was always grateful for her company when she returned home at some ungodly hour. Daisy had already gone to bed and any left-overs from supper had long since lost their appeal. As was often the case, Lily reached for the Alpen and enriched it with a dollop of double cream. She grabbed the magazine and swiftly read the article on the sports page that Cassie referred to. 'Hey! It's the same as before! It's about your car, Cassie.' Lily grinned at her friend. 'He's done it again. Good old Guy.'

Rather smugly, Cassie agreed. 'There's a few changes here and there, but you're right, it's almost word for word what was written in the *Chronicle.*'

'But it's months since he wrote that. I'd have thought the car was no longer hot news.'

Cassie shrugged. 'Oh, I think you're wrong there. These things take time – and you wouldn't believe how many people have referred to it since as the Throb.'

'*Le Throb.*'

'I know, but they leave out the *Le.*'

Lily scrutinised the picture of Guy in chinos, open-collared shirt and designer jacket leaning against a Fripon, arms folded and one foot across the other. 'Hmm, Guy Hamilton, ... *car specialist.* I must say, he looks rather dishy, doesn't he?' She peered even more closely, 'Is that a stud in his left ear?' She held up the picture for Cassie. 'It looks like an ear-stud, doesn't it?' Cassie nodded as Lily continued to study the article. 'And his hair's slightly shorter as well, more layered.'

Cassie watched her best friend's avid interest. She'd done just the same before passing the article over, thoroughly perusing it word for word, feature for feature. 'He's obviously destined for greater things,' she said.

Lily's brow creased as she raised her eyes to Cassie. 'Do you think so?'

'I've always thought so. That's why Keir hangs on to him like a dog with a bone.' Cassie pronounced Keir *Kee-erh*.

Lily's brow furrowed. 'You still don't like Kee-erh, do you?'

Stretching backwards and putting her hands behind her head, Cassie agreed. 'Correct.'

Lily was inquisitive. 'Has he asked you out again?'

Cassie shuddered. Since their encounter in his flat, Keir had steered clear of her at all times. 'No, I don't get to see him at all these days. Thank God.'

Lily yawned and put the magazine on the table. She pushed away her half-eaten muesli and groaned, 'Oh, Cassie, I'm dreading tomorrow. Absolutely dreading it.'

'Why?'

'Another wedding and I haven't been able to get through to Mrs Fairfield, the bride's mother who's organising it all, although she has spoken briefly to Nigel. I'd just like to have known that everything's happening as per the *latest* information. The numbers we're catering for have been changed so many times.' Lily sighed. 'But it's too late now. The food's practically ready apart from the final touches.'

Cassie pulled a face. 'Fancy getting married on a Tuesday.'

Lily stretched forward, slumping her head into her hands. 'Oh, they get married at all sorts of times, Cassie. In some ways it makes my job easier. Saturdays are busy enough without weddings.'

Cassie leaned forward and peered at her friend. 'Are you happy, Lily? I mean, you work such awfully long unsocial hours. Is all this what you expected?'

She pondered a while. 'No. But I do like the work. It's just the people who wear me out.'

'Slimy Nigel, y'mean?'

Lily nodded, 'Yes. And Chef. I can honestly say I loathe and detest bloody *Chef*.'

Smiling, Cassie added, 'But Will's good?'

'Yeah. Will's great.' Lily straightened herself. 'In fact, I think he's pretty fantastic.'

'What's this? Do you have designs on the guy?'

'Only on his workmanship. Although he's not so bad to look at, quite attractive really.' Lily's thoughts then switched to her cousin. These days every time she thought of Guy she was aware of a dull ache beneath her chest bone, around the heart area. Her eyes widened as she noticed Cassie's intense stare. Lily rallied her thoughts. 'But Will's well and truly stuck under Chef's thumb . . . and I'm beginning to think he feels secure like that.'

'Nothing's certain forever.'

'Some things are.'

'Only death.'

'Oh, Cassie! That's morbid!'

'It's the truth. Death is the only certain thing in life.' Playfully she thumped her friend's arm. 'It's true. So far as the rest is concerned, anything can happen.'

Lily yawned again and stretched her arms above her head. 'Well, I just hope nothing untoward happens tomorrow. I want the day over and done with then I can relax again for a while.' She slumped on to the table once more. 'I think I'll go to bed.' She stretched out her hand. 'Thanks, Cassie, for waiting up for me. You really are a treasure.'

'I don't wait up for you. I'm a nightbird, didn't you know?'

Lily narrowed her eyes. 'There's heaps I don't know about you, Cassie, absolutely heaps.'

'Yeah, well, there's heaps you don't want to know about me, I can tell you.'

Lily stood up. She didn't query that last statement, just smiled and said goodnight. Time and their abiding friendship had taught her when not to ask questions.

Chapter Twenty-Four

The following day started off well enough. The weather was good and as Lily buttoned up her despised but freshly ironed blouse and put on her newly brushed but equally despised jacket she felt refreshed and in the right mood to face the day. She pinned up her hair, as Nigel insisted, and took great care with her make-up then set off to walk the short distance to the Viking. Because of the ridiculous hours she worked, walking made life easier and kept her fit.

When she arrived, the first thing she did was go through to the kitchen to check on all the preparations. She had her lists in front of her and with the help of Sally, one of the kitchen staff, went through everything. Chef wasn't due yet and Lily was relieved about that, he'd only put obstacles in her way and tell her to come back later which would of course be impossible. She had a hundred and one other things to do. All the same, she was impressed with the food and realised that buffet feasts could be far more mouth-watering than four-course meals. Tempting morsels of stuffed smoked salmon, devils on horseback, samosas, pâté en croûte, spicy skewered chicken, butterfly prawns, *mignons de boeuf*, diced spiced and sautéd vegetables in delicate twists of filo pastry, cheese and anchovy aigrettes, and assorted salads and desserts were enough to entice anyone's palate.

Lily grinned and told Will, 'This looks wonderful.' She made a point of including Sally in her praise. 'You chaps in the kitchen certainly know how to create orgasmic delights, don't you?'

'Lily, you wicked girl! And I always thought you were much too prim to say such things!'

Her grin widened. 'I'm not prim, and it's good to be wicked every now and again, don't you think?'

Will stepped closer and wrapped one arm around her. She didn't mind. Will's touch was not nauseating like Nigel's. 'Well, you can be orgasmic with me any time you like, darlin'.'

Sally burst into a fit of giggles and Will flapped her with his oven cloth. This was the normal state of affairs in the kitchen when Chef wasn't around. But as soon as he entered there was a deadly hush.

Lily wriggled out of Will's clutches and started towards the door. 'Great stuff!' she said, throwing her hand in the air. 'I can see Mrs Fairfield is going to be another big fan of the Viking Hotel.'

But Lily was mistaken. Mrs Fairfield was not at all pleased with the Viking. She turned out to be a large American woman with plenty to say. Immediately she entered, before the bride and groom, she sought out the person in charge. With a huge welcoming smile Lily stepped forward. 'I'm awfully sorry, honey,' she said, 'but there are a few extra here today.' She looked behind Lily, which was disconcerting. 'I did speak to the Manager yesterday and he assured me a few more wouldn't make the slightest difference.'

Lily gulped. 'Yes, well, of course. That's where a buffet comes into its own.'

Mrs Fairfield gripped her arm and drawled, 'And I spoke to that Chef of yours a while back. Funny guy. Weird eyes, don't you think?'

Lily blinked. 'When was that?' she queried.

Mrs Fairfield didn't answer because the bride and groom had arrived looking like something out of a fairytale. For a good few seconds Lily just stood and stared at so much frothy white silk organza being swished about with lingering looks passed from the wearer to her groom. She began wondering how she'd feel if it was her wedding day and felt quite envious.

'Now we don't want a receiving line,' Mrs Fairfield ordered. 'Holds everything up and it's kind of draggy, don't you think? My daughter and her husband,' she laughed, unused to the word, 'will go straight through to the reception room and circulate as the guests arrive.'

167

Poor bride and groom, thought Lily. But she gestured in the direction of the reception room and Mrs Fairfield, the affable Mr Fairfield following, led the way. Laughing and joking, the bride and groom brought up the rear. Knowing they would be welcomed by the master of ceremonies, Lily waited for the bridesmaids and the rest of the guests.

Almost immediately she realised that the 'few more' was in fact a third. She'd been expecting seventy-five guests and the kitchen had catered for seventy-five or thereabouts, but there were easily a hundred guests milling around the reception room looking particularly hungry. Consequently the seating plan was wrong as well. Panic rose within her as she looked around for Mrs Fairfield.

The woman was already bossing the waitresses about. Lily drew her to one side. 'I think perhaps there are rather more than a few extra guests, Mrs Fairfield?' she said politely.

Adamantly, the woman shook her head, making her wide-brimmed hat wobble slightly. 'No, no. There's only a hundred – give or take one or two.'

'*A hundred?* But the final figure was seventy-five.'

'No, it wasn't! I spoke to your Chef a fortnight or so ago!' She chuckled. 'It was before I left for my much needed pre-wedding vacation.' She patted her cheek. 'To get myself a *real* tan. Anyway, I called in and the girl on reception said you weren't available and neither was the Manager, so I specifically asked to see the Chef. I could tell he wasn't too pleased at being interrupted but I definitely told him the guest list had gone up to a hundred!'

Trying hard to remain calm, Lily asked, 'And he made a note of this?'

Mrs Fairfield shrugged then looked around the room, paying particular attention to the quantity of food now being brought in. 'Probably, but what difference does it make? He's in charge isn't he? He's doing the cooking!'

But it isn't quite like that, thought Lily. She cleared her throat. 'So, Chef assured you he'd cater for a hundred?'

'Yes, of course he did. Why . . . hasn't he?'

Lily felt the colour on her face deepen and for the umpteenth time cursed the darned blouse she was wearing. Her fingers flew to the neckline as she eased it away from her damp skin, but foremost in her head was the fact that the mouth-watering bites of food being carried into the reception room and placed on the cleverly decorated tables were now going to be devoured in seconds and this wedding would look measly and mean which would, in turn, reflect upon her. It wasn't fair but it was a fact. Nobody in this hotel would blame Chef because he'd twist the facts to suit himself and land her well and truly in it.

Lily summoned a smile. 'If you'll excuse me?' She turned to leave the room but Mrs Fairfield grabbed her arm.

'There is going to be enough food, isn't there? That man's not going to let me down, is he? This is my daughter's big day.' She waved her hand. 'I mean, this place is supposed to be *the best* and I only ever wanted the best for Zoë.'

'Of course there'll be enough food. Please, just leave it to me.'

Lily's feet sped across the floor and Mrs Fairfield chased after her, stalling her again. 'Look, honey, there are several young kids here today. I mean, if there's some difficulty in the kitchen then what about some English sausages and . . .' she clicked her fingers '. . . whad'ya call them? *Fish fingers.* Yeah, they wouldn't go amiss.'

Breathlessly, Lily stared at her, hardly able to believe her ears. All this wonderful food at astronomical prices and she was talking about sausages and fish fingers! In that instant Lily really liked Mrs Fairfield. In fact she beamed at her, then nodded before continuing on her way first to Nigel's office.

'Nigel!' she said breathlessly as she entered and found him reading a magazine which he quickly shoved into a drawer. She'd learned very early on that he liked to make himself scarce during functions when in reality he should be out there, helping. 'Is there any possibility, please, you could sort out the seating for this wedding reception? We need another twenty-five chairs plus tables.'

Immediately he looked disgruntled and narrowed his eyes. 'This is your job, Lily. Don't tell me you've cocked up the numbers?'

She gazed at him for a few seconds before forcing a smile. 'I didn't cock anything up, and it needn't be a problem. Look, it's a long story, but suffice it to say Mrs Fairfield brought along an extra twenty-five people today.'

Standing up, Nigel argued, 'Well, it's not our problem then, is it? We can only do what we're asked to do.'

'*Nigel*! This is a service we're providing and it's no big deal adding more chairs!'

'Well, get somebody else to do it! I'm the Manager round here, not the general dogsbody.'

She hadn't got time to ask anybody else. Besides, they were all flying around like nobody's business. Lily implored him. '*Please, Nigel? For me?*'

Now this he did like. It was good to see Miss Precious & Untouchable begging. He moved round the desk, positioning himself directly in front of her. His hand found its way to her backside, which he squeezed, his face very close to hers. 'What's it worth then?'

She shifted away from him but was still desperate for his help. 'It's worth my thanks, Nigel. My eternal thanks.'

He stepped forward again and brought both hands to her buttocks. He squeezed her firm flesh, exciting himself as he did so. She was appalled and repelled and shot backwards. She actually considered fleeing the Viking forever. He drawled, 'Yes, well, I shall expect your eternal thanks when everybody else has gone home tonight . . . okay?'

With her best forced smile, she lied. 'You'll get it. Wholeheartedly. Just help me, please?'

He took her hand and placed it on the fly of his trousers. 'See what you do to me, Lily.'

Like lightning she pulled her hand away and shuffled backwards out of his office. 'I'm relying on you, Nigel.' Then she left.

Grinning like a Cheshire cat, he called after her, 'And I'm relying on you!' To do all sorts of things for me, he added salaciously beneath his breath.

She shuddered and made her way to the kitchen. As she entered Chef looked up, a smug expression on his face. 'Lily,' he purred, 'everything to your liking?'

How on earth should she play this? All she really wanted to do was smack him round the face but calmly she approached him. 'There is a difficulty with the numbers, Chef. I think perhaps you're already aware of this?'

Jokingly, he tapped his chest with his hand. 'Me? How should I know that? I just do as I'm told by you!'

Will, standing in the background, frowned and shook his head, warning Lily not to get heavy with the master. She swallowed hard. 'Is there any chance, Chef, that you could rustle up some more food? There's an extra twenty-five out there, some of them children.' Lily smiled pleasantly. 'Mrs Fairfield said she doesn't mind a few sausages and fish fingers for them but as things stand at the moment, there isn't enough of anything.'

Chef sighed deeply and put his hands on his hips. 'Well, now, Your Highness, I wondered how long it would be before you made a major slip up. But, you know, this is nothing to do with me. I've catered for the numbers you gave me.' He looked at his watch. 'And now I'm going home!' He laughed and turned to the rest of his staff, waving a hand at then. 'And so are my staff.' His eyes slid back to Lily. 'But please ... feel free to rustle up anything you like. No doubt you're a dab hand at sausages and fish fingers!'

Lily wanted to scream. Only Will's sympathetic smile in the background kept her from doing so.

And then Chef's attention was taken as a stern look crossed his face. He looked behind Lily and snapped, 'Who let you in here?'

Lily turned to see a tradesman holding an enormous tray of fresh asparagus. Even with all her problems she couldn't stop her eyes from wandering over the attractive-looking greenery.

The guy grinned. 'Going cheap. Freshly picked this morning.'

'Liar!' spat Chef. 'It's too late in the season for freshly picked asparagus.' He flicked his wrist. 'We don't deal with the likes of you. Go on, buzz off. Out, out!'

The amiable-looking tradesman shrugged and turned to leave. Chef proceeded to follow him out but called back to Lily, 'Have fun, young lady. Have fun!'

Immediately she turned to Will with imploring eyes. 'Are you going to help me?'

He held out his hands in despair. 'There's nothing we can do, Lily. We were asked to cater for seventy-five. If Mrs Fairfield has chosen to bring along an extra twenty-five then that's her fault, it really isn't ours.'

'But it's *not* her fault! She actually added them to the numbers a fortnight ago! She spoke to Chef herself. He's deliberately done this to land me in the shit!' Lily's hand flew to her mouth. 'Hang

171

on!' Like lightning she ran out of the kitchen and towards the back entrance of the hotel. Pulling open the door, she very nearly missed him. The tradesman had already stashed his asparagus in the back of his van, but she managed to stop him from driving away just in time. He wound down his window. 'I'll take it!' she said. 'Can you bring it back inside?'

Equally amiably he did as he was told. Like so many before him, he couldn't resist the smile on Lily Hamilton's gorgeous face. As he opened the back of his van, she spotted a basket of quails' eggs. 'Are they for sale too?'

'Certainly are.'

'Good. We'll have those as well.' She picked up the basket and led the way back to the kitchen where she handed them to Will before stripping off her jacket and undoing the buttons at the neck of her blouse. She rolled up her sleeves and donned an apron. Besides Will only Sally remained in the kitchen and the tradesman stood before them with his tray of asparagus. Lily gave him a beseeching smile. 'If you call back tomorrow, I'll pay you, promise.'

He put the tray down and grinned. 'Okay. See you tomorrow.' He wandered off, but not before giving her one last look. Will caught it. 'Another admirer, Lily! You just keep 'em rolling in, don't you?'

She ignored this comment because already she was putting the quails' eggs on to boil, setting the timer for three minutes, then preparing to chop the stalks from the vast pile of asparagus. 'Haven't got time to scrape,' she said. 'Sally! A large pan of boiling water, please, to plunge these in.' Lily looked at Will. 'Any suggestions? What's in the freezer that's quick and simple to prepare? Anything, anything! We can tart it up. Make it look special!'

The master of ceremonies arrived at the entrance of the kitchen looking decidedly glum. He moved towards Lily. 'Is it all right for the wedding guests to start eating? Mrs Fairfield has informed me they're all ravenous!'

'Is the seating sorted?'

'Yes. Mr Bates has organised that.'

'Okay, and the serving staff are ready too?' He nodded. 'Right, well, tell them to start. But have a word with Mrs Fairfield too and assure her more food is on its way.'

He raised his eyebrows before nodding then left the kitchen. Lily turned to Will. 'They'll probably eat that lot in no time.'

He frowned and looked at the first lot of asparagus Lily had already plunged into the bubbling pan of water. 'How are you going to serve all this?'

'Plain and simple. Dipped in butter on a silver platter. Delicious. Now, what else is there?'

He looked around. 'Well, we've got rosti on the dinner menu tonight. I've made dozens of 'em, mini portions, all prepared. They just need reheating.'

'Great! Is there plenty of smoked salmon in the larder?'

'Yes, of course.'

'Wonderful! Warm the rosti then top them with sour cream and slithers of smoked salmon. Then dill and lemon zest.' Immediately he set to work and Lily beamed at him. 'You're a treasure, Will. Thank you.'

He looked from her to Sally then back at her. 'It really is a pleasure, Lily. You must know that.'

Sally, enjoying the upbeat atmosphere in the kitchen for once, added, 'There's plenty of prawns in sesame seeds in the freezer. They can be deep fried in no time. Shall I do them?'

'Fantastic! And add some sprigs of coriander if we've got it. You're an angel!'

Sally wandered off and returned with four large bags and one extra. She held it out. 'And there's these. They're curled frankfurters, also for deep frying. Apparently they've got tomato ketchup inside. The kids'll love 'em!'

'Yes, yes. Do them, Sally. You're doing great.' The beeper started then and Lily scooped up the saucepan of quails' eggs, emptied the boiling water and poured cold on top.

Will added, 'And there's Mexican chicken on the menu tonight. I could parcel some spoonfuls into tortillas, fry them and finely slice them. A little guacomole on the side, a touch of sour cream, a little paprika – instant chimichangas!' He put his arm around Lily. 'Then I really do think we'll 'ave enough, don't you? You're not feeding the five thousand, darlin', don't get too carried away!'

'Fine, except for the fish fingers!' She looked towards Sally. 'Do we have any?'

Sally giggled and shrugged. 'Don't sound like the sort of stuff we normally have, but I'll see, shall I?'

'Please. And Will's right. If Mrs Fairfield complains, I shall resign.' Lily was already peeling the shells from the quails' eggs and slicing them in half. She would use these to form a plait across the asparagus as though holding it together.

'She won't complain! This'll be the best part of the 'ole bloody beanfeast, you mark my words!'

There was a delay before the rest of the food was served, but as soon as it landed on the tables the guests naturally gravitated towards it and were more than pleased to have a taste of everything. Lily, with her blouse rebuttoned and wearing her jacket, but with a very flushed face, returned to the reception room and was surprised to see adults helping themselves to fish fingers. Admittedly they were spectacularly served with criss-crossed slithers of shiny baked red pimento and al dente green beans but they were still meant for the children.

With a plate in her hand, Mrs Fairfield tapped Lily on the shoulder. 'Did you do all this? I must say the asparagus and quails' eggs are cooked to *perfection*.' More luck than judgement, thought Lily. Mrs Fairfield continued, 'I asked where you were and the master of ceremonies said you were in the kitchen. You're looking awfully flushed.'

Lily shrugged and took a deep breath. 'Am I? It's so warm in here.'

Mrs Fairfield indicated with her fork. 'That Chef of yours . . . I could have sworn I saw him leave.'

Lily swallowed hard, very aware that this lady missed nothing. She was tempted to be scathing but instead said, 'Chef prepared most of the food, Mrs Fairfield.'

'But not this, huh?' Lily frowned but still said nothing. 'Hah! As I thought. Do you know, I didn't like him the moment I laid eyes on him. He's got beady, furtive eyes. Don't you think he's got beady, furtive eyes?'

Lily laughed out loud. 'I really mustn't comment on that.'

'You know, honey, you're wasted in this place!' Mrs Fairfield took a deep breath. 'And I could get you a whole heap of work away from here. My friends are into entertaining in a *big* way. Somebody like you, with their wits about them, could clean up. I really like you.'

Lily stared at Mrs Fairfield who was being deadly serious.

'Well, I haven't been at the Viking very long and I do need this job to gain experience.'

With her spare hand, Mrs Fairfield gripped Lily's arm. 'Forgive me for saying so but you could gain a whole lot more valuable experience doing private parties. I'd have thought this sort of experience you could do without!'

Lily spied Nigel at the far end of the room and frowned as she remembered her absurd promise to him. Mrs Fairfield also looked in his direction. 'Oh, there's your Manager. I think I'll have a word with him. But would you be at all interested in some private work?'

Lily shrugged, not sure of anything at this point in time. 'Maybe.'

'Good, I'll call you. If you jot down your private number, later will do, I'll call you at home.'

Lily nodded. She saw no reason not to do that.

By the time Lily finally made her way back into the kitchen, Will had made another batch of rosti for the evening meal and replenished the depleted Mexican chicken. Chef would never know.

'I don't know what I'd have done without you, Will. And you, Sally. I'm so grateful.'

Will pointed his finger at her. 'You owe me. Just remember that.'

'Any time. I'm at your service.'

Then she heard her name called and turned to see Nigel standing there. With some trepidation Lily walked towards him. 'I'd like a word with you,' he said sternly, 'in my office.' And stalked off.

Pulling a face, she winked at Will and Sally then followed Nigel to his office, walking a couple of paces behind him all the way. He didn't talk to her. In fact, he looked most displeased. When they were inside his office he said, 'What have you been saying to Mrs Fairfield about Chef?'

She looked surprised. 'Not a lot. Why?'

'Well, she wasn't very complimentary just now. It's simply not done to criticise fellow members of staff.'

Taking a deep breath, Lily defended herself. 'Mrs Fairfield's feelings about him are nothing to do with me. She formed them all by herself.'

Nigel clenched his fists and hitched himself on to his desk. 'But you didn't help matters, Lily. Your attitude reflects very badly on the Viking.'

She was tired and more than ready to go home and really not in the mood for any of this. 'I actually think I helped things considerably this afternoon, Nigel. Has Mrs Fairfield complained about me?'

She noticed his balled fists. 'No, but that's not the point.'

'What is the point then?'

'The point is we all pull together. As I told you when I interviewed you, we're a small concern and everybody is responsible for doing their *own* bit.'

'Well, I've more than done *my* bit this afternoon, Nigel.'

'And so did Chef! He prepared some wonderful food today. And if there's one thing I can't stand it's rivalry between staff! You set out to make him look small this afternoon, and that's unforgivable.'

Lily took another deep breath then became aware of a thumping in her forehead. She put her hand there and turned to leave.

Nigel was furious at her lack of contrition. 'Where are you going?'

'I've nothing to say. I'm going home.'

He was off the desk in seconds and grabbing her arm. 'Oh, no, you're not!. You owe me, remember?'

She glared at him. 'Owe you what?'

'You know damned well what!'

'Nigel, you've just shredded my character and now you're expecting me to be nice to you?'

'They're two separate issues, Lily.'

'Not in my book they're not.' She tried to shake his hand away from her arm, but he held on. 'Please, Nigel, let me go!'

Angrily, he did so. 'You're a bitch, Lily! A real little *bitch*.'

'No, I'm not!'

He turned and thumped his fists on the desk. 'I can't stand women who play games!' He faced her. 'And that's what you do, Lily! What gives you the right?'

She frowned, totally confused. 'I really don't know what you're talking about. All I'm doing is my job.'

'And upsetting everyone else into the bargain.'

'I'm not, Nigel! I'm new here. I just need some help.'

176

Almost panting, he moved in on her. 'I'll help you, Lily . . . if you help me.'

'Huh! Sleep with you, you mean?'

'You knew what the score was when you took the fucking job!'

'If you believe that, Nigel, then you believe in fairytales.'

'Well, in that case, perhaps you should leave?'

She stood her ground. 'I will leave, Nigel. But not until I'm ready.' And with that she turned on her heel and walked out of his office. Fuming, he watched her go. Nothing worked with her, nothing. He'd tried charm, he'd tried understanding, and now he'd tried anger. She was immune to it all. In a flash Nigel Bates decided that Lily didn't like men. He reflected upon this further, coming to the conclusion she must be gay. He slammed shut his office door, resorting once more to his girlie magazines. But one thing was for sure. The sooner Lily Hamilton left, the better. She was too much of a distraction. How wrong can you be? He'd really thought she was his for the taking.

Chapter Twenty-Five

The atmosphere in the Viking went rapidly downhill after that. If Chef or Nigel was around, even Will and Sally avoided speaking to Lily. She felt she didn't have a single friend in the whole place and was at a loss to understand why. All sorts of thoughts flashed through her mind but she knew that these were the tactics used by management to freeze people out. It wasn't fair but what could she do? Although Lily had never been one to get on her soap-box and complain about workers' rights, she was sorely tempted to do just that. Nigel didn't own the Viking, it was owned by a bunch of businessmen and she knew exactly who they were. But when she considered this option she soon came to the conclusion that it would be unwise, could ruin her reputation and send her career into a downward spiral forever. Instead, with lots of pep-talks from Cassie, she soldiered on, making sure she triple-checked everything. She also tried to stay away from the kitchen and Nigel as much as she could. Effectively, Lily kept her head down and plodded on.

It was a good month before she heard from Mrs Fairfield again. The phone call came one Sunday evening just as Lily was about to go to bed. She recognised the woman's voice straight away.

'Lily Hamilton? Ah, good. This is Beverley Fairfield. Are you still working for that dreadful man?'

'Which particular dreadful man?' quipped Lily.

Mrs Fairfield laughed. 'What I mean is, are you still at the Viking?'

It was on the tip of Lily's tongue to say, Just! I'm hanging on by the skin of my teeth. Instead she said, 'Yes, of course.'

'Well, you've got guts, I admire you for that. Anyway, I was wondering if you'd be interested in doing a spot of private catering? It's for a dear friend of mine actually. A surprise sixtieth birthday party for her husband. Last-minute thing, terribly hush hush. They live in Girton, just off the Huntingdon Road. Lovely house with a huge garden and she's planning on having a marquee on the lawn linked to the house. She's dead set against using a hotel or restaurant and I suggested you. You mustn't let me down, Lily. I should think there'll be about sixty or seventy people there.'

Lily sucked in her breath and wondered how she could possibly cope. She had no equipment, no means of transport, no cooking facilities and no chef! And yet, this was just the opening she was looking for. Since Mrs Fairfield's daughter's wedding, Lily hadn't stopped thinking about the woman's offer of private work. 'What sort of food is she looking for?'

'Well, you know, honey, she wants to keep it simple but sort of classy so it'd be open to discussion. But of course she'd expect the whole package. You know, waitresses and flower arrangements – the works.'

'That won't be a problem,' Lily replied glibly then froze at her own stupidity. But already in her head she was deciding where to hire all the necessary equipment. The only real problem would be getting time off work. 'When is it?'

'In a month's time, four weeks yesterday to be precise. A Saturday night. Are you game?'

Lily laughed. 'Of course I'm game! Where can I get in touch with your friend?'

'Her name's Sheila Sibley, a lovely lady. In fact her husband owns the *Chronicle*. Do you get to read the *Chronicle*?' Mrs Fairfield waffled on before proceeding to give Lily all the necessary information she needed when already the mention of the *Chronicle* had raised tantalising thoughts of Guy.

'Would it be all right for me to call her this evening?'

'No, ring her tomorrow when her old man's on the golf course. But she's waiting to hear from you, Lily.'

'Fine, I'll ring her in the morning. And, thanks, Mrs Fairfield. I'm very grateful for what you're doing.'

'Oh, don't be. I recognise quality when I see it! Always have.'

Lily thanked her again and replaced the receiver. She turned to Cassie. 'I've just changed the course of my whole life!'

179

Her friend looked at her as though she was quite mad. 'Pardon me?'

Lily pointed to the phone. 'That was Mrs Beverley Fairfield – do you remember I told you about her? The wedding reception from hell?'

Cassie laughed. 'Oh, sure, that wedding.'

'Well, she asked me then if I was interested in private catering and now she's offered me a sixtieth birthday party.' Lily walked across the sitting room to her friend. They were alone as Daisy had already gone to bed. She sat on the floor and rested one elbow on the arm of Cassie's chair. 'I could do it with your help, Cassie, and Daisy's, I know I could.'

Cassie looked aghast. 'But I can't cook, you know I can't. I must be the only person in this house who can burn a boiled egg!'

'You don't have to cook. Hopefully neither do I. But I will need your help with the flowers and maybe, in order to keep costs down, serving?' Lily suddenly became all efficiency. 'And driving me about?'

Cassie's first instinct was to say no. Instead she frowned. 'What sort of party is this?'

Hunching her shoulders and not daring to look her friend in the eye, Lily elaborated. 'I told you, a sixtieth birthday party in a lovely house in Girton with a marquee for about sixty or maybe seventy people. The guy owns the *Chronicle*.'

There was a flicker of real interest in Cassie's eyes now. Lily didn't miss it, nor the rise of her friend's chest as she took a deep breath. 'But we're just not equipped to do all this.'

Lily's hand gripped her arm. 'Yes, we are! At least I am. That's what I was trained to do. If we keep our heads, Cassie, I can sort it. And just think of the money we'll earn!'

Cassie's clear blue eyes rested on her friend. 'You never cease to amaze me, Lily. We could end up in court! These guys might go down with food poisoning!'

'Or, alternatively, they could be so pleased with the service and the food we provide that they recommend us to all their friends.'

Cassie was allowing herself to be carried along on Lily's supreme confidence now. 'Okay, if you're stupid enough to put yourself on the line, I guess I'll just have to join you.'

Lily stood up and put her hands on her hips. Then she turned and walked over to the window, staring out at the darkness. 'Apparently most of the *Chronicle* staff will be there.'

There was silence as Cassie thought of Guy. 'Is that so?'

Lily turned. 'Guy still writes regularly for them. D'you suppose he'll be there?'

Cassie leaned back in her seat. 'How should I know? Give him a ring. Ask him.'

'I couldn't possibly do that!' Lily leaned on the window sill. 'We don't have that sort of relationship.'

Watching her friend, Cassie said, 'Well, maybe you should. It's obvious he likes you.'

Lily plunged her hands into her jeans pockets and pouted. 'Is it?'

Cassie rolled her eyes. 'As if you didn't know.'

Lily turned away and looked out of the window again. 'I'm not very good with these things. You should know that.'

Cassie raised herself from the settee. 'Well, if I had your looks, I'd take it as read that most men fancied me.'

'Rubbish! Looks aren't everything.'

Turning to leave the room, Cassie added, 'Maybe not, but you've got a whole bunch of other things to go with your looks, Lily. Take it from me, Guy *adores* you.'

Then she was gone and all Lily could do was reflect upon her friend's declaration.

Within a couple of days most things were fixed. There were no private functions at the Viking that weekend and Lily had even cleared with Nigel taking two days' holiday. He seemed remarkably willing to allow this; perhaps he thought she was applying for other jobs and needed the time for interviews. It didn't matter. One of her major problems was cleared. She'd arranged to visit Mrs Sibley and sort out the menu after which she could work out who to hire to cook everything.

But as she went about her job at the Viking Lily felt terribly sad. It hadn't worked out here, she'd made enemies instead of friends. She was a firm believer in assessing any situation from all sides and knew some of the blame must lie with her. Maybe she had led Nigel to believe she was game for anything, and maybe her over-efficiency had got up Chef's nose. The sad fact remained that Lily couldn't stay much longer and she didn't want to move to a lesser position in another hotel.

Sheila Sibley's house was grand. Mock Tudor, brick and pebble-dash, with huge bay windows, highly polished antique furniture and thick carpeting everywhere. And in the vast drawing room, huge French doors looked out on to a manicured lawn surrounded by colourful flower beds.

'I'd like the marquee there.' She pointed to the very middle of the lawn. 'Linked up to the French doors. We can eat in the marquee, then clear away for the live music and dancing.' She clapped her hands together. 'I'm getting so excited about everything, and when Beverley told me about you, it seemed exactly the right thing to do.'

'And do you think you'll be able to keep everything secret from your husband?'

Mrs Sibley patted Lily's shoulder. 'I'll certainly try. Now, we really must set to work and decide on this menu. I've got the drinks in hand. Another friend of ours is a wine merchant, so you won't need to worry about that side of things. And I don't know whether Beverley mentioned it to you but Andrew doesn't like spicy foods. He's terribly old-fashioned and as it's his birthday bash I feel I must pander to his likes and dislikes.'

'That won't be a problem. What had you in mind?'

'Well, my dear, there are two things he absolutely adores, plain-living darling that he is, and they're turkey and salmon. So if we could work something around those, that'd be splendid. Oh, and we must have some of that asparagus with quails' eggs that Beverley hasn't stopped talking about. What I'd like is a buffet-style hot meal where people help themselves, but I want it simple, not too many bits and pieces. Do you think you can cope with that?'

'Are we talking courses here, or just one main meal and then perhaps cheeses and desserts?'

'Oh, definitely only one main meal with pudding to follow. We'll serve the salmon and the turkey together and people can choose which they'd prefer. I thought we'd accompany it with the asparagus and perhaps a salad and then some sort of potatoes, unless you've any other suggestions?'

'What about boned stuffed turkey? I have a lovely recipe with

182

ham, veal, lemon and herbs. Not at all spicy, but very succulent and tasty. And then perhaps salmon Coulibiac where the salmon is served in latticed puff pastry with mushrooms, chopped eggs and seasoned rice. Equally delicious with a sauce.' Lily raced on, anxious to impress, 'And perhaps creamy *gratin dauphinoise* and Italian peppers – very colourful and quite suitable for late August.'

Mrs Sibley stared at Lily. 'Well, that all sounds rather gorgeous, my dear, but I'm sure he'd be just as happy with roast turkey and poached salmon.'

Lily blinked and lowered her eyes. 'Fine. Whatever you like.'

Her hand clutched Lily's arm. 'No! This is a party. We'll do it your way. I have a funny feeling Andrew will like anything you produce. I want it to be special, Lily.' She indicated her kitchen. 'Would you like to come and see?'

'Yes, I'd love to.'

'No doubt you'll get most of the food prepared beforehand, but if I say so myself it is rather a nice kitchen. I have three large ovens, one's in the utility room, and as long as you clear up after yourselves, you can use whatever you like.'

Lily breathed an enormous sigh of relief as she followed Mrs Sibley through the house to her extraordinary kitchen. The hiring of a field-kitchen would not now be necessary.

Several days before the Sibleys' party, panic set in. Although Cassie had all the flower arrangements in hand, and Daisy had been well versed in what she'd got to do and what she must not say, Lily was beginning to realise that without at least one more helper they were never going to be able to cope.

Cassie remained calm. 'But you can hire waitresses from anywhere, Lily. It won't be a problem. Leave it to me.'

'It's not a waitress I'm thinking about, it's another chef!' She slumped into her seat. 'And another chef will take all our profits. Have you seen what these agency people charge? But there's no way one person will be able to do all the preparation and cooking on the night.' She shook her head. 'And I can't do it! Correction – I don't want to do it! Oh, hell! I suppose I'll just have to do it.'

Daisy, who was clearing away the supper dishes, turned towards Lily. 'But I can cook, Lily. I'll help.'

She sighed, anxious not to hurt her sister's feelings but

knowing she'd be more of a hindrance than a help under such pressure. 'I know you can cook, Daisy, but I really do need you to help Cassie. I've got to be able to rely on you two for serving the food and clearing away.'

Daisy's forehead puckered. 'Yes, of course.' Then she beamed at her sister. 'And I'll keep everything neat and tidy. And make sure the flowers are all right.'

Cassie tapped a forefinger on her cheek. 'Why don't you ask Will from the hotel? He helped you before.'

A look of astonishment appeared on Lily's face. 'I couldn't possibly! That's poaching!'

Cassie tutted. 'So what?'

Lily shook her head. 'He wouldn't want to. He'd never agree.'

Cassie nudged her friend. 'But if you just asked, Lily?'

'Actually I can't, he's on holiday.' As soon as she said it, Lily's mind went into overdrive. Yes, Will was on holiday. Except she remembered him saying he wasn't going away. Perhaps there was a slim chance he might do a bit of moonlighting. Immediately she climbed out of her seat and went over to the phone. She picked up the directory. 'He lives in Histon.' Her finger was running down the lists. There was only one Cummings. 'Got it.' She picked up the receiver and dialled the number. 'If I remember rightly he lives with his mother. His father died years back.' The phone was answered by a woman. 'Mrs Cummings? Is Will there by any chance?' After what seemed an age he came to the phone. 'Will, this is Lily. How are you enjoying your holiday?'

He was surprised and flattered to hear her voice. 'Well, I'm not exactly doin' anythin', but it's nice to have a rest from Chef.'

Lily got straight to the point. 'Are you busy on Saturday?'

For an instant, Will thought she was asking him out. 'What's this? You asking me for a date?'

She laughed. 'Sort of. Actually I need your help. It seems I always need your help these days. Look, I know this is an almighty cheek, but I'm organising a party on Saturday night, a private party, and – I'm desperate for your input!'

'What party? Where?'

'Before I tell you, it's nothing to do with the Viking. You probably realise that my days there are numbered. I have to find other work and this is what I'd like to do. Private parties, and the like.'

Will hesitated, obviously weighing up her words. 'You always was wasted at the Viking, Lily. I did tell you that, straight off.'

'But what about you, Will? You're wasted there as well, although I know you're keen to stay and I understand that . . . but would you be prepared to help me out on Saturday? You'll be well paid.'

He chuckled and hesitated briefly. Then he said, 'Why not? Yeah, I'll go for it.'

His acceptance took her breath away. 'You will? That's absolutely fantastic! Look, can we meet somewhere this evening to discuss everything? Or perhaps you could come here?'

Once again he didn't hesitate. 'Tell me where you live and I'll be there.'

Of course, what Will had omitted to tell Lily was that he was bored stiff at home with only his ageing mother for company. His social life was non-existent.

Chapter Twenty-Six

Will Cummings not only helped Lily, he did the lion's share of the work. Because he had more time off he was able to get cracking with many of the preparations. Lily soon noticed that he was a man who liked to be told exactly what was expected of him, not a natural organiser, but left to his own devices he'd add very special touches. Together, away from the constraints of the hotel, he and Lily got on like a house on fire and she soon realised the extra chef wasn't going to be needed at all. Unfortunately the agency wasn't too pleased but Lily decided she'd worry about that when the next job came along. And Daisy and Cassie liked Will too. As Saturday approached, the panic magically turned into excitement.

It had been arranged with Mrs Sibley for the small group to arrive in the afternoon. Mr Sibley was out until much later and they were given the complete run of the kitchen. Cassie and Daisy set about their flower decorations. The colour scheme for the tables in the marquee was white linen tablecloths with yellow and blue napkins, all hired by Lily, so Cassie had chosen a mass of yellow lilies, sweet-scented white rocket, campanulas, white bleeding heart and ornamental blue globe thistles together with feathery grasses. Daisy worked alongside Cassie, mostly copying her, and now really quite adept in her newfound skill. The group of four, dressed in crisp white shirts, black jeans and purple and white striped aprons, harmonised completely, with Will's constant quips making them chuckle and Daisy's natural retorts making them laugh even more.

By the time Andrew Sibley was due to arrive home, most of the food was either cooking, ready for cooking or prepared for serving.

When Will first sliced through the turkeys, revealing the layers of ham and veal with lemon, parsley and thyme, the aromas in the kitchen were mouthwatering. At this point Sheila Sibley walked in and watched as he cleverly arranged the slices on heated platters for Cassie and Daisy to take through to the marquee. She was equally impressed with the Coulibiac and asparagus and the way it all looked so fresh, colourful and wickedly tempting. She felt enormously proud to be hosting such a feast. Her husband, Andrew, was beside himself because he hadn't suspected a thing. As more and more friends, colleagues and family turned up with presents galore, he became tongue-tied and speechless. Sheila plied him with champagne and fussed over him like a baby.

'He's here!' hissed Cassie to Lily as she returned to collect more food.

With a red face and wisps of hair escaping from her twisted top knot, Lily stared at her friend. 'Sorry, who?'

'Guy. He's here. With that woman we met in the Blue Boar. Jane whatever-her-name is.'

'That's because she's the Sports Editor of the *Chronicle* – I've seen her name and picture on the back pages several times.'

'Oh, yeah, that explains why she's draped over him like a rug!' Cassie picked up a bowl of Italian peppers and started to walk towards the door. She threw her friend a knowing glance and said, 'They seem pretty close to me, Lily!'

Lily watched her go, aware of her friend's deep interest in her cousin, then decided not to think about Guy Hamilton. She'd got more important things on her mind.

By the time everyone had finished eating and the tables had been cleared and moved back for dancing, Will wrapped his arms around Lily in the kitchen and hugged her tightly. 'I haven't enjoyed myself so much in ages.'

She looked into his face. 'I'm so grateful, Will. This would have been a disaster without you.'

'No, it wouldn't. You'd have knocked that other chef into shape, I know. When you back's up against the wall, you cope. I've watched you.'

187

She shifted slightly, loosening his arms. 'And I've watched you. We could be a great team, you and me, Will.'

He dropped his arms and ran his hand through his untidy curls. 'Yes, but parties like this don't come about often enough for us to try, Lily. It's been fun, and we've earned a nice little pile each, but to make somethin' like this pay, you'd need several parties each week.'

'But if we kept the organisation simple, just a few of us, we could make it work.'

'But we still need the parties, Lily.'

She was adamant. 'It won't happen overnight, I know that, but—'

Lily stopped talking as Cassie entered the kitchen and made a bee-line for the remains of a chocolate truffle cake. She scooped some on to a plate, poured double cream on top and started to devour it. 'I'm starving!' she said, dribbling cream down her chin. Smiling, she wiped it away with her little finger. 'And this is divine!' Aware that without Cassie also none of this would have been possible, Lily sidled up to her best friend and kissed her cheek.

Cassie frowned. 'What was that for?'

'For being you. And for being here and helping me.'

Cassie was modest. 'Nah, you'd have coped.'

'No, I wouldn't! I needed you. For a start, who'd have done the flowers?'

Her friend replied quickly, 'Don't forget Daisy. She did her bit, well and truly.'

'Yes, of course, Daisy . . . where is she?'

Cassie smiled uneasily. 'Chatting to Guy.'

'Is she really?'

'Aren't *you* going to go outside and say hallo?'

Lily shrugged. 'Perhaps. But don't forget we're staff.'

'Well, I'm sure Sheila Sibley won't mind you talking to her guests. She hadn't stopped singing your praises all evening!'

'Oh, dear, it's not all down to me.' Lily turned to Will. 'Will's done far more than I have.'

Cassie studied her. 'But it *is* all down to you, Lily. At the end of the day none of us would be here if it wasn't for you.' She turned to Will. 'She's the world's greatest organiser. I'm sure you agree with that, don't you?'

He nodded and opened his mouth to add more praise but Lily put her hands over her ears. 'Stop it, you lot. We were all in this together.' She moved towards the door then beckoned Will. 'Are you coming? Just to see what's happening out there?'

Smiling, he shook his head. 'No, thanks. I'm too shy. I'll finish up in here.'

Lily winked at Cassie. 'In that case, I'll go and find Daisy.'

'You do that,' smiled Cassie as her friend disappeared. And I think you're in for a surprise.

Lily passed her sister as she made her way along the hall towards the drawing room. Immediately Daisy went into a fit of giggles and clapped her hand over her mouth.

'Daisy? What's so funny?'

Her sister rolled her eyes. 'It's Guy. He's drunk!' Daisy's eyes widened. 'And he just kissed me, *on the lips*, and said I'd done a great job! He also said it was the best food he'd ever tasted and the flowers look gorgeous!' Daisy looked deadly serious for a moment. 'But he did say Cassie's flowers always look gorgeous.'

'Hmm, did he? Well, he can't be that drunk then, can he?'

Daisy frowned at her sister's brisk retort. 'Oh, it wasn't me who said he was drunk, it was Cassie.'

Lily smiled and touched her arm. 'Why don't you go and get something to eat? And, Daisy, thanks for all your help.'

'You don't need to thank me, Lily. I've really enjoyed it! Can we do this again? Mrs Sibley said all her friends want to know about you, I heard her.'

Laughing, Lily took a few steps forward to continue her journey, but turned back to her sister. 'I really hope so, Daisy. If they ask, we'll certainly go for it.'

Daisy punched her fist in the air. 'Great!'

Striding quite briskly now, Lily was almost to the French doors which led out along a small canvas-covered passageway linking the house to the marquee when she heard a distinct sucking and moaning sound. She turned and her eyes latched on to a couple sitting in an armchair in the far corner of the drawing room. The girl was sitting on the man's knee, wearing an extremely short skirt which had ridden up to her crotch. His hand was beneath the skirt, inside the girl's panties, stroking her backside. They were

heavily into their kissing, oblivious of everything. For a few brief
seconds Lily stared before carrying on. She didn't recognise the
man because the girl's long tousled hair covered his.

Then she bumped into Jane Richardson who held up her hands.
'Oops! Sorry.' She looked at Lily, sizing her up. 'Ah, you're
Guy's cousin, aren't you? The one who's done all the food.'

'Not just me. There was a whole group of us.'

'Well, it was wonderful! People couldn't get it down their
throats quick enough! Including me. Your telephone's going to be
red-hot after this!'

A shiver of delight ran through Lily. 'Thank you.'

Jane frowned. 'Have you seen Guy? I've been looking for him
everywhere?'

Unwittingly, Lily turned towards the drawing room and as
quickly it occurred to her who the man was, kissing and fondling
that girl. Almost guiltily she looked back at Jane. 'I really don't
know, I haven't seen him.'

Jane stepped forward, casting her eyes in the direction Lily had
looked. Her mouth dropped open and she took a few paces
forward. '*Guy!*' she exclaimed.

Both Jane and Lily watched as the girl shot off Guy's lap and
with a simpering expression wriggled as she pulled her skirt down
over her thighs. Guy didn't move, just sat there, his face aghast
with shame. But it wasn't Jane he was concerned about, catching
him out like that, it was the woman standing behind her.
Automatically he reached into his pocket and withdrew his
crumpled packet of cigarettes. With a shaking hand, he fumbled
about and lit one, but in all this time his eyes hardly left Lily's face
even though Jane was letting rip with quite a few choice
expletives, aimed mainly at the girl. Then she hissed at him, 'And
you're supposed to have given up smoking!'

Lily just watched as his eyes veered from her to Jane then back
again to her until suddenly she felt horribly in the way, like some
sort of Peeping Tom. She turned and started to go back to the
kitchen.

'Lily!' he rasped, clambering out of his seat. He had to steady
himself but within seconds was beside her, with Jane and the other
girl watching. He whispered, 'I'm sorry. So sorry.'

She glowered. 'What you do is your own business, Guy.'

He grabbed her arm and practically dragged her away from the drawing room. Outside in the hallway, out of sight of Jane and the girl, he faced her and Lily noticed the lipstick smeared all round his mouth. Even so, he was still the most desirable man she knew. 'Please,' he slurred, 'I just want you to know, I don't always behave like that.'

'What's it got to do with me, Guy? You can behave however you like. I really don't care.'

'But I *want* you to care.' He shook his head then brought a hand to his forehead. Their eyes locked and his were filled with remorse. 'Sometimes I can be such a *prat*.'

She said nothing. After a while he turned and walked away. She watched him go, noting he really was quite drunk. As soon as he went into the drawing room, Jane began hissing and swearing at him again. Lily noticed the girl had fled. She did likewise, back into the safe haven of the kitchen.

But it took the shine off the whole occasion for her. Cassie noticed the expression on Lily's face as soon as she walked into the kitchen but said nothing. The two friends had learned a long while ago when to keep their mouths shut. Even when Sheila and Andrew Sibley made a point of wholeheartedly thanking the four of them, and insisted upon adding a large tip to the cheque they immediately handed over, Lily felt downhearted. Then she struggled to pull herself together. Of course Guy was like that. A man like him must have most of the eligible Cambridge women, and further afield, falling at his feet. But the whole scene had tipped her over the edge. She wanted him now with a burning desire.

Chapter Twenty-Seven

'Sheila said that at least four people took our telephone number.'
Lily peered at Will as he drove her home, the back of his car
stacked with pots, pans and dirty tablecloths.

He chuckled. 'I can see you're going to be busy from now on,
Lily.'

With her eyes fixed straight ahead, she said persuasively, 'I
can't get you to join me then?'

He stole a look. 'What's it worth?'

Still churning with thoughts of Guy, Lily put her head back on
the headrest. 'A big kiss?'

His reply was swift. 'Okay, I'll hand in my notice tomorrow.'

She thumped him playfully. 'I'll bet.'

'No, you're on. For a kiss from the lovely Lily – *I'd do
anything!*'

'How much have you had to drink, Will? Ought you to be
driving?'

'I'm sober, absolutely sober.' He steered his car on to the
concrete area at the rear of Lily's house and turned off the engine.
Then he twisted in his seat to face her. 'You'd better make it
quick, before the others turn up.'

She put two fingers on his lips. 'No, don't let's make it quick.
Let's empty the car and, later, I'll give you a nightcap.'

His eyes dilated as he gazed at her, hardly able to believe what
he felt sure she was offering. 'Sure . . . whatever.' Will turned and
opened the car door, anxious to offload it and get indoors.

It was a while before Daisy and Cassie went to bed. Everybody
wanted to talk about the evening, the overheard conversations, the

compliments flying around about the food and flowers, whether or not there'd be any follow-up parties . . . and Guy. At least Daisy talked incessantly about Guy. Guy this. Guy that. Neither Cassie nor Lily made any comment.

As Cassie finally left the room to go to bed, she looked sideways at her friend. 'Don't do anything I wouldn't!' she whispered.

For a second, Lily was embarrassed and reconsidered what she was proposing to do with Will. And it was all because of Guy. Or was it? Perhaps it was more to do with exploring her own sexuality. She'd laughed about university and the lack of sex there but that had been deliberate. Maybe now was the time to bring down her defences. And who better to start with than Will?

He cupped her face in his hands. 'You don't have to do this, Lily. You look awfully scared.'

'Do I?' She shook her head. 'I'm not.'

He chuckled. 'I am.'

Lily took his hand and led him to her bedroom, locking the door behind them. It crossed her mind to tell him how inexperienced she was, but maybe he'd tell her the same about himself and right now she didn't want to hear that. What she wanted was some of the raw passion she'd seen exhibited between Guy and *the girl*.

She needn't have worried. Once inside her bedroom, Will's polite and easy-going attitude changed. He was out of his clothes in no time and helping her out of hers. His hands and mouth seemed to be everywhere, fondling, squeezing and sucking her breasts, gripping her buttocks then delving between her legs. Then he was lifting her on to the bed and crawling all over her. It took her breath away, but not in the way she craved. She gasped, 'Hadn't we better use some protection?'

'Christ, Lily. I haven't got any bloody protection!'

'But I might get pregnant.'

'You're not on the pill?'

'No. Please, Will. Perhaps—'

'It's okay. I'll withdraw. It's not a problem.'

Quite horrified now, Lily completely backed off. 'I really don't think so. I'm sorry, I can't let you do that.'

Unperturbed and back to his jolly self, he was off the bed in seconds, scrambling once more into his clothes, hopping towards the bedroom door. 'There's a garage down the road. I'll be back in no time.' He grinned across at her and blew a kiss. 'Don't move. Stay just as you are . . . angel.' And then he was gone.

She lay there for a good few seconds, remembering his ungainly actions and the way his hands had moved over her before she pulled the duvet around her chilled body. Lily ran her hand over her mouth where his tongue and lips had been and knew she was making yet another big mistake. But this one was worse because this time she knew better. Poor Will.

True to his word he was back in no time, like an excited schoolboy, clutching a slim packet in his hand. He entered the bedroom, threw it on to the bed and started stripping off before Lily had time to say anything. He practically jumped beneath the duvet and it was only then he noticed the t-shirt she was wearing. 'What's all this then?'

Lily shook her head. 'I'm sorry—'

'Sorry for what? What do y'mean?'

'I'm not ready for this. It's a mistake.'

He still couldn't grasp what she was saying and pulled her into his arms, running a far more gentle hand through her hair. After everything, it was soothing. She closed her eyes and buried her face against him. 'But I love you, Lily,' he whispered. 'I loved you the first moment I laid eyes on you. I want us to be together from now on. Always. Like this.'

Lily froze. This was just what she didn't want to hear. They'd worked so well together, and with Daisy and Cassie the four of them could have been a great team. But she could never love Will in the way he wanted and she could never risk being stifled by his love.

Aware of her silence, he raised her chin to look in her face. 'Don't you love me? It's all right. We don't 'ave to make love if you don't want to. I can wait. I can wait as long as you like. I mean, you wouldn't 'ave asked me if you didn't care. Would you?'

'Of course I care.' She hesitated before saying, 'But maybe I got carried away with this evening.'

He pushed backwards against her. 'What d'ya mean?'

Rather too bluntly she said, 'I want a business relationship, Will, not a love affair.'

He reared away, reminding her of a snake swiftly retreating,

194

unfurling himself into a standing position beside the bed. 'Well, what's all this been about then?'

She reached out her hand, at pains to put things right. 'It was a mistake. But, you see, I've never done this before and I just wanted comfort . . . I'm sorry, I never meant to hurt you. I like you so much.'

Then he turned on her in a way she'd never have thought possible. The sweet easy-going man she'd grown to respect and care for hurled the next words at her. 'Oh, yes, you just wanted comfort, did you? An' you expect me to believe that? Oh, leave it out, Lily! Nigel and Chef are right about you, you just like playing games.'

'No, I don't! That's so untrue!'

Hastily, Will was dressing again now. 'Seems I'm just like them poor buggers, don't it? 'Cept I got well and truly sucked in.' Hopping again in one trouser leg, he made for the door. 'I shall expect my money, Lily, for all the work I've done. You needn't think this 'as softened me up so you don't need to pay me.' He zipped up his black jeans and straightened himself before opening the door.

'Of course I'm going to pay you. Please, Will, don't go like this. I'm truly sorry.'

Will Cummings didn't give her another look, just slammed the door and banged and clattered his way out of the house. Once outside he revved his car's engine, shoved it into gear and drove off into the night.

Knowing that by her own stupidity she'd now lost her only ally at the Viking, Lily buried her face in her pillow and burst into tears.

Chapter Twenty-Eight

Guy sat with his agent, Peter Kent, and the sports editor of the *Daily Echo*, the rather camp but extremely popular Tom Cussons, drinking double espresso. Guy had so much sugar in his cup the spoon stood up by itself. The restaurant, one of the hot favourites of the moment, was quieter now, the frenzy of the lunchtime trade having thankfully died down. The Quintessential in Soho was diabolically slow if you were truly hungry, but what the hell? The atmosphere was still great.

'It's a jolly little quiz show, goes out mid-week at eight. You'll knock 'em for six, Guy. The punters'll love you, specially the women.' Tom Cussons sat back in his seat, sucking in his cheeks and assessing the man before him. 'And don't forget to wear something *thrillingly* sexy!'

Guy, who now had a regular spot writing about cars for the *Daily Echo*, smiled. 'I haven't got anything thrillingly sexy, Tom.'

Tom Cussons's hand came down very firmly on his. 'You know what I mean, sweet thing. Don't tease. And then you can write all about it in the *Echo*. You're on your way, Guysey. Watch this space, you're on the up!'

For a totally straight man, Guy was tickled pink by Tom's speech and mannerisms. He liked him, a lot. 'What if I can't answer any of the questions?'

'Oh, you don't have to worry about that, sweet thing! They give you all the answers before you go on!'

Guy laughed. 'I'm sure that's not true.'

''Course it's true. How else do you think they make these shows look interesting?'

Guy turned towards his agent, noting the glazed pounds, shillings and pence look in his eyes. The quiz show in question was a one off. A guest appearance. But something of a feat for someone who was still practically unheard of. 'Thanks, Tom,' Peter said, 'for suggesting Guy in the first place. We owe you a lot.'

He shrugged. 'Oh, don't thank me, just invite me to all your parties when you're rich and famous!'

Instantly Guy's memory returned to the party he'd attended at the weekend. Very vividly he recalled the look on Lily's face when he'd been caught with his hand up someone's skirt. He lowered his eyes, ashamed of himself. Jane had now walked, shown him the door (for which he was grateful – she could be exhausting!), and none of the women he met these days seemed even remotely real.

'And what's this other new show you mentioned?' asked Peter.

'*Ace Driving*? Oh, that's Andy McVay's idea. Going out on Sky early part of next year. Hoping to compete with the likes of *Top Gear*. Cute chap, Andy. I mentioned your name. He's terribly interested. Looking for four or five presenters.' Tom peered at Guy. 'You do drive, don't you, Guy? I mean, *really* drive?'

'It's my passion, Tom. I'm crazy about speed.'

'Well then, you're his man.' Tom turned to Peter. 'Push it, Pete. Don't hang about.'

'How do I get in touch with this Andy McVay?'

'It's not a problem, I can give you contact numbers. He's rather elusive, mind. Have to catch him at the right moment. But, like I say, he knows about you, Guy, so if Pete here gets a message through that you're on the box next month, perhaps he'll take the time to watch.'

Guy shuddered in his seat, not at all sure he liked all this pushing and clawing and flannelling. Maybe he was happiest just selling cars. Then again, the adrenalin rush that went with it all was becoming quite addictive.

'Then there's Seb Turner. He works for ITV's Nirvana Productions. Now he's talking about producing a programme on the dynamics of anything fast. Cars, boats, helicopters – y'know the sort of thing.' Tom slurped back the rest of his coffee. 'Cool chap, our Sebastian, . . . although they say he's a bit crazy about danger!' Tom covered Guy's hand with his own once more. 'Just keep the words flowing, Guy. Do what comes naturally. If you think of anything at all – unique, off-beat, quirky – write it down for posterity. Like I said, your career is on the up.'

Guy looked at Peter, who winked back at him, then again at Tom. 'I never realised that the rest of the nation is as enamoured of all this as I am. And it seems to be getting worse.'

'Yes, it surely is. I sometimes think people prefer an upmarket car to an upmarket house. And when you think about it, it's quite logical. I mean, it's only friends who visit your bloody home. But a car is what takes you further afield. If you're driving a fucking Merc people are hardly likely to assume you live in a grotty pad in Wapping. And there again, if you're honking along in a beaten up old Astra, they won't assume you reside in the leafy glades of wherever's poshest!'

Guy laughed. 'This is serious stuff. Perhaps someone should do a programme analysing the psychology of car sales.'

'Don't scoff, sunshine! It could well happen. But, please . . . not in my lifetime!'

Peter looked at his watch. 'Well, I'm sorry and all that, but I really must make a move.'

At this point everybody stood up and shuffled around the table. The bill had already been paid and Guy looked across the room to a table in the corner. A lovely woman dressed very smartly in a business suit with expensive designer jewellery had been giving him the eye for some time now. He smiled and she too left her seat and started to walk towards the door. He followed her out, closely followed by Peter and Tom. On the pavement, she turned and gave him an enormous smile, encouraging him to talk to her at the very least.

'Whooa!' hissed Peter in his ear. 'She's after you, mate.'

Guy knew then she was his for the taking. Was this the way he wanted to go? More parties with his hand up strange women's skirts? Rather abruptly he turned his back and quizzed Tom a little more about Sebastian Turner. When he looked again she was gone.

Keir didn't like it. He didn't like it at all. He'd assumed that Guy would climb the ladder of success in the world of selling cars – and he could just tag along, creaming off the surface. All this media stuff was beyond him. In layman's terms, Keir couldn't get a grip on Guy anymore, and he needed to get a grip. The trouble was, his friend was loving it all. So much so that his whole character had changed. From the flying about, hungry salesman he'd turned into a mini celebrity, someone others naturally watched and emulated. And it was all Jane Richardson's fault. She'd taught Guy a few too many tricks. The power Keir had once felt he wielded over his friend no longer existed. And Guy was *getting it* all the time!

Weeks went by and Keir hardly saw him now. He was panicking. After much brooding the old, old saying eventually sprang to mind. If you can't beat them, you simply have to join them.

Several weeks later, Guy threw down his pen and slumped back in his seat. He reached forward to pick up his whisky tumbler and downed the contents in one.

'Another?' asked Keir.

Guy held the glass in front of him and twisted it beneath the light, as though a decision on whether or not to have another drink was of major importance to him. Keir had noticed that along with giving up smoking, Guy was drinking less. He stood up and swiped the glass from his friend's hand. 'For God's sake, man, have another. It won't kill you!'

Guy smiled and was in fact pleased to have the decision taken out of his hands. As Keir refilled his glass he studied the words in front of him. In a couple of days' time he had an informal interview with Andy McVay and it had been suggested he should write down several ideas on how he perceived *Ace Driving* going: i.e., what he could do for it. This of course wasn't easy, so Guy had decided to go totally overboard and suggest all sorts of ideas. His title for his scribblings was: *Is this a Cart or is it a Chariot?* Privately, he'd always assessed cars on whether he considered them a cart or a chariot, and this was nothing to do with the price factor. He loved the Fripon which was definitely a chariot. He hated certain upmarket, expensive cars and christened them carts.

'By the way, I'm in London tomorrow – St Katherine's Dock,' he said as Keir handed him his replenished drink. 'Might be back late.' He grinned. 'Don't wait up for me.'

His friend smiled and sat down next to Guy, immediately looking over his shoulder. 'Can I read it?'

'Sure.' Guy handed him the two sheets of paper. He believed in keeping things concise.

Keir's eyes hungrily flew over the words, immediately recognising the shrewd wit which sprang from the page. He was jealous. He pointed to a word. 'You've made a mistake. There's an i in mercurial.'

Guy just smiled and made no attempt to alter the word. Keir passed back the sheets of paper. 'So, what's on tomorrow?'

'A lunch actually. You know the sort of thing. Curly sandwiches and warm white wine. A favour to Jane. Couldn't get out of it.'

'Jane Richardson? But why in London?'

Some friends of hers. Apparently they get together each year in the autumn and one of them has just bought this huge apartment overlooking the docks. Wants to show it off. Normally they meet in the Hilton, Park Lane. Just my luck to get the curly sandwiches and warm white wine.'

'Don't pre-judge. I mean, it's unlikely this person will do their own catering.'

Guy remembered Lily's food. If only. No chance. He mused, 'Must cost something in London to hire caterers. Cheaper to eat in the Hilton.'

'So why has Jane invited you along? I thought you'd fallen out?'

Guy suddenly grew weary of Keir's quizzing. He'd noticed of late that his flatmate asked numerous questions about trivial things. 'We haven't fallen out, Keir. We just don't see each other socially anymore.'

'Well, isn't this social, the thing you're going to tomorrow?'

'Yes, it is. But apparently they all take a partner and Jane has asked me. It's no big deal. I'm doing her a favour. I owe her, Keir. I owe her a lot.'

He shrugged his shoulders and pulled a face. 'I suppose she wants to show you off, you being a star now and all that.' He looked at Guy through narrowed eyes. 'She's too macho for me. I like more feminine women.'

Guy's eyes flickered but he didn't comment. He stood up and stretched himself. 'Well, if you don't mind, I think I'll hit the mattress.'

Keir looked at his watch. 'It's only eleven o'clock.'

'So?'

'Getting your beauty sleep, are you?'

'Nope. I'm just catching up.' Guy started to walk towards the bedrooms, and for the first time it crossed his mind that maybe it was time to move on, find a flat of his own. He couldn't stand all this having to explain where he was going and why if he wanted a relatively early night. What was wrong with Keir anyway? These days he hardly went out. It was like being married. He'd become clingy.

'Sweet dreams,' Keir called after him and Guy just raised his hand and made his way to his bedroom. Immediately Keir picked up the sheets of paper that his friend had been working on and re-read them. At the same time he finished the whisky he'd poured for Guy and seriously pondered his own future.

Chapter Twenty-Nine

Keir woke with a headache and for the first time in the history of his working life at Benson Motors rang in sick. He'd a lot on his mind and simply didn't feel like the day-to-day grind of over-seeing three garages. Why should he flog himself for very little reward? There was no way Jack Benson was ever going to make him a partner or raise his salary enough to make it all worthwhile. Okay, so he drove around in an extremely smart Daimler, but Keir wanted more than that. He wanted what Guy was getting. Excitement, women flocking round, never knowing what tomorrow held in store.

Guy left the apartment at about ten-thirty and was hardly out of the door when the phone rang. Keir rather reluctantly slouched from the breakfast bar and his mug of black coffee to pick up the receiver in the sitting room. 'Yes?' he said gruffly.

The woman on the other end of the line was very precise. 'Guy Hamilton, please.'

Keir frowned. Well used to dealing with such calls he decided to have a bit of fun. 'Speaking.' Then he turned on the charm. 'How can I help you?'

The woman cleared her throat. 'I'm ringing on behalf of Andy McVay. If possible, he'd like to bring his meeting with you forward by a day. Are you free tomorrow?'

Keir's eyes dilated and darted to the two sheets of paper on the table. Guy's mobile phone lay beside them. He'd obviously forgotten it. Swiftly he snatched up the sheets of paper. 'Sure, I'm free tomorrow.'

'Eleven o'clock then. You have the address and know the format. Mr McVay will look forward to meeting you tomorrow.'

Keir was about to query the address and format, but decided against it. 'Right,' he said, 'I'll be there. See you tomorrow.'

The caller said thank you and replaced the receiver. Keir narrowed his eyes and wondered what the address and format were. These days Guy told him so little. Rather heavily, he slumped down on to the settee and started to weigh up in his mind what he had to do.

The luxury apartment overlooking St Katherine's Dock was incredible. Guy and Jane fell in love with it straight away. Decorated in bold primary colours, mainly reds and blues, it seemed to ramble on in its cluttered but state of the art way creating an atmosphere of social ease and extreme wealth. Where did Jane find these people? wondered Guy. For such a relatively ordinary Cambridge girl, she seemed to have her finger in so many different pies.

They were welcomed by a housekeeper and Guy smelled food as soon as he walked in. He turned to Jane. 'Something smells good.'

She smiled. 'That's my surprise, Guy. Guess who's doing the cooking?'

He frowned, not daring to allow himself to think who he'd like it to be. 'I've no idea.'

'Oh, come on now. Think! That gorgeous creature whom you absolutely adore?' He still looked blank. 'Cousin of yours?'

'Lily? But she doesn't cook. She organises other people to cook.'

'Well, she's cooking today, I promise you.'

Guy swallowed hard. 'No kidding?'

'Nope. I told Jim all about her and he rang her straight away.'

'But what about her job?'

Jane shrugged. 'All I do know is she said yes to this.'

'Is she here on her own?'

Jane grabbed his arm. 'Let's go and see.' She pulled him into the main area of the apartment where vast floor-to-ceiling windows looked out across the docks with a sliding door leading on to a balcony. About ten people were standing outside enjoying the view and drinking champagne.

'Jane!' Jim Horwood, a financial adviser, had started out life on the same newspaper as her. He walked inside with outstretched arms then hugged her tightly before turning to Guy. 'And you must be Guy. Jane's told me quite a bit about you.' Warmly he shook his hand. 'Champagne?'

They both nodded and the housekeeper came forward with a tray. Jane and Guy each took a tall flute of Krug and Guy immediately put his down on a canvas-topped table which reminded him of a deck chair. They both looked around them. 'Love the pad, Jim. You've made a fantastic job of it. You must show me round. But first, is it okay if I take Guy through to the kitchen, wherever it is? Lily's his cousin,' Jane explained.

Jim raised his eyebrows. 'Is she really? My God, you don't look alike.'

Even though Jim beamed at him, Guy wondered whether to explain. Normally he didn't explain anything; in any tricky situation he just reached for his cigarettes. 'I'm adopted,' he said matter-of-factly, something he'd never found easy to admit.

'Ah, that explains it. Lucky you, having her in the family. She's gorgeous.' He patted Guy on the back. 'Marry her quick, boy, before somebody else snaps her up.'

Taking a deep breath, Guy just smiled and followed Jim and Jane towards the kitchen. And then he noticed Cassie in the same black jeans, white shirt and purple and white striped apron she'd worn at the Sibleys' party. She was putting the finishing touches to an arrangement of flowers on a vast smoked glass table with curved chrome legs. Surrounding it were twelve matching swivel chairs unholstered in dark grey leather. He moved swiftly towards her, gently touching her shoulder. In surprise she turned and fixed him with her normal confident stare. He suddenly felt engulfed in the depth of her violet eyes and no words came. In that instant Guy realised that for all this girl's bravado and quick wit she had deep feelings for him. Maybe he even felt something similar. If not for Lily. 'Cassie,' he said softly, then cleared his throat. 'I see you're at it again. The flowers look superb.' In a simple urn in the centre of the table were purple cornflowers interspersed with sprays of white baby's breath. Against the smoky grey table and chairs, the effect was soft and welcoming.

She turned back to her display. 'Oh, it's nothing. Just a simple posy.'

'Nothing you do is simple.'

204

She looked at him and he watched her eyes move towards the kitchen. 'Lily dragged me along again. I'm getting so used to waiting table I swear I do it in my sleep!'

Guy laughed. 'So does this mean she's said goodbye to the Viking?'

Cassie shrugged. 'She's thinking about it. If she gets enough private work. Besides, they're not very nice to her there. Correction, they're horrible to her.'

Guy looked surprised. 'They're horrible to Lily? Why?'

Cassie flapped her hand. 'Oh, it's a long story. Ask her, Guy. I'm sure she'd love to tell you all about it someday.'

Jim and Jane stood by, waiting for Guy to finish his conversation. Quickly he glanced at them then squeezed Cassie's hand. 'Speak to you later.' She nodded and watched him walk away. She took a deep breath and bit on her bottom lip so hard that she tasted blood.

Lily had her back to the kitchen door. Her hair, twisted back in its usual knot and secured with a slide, caught the light from the window and glistened red, gold and brown. 'Lily,' said Jim and she turned abruptly. 'Someone you know.' He held out his hand in Guy's direction. Jim smiled at Jane. Together they went back to their friends. For a second Guy watched their retreating figures before turning almost shyly to his cousin.

'Quite a long way for you to come, Lily?'

She tucked a stray strand of hair behind her ear and turned back to the stuffed and rolled chicken breasts wrapped in Parma ham which she was gently frying. 'Yes, Cassie did the driving. She's an angel.'

Guy moved closer. 'So you're cooking now?'

'Just this once! I got persuaded, well and truly. I need the money, Guy.'

'And you're working with Cassie?'

'Some of the time. Would you pass me that dish?' He picked up an oval-shaped dish and handed it over. He watched her scoop six portions of Parma ham and chicken into it, put it in the oven, then proceed to fry six more. He noticed her unpainted fingernails were tapered and clean and her hands flew adeptly from one job to another. 'We're trying to build things up.' She threw him a look and smiled. 'I really would like to leave the Viking.'

'Yes, I don't blame you. Frightful place. Don't know why you went there anyway!'

Lily shook her head and looked once more at the job in hand. 'It's a long story. I won't bore you with the details.'

'You can, anytime.'

And then the spinach started to boil over and Lily shifted the pan from the heat, hissing between her teeth, and Guy knew he ought to leave but didn't want to. 'I'd best get out of your way then.' But still he hesitated while waiting for her to say something. She was too busy but did turn her face to his and for several seconds their eyes stayed locked. She turned away again but in that few seconds he knew he loved her. Then he did something that would remain an aching memory in her heart for a long time. He moved in as close as could be, put his hands to her arms and kissed the back of her neck. 'I love you,' he whispered, and quickly left the kitchen.

He was out of the door before she caught her breath. Lily's mouth was agape and her hand flew to the area he'd kissed. Don't play games with me! she thought fiercely before facing her cooking once more. But her heart was no longer in it.

The lunch was a huge success, Lily's food playing a major part in this. Along with Cassie, she helped serve but made sure she kept her eyes away from Guy. He noticed and was hurt. He thought perhaps she'd smile at him in a special way after what he'd said. But Lily was too unsure of him to do that. Perhaps he said 'I love you' to loads of women. After all, look at the way he'd behaved at the Sibleys' party, how he'd treated Jane, and she was still with him.

At one point he did grab her attention. 'No Daisy today?'

Lily smiled, noting the deep brown of his almond-shaped eyes and the seductive curve of his mouth. Her eyes swept to the diamond stud he wore in his left ear and aware of her interest he touched it. 'Daisy had to stay in Cambridge to look after the shop.' Lily looked across at Cassie. 'She works in the florist's now.'

Guy smiled. 'Yes, I know. She told me.'

After collecting more plates Lily moved away. Those were the only words she spoke to Guy for the rest of the afternoon. Shortly afterwards she and Cassie washed up, cleared everything away and gathered their things together to leave. The party was still going on, but both young women were tired and ready to head home. Of course they said their goodbyes and Lily was aware of the way Guy looked at her. But then again, she noticed he also looked at Cassie in exactly the same way. Perhaps he loved her too.

Chapter Thirty

After rummaging around Guy's personal papers, Keir managed to find his agent's telephone number. With trembling hands he dialled the number. Peter Kent answered. 'Peter? Ah good, you don't know me but I'm a friend of Guy's. Keir Doughty. I had a call today from Andy McVay's assistant about Guy's meeting with him and as he's not here I just wanted to confirm a few things with you.'

Peter hesitated and said rather flatly, 'Where's Guy?'

Keir laughed, 'Oh, you know Guy. Out putting it about!'

Peter bristled and thought, Some friend. 'That doesn't sound much like Guy.'

Keir swiftly corrected himself. 'No, of course not. Only joking. Anyway, in my newly appointed position as his social secretary I thought I'd go over with you the details of this meeting so I can make sure he knows exactly what's expected of him.'

'Well, I'm very sorry, Keir, but I don't know the details. Guy has a habit of sorting these things out for himself. In fact, I've always thought him very capable. Very together.'

'Yes. Yes, he is. But it's Canary Wharf, isn't it? McVay's offices?'

'Yes, I believe it is.'

'And the format?'

'Format? What format? I have no idea. You'd better ask Guy.'

'Well, what about dress code? Smart casual, do you think, or suit and tie job?'

Peter was beginning to get an uneasy feeling about this telephone conversation. 'I'm quite sure Guy can decide that for himself.'

Keir realised then that Peter Kent wasn't having any of it so changed his approach, becoming angry and curt. 'Hmm, well, don't blame me if he completely cocks up this one.' And with that he replaced the receiver. It was only then that he realised that Peter Kent would now try and get in touch with Guy so snatched up his mobile phone and stuffed it in the back of a drawer. Then he unplugged the main phone. After doing that he smacked his hands together and poured himself a large whisky.

As Guy had implied, he didn't return to the apartment until well after midnight. Keir had given himself an early night – it was his big day tomorrow – but heard him come in. He didn't stir, just rolled on to his side and did his utmost to try and sleep. The following morning he rose early, dressed in a blue button-down shirt (no tie), casual navy trousers and an ultra-smart paler blue jacket. As he looked in the mirror he ran his hands through his short dark crinkly hair and smiled. Keir was a handsome man, in a 1950s sort of way. Sadly, he was out of step with the times. He walked through the flat towards the kitchen and made himself a coffee. The previous evening he'd tucked Guy's two pages of notes into his jacket pocket and as he drank his coffee he patted the spot where he knew they'd be. After checking he had his own mobile phone he was about to leave when Guy called after him.

'Keir! You haven't seen my mobile anywhere, have you? I've bloody lost it!'

He turned and did his best to look blank. 'No.'

'Sod it. Where on earth can I have left it?' Standing in just his shorts, Guy ran a hand through his dishevelled hair. 'Nobody rang for me yesterday, did they?'

Panic surfaced in Keir. 'Like who?' he said abruptly.

Guy shrugged. 'Andy McVay's lot. They were going to confirm that the meeting's on for tomorrow.'

Keir lied, 'No. Nobody rang. Look, I must be off. I'll be late.'

'Where are you going?'

With a look of alarm on his face, Keir said, 'To work. Where'd you think?'

Guy smiled. 'You don't normally dress like that to go to work.'

Immediately, Keir's face relaxed. 'Well, I do from now on. I'm bloody fed up with toeing the line. It's time even I branched out, don't you think?'

Guy frowned, thinking it was a bit of an odd thing for Keir to say, and walked over to the kitchen to make himself a cup of coffee. 'Have a good day then.'

Keir made for the door and muttered, 'I'll certainly try.'

After finally finding a parking space, he was still twenty minutes ahead of schedule as he entered the famous Canary Wharf building. He had no trouble finding Andy McVay's offices and after introducing himself to the receptionist as Guy Hamilton, was asked to wait with two other men and an attractive dark-haired woman. They all introduced themselves and he soon realised that all three were hopeful of presenting *Ace Driving* and was somewhat relieved to see the two men were dressed similarly to him, or so he thought; they probably wouldn't agree. Eventually they were all served with a glass of champagne which Keir declined, he never could stand champagne, and almost immediately afterwards asked to go through to McVay's office.

It was a bit of a shock entering the enormous square room because as they filed in a cameraman filmed their every move. The results were boldly displayed on a large screen set high on the wall and situated behind the four seats in front of McVay's long and wide teak desk. While chatting amiably to the four of them, he could simultaneously see how they came across on screen. Lucky for Keir he came over quite well, appeared more than confident and was in fact much better looking on celluloid. The meeting took the form of a light-hearted discussion, filling them in on the new *Ace Driving* format, the types of cars they would be reviewing each week, how they should review them, the driving they would be expected to do, and so on. It became obvious that McVay was hopeful that the four people sitting in front of him, hand-picked in one way or another, would all be presenters and Keir was relieved that nobody appeared to realise that he wasn't in fact Guy Hamilton.

About an hour later sandwiches were served and the cameraman stopped filming. More champagne, just a glass, was produced and again Keir declined. His eyes hardly leaving McVay, Keir was interested to see that he declined as well. Then he looked across at the large tray of sandwiches, noting that they had the normal sort of fillings except for some wheatmeal ones with sliced banana in them. He was almost tempted to laugh, it was like being back at nursery school, but he quickly noticed that Andy McVay was eating them. After that Keir copied him and ate banana sandwiches as well.

Much to Keir's horror, after lunch they were informed they were to be taken by minibus to Woolwich, the old disused docklands area where several *Top Gear* programmes were filmed. It soon became obvious that all four were going to be put through their paces in order to show their driving skills. Keir loved cars, they'd been his life, but he was no speed merchant – no Guy Hamilton. A steady pace always suited him better. He panicked and excused himself, quickly making his way to the gentlemen's toilets. Here he went into the first available cubicle, locked the door and immediately withdrew a hipflask of whisky from an inside pocket. He took an enormous slurp. Then he withdrew a wrap of speed from another pocket and poured half on to the back of his shaking hand. With an already rolled up crisp five-pound note, Keir snorted this up then slumped back against the door, catching his breath. He'd just have to brazen this part of the day out.

It was a sunny early November day and Keir was relieved to be able to wear his sunglasses. At least nobody would notice his dilated pupils. By the time the minibus reached its destination he was feeling good. On top form. Raring to go. It always worked, the old speed. And Keir was sensible, he didn't use it too often. Only when needs must.

The four cars waiting to be driven at Woolwich's disused docks were a 1.2-litre Vauxhall Corsa, a 2-litre Mondeo, a Porsche Carerra and an M-series BMW. The four would-be presenters drew straws to see which car they'd drive and Keir ended up with the Mondeo. He shrugged good-naturedly, in fact secretly relieved, and waited his turn. The cameraman would be a passenger with all four and they were expected to give a running off-the-cuff commentary on their thoughts as they drove the cars they'd drawn.

By the time he took his seat behind the wheel of the white Mondeo, Keir hadn't a care in the world. Fortunately he'd been able to have another couple of nips of whisky without anyone seeing and revved up the car and set off at a spanking pace, driving recklessly perhaps, but not so recklessly that the cameraman felt

211

in any sort of danger because he just kept the film rolling. Keir chatted on about the car, with Andy McVay tuned in at the other end, pointing out its excellent road-holding, punchy acceleration and smooth ride. He added that he wasn't too impressed with its vapid exterior or touchstone interior looks, couldn't personally stand white cars, but what the hell – it *was* a Ford. He remembered all the phrases he'd heard Guy use and parroted them, summing up at the end that the Mondeo was no cart but a chariot with grace and guts. The cameraman came out smiling and so did Keir.

Concentrating carefully with arms folded he watched the last two rides. At the end of the session all four participants were enormously relieved and on its way back to Canary Wharf the minibus was filled with merriment and laughter. Only Andy McVay sat thoughtfully in his seat, weighing up his protégés. There was no doubt in his mind, his favourite was Guy Hamilton. He was different. Aloof and yet bold and witty. He would definitely be given the coveted position of main presenter on *Ace Driving*.

It hadn't taken Guy long to realise that the phone in his apartment was unplugged. He assumed the cleaning lady must have done it accidentally. Shortly afterwards he searched high and low for his notes on *Ace Driving*. While doing so, and supposing Keir must have shoved them away in a drawer, a habit he had, he found his mobile phone. At this point Guy knew something was wrong. There was no way anyone would have mistakenly put his mobile phone in the back of a drawer. Even the cleaning lady didn't do such idiotic things. It must have been deliberate. Then he remembered Keir's informal clothes earlier that morning and for some reason a feeling of dismay overwhelmed him. First he rang his agent, who said he'd been trying to get hold of him since yesterday and immediately repeated, almost word for word, Keir's garbled phone conversation. Hardly able to believe it or understand what his friend was playing at, Guy immediately rang Andy McVay's office and was informed the meeting was not tomorrow, it was today. In fact, it had already started. He slammed down the receiver, grabbed his jacket and keys and headed for the door.

By the time he reached Canary Wharf the four participants were at Woolwich docks. All he could do was wait impatiently in the reception area of Andy McVay's offices. If ever Guy needed a cigarette it was now, but he didn't have any on him and wasn't about to go in search of them.

After what seemed an age, the small group of people walked back through reception towards McVay's office and Keir spotted Guy straight away. He recoiled slightly, as though trying to make himself invisible, but within seconds Guy was upon him, glaring at him with the sort of hostility Keir had never seen before in his eyes.

'What's all this?' demanded McVay, noting the stranger's angry stance.

Guy turned to the man he rightly assumed must be the producer. 'I'm Guy Hamilton. I believe that *he* might have been trying to pass himself off as *me*.'

McVay frowned and looked at Keir who shook his head then rolled his eyes. In a gentle voice he said, 'I can explain.'

McVay pointed to his office and the rest of the crew. 'You lot go through. We'll be with you in a minute. Right, you two, over here.' He directed them towards a table and chairs set near a window at the far end of the room. If ever Guy had wanted to hit somebody in the mouth it was now. How could Keir have done this to him?

'So,' said Andy McVay, 'you're Guy Hamilton?' Seething and anxious to tear Keir to shreds, he nodded. McVay looked at Keir. 'So who are you?'

A crafty smile crossed Keir's face. 'Actually, I'm Keir Doughty.' He shrugged. 'Guy and I, well, we've been friends for years.' He turned to Guy. 'And as I see it, Guy, this is payback day. And it's well and truly overdue.'

'*Payback day?* What's that supposed to mean?'

'It means, I'm taking what's due. All the ideas you've stolen from me, all the help I've given you over the years, all—'

Guy grabbed his arm and spun him round to face him. '*What did you say*? What the *fucking* hell are you talking about?'

Keir looked at McVay. 'See what I mean? He can't keep his temper for a second and he drinks like an addled fish!' He added the bit about drinking because he had sussed out that Andy McVay was not a drinker. Years and years spent carefully watching other people had left Keir able to size them up accurately after only a very short association.

Guy struggled to calm himself. 'Why are you saying these things, Keir?' He turned to McVay. 'It's all lies. You surely can't believe all this? Everything he's just said is lies!'

McVay frowned thoughtfully then asked, 'Tell me, Guy, why is it that Keir's here today and you're not?'

'Because he bloody shafted me, that's why! He took the phone message from your assistant yesterday and didn't pass it on! He even hid my bloody mobile phone!'

Keir burst into laughter and tossed his thumb in Guy's direction. 'Oh, and I forgot, he also lies. Or, correction, imagines things.'

McVay stared at Guy, whom he'd thought rude and out of order, then at Keir. He realised that as far as he was concerned it really didn't matter. Keir was the man for the job, whatever tactics he'd used to land it. He gave Guy his attention. 'I'm sorry about the mix up and I can understand that you're upset. But the bottom line is, you're simply too late.' He shrugged then turned on his heel and walked away.

Guy also turned. Raising his fist, he smashed it into Keir's mouth. He fell back, crashing on to the chair behind him, and Guy watched for a second, stroking his knuckles, before striding off. McVay, who'd turned at the fracas behind him, stared in shock as Keir scrambled to his feet with blood oozing from a cut at the corner of his mouth. Guy pushed past McVay, paused in the doorway to look back then left, slamming the door behind him.

Part Three

Chapter Thirty-One

As Lily and Cassie touched down at Newark Airport near New York it was raining. They left the Virgin gate and joined the mammoth immigration queue zig-zagging its way in a single file to four or five desks where passports and tickets were examined. 'Bloody New York,' hissed Cassie and smiled at her friend whom she noticed looked tired and drawn. 'Perhaps we should have stayed home. All this palaver and the weather's worse here than it is back home.'

Lily looked around herself. 'No. I need this break.' She smiled. 'And I'm dying to see where you were brought up.'

Sure, thought Cassie. She stole another quick glance at her friend's face and reflected further upon the crazy workload she'd landed herself with over the last few months. And it was ongoing. These precious days away had been well and truly snatched. At long last Lily had given up the dreadful day job at the Viking, and Cassie had somehow or other managed to cut down her hours with Mrs Sniffnel. She no longer worked in the shop, just did Benson Motors flower arrangements and various hotels. Daisy worked, with Mrs Sniffnel, who was now fully recovered, and the pair of them seemed to get on very well. But there had to be an easier way for Lily's new business. She was flogging herself to death all the time with countless dinners and parties and corporate lunches in both London and Cambridge. At first it'd been fun, but six months down the line Cassie was beginning to wonder if she wouldn't prefer just working for the mellowing Mrs Sniffnel. The idea of this long weekend break was to discuss their future and decide how they were going to organise their workload. A plus was the money, which was good, especially in London, but constantly hiring in staff and equipment was exhausting.

They eventually got through immigration and made their way out of the airport towards the famous yellow cabs waiting to take passengers into the centre of New York. Here they joined another queue and both girls shivered in the inclement weather. Another twenty minutes and they were seated and being driven at high speed towards Manhattan, West 46th.

The Paramount Hotel, designed by Ian Schrager for the young and trendy, had been selected by Cassie because it was very close to where she'd once lived. As they entered the dimly lit reception with its spectacularly curved but stark stairway and its hip furnishings, though certainly no outward show of luxury, Lily was reminded of enrolment day back at university. There were so many student-type black-clad figures milling around. She smiled as they waited to register and collect their tiny plastic room card. With just a small bag each, they took the lift and made their way to their room. Once inside, the somewhat austere white furnishings seemed clinical to Lily, not at all warm and welcoming, but she would never have hurt her friend by saying so. Instead she threw down her bag and flopped on to the double bed which was theirs to share for four nights.

Cassie walked over to the window and raised the blind, looking out on to high-rise buildings with numerous chimneys belching out steam from air-conditioning systems and just a glimpse of Broadway through a convenient gap. In the dusk of early evening everything looked brown and grey. She sighed as memories from her bittersweet childhood came flooding back and nostalgia gripped her in a way she'd least expected. How long had it been? Seven, or was it eight years? She pulled herself together lest she cry and concentrated on enjoying herself.

Cassie looked at her watch, now set for New York time, and saw that it was six p.m. Eleven back home. She was hungry and remembered her aversion to in-flight food. Funny really, because Lily, who in Cassie's opinion was the best cook ever, had eaten everything put in front of her. 'Joe Allen's is just across the street. Shall we go over and eat?'

All Lily really wanted to do was crawl beneath the sheets but she raised herself, propped up on her elbow, and nodded. 'Sounds good. Do we have to change?'

' 'Course not.' Cassie moved towards her friend. 'Come on, lazy, you can catch up on your sleep later.'

Lethargically, Lily shifted from the bed. 'I fancy a drink, actually. Something very, very strong, like a triple vodka and tonic with masses of ice and slices of lime. Do they do that here?'

Cassie turned and smiled. In an exaggerated accent she said, 'Honey, this is New York City. They do *everything* here!'

Lily was standing now. She ran a hand through her dishevelled hair and twisted to look in the mirror. Cassie grabbed her. 'You look great. Come on, let's go, or I'll pass out from hunger.' She practically dragged Lily from the room, making her laugh with her insistence. 'We're gonna have a great time here, Lily, *if it kills us*!'

Joe Allen's, so similar to its sister-restaurant off Shaftesbury Avenue in London, cheered Lily up. Both she and Cassie ate delicious Caesar salads, steaks and fries, and along with the vodka and tonics a bottle of house red. 'Do you know something, Lily?' said Cassie as she raised her glass to finish her wine, 'the thing I love most about you is your ordinariness. And yet, nobody could ever really describe you as ordinary.'

'That's because there's no such thing,' Lily replied matter-of-factly.

'But we all like to feel comfortable, don't you agree?'

'Yes, I do. Then again we also like what stretches us and makes us feel out of the ordinary! I mean, take our business. People employ us to provide something special, not something ordinary.'

'Yes, well, you've moved away from my meaning. I'm talking about you, Lily. The way you behave. Your lack of pretence. But I just can't find the right words.'

Lily grinned and also finished her wine. 'Why don't we forget me and talk about you?' She swept her hand around. 'I mean, why on earth did your parents leave here to go to provincial ol' Ely, of all places. It seems such a strange thing to do.'

Cassie shrugged. 'Freedom and money! My mom missed the open spaces of her childhood and when her parents died she couldn't wait to get back. After the rat-race here, who can blame her?'

'And you? Do you ever miss it here? I mean, really miss it?'

After several seconds of really considering this question, Cassie shook her head. 'No. I guess I'm in love with Cambridge. Apart from its ancient charm, what better job could I have than working with nature's greatest gift, beautiful growing things?'

'But you could have done that here.'

'I still like Cambridge. And London. Since we've been charging around, I've seen a lot of London and it has a pace of its own.'

'Yes. The same as this place, no doubt.'

'You're not stuck on New York already, are you, Lily?'

'No, we've only just arrived. Although as we approached the city from the airport that famous skyline nearly blew me away. Are we going to do the works? Statue of Liberty, Empire State Building, St Patrick's, Madison Square Garden . . .'

'Sure, if you like, but I want to see the Park, and do Macy's, and skate on the ice-rink at Rockefeller Center, and try some clothes on in Bergdorf Goodman's.' Cassie laughed. 'I never dared before – and eat in some real classy restaurant. Oh, and take a helicopter ride!'

'And visit the Guggenheim and the Metropolitan. And eat oysters at Grand Central!'

'Hey, we'll never fit all this in.'

Lily sighed. 'Well, it doesn't matter. What's most important is that you show me where you lived.'

'It's just down the street actually. Not far at all. I told you, Lily, it was an apartment over a piano bar. Nothing special, nothing special at all.'

'But I still want to see it.'

'As long as you understand there isn't anything to see. I'm certainly not going inside.'

'You're not?' Lily looked surprised, but how could she know that Cassie was nervous of bumping into her so-called uncle?

'No. It's past history. I don't miss the place at all.'

Lily knew then there was something her friend wasn't telling her and wondered whether to probe a little. She never had before. Perhaps now was the time. 'Did something happen to you in that apartment when you were younger?' She smiled, gently. 'I always feel that maybe there's a dark secret lurking somewhere in your past. You could tell me, you know.'

Lily wasn't prepared for the look of astonishment on her friend's face. 'Whatever makes you think that?' Cassie rapidly shook her head and was curt to say the least. 'I haven't any dark secrets. What a stupid thing to say.'

Lily flinched at her rebuke and quickly averted her eyes. When Cassie finally allowed herself to look at her friend's face she felt sorry for the harsh words she'd uttered, but just couldn't bring herself to explain. Apart from Guy, she'd never told a soul and wasn't about to start now. After all, there just might be a small part of Lily that thought Cassie had actually asked for it all, deserved it. Cassie couldn't face that. 'Shall we make a move?'

Lily smiled. 'Yes, I shall sleep like a log tonight.'

With a laugh Cassie said, 'You'll be lucky. I bet you wake up about four. Jet lag plays havoc with your sleep pattern, however much you think it won't.'

'Well, I don't think anything's going to stop me sleeping tonight.' Lily watched as her friend attracted the attention of a waiter who brought their check. The two girls paid then slowly walked back to the Paramount Hotel.

But Lily didn't sleep like a log. She woke and looked at the clock on her bedside table and saw that it was three forty-seven, so Cassie hadn't been far out in her assessment. She turned and assumed her friend was asleep. Silently she climbed out of bed and walked over to the window. Lily drew back the drape and pulled up the blind and New York's lights lit up the bedroom. She peered outside and was pleased to see it had stopped raining. She cast her eyes around the area and wondered about Cassie's life as a child, feeling sure she was hiding something. She started as she felt something brush her arm and found Cassie standing right behind her. Both girls were wearing long t-shirts and Cassie smiled. 'Told you, didn't I? Said you wouldn't be able to sleep.'

'It's really strange, I don't feel at all tired now.' Lily looked around the hotel room. 'I wish we could make coffee or something.'

'We can order it on room-service.'

Lily pulled a face. 'Bit extravagant, don't you think?'

'What the hell! We're on holiday.' Immediately Cassie walked over to the bed, turned on the reading light and picked up the phone, dialling room-service. She looked at her friend, 'Coffee? Tea? Hot chocolate?'

'Hmm, hot chocolate would be nice.'

Cassie ordered two hot chocolates and replaced the receiver. She curled up on the bed, drawing her legs beneath her. 'It'll be ages. What about raiding the drinks bar over there?'

'Cassie! We've had a river of alcohol already!'

'Come on, Lily. What's happened to the wicked girl of yesteryear? Let's live dangerously for once!'

With a smile Lily turned to unlock the mini-bar and looked inside. 'What do you fancy?'

'Is there any brandy?'

She ran her fingers along the small bottles and said, 'There's some Armagnac, will that suit you?' There was silence then. She turned and caught the transformation of her friend's face from bright and cheerful to deep despair. Cassie's face actually crumpled as she lowered her eyes, remembering the last time she'd drunk Armagnac. The memory came flooding back and she couldn't stop it. Guy and her, making love. Had it really happened or was it a figment of her imagination? The pain in her heart seemed too much to bear. Lily saw it and walked over, sliding across the bed to put her hand on Cassie's. Very softly she said, 'You have to tell me, Cassie. You have to tell me what all this is about, because if you don't, you'll break my heart.'

Mine is already broken, thought Cassie, and raised her eyes to her beautiful friend, refreshed from a couple of hours' sleep. How could it be that after hanging around airports for most of the previous day, a seven-and-a-half-hour flight, a hasty meal across the road then falling straight into bed, Lily could end up looking like this? Ravishing, alluring. How could Cassie ever hope to compete with her? Anger threatened to erupt as once more she wanted to tell her friend to mind her own business. But how was Lily to know that Cassie's past was now connected to her own cousin? How was she to know that along with sharing her secret, and her body, she'd also given him her heart?

'It's just . . . memories, that's all. They creep up on you when you least expect.'

Lily probed once more. 'Far distant memories or more recent ones?'

Cassie stifled a sob in the back of her throat. 'Both, I guess.'

With a swift movement, Lily shifted off the bed and withdrew the bottle of Armagnac from the mini-bar. She poured it into a wine glass then helped herself to some vodka. She moved back to her friend and passed over the Armagnac. 'Cheers,' she said, clinking glasses. 'And if you don't want to tell me, Cassie, on my honour I'll never ask again. But some things are better shared and I want you to know that I care, as you've continually cared for me. In fact, I love you almost as much as I could love anyone, so I'd be more than honoured if you'd share the bad times with me as well as the good.'

Studying her friend, Cassie stifled another sob. She loved Lily too. She took a sip of the Armagnac then reached out, clasping Lily's hand. Taking a deep breath, she began, 'I love you too, Lily . . . but you have to understand, you're a hard act to follow. I guess I tend to live in your shadow and at times I feel a little jealous.'

For several seconds Lily was silent. 'Why?'

Cassie nearly choked on another sip of her drink. 'Oh, come on, Lily. Do I really need to explain?'

Her face creased in confusion. 'Is it because of my work or what?'

'The way you look, Lily! It's because of the way you *look*. I don't give a shit about the rest. But when we walk into a room together all eyes are upon you. When I walk into a room without you quite a few of them'll fix on me.'

'But that doesn't make people like me, does it? As I have found to my cost a lot of people hate my guts!'

'No, they don't! It's because they can't control you or they're just plain jealous, like me! You're so beautiful, Lily!' Cassie stopped then as she saw something familiar in her friend's eyes, something she'd never seen there before only she recognised it straight away. She ought to, she'd seen it often enough in her own eyes. It was torment. She looked down and shook her head. 'You can't help it, bless your heart. You can't help being beautiful in the same way as dear ol' Daisy can't help being – well, being Daisy.'

'And is that why you're so unhappy here in New York? Because you think I'm more beautiful than you?'

'I don't think it, Lily! I know it!'

'No, you don't! You just *stupidly* think it! Who said, "Beauty is in the eye of the beholder"? And you *are* beautiful, you know darn' well you are. I have to say, I don't believe a word of this crap. I believe you're screwing yourself up over something else and this beauty business is just . . .' Lily widened her eyes and looked up, struggling to find the right words '. . . is just the whipping boy!'

Cassie smiled at this and gulped back some more of her drink. She pondered a while and braced herself. 'If I tell you everything, it could change our friendship.'

'It probably will, but whatever you tell me won't stop me caring.'

Cassie's eyes implored her. 'But it might, Lily, it just might.'

Grabbing her friend's shoulder, she said, 'But I've told you everything in the past and you've stuck by me, even though you probably thought I was a chump!'

'Well, what happened to me is nothing like what's happened to you.'

'Okay, tell me then.'

'*Okay* . . . I'll try.'

There was a knock on the door and Lily slipped off the bed and walked over. A porter brought in a tray with two cups and saucers and two small thermos flasks of hot chocolate. He put it down on a table and Lily rummaged through her handbag to give him a tip. He took it and allowed his eyes to wander slowly from her face down the length of her body. He was oblivious of Cassie on the bed a few feet away. Lily hastily moved towards the door, pulling her t-shirt over her thighs. Rather reluctantly he left. Swiftly Lily turned to Cassie. 'And if you think I like that sort of ogling, you're quite mistaken!'

Laughing, she said, 'I know you don't, Lily. Please forgive me?'

Immediately she started to pour the hot chocolate. 'Nothing to forgive. In fact, I always want us to be honest.' She looked up at her friend. 'So remember that, Cassie Milbank, *I always want us to be honest*.'

Cassie took the cup of hot chocolate from her friend and both girls made themselves comfortable on the bed. Cassie sipped some of the chocolate then cleared her throat. 'I suppose I'd better start at the end and work backwards.' Lily frowned but said nothing. 'Perhaps you're right about your beauty being the whipping boy for my unhappiness. But, you see, the truth is,' Cassie hunched up her shoulders slightly, 'I'm in love with someone who simply doesn't love me.' She saw the interest in her friend's eyes and averted her own, in case she lose her nerve. She rushed on, 'It's not a crush, in case you're thinking it might be, it's very real and it bloody well hurts like hell all the time. Never a day goes by when I don't think about him. Really dwell upon his every move. But he'll never love me, not ever, and do you know why?' Again Lily said nothing but her eyes were wary now 'Because he loves you, Lily. *He bloody loves you.*'

Lily swallowed hard. Of course she knew who Cassie was talking about. Her pulse quickened and part of her didn't want to hear any more. She struggled with her next words. 'And have you been close to this person? I mean, really close?'

Cassie put down her cup and saucer, took Lily's and put those down as well. She squeezed her friend's hands and very softly said, 'Once. Just once.'

Lily's heart stopped beating. 'When?'

Steadfastly keeping her eyes on her friend's face, Cassie sighed and bit her bottom lip, but knew she had to continue. 'It was that time I gave him a lift in my car, remember? I think you suspected something when we talked about it afterwards.'

Lily's face contorted. 'But when you say really close, what exactly do you mean?'

Briefly, Cassie closed her eyes. 'It means, as close as can be.'

Lily pulled her hands away. 'You made love? You had sex with Guy?'

Taking a deep breath, Cassie ran her hand across her forehead. 'It was only once, and I'm telling you about it now because he put me out of a misery I'd been riddled with for years. We did have sex, but it wasn't some ecstatic romp or anything. It was very different.'

'How do you mean, different? What misery?'

Cassie prepared herself and lowered her eyes. 'The misery of my childhood . . . Because, when I was young, I was abused, sexually abused I mean, and then later, as I developed, I thought I'd been damaged in some way.' Cassie ignored her friend's gasps and threw back her head, laughing. 'My God! Doesn't it all sound corny?' She levelled her eyes at Lily and saw the tears there. 'But when you've lived for years with a fear like that it's just one great big bloody relief to know that you're normal after all.'

Lily sucked in her breath. 'Oh, Cassie, who abused you?'

'*A geek.* A sort of uncle.'

'When? How old were you?'

225

'Well, he started when I was five but it went on until I began to develop.'

Lily's hand flew to her mouth. 'Cassie, this is dreadful. Why didn't you tell me? You could have told me. You *should* have told me.'

'I couldn't! I couldn't tell anyone! I thought I was a freak and this *uncle* threatened me with all sorts when he was doing it to me. You learn to bury it, Lily. You learn to bury it deep.'

'And Guy? He knows all about this?'

Cassie threw out her hands. 'It sort of all came out. I froze, y'see, when he . . . when he touched me, and he knew something was very wrong, and he was just so caring and wonderful. I just can't tell you how wonderful he was to me.' Cassie raised her face as though remembering it all, then smiled at her friend. 'He checked me out and told me I was in good shape. In fact, he restored my faith in myself, in men, in the whole of the universe. Up to then I was at rock bottom. But the trouble is, I really fell for him. I mean, I always fancied him rotten but that's not love, is it? And I just can't rid myself of it though I've tried, . . . I just keep on loving him even though I know he loves you and I'll never be able to have him.'

'You don't know that, Cassie. How can you possibly know that? Has he . . . has he ever told you he loves you?'

Cassie grimaced. 'Of course not. He doesn't.'

Lily remembered his words of love to her, but then she remembered the way he'd looked at Cassie on the same occasion. 'He might.'

'He doesn't! He loves you, and if you can't see that you must be blind.'

'Well, why doesn't he do something about it then? Why doesn't he make a move?'

Cassie stared at Lily then held out her hands. 'He's scared, I guess. Scared you'll reject him. Or maybe he feels bad about the family thing. I'm telling you, Lily, if you were to make a move on him, he'd snap you up like a shot.'

'Well, I'm not going to make a move on him. Never.'

'Why?'

'Because I don't believe you. I think Guy likes all women.'

'He might like all women, but he loves only you. It's in his eyes and in the way he moves. When you're around he stops functioning normally, just concentrates on you.'

Lily reached over and picked up her hot chocolate and started to sip it. She cupped her hands around it, trying to get into her head the fact that her dearest friend had made love to Guy. She'd known something had gone on but at the most had suspected a dinner together or some other sort of closeness. Never this. It was Lily's turn to be jealous now and she stole a look at her friend and seriously wondered why Guy would make a move on her if he didn't feel something for her. Lily needed to think about all this. She needed to think about it a lot.

Cassie sensed her friend's pique. Gingerly she asked, 'Are you angry with me because of Guy, or because you think there was more to this child abuse thing? Maybe you think it was all my fault?'

Lily's eyes widened to nearly twice their size. 'How could I possibly be angry with you about either? Certainly not the abuse thing! Cassie, so far as Guy is concerned, don't you see, I'm just like you? I'm bloody jealous!'

'So you do care about him? You see, I never really knew. I kind of suspected you did, but I was never a hundred percent sure.' Cassie noticed that Lily's hands were wrapped so tightly round her cup her knuckles were white. She considered then what a pair they were. What a pathetic pair. Wasting their precious holiday torn apart with despair over a man whom neither had seen for months.

Lily cleared her throat and decided to follow her own credo and be honest. 'I suppose I really started to care for Guy in a big way after that first party we did. I saw him snogging this female.' Her eyes on Cassie's face were anguished. 'He had his hand right up her skirt, inside her knickers even, and she was squirming on his lap and really losing it. I reckon she'd have done it with him, there and then, in the middle of the Sibleys' drawing room! It threw me, Cassie, really, really threw me. Since then, like you, I haven't stopped thinking about him.'

'Is that why you decided to go with Will that night? Because Guy aroused such feelings in you?'

Looking ashamed, Lily nodded. 'Yes. How did you guess?'

'Pretty easily actually. I saw Guy with her too but it aroused different emotions in me. I'd have liked to yank the bitch off his knee by the hair and smack her in the mouth!'

Lily laughed then her face straightened. 'But why would he behave like that, for all to see?'

227

'Simple! He was drunk. And I have a hunch it was his way of disentangling himself from that Jane woman.'

'From Jane? Is that what you really think? But he's still with her.'

'No, he's not. They're just friends. I heard them talking about it at that lunch party we did in St Katherine's Dock. Guy loves you, Lily. Everyone else is immaterial.' Cassie poked her friend. 'And Daisy agrees.'

Lily laughed again. 'Well, she would agree with anything you say.'

'Oh, no, she wouldn't. In fact, it was Daisy who said it first.'

'Was it really? Well, we all know we can't rely on Daisy for the truth.'

'Lily! I'm staggered to hear you say that. That sister of yours is one of the most intuitive females I know. She may not be razor sharp, but she's sure as hell got some pretty accurate powers of observation.'

Lily looked resigned and put down her cup, suddenly reaching forward in a loving way to touch her friend's face. 'Let's not talk about Guy anymore, Cassie, please. Let's forget all about him for this weekend. He'll only spoil things for us.' She searched Cassie's face. 'What I would like to talk about is this awful uncle of yours. I'd really like you to start at the beginning. Will you? And tell me absolutely everything. I want to know it all ... please? Every last detail?'

Cassie blinked and almost immediately started to talk. She was surprised how easy it was to pour it all out, this time allowing herself to remember and speak about even the worst details. The two young women talked until daylight and beyond when, quite exhausted, they fell asleep once more.

Lily woke first, with a start, and looked at the bedside clock. It was 11 a.m. She rolled on to her back, remembering the long night and all that Cassie had told her. She turned to look at her friend, still asleep, and felt differently towards her. What a burden she'd had to bear over the years. What a terrible burden. Poor Cassie. But it wasn't just that. Lily felt differently towards her now because of her sexual link with Guy. At the thought of this, something pricked her memory; a dream from last night. Guy was with Cassie and she was sitting on his knee. But they weren't kissing

228

and fondling each other, not at all. In fact they were weeping. How strange. Both of them wept. Perhaps it was because of Cassie's dreadful past.

Lily sat up in bed, turning once more to look at her friend, still asleep. Taking a deep breath, Lily swung her legs off the bed and stood up, walking over to the window. She peered out on to a bright and sunlit day and immediately felt uplifted. She resigned herself then to what was past being past. Anyway, perhaps Guy wasn't destined to belong to either of them. Perhaps, as Lily stood looking out on to New York's 46th Street and Broadway, he was ensconced somewhere quite happily with another far more gorgeous female. Who could tell? They'd heard no word from him for a long while.

Chapter Thirty-Two

Guy's life had taken an unforeseen twist. After his departure from Andy McVay's office in Canary Wharf nearly six months previously, he'd driven home like a madman, sometimes touching 140 m.p.h. in his Porsche 911 and not giving a thought to his own safety or even the safety of other more sensible beings on the M11 that day. On his return to the flat in Newnham he'd rung the locksmith who'd promised to be there within an hour, then gathered together Keir's things, at least the portable ones, and thrown them into bin-liners. Then he'd taken the bin-liners to Benson's Hills Road garage where, yes, he'd even seen Naomi for the first time since she'd swiped him round the face in their former marital home. She'd stared at him, not seeming to notice the way he unceremoniously dumped three crammed full bin-liners with Keir's belongings on the floor inside his office. It was as though she was seeing her ex-husband in a new light.

Over the last couple of years Guy had changed dramatically as his confidence had grown. The fury on his face today because of his best friend's double-dealing only enhanced his good looks and she wanted him back with such a force she practically ran after him as he stalked back to his car to fetch even more belongings of Keir's.

After he'd deposited every last thing, he turned brusquely to her. 'Tell him, will you, that I never want to see his rotten face again? Tell him that if he ever tries to come near me again I won't just punch his mouth in, I'll punch the lights right out of him!'

She'd frowned then. 'Who? Who're you talking about, Guy?'

'Keir of course. Keir Doughty.' In all this time Guy had hardly looked at her except to notice she'd lost a lot of weight and her hair had grown and looked decidedly brassy. Even in his current state of mind it did occur to him he'd had a very lucky escape so far as she was concerned.

But he was heartbroken. He'd thought his position as presenter of *Ace Driving* was in the bag. How come Keir had nabbed it from under his very nose? How come Andy McVay hadn't been put off when told of his appalling behaviour? On the contrary, he'd seemed impressed. Guy had come so far, so very, very far, and now his reputation must surely be in tatters. For all he knew, Keir would probably sue him for assault. Well, let him sue. Guy didn't care. At this point he didn't care about anything.

Naomi tripped behind him as he returned for the last time to his car. She even dared to grab his arm and in a fury Guy swung round, pulling it out of her grasp. With the unexpected force of it she practically toppled over and he had to reach forward to stop her fall. 'Guy!' she said breathlessly. 'I can see you're in a state, but we have to talk.' He gave her his attention then, thinking perhaps she was going to tell him something important about Keir. 'Don't you see, we have to talk?'

Still clutching her tightly, Guy peered into her eyes. 'You know something?'

She took a deep breath. 'Only that we've made a mistake and that I'm sorry, really sorry for everything. But we could start again. Afresh. It's not too late, is it?'

He glowered at her, hardly able to fathom her meaning. He'd inadvertently walked back into her life and she'd presented him with this. If he didn't despise her so much he'd have felt sorry for her. Instantly, he let go and turned towards his car. 'Guy!' she squawked. 'You can't come back here like this and then leave again!'

He jerked round. 'I didn't come back here to see you, Naomi! I've nothing to say to you! We're finished, don't you understand that? We were finished before we even began!'

Her mouth tightened and her eyes hardened. 'You fucking bastard! You come back here, throwing your weight about as though you own the place, and then you insult me! I was your wife and if it hadn't been for me you'd be nowhere today. You're scum, Guy Hamilton, and whatever it is that Keir has done to you, I'm glad! You deserve it!'

'Well, you would say that, wouldn't you?'

'Yes, I would! And I'll tell you something else about Keir, shall I?' Her face creased into a smile, a familiar smug smile. He had seen it many times before. 'At least he knows how to fuck! Which is more than can be said for you!'

As disenchanted with her as he was, she'd caught him off-guard. He searched her face now. 'You and Keir? While we were married? It was him?'

She lied. 'While we were married *and* before. If you must know we were together on the eve of our wedding and it was a darn' sight better than anything you ever did the next day!'

Guy balled his fist and was tempted, but stopped himself in time. Enough was enough. He pointed at her instead. 'You're a dirty little cow, Naomi. Correction!' He allowed his eyes to wander over her. 'A dirty *scrawny* cow!'

She went to strike him but he was too quick for her and into his car in a flash. She banged her fist on the roof but Guy just turned the ignition and drove off. Briefly he looked in his rearview mirror and, true to character, she was standing there, jumping up and down and waving her fist at him. He wanted to laugh but a much stronger emotion had taken hold: bitterness and hatred for the man he'd trusted and considered for years to be his very best friend.

Keir didn't return to their flat. Perhaps he lacked the courage. Guy never heard another thing from him. His agent, Peter Kent, rang the following day to say that Keir had undoubtedly landed the job as chief presenter on *Ace Driving*. But Peter was as disgusted as Guy and proved to be very supportive, assuring his client that all was not lost. As he saw it Keir had only landed the position through lies and subterfuge. Peter's advice was to lie low for a while, let the bastard dig his own hole, which he inevitably would. When the time was right they'd be there to give him the final push. Strange though it might seem, Guy had drawn comfort from these words and from that day forward he and Peter were firm friends.

232

Chapter Thirty-Three

The jet lag seemed worse coming home. Lily and Cassie arrived back at the house in Grantchester Road after spending four divine days in New York and wanted nothing more than to spend another four days getting over it. After that first night, Guy was not mentioned again. Instead the two young women covered as much of the city as they possibly could in such a short space of time and even fitted in the famous West 30th Street helicopter ride. They took a brief look at the piano bar on 46th Street where Cassie had lived and moved quickly on, ate a dozen assorted oysters each in Grand Central Station, devoured soft-shell crabs in the River Café in Brooklyn, enjoying its wondrous view of Manhattan across from the famous bridge, and eulogised about the cornmeal and sage-fried rabbit in the Union Square Café on East 16th. Lily hated the sardine-style packed lift zooming up to the top of the Empire State Building but adored Central Park, especially the seals, and the Metropolitan Museum, including the hot dogs they ate outside directly after so much culture. Cassie loved it all and seriously wondered if she might one day have the courage to come back again to live here.

They arrived home in the early morning and were greeted by an excited Daisy who'd taken six phone calls in their absence, enquiring about their catering services. Cassie turned to Lily and wagged her finger. 'Now remember what we said. Delegate, Lily! We employ extra staff, okay?'

Daisy looked astounded. 'But your costs will go through the roof!' This was a term she'd heard used regularly by the girls.

Cassie was adamant. 'No, they won't. This business has to pay its way without Lily dying from exhaustion.' She looked at Daisy and smiled. 'We discussed all this at length while we were away, Daise. If it doesn't work out we quit, it's as simple as that.'

Daisy looked worried. 'And I can still work at the shop?'

'Of course. If it's what you enjoy?'

'It is, but I also like working with you two.' She looked afraid. 'You're not thinking of leaving me out, are you?'

Taking a deep breath, Lily contemplated saying that it didn't matter whether Daisy was in or out. 'Only some of the time. When you're too busy.' Daisy brightened. 'And guess what we're going to call ourselves?' Daisy pulled a face and racked her brain. Lily laughed, recognising that her sister really thought she had to guess. 'Fare & Flair. We're calling ourselves Fare & Flair.'

Daisy's eyes widened. 'That's good. You two have always been fair.'

'No, not that fair. Fare – as in food.'

Folding her arms, Daisy said, 'Oh.' Then her face lit up. 'Oh, yes.' She brought her hands together. 'I do see. That's great.'

Simultaneously Lily and Cassie drew a deep breath, but Lily was already riffling through the mail. She ripped open one particularly interesting-looking letter and her eyes flicked over the page before excitedly she passed it to Cassie. As quickly, Cassie read it and looked both surprised and resentful. 'Mr Doughty on TV? Wonders will never cease! What on earth is he on about?'

'Well, you should know. You're the one who works at Benson's.'

'Hah! I might call in there but these days I flit in and out as quickly as possible. And I never listen to gossip.'

'Well, in that case you obviously missed out on the fact he doesn't even work there anymore.'

'Hmm, too true I did. Funny that. He's half the reason I don't hang about. Maybe it's time I did enter into the spirit more at Benson's.' She scrutinised the letter further. 'Strange we never knew anything about all this, though.'

'It's Sky TV. We don't have Sky, not that we ever watch television anyway, but it does say a party to celebrate the highly successful eight-week run of *Ace Driving* so he *must* have left Benson's.' Lily tilted her head. 'I wonder if this is anything to do with Guy?'

Cassie nudged her friend. 'Well, why don't you ring him and find out?' Lily pulled a face and Cassie quickly continued,

'Although, I must say, I'm surprised. I would have thought Guy'd be presenting the programme, not bloody Keir.'

Daisy raised her forefinger. 'Oh, dear. Yes, I remember now. It was a Keir who rang here. He was three of the calls. That's because he rang three times. He's *desperate* for you to do the food for his party . . . in London it is!' Daisy put her finger on her chin. 'Now where did he say?' She shook her head petulantly. 'Oh, fiddle, can't remember!'

Lily looked at her sister and felt a lump in her throat. She was so special with her childlike ways. She tried so hard. 'You're doing great, Daisy. I don't know what we'd do without you.'

'Well, you went on holiday without me!'

Lily and Cassie flashed a knowing glance at each other. 'But that was only because Mrs Sniffnel needed you in the shop, you know that.'

Daisy's hand flew to her mouth. 'Oh, yes, I forgot to tell you! She's retiring!' Daisy turned to Cassie. 'She wants you to take over completely, Cassie, become overall manager. I told her you wouldn't be able to. I told her how busy you are with Lily, but she'd really like you to fit it all in somehow or other.' Daisy's hand flew to her forehead and she rolled her eyes. 'Oh, dear, I was supposed to tell you that as soon as you came home. Mrs Sniffnel made me promise. I think she thinks I'm forgetful, but I'm not really. At least, I always remember in the end, don't I? Anyway, she wants to retire quickly, like now I think . . . Oh, dear, it might not be now, it might be next week. *Oh, I don't know*, I forget my brains these days!'

Amused by Daisy's little outburst and surprised by what she'd said, Lily and Cassie looked at each other and immediately Cassie saw the question mark in her friend's eyes. What now? In her heart Cassie really wasn't sure. Suddenly being presented with an opportunity to take over a florist's in the middle of Cambridge, one with a fine reputation through her own expertise and hard work over the years, could throw Fare & Flair into disarray.

'I can't run Fare & Flair without you, Cassie, not in the way we planned, but you really don't have to be there all the time. I mean, couldn't you and Daisy get some extra help in the shop then we could work it all out between us? Don't you think that's possible?'

'Lily, I don't expect you to run it without me. I'd be offended if you tried.' Cassie grinned. 'You must know I'm *indispensable*, and I'm with you all the way.'

Relief washed over Lily. 'But maybe you could still manage the florist's?'

Cassie waved her hand. 'Yeah, why not! Just call me Superwoman!'

Daisy giggled then her face became quizzical. 'Did you bring me a present? You did say you would. Both of you. Remember?'

Cassie held up her hands. 'Sure we did. But first, how about a cup of tea?'

Once more, Daisy's hand flew to her mouth. 'Oh, sorry. Of course, I'll make it now. Would you like some breakfast as well?'

Cassie was hungry. 'Sounds good.'

Already Lily was making her way upstairs lugging her heavy bag with her. 'Leave me out, if you don't mind. I just need some sleep.'

'Lazy bones!' shouted Cassie. 'You'd better get your butt into gear, Lily Hamilton. There's big business out there for the taking!'

Lily yawned and continued on her way to bed.

Fortunately Keir's apartment was in the Docklands area of London and easy for Lily to get to from Cambridge. A straight trip along the M11. In between everything else, she'd taken driving lessons and was relieved, like Cassie, to have passed her test first time. This had been about a month before their trip to New York. Since passing Lily had done so much driving it seemed as if she'd been doing it forever, and she loved it. A bit like her cousin Guy, Lily liked speed and in her new Cavalier Estate she bombed along, keeping her eyes constantly peeled for police cars.

Keir had given her strict instructions on where to park and she was pleased to be punctual. In the last few days she'd been working hard at home, planning the future of Fare & Flair. Then she'd put together a business plan showing how she and Cassie wanted things to progress and made an appointment with her bank manager in the hope of acquiring a much larger overdraft.

Looking particularly stunning in a pale green trouser suit and with her hair cut into long layers which fell attractively on to her shoulders, she made her way towards Keir's apartment. As she entered the converted tobacco warehouse it was like a new beginning because her role was somehow different this time. Okay, so she'd put in an appearance at as many functions as possible in the future, overseeing everything, but she was merely the organiser now, the planner, as was Cassie, and if people wanted their excellent services they'd have to pay dearly for them so she could afford to hire plenty of staff. Lily was as competitive as the next person, more so. She was determined to succeed and that meant making money. It was her intention to start the process with Keir Doughty.

As Lily rang the doorbell she remembered Cassie's reluctance to have anything to do with this man and wondered why. Her friend had omitted to tell her about the episode at the flat he'd shared with Guy because, as was her nature, she shut out the things she didn't want to remember. But Cassie had quizzed the staff at Benson's about his departure and they were excited about his shift to stardom and avidly watched *Ace Driving*. Kelly, who still worked there, had told Cassie that Keir looked gorgeous on screen and was sure to go far. She omitted to mention his rift with Guy.

Lily only vaguely remembered Keir from Guy's wedding, and was excited because of the contacts she could undoubtedly make through this party, and, more importantly, because she was sure Guy must be involved somewhere along the line. Wearing navy trousers and a rust-coloured silk shirt, Keir answered the door and ran a lazy hand through his hair which was now fashionably longer. Lily frowned because she didn't remember him at all. But Keir remembered her all right and in his opinion she still remained the most beautiful female he'd ever laid eyes on. Smiling very slowly, he extended his hand and drew Lily into his apartment, like a spider to the fly. Keir was delighted to see her again. Stealing precious Lily would be the final offensive on Guy Hamilton, his erstwhile friend and new enemy, and would go a long way to paying him back for Keir's two broken teeth.

Lily had thought the St Katherine's Dock apartment palatial enough but this was almost twice the size. Unfortunately there was no view of the river but a huge balcony did provide a view of Canary Wharf and a glimpse of the Dome. As Keir guided her further and further into his domain, she cast her eyes around, noting the stripped beechwood floor and a couple of sofas with a marble-topped table on stainless steel legs standing in between.

Little did she know that this was almost an exact replica of the furnishings in the flat Keir had shared with Guy in Cambridge – which was just as well because she didn't much like it. It was uncompromisingly male and reminded her of home. Her Ely home that is. A place for everything and everything in its place. Where were the home comforts? The scattered cushions, footstools, tables to lob things on. And books. There were no books at all. Just a couple of *avant-garde* lamps. And the colour scheme was pale. Lily liked strong colours. Vibrant colours.

'This place has cost me a bloody fortune,' Keir mumbled under his breath, perhaps because he was aware she wasn't impressed. 'And although I want this party, I don't want anything spoiled.' He looked at her as though this should be her responsibility as well.

'Of course you don't. But your friends are big boys now ... aren't they?'

Her quick retort reminded him so much of Cassie Milbank. He cleared his throat, 'Hmm, yes.' He couldn't resist asking, 'And I understand Ms Milbank is your partner?'

'How do you know that?'

He tapped his forehead. 'There's nothing I don't know.' Holding her eyes, he smiled. 'You two are becoming famous. I think it might be something to do with *your* stunning looks and Ms Milbank's stunning *flowers* ... and the food, of course.'

Something about the way he spoke and looked at her unnerved Lily. She was beginning to understand Cassie's dislike of him. 'Yes, the flowers are important.'

He folded his arms and stuck out his chin. 'And I'd like plenty at this party. I'd like Ms Milbank to really show her hand.' He gave Lily a sidelong glance. 'Will that be possible?'

He really has a thing about Cassie, she thought. 'I'm sure Ms Milbank will be happy to oblige.'

Keir threw back his head and laughed in an exaggerated way, high-pitched and barely controlled. 'Well, I wouldn't be so sure if I were you.' He stared at Lily and she noticed that his eyes appeared vacant. Her immediate conclusion was that this man was into drugs, she'd seen it many times at university. He must be a user of some sort.

'How's Guy?' she asked, anxious to change the subject.

Keir spluttered and laughed again. 'You mean, you don't know?'

She looked askance. 'Know what?'

Melodramatically, Keir crossed his forefingers in front of him. 'Daggers drawn, we are! Enemies to the bitter end!' He smiled sardonically. 'I stole his thunder and the poor boy's angry with me . . . to say the least.'

'What do you mean, stole his thunder?'

'We both wanted to be presenters of *Ace Driving* – and I got the job. Now Guy can't find it in his heart to forgive me.'

Surprised, Lily stared at him. 'You mean, you've fallen out with Guy because you got the job?'

He brought his face very close to hers. 'Yes, Lily. He actually punched me in the mouth – see?' He drew back his top lip to reveal two exquisitely capped teeth. 'I could have sued him, but I decided not to.'

'Wow, that was big of you.'

He glared at her. 'It was actually. Look here, young lady, I'm doing you a favour asking you to organise this party. If you don't want the job, just say so.'

I don't like this man, thought Lily. Walk away. Quickly. Now. 'Guy's my cousin. He's family. Surely you understand my loyalty to him?'

Keir switched, became charming once more. 'And I bloody miss him. He was my best friend. I couldn't help it if Andy McVay preferred me. Surely you understand my position too?'

'If what you're saying's the truth, of course I do.'

He tapped her shoulder lightly. 'Remember, Lily, I never lie.'

She was embarrassed and wanted to move away. 'So how many people were you thinking of inviting to this party?'

He cleared his throat. 'About fifty. And I want the best. The works. Fine champagne,' he gave her a sidelong look, 'but none of that Krug stuff. Can't afford that. And I'd like a running buffet . . . and beautiful flowers.'

She looked around the room. 'Actually, Cassie could really go to town here. Because of your colour scheme, she could ring the changes.'

He looked insulted. 'I hope you don't mean bright colours? Keep it subtle at all costs.' He thought then said, 'Yes, white. I'd like the flowers to be white. Is that possible?'

She knew better than to argue. 'Of course. If that's what you want?'

Keir stroked his chin and smiled at her. 'What must you think of me? I'm forgetting my manners. Can I offer you a glass of something?'

She shook her head. 'No, thanks. I'm driving.'

'Oh, come on now. Just a little one?'

She was uptight and didn't like the feeling. What harm could one drink do? 'Okay, white wine wouldn't go amiss.'

Immediately he started towards the kitchen, looking back over his shoulder. 'Cloudy Bay – do you like Cloudy Bay?'

She grinned. 'I love Cloudy Bay.' Perhaps Keir Doughty wasn't so bad after all.

Cassie's mouth dropped open. 'They've fallen out? Guy took a swing at him?' A tiny smile creased the corners of her mouth. 'Good for Guy.'

'But not if it was just over Keir's landing a job. I mean, in their business the competition must be red-hot.'

Cassie shifted back in her seat and tucked her feet beneath her. 'Don't you believe it! That man's lying. There's more to this, you can bet your sweet life on it.'

'But why would he lie? And let's face it, Cassie, he got the job, didn't he? And he's doing very well.'

'Hmm. Well, I'd like to hear Guy's side of the story before I pass judgement.'

Lily looked across the room at her friend and recognised her abiding loyalty. Or was it that she simply couldn't stand Keir Doughty? 'But one thing's for sure, Cassie.' She raised her eyebrows. 'Keir certainly has the hots for you.'

Narrowing her eyes, Cassie inclined her head. 'I don't want to know, Lily, so don't try buttering me up with statements like that. I've told you, we'll do this job because of the contacts we can make, but please don't ask me to be anymore than civil to Mr Doughty. I loathe him. Really, really loathe him.'

Lily smiled. 'This is so amusing. You always call him Mr Doughty and he always refers to you as Ms Milbank.'

'Good! Let's keep it that way.'

'But white flowers ... and the place is crying out for some colour!'

Cassie slapped her thigh. 'If Mr Doughty wants white flowers, he can have them. And don't worry, Lily, I'll make his place look wonderful, rest assured.' She looked down at her nails. 'Did you give him some idea of the cost?'

Taking a deep breath, Lily admitted, 'Yes, and I have to say he flinched. But what the hell? He wants our services, he'll damn' well have to pay for them.'

'We must be careful, though. We don't want him telling everyone we're too expensive.'

'We're not! And I'm sure he won't.' Lily sat forward and put her elbows on her knees, cupping her chin. 'We must make this really special, Cassie. It must be service *par excellence*.'

'It will be! Tell those clever freelance chefs exactly what you want right down to the last detail, and make sure they do it!'

'And on this occasion we must both be seen to be there, Cassie.'

She pulled a face. 'Of course. Invisibly visible! I'll just keep my distance from the creepy host.'

241

Chapter Thirty-Four

It was late April when Cassie arrived at Keir's apartment on the day of his party with armfuls of white daffodils, white tulips and several statuesque white foxtail lilies. A bundle of white fountain grass was the only other adornment with its graceful feathery plumes. As she walked through the door she immediately noticed the likeness between this apartment and the one Keir had shared with Guy, and was mightily relieved the client was out. Lily was making her own way there later. Cassie made a return journey to her car to fetch containers, oasis and vases for her arrangements and was hardly back in the apartment before Keir arrived and stealthily came up behind her.

'Ms Millbank,' he drawled.

She twisted round and was surprised to see a very different Keir from the one she'd deliberately shut out of her life. Wearing jeans and a sweater he looked almost approachable, and the way he smiled held warmth instead of sarcasm. 'Mr Doughty.' She coughed. 'Your girlfriend let me in.'

His face straightened. There was a tightness around his mouth. 'She's not my girlfriend. Whatever made you think that?'

Cassie enjoyed watching him squirm. 'Perhaps it was something to do with her attire.' She turned back to her flowers. 'Wasn't that the top half of your pyjamas?'

'I don't wear pyjamas,' he said curtly but decided not to dwell on the girl he'd been sleeping with, a researcher for *Ace Driving*, and instead allowed his eyes to wander over Cassie's blonde hair which now reached the middle of her back and gleamed with good health. She was still the same in his opinion, still voluptuously gorgeous, and stirred a wealth of desire within him like nobody he'd ever known. He had to have her. He had to break her spirit somehow. After Lily, that is.

'The flowers are lovely. Where are you going to put them?'

She turned then. 'Where would you like them?'

He laughed, 'Oh, I think I'll leave that to you. I haven't a clue.'

He seemed almost human. 'That's all right then.'

Keir rubbed his hands together. 'What time's Lily going to be here?'

Cassie looked at her watch. 'Soon, I should think.'

He touched her shoulder. 'Glass of wine?'

She shifted just enough to allow his hand to drop. 'Great. Love one.'

He rubbed his hands together again. 'Right. I'll get you one.'

She watched him walk away, waited until he was out of sight then looked around before once more picking up her vases and reflecting upon how she was going to arrange the flowers around the vast curving room.

Dressed in a plain black dress with high-heeled shoes and her hair worn loose around her shoulders, Lily left the kitchen where two young chefs laboured over tempting morsels of food and cast her eyes around the clamour of people quaffing champagne and talking loudly in order to be heard. Gingerly, she moved into the masses, seeking out the three serving girls she'd employed for the evening. Her eyes caught one of them dressed in black jeans, white shirt and purple and white striped apron with the logo Fare & Flair on the right-hand side of its hem. Lily moved swiftly towards her. 'Everything okay?' With a smile, the young waitress nodded and Lily moved on, doing her best to look inconspicuous. But someone caught her eye, just fleetingly, before he disappeared on to the illuminated balcony where more people were gathered. So much for Keir's fifty people, thought Lily. She had catered for that amount, allowing plenty per person, but there were at least seventy people in the apartment that evening.

She eased her way towards the balcony and the man who'd caught her eye. He was middle-aged and had a distinctly familiar look about him. Lily put one hand on the glass sliding door and peered outside. He was laughing now and she shrank back because he was with Keir. She was about to leave and go back to the kitchen when the man raised his face and looked directly at her. He smiled warmly and for a second she stopped breathing. With her mouth open she watched as he nudged Keir and appeared to enquire who she was. Rapidly, Keir moved towards Lily and, taking her by the hand, dragged her towards the older man.

'Lily, meet Seb.' Still holding on tight to Lily's hand, he continued, 'She's responsible for all the food tonight.' His eyes searched around. 'And her partner, who seems to have disappeared, is responsible for the flowers.'

Seb held out his hand and Lily disentangled hers from Keir's to shake it. 'Sebastian Turner,' he said. 'And well done. The food's excellent.'

She couldn't help herself. She openly studied him before quickly saying, 'You look so like somebody I know.'

Seb laughed. 'Oh, please, no! Not another poor bastard like me.'

Lily looked at Keir who was smiling but oblivious of the connection she was trying to make. 'Don't you think so, Keir?' Her eyes moved once more to Seb's face.

He shifted back a little and made a big point of examining the older man. 'Sorry, haven't a clue who you're on about.'

Lily shrugged and felt uncomfortable. Perhaps she was being presumptuous. 'Lily, let me get you a glass of champagne,' insisted Keir who appeared not to be drinking himself. She knew otherwise. All evening he'd made frequent trips into the kitchen for enormous slugs of whisky from a glass he kept filled in there. It had all been done in a *bon vivant* way and he'd offered the same to the chefs, who'd both declined, but Lily reckoned he'd already knocked back a bottle. Though nobody would know. He didn't appear in the slightest bit drunk.

'No, no. I'm quite all right.'

'No, I insist.' He disappeared and Lily looked once more at Seb.

'Who is he then? My lookalike.'

She shook her head. 'Oh, nobody. I'm sorry. You must think me awfully rude.'

'Not at all. I'm just dying to know who you're talking about?'

His eyes . . . they were the same colour and the same almond shape. He even had the same way of looking at you; and the shape of his head and the way his grey hair fell across his forehead – it

244

was eerie. He was slightly shorter but still held himself in the same upright manner. Even his style of dress was similar. She found herself saying, 'It's uncanny, really it is.' Lily turned to seek out Keir again, noticing him straight away. Although he was carrying a glass of champagne for her he was laughing with another group of people. 'I'm really surprised Keir hasn't noticed.'

Seb took a pace forward and with his forefinger touched Lily's face, turning her attention back to him. She blushed at his approach and their eyes locked for a few seconds. 'Beautiful lady, who are you talking about?'

She was relieved when his finger dropped from her face. It unnerved her. She said flippantly, 'Actually it's my cousin. His name is Guy. Guy Hamilton.'

Still with a smile, Seb shook his head. 'Well, you've got me there. Don't think I know any Guys . . .' Then his eyes widened as though a recollection had pricked his memory. He chuckled casually. 'But while we're on the subject . . . how old is your cousin?'

She racked her brain. 'I'm not sure. Early thirties, I suppose. Something like that.'

He was looking at her now with undisguised interest. 'Your cousin, you say? Where are you from, Lily?'

'Cambridge. Although originally we're both from Ely . . .' Lily stopped in her tracks, first because of the look on Seb's face, and secondly because she was suddenly yanked away by Keir.

'Someone you must meet, Lily!' he breathed in her ear while looking apologetically at Seb and placing the glass of champagne he'd brought for Lily on a nearby table. 'You want to make contacts, don't you? This guy is executive producer of *Ace Driving*. Andy McVay's his name, and, boy, he could do you a few favours!'

Peering up at Keir, Lily noticed the haze in his eyes and the smell of liquor on his breath. When she focused ahead she came face to face with a balding, bespectacled man of about forty-five. He was drinking what looked like orange juice, but there was no telling she'd learned. 'Andy, meet Lily Hamilton. She organised this bash for me today.' Keir looked down at her and smiled secretly as though their relationship was of great significance before returning his attention to Andy. 'Isn't she gorgeous?'

Did he really need to add that? Lily pulled her arm away from Keir's grip and struggled to smile at Andy McVay. He held out his hand. 'Pleased to meet you, Lily. I must say, I've loved the food so far. Can't wait for the pudding. Is there any?'

'Of course.'

Andy sipped his juice. 'Anything with bananas? I'm rather partial to bananas.'

Lily flashed a look at Keir who beamed back at her. 'Yes. We've made banana fritters and a rather special banana and praline tart at Keir's request.'

'Wonderful!' exclaimed Andy, and patted Keir's shoulder. 'You certainly know how to look after me, don't you, Keir?'

He looked suitably deferential. 'I aim to please.'

Andy McVay turned his attention back to Lily and sized her up before saying, 'I could put a fair bit of business your way, ducky, if you're prepared to be flexible in what you cook?'

She didn't hesitate. 'I'll be as flexible as you like. What exactly are you thinking of?'

He poked himself in the chest. 'Well, I'm a vegetarian, but I like interesting vegetarian food, none of this moulded quorn rubbish! And I know a lot of people who want to eat crazy food – y'know, seriously wacky – so if you're game . . . ?'

'Whatever takes their fancy.' Lily took a deep breath, wondering what on earth wacky food was? 'We're prepared to cook whatever's asked for. It shouldn't be a problem.' She smiled, 'But now I think I'd better go and see about the desserts.'

'Yes, you do that, and save a couple of those tarts for me, Lily.'

She smiled again. 'I promise.'

He called after her, 'Do you have a card? A business card? I'll need to get in touch with you.'

'Oh, I can do that for you,' interrupted Keir, already following Lily.

She insisted, 'But I'll still give you our card.'

Andy McVay looked from Lily to Keir and wondered what on earth their relationship was. He assumed correctly that Keir was after her but that she wasn't in the least bit interested. He was relieved. It was taking time and precision handling, but he'd wait. In his opinion Keir was well worth waiting for.

Keir finally managed to stall Lily. 'Your champagne, I left it on the balcony. Come on, have a drink with me. All work and no play . . .'

He grabbed her hand once more and led her back on to the balcony. She really didn't have any choice. Sebastian Turner was still there, leaning over the rail looking pensive. He turned as they approached and seemed extremely pleased to see Lily again. In fact his face lit into a welcoming smile so reminiscent of Guy's that in a flash she thought she knew who this man was – who he had to be. She also suspected she was treading on dangerous ground and drew in her bottom lip, biting it hard.

'Look at that!' moaned Keir. 'Somebody's nicked your *fucking* champagne. Thieving gits!' He turned to go back into the apartment after placing a firm hand on Lily's shoulder and saying, 'Hang on, I'll get you another.' Before she could object he had gone.

Lily looked at Seb, waiting for him to speak. With a lazy smile he said, 'I'd really like to finish our conversation, Lily. I think you were telling me about Ely?' He ran his forefinger beneath his chin. 'So, this cousin of yours . . . tell me, would you, what's his mother's name?'

She hesitated. 'Why?'

He chuckled and leant back against the rail. 'Oh, just a hunch.' He tried to appear nonchalant. 'I think I might know them.'

'Lynda. She's my Aunt Lynda.'

He gripped the rail. 'Is she now? Who's your uncle?'

'Guy's father, you mean?'

'Yes, Guy's father.'

'Tom Hamilton.'

Seb looked pensive. 'So, tell me, this Aunt Lynda – was her name Nichols by any chance before she married Tom Hamilton?'

Lily gulped, racking her brain. 'I really couldn't say. Why?'

He shrugged. 'Like I said, just a hunch.' He turned away slightly. 'And where is this Guy?'

She looked around the partygoers, extending her hand. 'Well, as I understand it, out and about doing what all these guys do!' Lily smiled then. 'He loves cars – and speed! And he's a brilliant writer. Writes for the *Daily Echo* and the *Cambridge Chronicle*. In fact, he and Keir used to be good friends – a while back.'

Seb's face went quite white. He cleared his throat. 'That's interesting.'

Lily held his gaze and felt she'd stumbled on something she couldn't handle. Then again, Seb's likeness to Guy and his knowledge of Lynda could simply be coincidence. All the same, she wondered about a man who could walk away from his pregnant girlfriend, never to return, as she understood Guy's natural father had done to Aunt Lynda. She decided to be bold. 'So how do you know Lynda?'

Keir was making his way back towards them. Seb said quickly, 'If I give you my phone number, Lily, will you get in touch with me? After tonight, I mean? I'd really like to meet your cousin.'

'Here you are!' Keir pushed a filled to the brim flute of champagne into Lily's hand. He then patted Seb on the back. 'So have you found out who he is then?'

'Sorry?' queried Seb while alerting Lily with his eyes to stay silent.

Keir peered from him to Lily then tapped his forehead. 'Weren't you wondering who Seb looks like, Lily?'

'Oh, that.' She laughed nonchalantly. 'No, not at all. Now that I'm close up I can see he looks nothing like him.'

Convinced, Keir wrapped his arm round her. 'So what about this little bombshell, Seb? Don't you think she'd look good in a helicopter?'

Lily felt trapped. She didn't at all like being hugged by Keir, but decided it would be rude to shift away. Seb considered her. 'Yes, she'd look pretty good in anything, but the lady's into parties, Keir, not *Top Speed*.'

She held his gaze. '*Top Speed*? Is that the name of a programme? Are you in television?'

Keir looked down at her. 'Didn't you realise, Lily? You're in exalted company. This guy owns Nirvana Productions.'

She'd never heard of Nirvana Productions but knew she ought to be impressed. Keir certainly was. Lily moved away from his grip. 'Seb – tell me about *Top Speed*? Is it on television?'

'It will be,' butted in Keir. 'Seb's looking for writers and presenters.'

Raising her face to his, Lily saw the look in his eye. All this fame stuff had gone to his head. She returned her attention to Seb. 'What exactly is *Top Speed*?'

Lazily, he smiled then gestured with his hands. 'Anything that

248

moves swiftly. Power boats, fast cars, motor bikes, helicopters and so forth.'

'And is this for Sky TV?'

He shook his head. 'No, ITV.'

Keir tapped Seb's shoulder. 'Well, *I'm available*. Or at least I can make myself so. My contract does allow me to shift about.'

Seb smiled. 'I'll bear it in mind.'

'You do that.'

Lily was anxious to get away from their overbearing host. She smiled at Seb. 'I'd better go and check on the puddings.' She sipped her champagne and held up the glass. 'Is it all right if I take this with me?'

'Of course,' Keir said, moving closer to her. 'By the way, where's Ms Milbank?'

Lily sighed, aware that he was not going to be at all pleased. 'She left, Keir. A headache. You know how it is. But the flowers look marvellous, don't you agree?'

Keir looked extremely put out. What was the point of paying for this pair if he couldn't show them both off? 'She didn't even say goodbye.'

'That's because you were getting ready at the time, Keir. We try to make it our business to be unobtrusive.'

'Well, neither of you could ever be that!' He reached out and blatantly patted Lily's bottom. She flinched at his nerve and spilled some of her champagne, eyes darting towards Seb. In that second she could see what he really thought of Keir. She ran her hand over her dress, removing the residue of the spill, and proceeded to walk away.

Keir was beside her, whispering in her ear, 'Time of the month, eh?'

'I beg your pardon?'

'Cassie! Time of the month? Her headache?'

How impertinent could you get? She decided not to answer but he grabbed her, spilling more champagne. 'I'm sorry. It was a joke. I didn't mean to offend you.' He looked around the room. 'I'm really pleased with what you've both done tonight. Tell Cassie for me, will you? I'd like her to know. Say I'm sorry about her headache. Please?'

'Of course.' Lily smiled. 'Now, I really must go and see to the desserts.'

'Yes, off you go. Must keep Mr McVay happy.' Keir grinned and looked around. 'After all, he's paying for this little lot!'

Lily wasn't at all surprised. She continued her journey to the kitchen.

With the party still in full swing, Lily was preparing to leave. She'd made sure everything was in reasonable order, the chefs had long since left, and the two waitresses still working knew exactly what was expected of them before they could leave. She was not particularly looking forward to her long drive home and almost crept towards the front door in the hope that Keir would not see her. Throughout the evening he'd made a point of introducing her to everyone, as though she was someone he'd plucked from nowhere, not a successful party planner. He was ebullient, to say the least, and as the evening turned to early morning, the effects of the massive amount of whisky he'd drunk began to show. Even Andy McVay, who had for months wrongly assumed Keir didn't drink, noticed his top presenter's condition and smiled, thinking everyone had to let their hair down once in a while. And, after all, he had organised a damned good party.

'Lily!' She turned to see Seb Turner coming towards her and her heart plummeted. 'I was hoping to catch you,' he said breathlessly and she noticed that in the harsh hall light he looked a lot older than he had in the softer glow of the balcony. He cleared his throat. 'I wonder if you would mind giving me your cousin Guy's telephone number?'

She hesitated before answering. 'In all honesty, I don't know it off-hand. We're not that close.' What a lie, she thought privately.

Seb looked surprised. 'Oh, I got the feeling you were.'

She floundered, 'Well, we are and we aren't. I mean, he's a good bit older than me and left home when I was still quite little. But we do get to see each other once in a while, through business mainly.' She looked him in the eye, unable not to show a little of her true feelings. 'He is an incredible person, Seb.'

He chuckled as though pleased, then turned back towards the hubbub of the party. 'That's not the impression I got in there. I was speaking to Andy McVay just now. Do you know him?'

'I've met him, yes.'

'Well, you probably know he's the brains behind *Ace Driving*, the programme Keir presents? Anyway, after our little chat earlier on I decided to do a bit of probing about Guy Hamilton and McVay told me there was a real row between Keir and your cousin before filming got underway. Apparently it was Guy who was up for the job first until Keir pulled a fast one and got in there. A really crafty move, quite impressive in a way. Made Guy look pretty stupid. Anyway, it seems young Hamilton wasn't at all pleased and thumped Keir in the middle of Andy's office! And Andy definitely wasn't impressed by such appalling behaviour. Then Keir went on to say that Guy had always stolen his ideas and was a bit of a drunk, and a womaniser and liar too.'

Lily stared at him in astonishment. 'That's rubbish! Absolute nonsense! Would you like my opinion?'

'Of course.'

She pointed back into the room. 'If anyone's a liar, it's Keir.' Then she took a deep breath and decided she'd said enough. He hadn't paid her yet. 'Look, perhaps I'd better go.'

Seb reflected upon all this. 'Well, for someone who's not close, you seem to be mighty fond of your cousin, Lily.'

She frowned. 'Yes, I suppose I am.'

'But you can't give me his phone number . . . or won't?'

She opened her mouth to speak, then closed it again. 'He's in the business, Seb. Writes for the *Daily Echo* and the *Cambridge Chronicle*. I'm sure you've got the contacts to rustle up his phone number, and it would be better coming from you. I'd prefer to stay out of it, if you don't mind.'

'Of course. I understand. I'll get Andy McVay's assistant to give me the low-down. Guy's probably got an agent so I'll arrange an interview with him that way.'

She smiled and turned to leave. Seb grabbed her arm. 'Don't suppose you'd be free for dinner one night, would you?'

Staggered, she looked up at him before finding her tongue. 'But I live in Cambridge.'

'Not a problem. I'll come to Cambridge.'

Her reply came out too quickly. 'No, I don't think so.' Then she added lamely, 'I am very busy at the moment.' Why was it that she always messed up turning down such invitations? She ended up feeling stupid and Seb Turner looked disappointed. But, really, he was in his mid fifties at least.

'Bit old for you, am I?'

He'd hit the nail on the head. Lily was honest. 'A bit.'

He shrugged good-naturedly. 'Too bad.' He turned and went back to the party where he knew he'd find plenty of gorgeous females who wouldn't give a toss how old he was. They wouldn't see past his affluence and the power he wielded. Pity Lily did. He turned briefly to catch a fleeting glimpse of her magnificent hair as she left the apartment.

Chapter Thirty-Five

Guy!' Peter Kent said excitedly down the phone. 'I've had Sebastian Turner on the blower to me this morning. He wants to meet you! Nirvana Productions are coming out with a new programme called Top Speed – perhaps you remember Tom Cussons mentioned it a while back? Anyway, if he likes you, you might get to be one of his presenters.'

For a few seconds Guy was speechless. 'What's Top Speed, Peter?'

'What the hell! Who cares? You're in with a chance!'

Guy laughed. 'I care, Peter. I'm not presenting some programme about traffic offences!'

'No, of course not. It's fast cars, Guy, and speed boats, helicopters, motorbikes, anything that goes at high speed.' Peter laughed. 'He did ask if you could fly.'

The conversation they'd had with Tom Cussons now returned to Guy. Normally he forgot nothing but such a lot had happened since then. He asked anxiously, 'And what did you say?'

'I said no. But that you'd be prepared to learn.'

Smiling, Guy changed the phone from one ear to the other. 'So when do I get to meet this Sebastian Turner?'

'Tomorrow lunchtime. Clinch it, Guy. Don't let that bastard Doughty get a look in.'

Guy chuckled. 'I'll try, Peter. I'll definitely try.'

Some days everything goes right. And for Guy that day was one of them. He left his apartment with the idea of visiting Guilio's in Cambridge to buy something new to wear the next day; it'd been a while since he'd bought anything. He parked in the Lion Yard and was hurrying along Sussex Street towards King's Street when he saw Lily. They spotted each other at exactly the same time and simultaneously their faces lit up.

'Guy,' she said as he firmly placed both hands to either side of her arms and kissed her cheek. 'I haven't seen you in ages.'

'I've been about. How's business?'

'Not bad. Quite good in fact. I've just . . .' She hesitated and decided not to mention Keir's party.

'Just what?'

She turned and looked towards Sidney Street. 'Been in Marks and Spencer.'

He raised one eyebrow. 'Oh. Anything interesting?'

She grinned, feeling foolish. 'Well, the food's divine.'

'But not as divine as yours.'

'Thank you.' She tried not to allow her eyes to linger on his face. 'What are you doing?'

'I'm after some new clothes.' He touched her elbow. 'Have you got a minute? You could help me choose.'

Lily had a thousand things to do but couldn't resist the opportunity of spending some time with her cousin. 'Sure, I'd like to.' He led the way to Guilio's.

Wearing a charcoal grey Armani suit with a silvery-grey shirt, Guy left the fitting room and stood before Lily. 'Well?'

He looked wonderful and she felt ridiculously happy being with him. 'Fab,' she said. 'You look really famous.'

He peered at her as though surprised at her use of the word. Then he moved forward and examined himself in a long mirror. 'But will it impress Sebastian Turner, I wonder?'

Lily was astounded. It certainly hadn't taken Seb long to get in touch. She coughed and asked, 'Who?'

Already making his way back to the changing room, Guy looked over his shoulder. 'I have an important interview tomorrow, Lily.' He held up crossed fingers. 'Wish me luck. My future depends on it!'

As he disappeared she called after him, 'Buy the suit, Guy – and the shirt.'

He answered, 'I intend to.'

Of course he did. Guy Hamilton didn't need her to tell him how good he looked. She sighed, remembering Seb's remark about

Guy's being a womaniser and forced such thoughts away.

As quickly he was dressed again and out of the fitting room. He took the suit and shirt over to the desk and paid for them with a gold card. Lily watched him and wondered if she'd ever again be in his company like this. Surely his future was now assured? She felt sure Seb would take Guy on and if that was the case he was set for stardom. And where would that leave her? She was just like Cassie. Lovesick.

But Guy took her arm as they left the shop and said, 'Fancy a drive out and some lunch?'

Even though she didn't have time she very quickly agreed and together they walked back to the Lion Yard where both their vehicles were parked, only she followed him to his Carrera where he opened the passenger door for her to sit down then closed it carefully behind her, as though she was precious. Then he opened the boot, slung in his carrier bag as though it didn't contain hundreds of pounds' worth of clothes and before long they'd left the car park and headed out of Cambridge.

He turned to her. 'Where do you fancy?'

She hadn't a clue. Lily just wanted to be taken where he fancied. Anywhere. 'I really don't mind.'

'Let's go the The Star at Lidgate. It's the other side of Newmarket, but I like the atmosphere there.'

'Fine. Wherever.'

In no time they were on the A11 and Guy was putting his foot down. Exultantly, Lily sat back and looked briefly sideways at his face. He smiled at her. 'Do you like speed, Lily?'

'Yes. But this is something else! I've never been in a Porsche before.'

'It sure is. Believe it or not, I'm in love with this car.'

'Oh, I believe it.' Perhaps that was the crux of his personality: his love for cars pushed everything else into the shade. As her eyes left his face, she remembered his words of love to her and felt perplexed. She stole another look. He seemed oblivious of her, just concentrating on his driving skills, which were more than competent. Lily snuggled back in her seat to enjoy the ride.

The Star, with its wealth of ancient beams and inglenook fire-places, was surrounded by thatched and timbered cottages in the heart of Suffolk's Lidgate and was enjoying a brisk lunchtime trade, but they found a table for two in the bar area and ordered the special luncheon of the day: Newmarket sausages and sauté potatoes. While they waited for this to arrive, Lily sipped her white wine and watched as Guy drank his beer. 'So tell me about Sebastian Turner?' she asked.

His eyes met hers. 'Not a lot I can tell you. He works for Nirvana Productions and is looking for presenters on a new programme he's putting out.'

It was on the tip of Lily's tongue to correct Guy and say that Seb owned Nirvana Productions, but she stopped herself in time. 'Will this mean you'll leave Cambridge?'

He appraised her for a few seconds and wiped his mouth with the back of his hand. 'I'm not sure. I'd like to land the job first, before I make any plans.'

Oh, you will land the job, she thought. Most definitely. Then she made a slip-up. Deception wasn't something Lily practised. 'So what's it called? Top Speed?'

He stared at her, surprised. 'How do you know that?'

She flushed and took a gulp of her wine. 'I must have heard you say so.'

'I didn't say so. I wouldn't have said so. I don't intend to mention any details about this programme to anyone.'

He appeared angry with her and she wondered if he often became angry. Obviously he did as far as Keir was concerned. Lily lowered her eyes then opted for honesty. 'I may as well come clean. I sort of know him. He was at a party I did over the weekend and he mentioned his new programme. I'm sorry, I should have said, but it just didn't seem appropriate.'

Guy glowered at her. 'What party?'

Lily felt the heat rise to her face and felt ridiculously embarrassed. Then she wondered why she should feel embarrassed. She'd been the one to champion him. 'Keir's party.'

'*Keir's party?* Keir Doughty?'

'Yes. Look, I'm sorry, Guy, but at the time we accepted the job neither of us knew that you and he were, well . . . not friends anymore.'

Guy was appalled. 'And now that you do know?'

'I don't like him, Guy! And Cassie doesn't like him either. But business is business.'

'Yes, well, there are some people to whom that doesn't apply.'

256

Guy downed the rest of his beer and looked around. Inside he was seething. But more than that, he was crushed. Did that man plan to dog him all his life? He forced himself to ask, 'Well, as you know so much, does this mean Keir's up for the job as well?'

She was hurt by his tone. 'I don't know, although I noticed Seb didn't appear to be overly keen on him.'

'Seb? Is that what you call him?' There was a trace of bitterness in Guy's voice.

'Not me. Everybody does.'

'So what did you tell *Seb*? Anything interesting about me?'

'I said that you're an incredible person.'

Guy's eyes widened and for a second he was speechless. 'Thanks,' he mumbled, but still couldn't forget his anger. Any mention of Keir had that effect on him.

The sausages arrived and Lily and Guy started to eat. Neither spoke for a while. Lily deeply regretted her words and wished she'd never opened her mouth. Then she decided it might be best to try and cheer him up. Make a joke even. Bravely, but perhaps stupidly, she asked, 'That lunch party at St Katherine's Dock, do you remember?' Guy nodded thoughtfully and she grinned. 'Why did you say you love me?'

But he didn't respond warmly, not at all. He was thrown. Guy just put down his knife and fork and slumped back in his seat. He knew the answer easily enough – because he did love her. How could he not? Seeing her now, concern written across her lovely face, he had a mind to declare this love once and for all. Then he remembered Keir. What if he'd been dabbling with her in the same way as he had with Naomi? Guy couldn't stand that. It would crucify him. 'I do love you, Lily. You're family.'

'Oh . . . yes, and I love you too,' she said blithely.

He cleared his throat and started to eat again. 'How's Cassie?'

Lily's eyes darted to his face and he looked straight back at her. She imagined them then, making love. How did they get that close? 'She's fine. Why don't you give her a ring sometime?'

'Why should I do that?'

'I thought the two of you were close?'

He queried her meaning. 'Did she say that?'

Lily stopped herself before it was too late. Why was this all going so wrong? 'She cares for you, Guy. That's what she said.'

He looked grateful. 'Does she?'

257

Jealousy overwhelmed Lily. 'Yes. We all do.'

'And Daisy? How's she?'

'She's doing great.' Lily pushed her plate away. 'I'm not hungry.'

He took her plate and forked her saugages on to his. 'Pity to waste them.' Pensively he ate the lot. Lily sipped her wine and watched him.

The car went at a gentler pace on the way back to Cambridge. Lily tried various subjects of conversation but nothing seemed to work. Guy drove back into Lion Yard and took another ticket then she directed him to her car. She was already opening the door when he grabbed her arm. 'I'm sorry, Lily. I've been dreadful company. Will you forgive me?'

'There's nothing to forgive. I understand.'

He raised his eye brows. 'No, you don't. It would probably take me a month to make you understand.' He gave her the ticket. 'Take this and give me yours.'

She looked down at the ticket and realised he was offering to pay her hefty parking fee. 'There's no need.'

'There's every need. Please, Lily.'

Something in his eyes was insistent. Perhaps it was another way of apologising. She climbed out of his car and went over to hers to swap the tickets. Then she passed hers over to him. 'Thanks for the lunch.'

He was out of his car in seconds and, cupping her face with his hands, pulling her closer. He kissed her mouth. It started off innocently enough but she responded with such fierce passion that Guy found himself locked in an embrace that left him feeling giddy with a mixture of surprise and desire. When each finally relinquished their hold on the other they looked nervously around the car park but nobody appeared to be looking. With an embarrassed smile, his eyes rested on her face. 'Phew – you've taken my breath away, Lily.'

Still with his arms resting lightly on her shoulders, she sighed. 'Have I? I'm sorry, but I suppose I've waited a long time for that kiss.'

He chuckled. 'Have you? I'd never have guessed.'

She concentrated on his face and he was aware of her scrutiny. She sighed again. 'I find that hard to believe.'

He let go of her then and touched her mouth with two fingers. 'You're out of bounds, Lily. My baby cousin. Surely you understand that? The family wouldn't approve.'

She felt like swearing but instead said, 'The family? I think you're a little obsessed with the family, Guy. Anyway, I think you're also wrong but even if you're not, who cares?'

'Well, for starters, I suppose I do.'

She frowned. 'Does that mean I'm to remain out of bounds?'

He pulled her closer and gently kissed her lips. 'Perhaps not.'

Lily was struggling against her own excitement. All sorts of thoughts passed through her mind. Not least: Stay calm, don't appear over-eager. And, best of all, Wait 'til Cassie hears about this. But all she said was, 'Good.'

'I'll ring you then, shall I?'

She wanted to say, Can't we make an arrangement now? But whispered, 'Please do.'

Guy let go of her then and, grinning, climbed back into his car. 'I'm blocking your way.'

Lily grabbed the door, anxious he shouldn't just drive away. 'Good luck tomorrow, Guy.'

He nodded. 'Thanks, Lily. And I will be in touch.' His smile was warm.

'Yes . . . I'll really look forward to it.' She was sounding much too eager.

He blew her a kiss and within seconds had driven off. All she could do was go back to her Cavalier and, with trembling anticipation, drive home.

Chapter Thirty-Six

Guy didn't know what to expect. The brief glimpse he'd had of Keir's interview with Andy McVay was now distorted, like a nightmare in his mind. But he did recollect a great many people milling around looking important. Today couldn't possibly be the same because Sebastian Turner, or Seb as Lily had called him, had arranged to meet in a restaurant and the restaurant was not at all what he'd anticipated. Guy, thinking it would be the sort of place where the successful gather, was mistaken. Ralph's in Chelsea was one of the most unpretentious eating houses he'd ever been in.

He arrived bang on time and was informed by Ralph himself, a typical Londoner, that Seb hadn't arrived yet. Guy was offered a drink, he had a beer, and shown to a table near the window with a view of a wharf. Very nervously he sipped his drink and waited a good ten minutes before the man himself turned up.

He walked towards Guy with his hand extended. 'I told Ralph to look out for you. Very pleased to meet you, Guy. Sorry to keep you waiting.' Immediately he was put at his ease as Seb Turner made himself comfortable and looked out on to the sunny day. 'Did you park all right? I only thought about it afterwards. Car parking can be tricky for you out of town people.'

Guy nodded, feeling a bit like the country cousin. 'It's okay. I parked in Blackhorse Road and tubed in.'

'Oh, familiar with it all, are you?'

'Fairly.'

'That's good. But you like living in Cambridge?'

Guy was surprised Seb even knew he lived there. 'As a matter of fact, I do. But, you know, Cambridge is only half an hour down the M11. It's the bit afterwards, the outskirts of London, that takes all the time.'

Seb nodded thoughtfully. 'Of course.' He cleared his throat. 'So, have you always lived in Cambridge?'

Guy hesitated. He'd never really liked discussing his family. The whole issue made him uneasy, although he wasn't quite sure why. After all, he did love them. 'I was brought up in Ely. It's a small—'

'I know Ely, Guy. I know it well. Went to school there actually. King's.'

Guy raised his eyebrows. 'You went to King's? How extraordinary.'

'Not really. It's a pretty ancient school – like me.' Seb laughed. 'In fact, I was quite attached to the place. It was the nearest I ever got to home. Mind you, it's years since I've been back.'

'Did your parents live there?'

Shaking his head, Seb looked sad. 'No, I was a boarder at King's. School House actually. In those days my parents spent most of their time in Hong Kong. My father was a pilot, ran his own airline. Freight.' He smiled. 'The old bugger taught me to fly when I was a kid and, believe you me, that was in the days when flying really *meant* flying. In fact, we often used Cambridge airfield. But that was years ago.'

'Are they still alive? Your parents, I mean?'

'No, sadly not. Both of them died a few years back. Pity. I miss 'em more now than I would have thought possible.'

'Do you still fly?'

'No, I never had a proper licence. Unlike my father. But the fascination's still there, hence the new series.' Then he studied Guy. 'Are you interested in learning to fly?'

His eyes glowed. 'It's something I've always promised myself I'd do one day. I'd love to have a go.'

Seb tapped his hand. 'Good. Because that's the first thing I want you to do. And we'll film you learning!' Guy's heart missed a beat. Seb spoke as though the job was in the bag and already he was warming to the older man. He had to pull himself up sharp. The last thing he wanted was to appear complacent. 'Will that bother you?'

'Not at all.' Guy laughed and Seb liked the timbre of his voice. It was a confident laugh yet filled with expectation. Seb sat further back in his seat, controlling a sudden urge to touch this young man opposite him. Over the last few days he'd been doing quite a bit of homework on Guy Hamilton and it was amazing what he'd found out, the most important piece of information being that he was born Guy Nichols. Now he just wanted to make up for lost years – wasted years. Outside work, Sebastian Turner's life was steeped in regrets. He'd never married, although had ample opportunity, never fathered any other children and his personal life was now undeniably hollow. The only contact he'd ever had with Guy's mother, after he'd left her, was a message along the grapevine that she'd had a son and was going to call him Guy. On hearing this, thirty-two plus years ago, he'd run a mile and decided never to return to Ely again. Now he hated himself for behaving in such a way. What weakness he'd shown. What wretched weakness. Hopefully his son had more of his mother's grit in him.

Ralph arrived at the table. 'Ready to order?

'Lamb's kidneys, veg of the day and sauté potatoes for me, Ralph, and a bottle of your claret.'

Guy blinked at Seb's instant choice then shrugged in a relaxed fashion, holding out his menu. 'Why not make that two?'

'You like kidneys?' asked Seb as Ralph walked away.

'I do. Don't get to eat them much. I like liver as well.'

Seb nodded. 'Me too. So many foods are frowned upon these days.'

'No chance of you becoming a vegetarian then?'

'I'm not averse to vegetarianism. What I'm averse to is people who turn up their nose at choice. That's what I don't like.' There was silence while Guy finished the rest of his beer. 'You want another?' asked Seb. 'Or are you going to join me in some red wine?'

'I'll have a glass of wine, if that's all right . . . but I am driving.'

'Of course.' Seb dragged his eyes from the young man's face. 'Now, before we start talking about *Top Speed*, I'd like to ask you two questions.' He ran a hand across his own face as though testing the smoothness of his early-morning shave. Then abruptly pointed a finger at Guy. 'What makes you think you'll look good on the small screen?'

Guy chuckled. 'I don't think any such thing! I'm not so vain. But I do like the idea of trying out the *Top Speed* machinery!'

Seb tapped his hand. 'But you have to look good doing it else it

262

doesn't work. Your agent told me you'd been on a sports quiz and that you looked damned good, sounded good as well . . . but it was only once so they obviously haven't invited you back? Why'd you think that is?'

'It was at the end of their series. They said they would in the autumn.'

'Hmm. But do you feel comfortable in front of the camera?'

Guy looked blank for a second. He'd always taken a pride in his appearance but vanity had never been a strong point. He wondered if Seb Turner was trying to trip him up. He decided to throw the ball back in his court. 'I suppose so. Do you?'

Seb smiled, briefly wondering if Guy had seen the likeness. 'What have I got to do with it?'

'Well, you're the one in television. All I do know is I'd be extremely pleased to be given a chance. Would you want my own commentary as well?'

'Of course! We're looking for people who've got plenty of witty but wise words to say about the fast machines they try out. And we're looking for nerves of steel. Do you think you've got nerves of steel, Guy?'

'Who knows? Let's just say I like speed, and the fear bit is part of the thrill.'

'But is it danger that turns you on?'

He's trying to trip me up, thought Guy. In fact Seb Turner was trying to find out if Guy felt the same way about speed and danger as he did. It was irresistible – up to a point. For him there definitely was a cut-off point and because of that he'd stayed alive.

'If by danger you mean life-threatening, then no. That holds no thrill. For me the excitement is in pushing my own prowess. Sensing that I can outmanoeuvre any danger, if you see what I mean? It's a mental thing.'

'Good, I like that. You seem an honest sort of bloke, Guy. Are you?'

All these direct questions. It would be so easy to lie. 'Yes, of course.'

'Which brings me to my second question. This might not be so easy to answer.' Seb cleared his throat. 'Why did you hit Keir Doughty in the mouth when he landed the job you wanted?'

The laughter died in Guy's throat and he stared at the man opposite him. 'How did you know about that?'

263

'Son, in this business, there ain't no such thing as secrets.'

'Well . . . I can't answer that without telling you the whole story and I'm sure you're not interested?'

'Try me. I most certainly am.'

'But it would be my side only, wouldn't it?'

'Well, maybe that'd even things up. Maybe I've already had his side.'

'Oh, I don't doubt you have!'

'Well, get your own back, Guy. Spill the beans.'

'I'd rather not. I'd rather forget it all. It's past history. Can't I be judged for myself? All I'm asking for is a chance, I won't let you down.'

'And you won't go knocking people about if they annoy you?'

Guy smirked. 'Well, that depends on their resemblance to Keir Doughty, doesn't it?'

'So if I were to offer him a job on the same programme, you'd have a problem?'

Guy groaned. 'Definitely.'

'What if I said that *is* a possibility?'

Guy reflected upon this and suddenly selling cars back in Cambridge seemed a darn' sight more attractive than any amount of frolicking about on television with glamorous machines. He braced himself, remembering his agent's words. Clinch it. He smiled. 'It would make it more of a challenge – but at least I'd get the chance to make him eat his words. Whatever they were.'

'So, suffice it to say, the smack you gave him was well deserved? You don't regret it?'

Guy laughed again. 'I most definitely *do* regret it, and I regret ever having trusted the bastard in the first place.'

Their meal arrived and both men stopped talking until the waitress serving them had left. 'You've convinced me,' Seb said then. 'And if it makes you feel any better, I never intended offering him a job anyway. I don't like the bastard any more than you do!'

The two men looked at each other with complete understanding then both laughed before starting their meal. From then on the job was in the bag.

Guy rang Lily but she wasn't there. He actually spoke to Cassie and the words he wanted to say somehow or other just stuck in his throat. Maybe it was because she still stirred feelings within him, confused feelings, and he didn't feel able to tell her of his desire to see Lily. Instead he asked how they all were, told her that he was about to start filming Top Speed, said he'd be in touch again and put down the receiver. Cassie hadn't a clue what it was all about because although it had been Lily's initial reaction to rush home and tell her everything, in fact when it came to it she hadn't. The last thing Lily wanted to do was hurt her best friend so she decided to wait until Guy's telephone call came. Cassie passed on his message and of course Lily was hurt.

'Didn't he say anything else?'

Cassie frowned. 'No. Just said he was about to start filming. Why don't you ring him, Lily?'

She shivered with disappointment and shook her head. 'I'm sure he'll ring again if he wants to speak to me.'

Cassie studied her friend. Pride. What a stupid sentiment it was. But she didn't say this because the sound of Guy's voice had actually stirred once more all the old feelings she'd tried so hard to stifle.

Within two weeks Guy was learning to fly a Robinson two-seater helicopter from an airfield close to Southend while constantly being filmed by a roving cameraman called Fred, whose language was peppered with the very worst expletives cleverly wrapped in witticisms which kept Guy laughing long after they'd retired for the day. Overnight his life had changed. He not only clinched the deal with Nirvana Productions, he also appeared to make a friend. Seb Turner couldn't do enough for him and turned up regularly to watch his attempts at flying which, after a bumpy beginning, were impressive to say the least. Guy proved to be a natural aviator in the same way as he was a natural driver of fast cars. There was much hilarity during the weeks that followed and although there wasn't room for Fred in that first two-seater helicopter, his camera was attached to the machine in such a way that Guy's actions and words were easily recorded. It soon became obvious he appeared to have no fear and his reflexes were so finely tuned he even astonished his instructor. And as the words tripped off his tongue everyone realised that along with nerves of steel he had a mind as sharp as a razor. More importantly, when they ran back the film he looked fantastic on the small screen. In a nutshell, Seb was so overjoyed to have found him.

The first Top Speed episode was scheduled to go out in June. Its format was to introduce the presenters, explain a little about their hectic lifestyles and habits – in short why they enjoyed Top Speed machinery. There were two other presenters, both females, one Seb's current girlfriend Julie. All filming was done in and around the British Isles and Guy soon became used to living out of a suitcase with Fred dogging his every move. Once or twice Fred even followed him to the men's room, deliberately of course. That was when Guy's hand went very firmly over the lens.

Chapter Thirty-Seven

'Lily!'

Her heart literally stopped beating. It had been three weeks. 'Guy,' she replied as calmly as possible. It was quite early in the morning and she was wrapped in a bathrobe with streaming wet hair.

He chuckled. 'At last! You're an elusive character, Lily, I must say.'

She frowned. 'Am I?'

'Well, I have tried several times to ring you. I always seem to get somebody else.'

'Oh, really. Who?'

'Well, Cassie the first time. After that voices I didn't recognise.'

Anger combined with relief that at least he had tried welled within Lily. Her housemates were notoriously unreliable when it came to phone messages. She took a deep breath. 'How's it going? I'm sure you must be incredibly busy.'

'I am, but it's going great. A bit crazy, my feet hardly touch the ground. But look, I've got a free day and I'm taking myself off to Snetterton for a spot of driving on a skid-pad. I was wondering if there was any chance we could get together later on?'

She was up to her neck in work but not about to let an opportunity like this pass her by. 'What exactly were you thinking of?'

'Anything. Are you busy this evening?'

She couldn't lie. 'Well, actually I am. You see, sometimes my clients insist I'm around and of course it pays to keep them happy. Tonight is one of those.'

A small silence. 'What about this morning?'

Accounts, letters, umpteen things to do. She laughed, 'Are you suggesting I come to the skid-pad with you?'

'Would you?'

To hell with the paperwork! What an idea. 'Yes, but do I get to watch or take part?'

'How about both?'

'Sounds great. I'd love to come.'

'Okay, I'll pick you up in an hour.'

Cassie wasn't there, she was at the shop with Daisy. Both of them had left early. Lily picked up the receiver again and dialled the florist's. Cassie answered straight away. 'You'll never guess!'

But she did guess. Immediately, as if by telepathy. She looked at her watch. 'I think I can.' Maybe it was that lilt of happiness in Lily's voice. 'You've heard from Guy?'

Lily giggled. 'Oh, Cassie, you must have a sixth sense. And I'm going to a skid-pad with him!' She bit her lip at the silence on the other end of the line. 'You okay, Cassie? You're not, well, upset or anything, are you?'

'Lily, please. Of course I'm not upset.' It was just the knot in her stomach and the way the next lie tripped so easily off her tongue as Cassie pulled herself upright and smoothed back her hair with her free hand. 'In fact, I'm glad. Where exactly are you going?'

'Snetterton. Look, I have to dash. I need to dry my hair, get dressed and put on some make-up. But I'll be back before tonight so if anybody needs me, make some excuse, will you?'

'Sure. And, Lily . . . do have a good time.' She cleared her throat. 'And give Guy my love.'

'I will, Cassie. Thanks.' Lily then hung up and Cassie, on the other end of the line, clutched the receiver to her heart for a few seconds before returning it to its cradle.

It was thrilling! Exhilarating! Driving an old Ford Escort and wearing a helmet, Lily was instructed in how to handle the car on a wet surface by swerving into a skid, steering into the skid, then pulling back into a comparatively straight driving position. At first it was alarming, but then she got the hang of it and loved the feeling of control. Previously, she'd spent quite a while watching

Guy and had actually sighed at his expertise and easy technique. To her eyes he didn't need any practice, he was a natural born driver, but she respected him all the more for his total lack of conceit. She couldn't help noticing that everybody else did as well.

After her endeavours he opened the Escort's door and pulled her into a standing position, smacking a kiss on her cheek. 'You did brilliantly, Lily! You showed no fear at all.'

She removed the helmet and laughed. 'Don't kid yourself, I was scared stiff.'

'I'd never have known.' He looked around. 'Don't you just love this sort of thing?'

She nodded, deciding that she did, and shook out her hair. 'Beats catering any day.'

He squeezed her shoulders. 'I'm going to buy you lunch, Lily, I'm bloody starving after all that.'

She allowed herself to be led away, Guy's arm resting lightly around her shoulders. Lily wondered whether to pinch herself. Was this really happening?

It was as though the previous lunch they'd shared in the Star was light years away. Guy was a different person. Lily put this down to his new career and restored faith in his own ability, something she'd never doubted and knew for a fact none of the family had either. When he reached over, picked up her hand and kissed it, she asked, 'Does it really bother you so much what the family think, Guy?' She took a deep breath and looked around. 'I mean, you've always seemed to me to be so confident, so sure of your own destiny. Why worry if a few aunts and uncles disapprove of our relationship? Not that they will, mind.'

Still holding her hand, he sighed and considered his answer before speaking. 'I suppose I worry because I've always felt I have to try extra hard to win their approval. Anyway, it's not particularly the aunts' and uncles' approval I want.' He lowered his eyes. 'I suppose it's my father's.'

'But Uncle Tom adores you, surely you realise that?'

'Does he? He adores my mother, but maybe I've always been a thorn in his flesh. Not all his fault, I hasten to add. I know I was a bit of a bugger when I was a child.'

'Weren't we all? But I can't believe that. Surely he never made you feel like a thorn in his flesh?'

Guy weighed up the question. 'No, but he found fault with me all the time. To be honest with you, Lily, I was glad to get away and had no intention of returning home once I had.'

'But why do you think he'd disapprove of us having a relationship?'

'Because it's like I'm nabbing all the best bits. He's better now, but he still thinks I'm above myself as it is. And, let's face it, if anything went wrong, I'd never hear the end of it.'

She panicked. 'What do you mean, went wrong?' Lily panicked even more when she saw the look on Guy's face. He actually flinched. She realised then that perhaps she was taking too much for granted. Maybe he only wanted a loving friendship. The thought of him loving and leaving her filled her with a new horror.

Guy smiled and shrugged. 'What I mean is, my track record isn't all that good. In all honesty, Lily, I'm a failure when it comes to relationships and my father enjoys reminding me of that.'

'But Aunt Lynda is enormously proud of you, and so's Uncle Tom.'

Guy's eyes stayed fixed on her face. Then he said, 'How can I possibly expect you to understand? You've always been so special to everyone. The cherub, as it were, the bright and beautiful one.'

She snorted in an unladylike way. 'Rubbish! What about Daisy?'

'Lily, Daisy's different. And don't tell me you don't see and feel that. I've seen the way you treat her with kid gloves, and I'm sure it's because you recognise she often gets pushed aside.'

Lily frowned. 'And you think that's because of me?'

Guy considered the question again. 'In a way, perhaps. But it's not your fault, it's just the effect you have on people.'

'I'd like to remind you, Guy, that I was a child when you left Ely. You haven't exactly been around much to notice these things.'

'You don't need to be around very long to recognise the effect you have on people.' He let go of her hand and sat back in his chair. 'Lily, the first time I saw you – when you were grown-up, I mean – was at Grandpa's seventieth birthday party and *you* . . .' He sighed and leaned forward again, putting both elbows on the table. '*You took my breath away*! I couldn't get you out of my mind for weeks.' He laughed. 'And the next time was at my wedding. Believe me, as I walked back down the aisle, *married*, I wished to God I wasn't! Now that doesn't exactly make me a very straightforward person, does it?'

Deeply flattered, she chortled, 'But, Guy, a hell of a lot of people absolutely detest me. I suffered, really suffered, when I worked at the Viking.'

'Did you?' He looked surprised. 'Well, all I can say to that is – if they made you suffer, it was because they were jealous of you.' He smiled knowingly. 'Or maybe, if it was the men, they made you suffer because they wanted you and you didn't want them.'

That struck a chord and Lily looked down at his hand enfolding hers. 'But that's different from family, isn't it?'

'You're still very young, Lily. Sadly, I'm a good ten years older than you and I've been married and am now divorced. It's an ugly business. I should have more sense than to taint you with all that.'

She grinned. 'You could only taint me, as you put it, if you let me get really close.'

For a fleeting second he looked alarmed. 'I'd like you to get close, Lily, but I'm frightened that if you do, you'll be just like my ex-wife. Become disillusioned then walk away.'

'She left you? It wasn't the other way around?'

Guy retreated into his seat. 'Well, strictly speaking I left her, but it was because she found me unsatisfactory and didn't behave very well. A brief piece of advice: never trust a best friend . . .' His words died in his throat as he realised what he'd said.

'Keir, you mean?'

'Yes, Keir.' He was pleased she hadn't supposed he meant Cassie. He would never refer to Cassie even in the same sentence as Keir. 'He screwed my wife, then he screwed me!'

She reached across the table. 'I'm truly sorry, Guy.'

He grabbed her hand. 'So stay away from him, Lily. For me.'

'Of course I'll stay away from him. The only reason I saw him was because of business.'

'Keir has no scruples. He'd suppose that if you were game for business, you'd be game for anything.'

'Well, I'm not.'

Guy smiled, then turned to attract the attention of the waiter to ask for the bill. He looked back at Lily and asked, 'What time do you finish tonight? I shall be off again tomorrow and God knows when I'll be able to see you again.' He saw her face fall. 'I'm sorry. I do want to see you again, Lily.' He grinned. 'Despite my hang-ups about the family.'

'I suppose I could get away by about ten.'

'Okay, ten it is. Where shall we meet? Can I pick you up?'

'No. Perhaps it's best if you come to my place. At least that way you can talk to Daisy and Cassie if I'm late.'

Guy nodded and smiled. Yes, he'd quite like to see Daisy – and Cassie.

Chapter Thirty-Eight

Guy arrived early. Cassie let him in and welcomed him into the sitting room. He noticed her face was flushed and she appeared disconcerted, but he also noticed she looked radiant. Gorgeous in fact. It was hard not to stare. He sat down and declined a drink. This was followed by an uncomfortable silence. 'Where's Daisy?' he asked by way of breaking the ice.

'She's having a bath. She knows you're coming and she'll come down again to see you. Daisy adores you, Guy.' It was as though Cassie was desperate to put the onus of adoration on to somebody else.

He replied easily, 'And I adore her.'

Cassie sat down opposite him. 'Did you have a good day? I had a brief conversation with Lily earlier on. I understand she's now an expert on a skid-pad.'

Guy laughed. 'Too true she is. She's like you, Cassie, a damned good driver.'

'Am I? That's nice. Thank you.'

'It's true. I was most impressed by your driving.' He noticed the fleeting expression of pain in her darkest blue eyes and hurried on, 'Have you still got the Fripon?'

'Yes.' She lowered her eyes. 'Paid for now.' Cassie looked towards the sitting-room door. 'Oh, that's Daisy now. I can hear her clattering about upstairs.' She giggled and put her hand in front of her mouth. 'She can be a bit clumsy sometimes. Poor Daisy, she can't bear to leave any mess anywhere and sometimes ties herself in knots clearing away!'

Guy stretched in his seat and Cassie's eyes danced over his long legs. 'So do you like living in Cambridge?' he asked.

'Love it. We all do. It works well. Somehow or other the three of us manage to combine business and pleasure quite comfortably. We're all like sisters really.'

Guy frowned. 'You're lucky. Mind you, I thought I'd managed the same thing for a while.'

Cassie narrowed her eyes, picking up his drift. 'Well, I'm afraid I always saw through Mr Doughty. I never liked him.'

Guy regarded her. 'You're the first person who's ever said that to me. Actually, it's music to my ears because it makes the fact I absolutely loathe him easier.'

'Lily feels the same too.'

'But she doesn't make her feelings quite so obvious.'

Cassie countered, 'Well, perhaps she doesn't loathe him but neither of us likes him.'

'So I can rely on you not to work for him anymore?'

Cassie nodded, noting the obvious importance of this to Guy. 'Yes, of course you can.'

All conversation halted then as a loud thump was followed by a piercing cry and the clattering sound of someone tumbling down the stairs. In alarm Cassie and Guy looked towards the door then hurried out of their seats to see what on earth had happened. At the bottom of the stairs, Daisy lay in a heap.

Cassie raced towards her. 'Daisy! What on earth happened?'

Her bottom lip trembling, with Guy's and Cassie's help she pulled herself into a sitting position. 'I fell. I tripped on the tie of my dressing gown. *I fell!*' Then she burst into tears.

In dismay, Guy raised his face and Cassie did the same. Their eyes met. Quickly Guy averted his. 'Careful, Daisy. Here, let me help you up. Put your arm around my neck.'

Daisy did this and, hanging on to both Guy and Cassie, somehow or other managed to stand. 'Oh! It's my foot! Hell's bells, I've broken it! I must have broken it!'

'Well, don't put any weight on it. Just lean on me. Come on, Daisy, perhaps if you could turn and sit on the stairs we could look at your foot.' Guy guided her into a sitting position on the stairs and he and Cassie examined her bare foot.

'I think you need to go to Addenbrooke's, Daisy.' Cassie ran her hand gently across the foot and she winced. 'It might not be broken, but we should certainly get you checked out.'

Guy agreed and said, 'Well, I'll take her. It's only down the road.'

274

'No, don't be silly! Lily'll be devastated if you're not here. I'll take her. You must stay.' Cassie looked at her watch. 'She won't be long.'

Daisy pouted. 'But I can't walk. I'll need Guy to help me. You're not strong enough, Cassie.'

Guy smiled in agreement. 'She's right. How about we go in your car, leave a note for Lily, and she can follow us down there. And then, if you like, bring me back here.'

Cassie saw the logic in this. 'Okay. But I'd better get you some clothes, Daisy. You can't go to casualty like that.' She clambered around her and raced up the stairs.

Guy squeezed Daisy's arm. 'Don't worry, it's probably just a strain. You'll be all right in no time.'

'But I don't like hospitals. In fact, I hate them! Even the smell I don't like. Oh, I wish Lily was here.'

'Well, she will be soon,' he said soothingly. 'Is there a note-pad anywhere? I'll write her a note.'

Daisy pointed to the kitchen. 'There's a pad in there.'

Guy patted her hair and left for the kitchen where he wrote a hasty note to Lily explaining what had happened.

Within minutes Cassie was downstairs again, helping Daisy into some clothes. Guy waited in the kitchen, anxiously looking out of the window in the hope that Lily would return before they left. She didn't, so with Cassie he helped Daisy into the car and then sat in the back as she drove to Addenbrooke's.

Lily was directed to the cubicle where Guy and Cassie waited with Daisy who, with crumpled face, was lying on a trolley-bed. A doctor had taken a brief look at her foot and was filling in notes ready for her to go to X-ray. Daisy's face broke into the semblance of a smile when her sister entered the cubicle. Just briefly Lily looked at Guy, smiled shyly, then gave her sister her full attention. 'What's all this then? What have you been doing, Daise? I told you not to try those acrobatics on the stairs.'

Her attempt at humour did nothing for Daisy's mood. 'It's not funny, Lily, it hurts like mad. Where have you been? We've been waiting ages for you.'

Guy, watching the interaction between the two sisters, noticed how tired Lily looked. He wanted to reach out and pull her into his arms but instead his eyes were drawn to Cassie who was also watching the two sisters. He noticed the concern on her face and and realised he was witness to a most unusual relationship between three women. There appeared to be no restraint or animosity whatsoever, apart from Daisy's grumpiness, just genuine concern. He envied them then. In all his life he'd never come across such affection.

Lily reached out and hugged her sister as the porter arrived with a wheelchair to take Daisy down to X-ray. 'Oh, do I have to get into that thing?' She quickly looked across to Guy. 'Guy can help me. I'd much rather go with him.'

'Daisy, behave yourself!' said Lily, smiling at the dark-haired porter with the ruddy complexion who proceeded to help Daisy off the trolley-bed. He was a man of about thirty-five, medium height, quite stocky, with the most kindly brown eyes she'd ever seen. They stayed on Daisy's face for just a fraction too long after he'd helped her into the chair. She noticed and actually blushed. Cassie smiled and winked at her. Lily, with rolling eyes, just looked across at Guy, quite relieved that Daisy had been charmed by the porter.

'Now,' he said, 'my name's Harry and don't you worry about another thing, love. So what's your name?'

In a newly subdued voice, she replied, 'Daisy.'

'Daisy. What a pretty name. Well, Daisy, I handle this chair like nobody else. So, tell me, what have you been doing to yourself, pretty little thing like you?'

'Huh! I'm not little, and I'm certainly not pretty! Lily's the one who's pretty. I'm fat!'

The porter looked briefly at Lily, then bent over to look into Daisy's face once more. 'Call yourself fat? Huh! You should see my old mum. Now *she*'s fat. Anyway, no matter, because I'm telling you now, Daisy, most men like women with a bit of meat on them.' He looked at Guy. 'Don't they, sir?'

Grinning, he nodded in agreement. Then, he held out his arm to Lily, turned to Cassie, and the three of them followed the porter and Daisy to X-ray.

It was an age before they all arrived back at the girls' house in Grantchester Road. The metatarsal or outer bone in Daisy's foot had been fractured and she was now plastered up to her mid-calf. She'd been provided with a pair of crutches and told to rest for several days. The plaster would come off in three weeks. She was helped up the stairs by Guy and into bed by Cassie. Lily took Guy into the sitting room and closed the door. Together they sat on the sofa and she lolled her head back against the cushions. 'Phew! What a day.'

He raised his hand and brushed his finger down her cheek. 'You look tired, Lily. Would you like me to go?'

'*No*. Not yet. You said yourself I probably won't see you again in ages.'

'I can ring you, though.'

'Won't you be getting *any* time off?'

'Yes, but it's not easy to make arrangements. And you don't exactly have a nine to five job yourself, do you?'

She moaned then studied him, eyes lingering on the set of his jaw and the way his eyes crinkled at the corners when he smiled. He was an enormously attractive man and she knew that as soon as Top Speed was screened he'd be pursued by countless women. How could she bear it if she hardly saw him? She whispered, 'What now then?'

Oh, Lily, he thought, I'd like to make love to you. I'd like to push you down on this sofa and meld your body with mine. But it was far too soon and he respected her far too much. This was no ordinary relationship, it really mattered. He had to get it right. Naomi had been the hottest female he'd ever encountered, far more predatory than Jane Richardson, and within hours of their first date he'd found himself kneeling in the passenger footwell of his car, ramming himself inside her – and look how that had turned out! Guy reached forward and tenderly gathered Lily into his arms to kiss her. She responded with tantalising urgency and he wondered whether to throw all caution to the wind and take her, there and then, but a picture of his father flickered through his brain and he knew he couldn't. He said, 'You must know how I feel about you. *I love you*, Lily. I always have, but I can't . . . take advantage of you.'

Her brow furrowed into tiny worry lines. 'Why?'

He shrank back a little. 'You wouldn't really want that. You must know it would spoil things.' He looked around the room. 'I don't want to make love to you furtively while your sister and best friend try to ignore the noise – and sleep.'

Lily swallowed hard, remembering how easy he'd found

277

it to make love to Cassie. 'It needn't be like that, Guy.'

He raised her chin with his hand. 'It would be, I'm afraid. You'd wake up tomorrow and think how unsatisfactory it all was, and I wouldn't be able to help it because I happen to want you so *fucking* much.'

'I do have a perfectly private bedroom, you know.'

'And let me guess – next to Cassie's?'

Lily pouted. 'So?'

'No, I really can't do that. Not with you. It would be impossible. I love you. We'll wait.'

Lily looked down at her feet and felt the embarrassment colour her cheeks. What must he think of her? She hurried to explain, 'I don't make a habit of asking men to my bedroom, you know.'

He laughed. 'I never for a minute thought you did.'

She looked at him then. 'If I said I loved you too, would you understand?'

'I know you love me, Lily. It's in your eyes.'

'Is it really? Am I that obvious? In that case, when then?'

He brushed his mouth against hers. 'When I can very privately make love to you – and then make love to you over and over again. Okay?'

The very thought made her weak with desire. She croaked, 'Promise?'

'I don't need to promise, Lily, it's a sure thing.' He kissed her nose. 'And when that happens, you'll thank me for waiting. That's my promise to you.'

She believed him. She had no choice.

Chapter Thirty-Nine

It was late June and the first episode of *Top Speed* was being televised. With Cassie and Daisy, Lily sat watching, hardly able to tear her eyes away from the screen. She'd seen Guy several times since Daisy's accident for snatched lunches, snatched kisses, nothing more because it always seemed to happen at inopportune times. But he'd rung her many times and sent flowers and cards complete with loving messages. The carefree and lovable character now becoming popular throughout the country was one Guy Hamilton. But she loved the private man, the considerate and caring man, with a passion she hadn't known she'd possessed. He'd stuck to his principles about hasty lovemaking and part of her, the frustrated part, thought that was related to some hang-up he had about the family. Lily was beginning to fear that if they put off the inevitable for too long, it would be put off forever!

Immediately after the first programme, Cassie stood up and turned off the television. She looked at Lily and Daisy with her hands on her hips. 'Well?'

'Cool!' eulogised Daisy. 'Didn't he look dishy? And that girl . . . Julie, was it? The one with the speed boat – she's dishy too.' Daisy rolled her eyes. 'Isn't she lucky working with Guy?'

Sticking out her chin, Cassie looked across at her friend and business partner. He'll be a household name now, she thought, lusted after by countless women, and realised that Lily, almost there in her relationship with him, must be silently suffering too. She turned her attention to Daisy. 'I should think he hardly sees her, he's too busy doing his own stuff.'

'Shall we ring him and congratulate him?' asked Daisy enthusiastically.

Lily looked across at her and smiled. 'He promised to ring me tonight. Hopefully I'll get to see him too. I tell you what, Daise, I'll make sure you speak to him as well.'

'Oh, yes, please. I'll tell him I think he's brilliant!'

Lily frowned and bit her lip. Then Cassie tugged at her arm and with a comforting smile said, 'How about a drink to celebrate Guy's success?'

Lily's eyes lingered on her friend's face. She knew that Cassie understood. That was part of the trouble, Cassie understood everything. Sometimes Lily wished she didn't. She looked at Daisy. 'Do you fancy a drink?'

With her foot on the mend, Daisy stamped it and nodded, 'Yes, please. I'd like some of that Hooch. Have we got any left?'

'I'm sure we have.' In a straggly line, the three girls left the room and made their way into the kitchen.

As she followed, Daisy repeated, 'I can't wait to tell Guy how good he is.' She reasoned with herself, 'And I bet he'll be pleased because everybody likes praise, especially from family. I think Guy particularly likes praise from the family. After all, we're the ones who really love him best, aren't we?'

Lily nodded and tried to appear nonchalant at her sister's words but they had a sting in them somehow.

Guy arrived back at his Cambridge flat five minutes before the first episode of *Top Speed* was screened. He'd raced down the M11 from London at 100 m.p.h. in his Porsche, determined to watch the programme then shower and change in order to see Lily. His only reason for returning to Cambridge was to see her. He knew she was free and was longing just to hold her in his arms. In fact the longing was intensifying and it was his intention tonight to pick her up and bring her back to his flat. Even so it would be fleeting as he was off to Glasgow the next day.

For some reason, maybe nerves, during and after the programme he was dying for a cigarette – would he ever rid himself of the craving? What with the perpetual excitement, the hectic pace of his life, just every now and again the desire to smoke overwhelmed him. To stave it off he walked through to his bedroom, shed his clothes and wandered straight into the adjacent bathroom where he stepped beneath a bracing hot shower. As he washed himself he thought of Lily. Just lately he'd done a lot of serious thinking about her. His life had changed so much and he realised that this impossible situation they found themselves in could only be remedied if they actually moved in together. At least that way they would have their nights alone. But first he wanted to clear things with the family because he was sure they knew nothing about this blossoming relationship. He stepped out of the shower, towelled himself dry, then walked over to the phone to ring her. Just as he was about to pick up the receiver, it rang.

It was Seb, verbally patting Guy on the back. And himself, of course. The programme had turned out well, would surely be a huge success, and the format was exactly as he'd wanted it to be. Sounding more than a little nervous, he cleared his throat. 'Er, have you heard from your family?'

'Not yet. I'm just about to ring my cousin Lily, then I'll give my mother a ring.'

'Ah, yes, that beautiful cousin of yours. You must ring her. She spoke so highly of you.' Seb chuckled. 'Stuck up for you, in fact.'

Guy stopped functioning for a few seconds then fumbled his words. 'What do you mean, stuck up for me?'

'Didn't she tell you? I saw her at Keir's party.' Seb liked to be direct and was now anxious to shift his relationship with Guy on to a more honest footing. If he didn't tell him soon who he was, his mother undoubtedly would. It would be better coming from him. Safer.

Guy's memory drifted back to his lunch with Lily at the Star. 'Yes, she did. But to be honest with you, we try our hardest not to discuss Keir.'

'Hmm, can't say I blame you.' Having become so close to his son over the last few months Seb was aware of the tension in Guy's voice at the linking of Keir's name with Lily's. He remembered his own feelings for her, how he'd made a fool of himself by asking her out. Perhaps Guy feelings ran deeper than mere liking. Instinctively he knew they did.

Guy mulled something over in his mind then spoke. 'Seb, you saw Lily with Keir . . . how exactly did he behave?'

'For Christ's sake, Guy, he's a piss-artist. I admit he was all over her like a rash but she didn't want to know, simple as that.' Seb chuckled. 'Sounds as though you're more than a little keen on Cousin Lily.'

Guy attempted a laugh, not at all anxious to go making statements about his personal life just yet. 'No comment. Although if I thought Keir Doughty had so much as laid a finger on her, I'd kill him!'

'In that case, you ought to grab her while you can. Put her well and truly out of his reach!'

Guy swallowed hard. 'That sounds like the voice of experience.'

The pitch of Seb's voice suddenly changed, softened. 'Experience, yes, but I'm afraid my track record wouldn't encourage anyone to take advice from me. Which brings me to the real reason I'm ringing, Guy. While we're on the subject of family, I think it's time you learned the truth about me.'

There was silence as Guy struggled to switch his thoughts from Lily to Seb. What a strangely personal conversation this was turning out to be. 'Learned what about you?'

Seb froze as he realised this wasn't going to be easy. His son could hate him. Probably would. In fact, he deserved to be hated. Perhaps now wasn't the time, especially over the phone. 'Oh, nothing. I'll catch you another time.'

'No! You can't do that. Learned what about you?' Guy panicked. 'You're not ill, are you?'

Seb sighed almost in relief at his son's reaction. 'No, Guy. I'm not ill. You might wish I were when I do tell you.'

Realisation suddenly struck him. 'Oh, I get it. Is this about Keir? You're giving him a job?'

Seb let out a harsh laugh. 'No, it fucking isn't about Keir, and I'm fucking well not giving him a job! Here's me trying to open up my heart to you and all you can think about is Keir!'

'I'm sorry. I'm just utterly perplexed, that's all.'

'Well, as I said, perhaps now isn't the time. Besides, we need to talk face to face.'

'No! *Now*. Please. Hey, you're not going to fire me, are you?'

'*No, Guy!* For Christ's sake, why would I fire my own *son?*' Seb took a deep breath. He'd done it now and felt truly scared. It was a good job he was sitting down because his legs had turned to jelly. He even considered replacing the receiver for fear of what he might hear. The silence that ensued seemed to go on for ever. In a gravelly and emotional voice, he asked, 'Guy? Are you still there?'

With surprising calm, he replied, 'If this is true, how do you know?'

Nervously, Seb answered. 'I just do, Guy, believe me. In fact there's not much I don't know about you. Your mother was Lynda Nichols and I am your natural father.'

Guy almost choked. 'Nichols? But how did you find all this out?'

'I just did.'

'But you must have had some idea in the first place? What made you even think I was your son?'

'Well, it was that cousin of yours actually. She saw the likeness.'

In a flat angry voice Guy asked, 'Lily? She told you all this?'

'No! Lily didn't tell me anything. She just said I looked like you and we got talking. I quizzed her, and if I remember rightly she was bloody uncomfortable about it all, worried even. Look, I've wanted to find you for years! I know I have no right, I do know that, but when Lily said I looked so much like you, and that your name was Guy . . . well, everything just fell into place.'

Coldly, Guy asked, 'And is that why you gave me the job?'

'*No way!* I gave you the job because you bloody well deserved it!

Guy's thoughts returned to that cosy interview in Ralph's near Chelsea Wharf. And as quickly he thought of the programme screened that evening. It had been good, there was no denying that. Then he thought of his mother, the woman he'd loved so fiercely ever since he could remember. And she'd never spoken of his real father. Not even when he'd asked as a small boy. She'd never spoken of him, ill or otherwise. 'What do you want me to say, Seb? I need time to think about all this.'

'Guy, I don't want you to say anything. I suppose, eventually, I'd like your forgiveness.'

'Mine? It's not me you should be asking for forgiveness!'

'I know! I know! I was weak and stupid. But . . . I didn't love her.'

Guy's thoughts moved to Naomi. He hadn't loved her either. Perhaps he was as bad. He flung his next words at Seb, hoping to wound him. 'Well, actually, you did us a favour. We're happy and both love *my father* very much.'

It worked. The truth hit home. Even so, Seb tried to explain.

'Good, I'm glad. Guy, if I could only go back, believe me, I wouldn't desert her. The whole episode set a pattern of non-commitment for the rest of my life and it's caught up with me now. I've got no one. At least, no one who really cares. But it's easy to be wise with hindsight. The truth is, I was a bloody fool.'

'You should have told me. I need to protect my mother. This could really hurt her, and my father.'

Seb drew a deep breath. 'I know. I'm sorry.'

'Look, I'll have to go. I must ring her, and explain. No, I'll go and see them. She'll have recognised your name on the credits. You should have bloody told me, Seb. So should Lily!'

'Oh, no, please don't go blaming her. She knows nothing about all this.'

'I'll blame whom I like! You know what you did, don't you, all those years ago? You set me apart from everyone! I *never* bloody belonged. I always knew it, and always blamed myself. I still don't belong, not really. All of them – I'm so different from them all, and it hurts. All the time it fucking hurts.'

'Guy, I bet you're wrong! I bet they're all so proud of you, every last one of 'em. How could anyone not be? I am, and I've only known you for a short time.'

Guy's next words tumbled out. 'But you're my own flesh and blood! You're my father!' He hesitated, drawing breath, feelings of betrayal and guilt towards his adoptive father overwhelming him. 'Look, I really must go.'

'I'll be in Glasgow tomorrow, Guy. I'll talk to you then.'

'No, don't! Stay away, Seb, at least for the time being. I need some time to take all this in. Please, just stay away from me, will you? If you want me to do a good job, just stay away.'

'Okay, okay. I'll stay away. Of course I will. Look, I'm sorry I didn't tell you straight away. I realise now I was wrong.'

Guy snapped, 'I hate being kept in the dark – by anyone!' Something broke in his voice as he groaned at his own words. He knew he could find nothing else to say to Seb. Quietly, he replaced the receiver and brought his hands to his head, dragging them through his hair. He wanted to cry, to shout abuse, but what was the point? He wanted to kick something but stopped himself. He dropped his hands and looked around the flat which seemed empty somehow. All thoughts of Lily moving in were temporarily forgotten as he remembered his mother. She was his priority now.

He dropped the towel he clutched to the floor, stumbled across the bedroom to grab some jeans and a sweater, dressed quickly, grabbed his jacket and car-keys and headed for the door – and Ely.

Lynda Hamilton had been trying to ring her son since she'd watched the credits roll at the end of *Top Speed* and his line was constantly engaged. Up until that point she'd been filled with excitement and pride as she'd watched her son fly the Robinson and at the same time describe so easily how he felt. Then she'd seen a name from her past, produced by Sebastian Turner, and her heart had turned cold with fear. She'd hardly dared to look at Tom who fortunately hadn't a clue who Seb was. Over the years very little had been said about her former lover except that he was a mistake and she was well rid of him. But the truth was Lynda had been desperately in love with him and deeply wounded when he'd deserted her in such a callous fashion. At first friends kept her informed of his whereabouts. He was in London. He was a writer. He was struggling – good – and then no more. After Guy was born, she stopped asking and her own personal struggle began. A long and lean five years later, Tom Hamilton entered her life and changed everything. Aside from adoring her, he'd showered her with all she could ever want and tried so hard to be a good father to Guy, which wasn't easy. What a pity they had been unable to have children of their own, perhaps that would have bound them all together. As much as Lynda loved her son, she knew only too well he had a fierce determination and could be as stubborn as his adoptive grandfather, Bill, who had been very stubborn indeed. If Guy dug his heels in about something, whether it was to do with people or things, it took something monumental to shift his opinion. Lynda always felt he'd made his mind up about the Hamiltons the moment he'd met them all; he hadn't liked them and that was that.

'I should think he's gone out to celebrate!' said Tom, noting his wife's pique. He put a loving arm around her. 'And who can blame him? You must be so proud, Lynda. I know I am.'

She retorted, 'The phone's engaged. He can't have gone out.'

'Okay. There's no need to snap my head off! I'm sure he'll be in touch. He's never let you down yet.' Tom's feelings towards Guy had changed these days. Since his own father had died and he'd seen how distraught Guy had been about that, he'd felt closer to him somehow. And he was also proud and felt in some part responsible for his meteoric career. After all, hadn't he bought that first go-kart?

Lynda looked contrite. She ran a hand across her forehead. 'I'm sorry, Tom. It's just, well, I'd like to talk to him, that's all.'

'Course you would, and I'm sure you will. Come on, love, shall I make you a cup of tea?'

She smiled. 'That would be lovely. Better still, I'll make you one.'

'No, I insist. You go and sit down. I'll bring it through.'

Lynda smiled weakly and decided to do as she was told.

Guy made it to Ely in record time. He parked outside his parents' home and hastened up the familiar garden path to the back door, which was always unlocked. He entered the house and called out. He was greeted by his father. 'Guy! We never expected to see you here!' Tom walked towards his son and embraced him. 'Well done! We were very impressed!'

Guy peered at him. 'You were? Really?'

'Damned right we were.' Tom stuck out his chest. 'And I liked the bit about the go-kart. It was good of you to mention that.'

'It's the truth. I was hooked on the whole concept of speed after that, Dad. You know I was.'

'So is it all flying for you in this series or are you going to be driving cars as well?'

'Everything! I'm driving in Glasgow tomorrow . . . and flying a Bell Jet Ranger.' Guy's face was full of enthusiasm for what he was doing. 'I get paid for doing what I enjoy most. I think that makes me one hell of a lucky chap.'

Tom patted him on the back once more. 'You'd better go through. Your mum'll be really pleased to see you. She tried to ring. Got uppity when your line was engaged. I think she feels she should have been the first to congratulate you.'

Guy looked away. 'I'll go and see her. Thanks.'

'Can I get you anything? I made some tea earlier on. It'll be cold now. How about I make a fresh pot?'

'No, don't do that. Although a coffee wouldn't go amiss.'

'Okay, coffee it is. You go through and I'll be there directly.'

With some trepidation, Guy walked through to the sitting room of the house he'd shared with his parents from the age of six until eighteen when he'd left for university. It hadn't changed much and although he'd never been exactly happy living there, it was still his home and stirred up all sorts of strong feelings in him.

'Mum,' he whispered as he walked towards her. Lynda was sitting facing the blank television. She turned quickly and relief washed over her at the sight of her son.

'Oh, Guy! Guy!' she repeated over and over again as she scrambled out of her seat and wrapped her arms around him. 'I tried to ring you, darling. We're so proud of you. So very, very proud of you.' She squeezed him tightly and it was only when she searched his face, as he did hers, that she realised her worst fears were justified. She struggled with her next words. 'It is him, isn't it? I knew it! I knew it as soon as I saw his name . . . You should have told me, Guy. Warned me. It came as a big shock, I can tell you. You should have told me.'

He let go of her and urged her back down then half-knelt before her with one hand on the arm of the chair. It was pose he'd often adopted as a child when he'd wanted to talk to her about something, only he was a man now and it looked strangely awkward. 'I didn't know, Mum. At least, not until tonight. Seb rang me and told me then. I think he must have guessed you'd realise who he was.'

'Well, that was big of him, I must say!'

Guy stared at his mother, seeing the deep hurt in her eyes and sensing her fear of the possible repercussions. 'Does Dad know?'

'Of course not! I wasn't sure myself.'

As if on cue, Tom walked into the room, but instead of coffee he carried a tray bearing three glasses and a bottle of champagne. He grinned. 'I've been waiting for the right moment to open this.' He put the tray down on a table and proceeded to untwist the cage of wire around the cork. Briefly he looked at his wife and son. 'Why so glum? What's the matter with the pair of you? This is supposed to be a celebration, not a wake!' Both Guy and Lynda watched as he eased the cork out of the bottle with his thumbs. It popped and he proceeded to fill the glasses, each time waiting for the fizz to die down so that he could top them up. Nobody spoke. They all watched as though fascinated. He put the bottle back on the tray and handed two of the glasses over then took his own. 'A toast then,' he said cheerfully, 'to Guy and *Top Speed*. Well done. Your mum and I are very, very proud of you. And thanks for coming over, that was very thoughtful of you.' He winked at his son and knocked back half the contents of his glass. Tom pulled a face. 'Urgh! I never did know why people like this stuff.' He picked up the bottle and examined the label. 'Supposed to be good though.'

Still sitting on his heels, Guy sipped his champagne. 'It is good, Dad. One of the best. Thanks, I appreciate it.' He looked at his mother, who sipped her champagne.

'Mmm, it's lovely, Tom.'

Guy put his glass on the table and stood up. He looked at his father and gathered his courage, knowing that what he was about to say could knock their relationship back to where it had started. He hoped not. 'There was another reason for my visit tonight.' He looked at his mother. 'I had to come because I was worried about Mum. And you, Dad.'

'Worried about your mum? And me? Why?'

'Because after the programme I had a phone call from my producer and he told me something that really shocked me. *Really* shocked me.' Guy's eyes were still on his mother who was now burying her face in her free hand. Tom also looked at Lynda and moved towards her, putting a hand on her hair.

'Lynda?' he asked. 'What's all this then?' He looked at Guy. 'Somebody had better explain what this is about because I'm bloody lost. I thought we were all supposed to be celebrating. What phone call? Come on, Guy, tell me?'

Lynda didn't wait for her son. With distraught eyes she looked up at her husband. '*Top Speed* is produced by Sebastian Turner, Tom, and Sebastian is Guy's natural father.'

At first the words seemed to bounce off Tom. Still with a smile on his face, he looked from his wife to his son then slowly realisation of what she'd just said dawned and his face clouded over. He stared at his wife. 'And you knew about this? All along you knew?'

'Of course she didn't know, Dad. Neither did I until tonight. Seb rang me after the programme and told me then. That's why I came straight over.' Guy put a hand to his temples and rubbed an area over his right eye, making it quite red. 'I never meant to hurt you both, you must know that. All this has come as such a shock to me.'

Tom stared at his son and instantly recognised the misery on his

288

face. He knew what to look for now, since he'd seen the same misery at the deathbed of his own father. Then he looked at his wife and she, well, she just looked totally wretched. His heart went out to them both.

He put down his glass and walked towards his son, very lightly touching his arm. Quite boldly, he said, 'He might be your natural father, Guy, but he can't possibly feel how I do right now. After all, it was I who brought you up.' He tapped his chest. 'And it's us, your mother and I, who're responsible for how you turned out – not this Sebastian Turner. So he's not going to rob me of my moment of glory.' He turned and picked up his own glass and Guy's, putting Guy's firmly back in his hand. Tom glanced down at his wife who sat looking up at him with wonder and love in her eyes and smiled at her, chinking his glass against hers. 'To us!' he said. 'And as my old man used to say – bugger the rest of 'em, they just aren't important enough!'

'Oh, Tom,' Lynda blurted out, struggling to stand up now and being helped by both her husband and her son. 'Thank you. Thank you so much.' He bent forward and kissed her.

'Don't thank me. It's me who should thank you. Both of you. You've enriched my life so much, the pair of you, and like I said, nobody can take that away from me. They can try but they won't bloody succeed.' He chinked his son's glass and downed the second half of his champagne. He grinned. 'See, I could get used to this stuff. It don't taste half so bad the second time.'

With blurred eyes, Guy looked from his father to his mother, then back again at his father. He drew closer and embraced him, so relieved that it didn't matter, it didn't change anything, Sebastian Turner's being his real father. He'd been afraid it would. In a nutshell, Guy couldn't bear to lose the respect and love of the only father he'd ever known, the one standing before him: Tom Hamilton.

Chapter Forty

Lily could not believe it. Guy had never let her down like this before, and tonight of all nights. She looked at her wristwatch. It was eleven o'clock. She'd even swallowed her pride and rung him, three times, but there had been no reply so he wasn't even there. At first she'd thought he must be on his way to see her then decided he'd gone out to celebrate. Or perhaps he hadn't even bothered to come home. But none of that explained why he hadn't rung her. As the minutes ticked away into hours a burning anger mounted inside her. In the end she made some excuse and went off to have a bath. In the privacy of the bathroom she submerged herself in water and moped until there was a tap on the door and Cassie poked her head round.

'Fancy some Horlicks?' Lily pulled a face and shook her head. Cassie stepped forward. 'Well, in that case, do you mind if I come in?'

Actually Lily did mind, but again she shook her head and muttered, 'If you like.'

Cassie sat on the loo seat and looked across at her friend amidst an abundance of sweet-smelling bubbles. She'd tied and twisted her hair into a knot on top of her head and wet tendrils adorned her lovely face. She looked beautiful and flushed from several vodka and tonics, but apart from that pretty miserable. Cassie cleared her throat. 'I just want to say there must be some perfectly valid reason why Guy hasn't rung you tonight, Lily. Something's happened. He's obviously got held up somewhere.' She stretched out her hand. 'I mean, his life must be crazy right now.'

Lily snorted. 'He does have a mobile phone, Cassie. I'm sure he could at least spare a minute to dial my number.'

Cassie took a deep breath. 'Unless something out of the ordinary has happened.'

Lily's eyes flashed and she shifted herself into an upright position, putting a hand across her mouth. 'My God, you don't think he's had an accident, do you?'

Cassie shook her head. 'No, I don't. Oh, Lily, of course I don't. But I do think there's been some hiccup that has kept him away from you. It's just I can't bear to see you so miserable, and all relationships have to suffer this sort of setback, you know.'

Lily snapped, 'Setback, is that how you term it? And how would you know?'

Cassie sighed and lowered her eyes. 'Ouch! That was unkind.'

Lily leaned out of the bath and stretched out her hand to her friend. 'It was and I'm sorry.' Cassie took her hand and squeezed it. 'I just love him so much, Cassie, and all the time I keep thinking it shouldn't hurt me like this. I can't spend my life like some frustrated jealous heap of misery!'

'You won't! Of course you won't. For Christ's sake, you're almost there! But the pair of you ... your timing is slightly out because he's at a crucial and exciting stage in his career and to a certain extent so are you!' Cassie squeezed her hand again to make her point. 'And *you've* done amazingly well. Even I find it hard to keep doing my little bit so God knows what it must be like for you – and for him! This isn't all Guy's fault, Lily, because I can remember times in the last few weeks when he's rung or even called here and you've been out.' She drew breath. 'Look, what I want to say is, I'm sure it won't always be like this, it will calm down eventually, and my advice to you is to stay cool. Please.'

Lily slithered into the depths of the bath once more. 'I still don't see what could possibly have happened that stopped him from picking up a phone.' Her eyes became fierce. 'And I almost hate him for it!'

'Well, you shouldn't. You're pre-judging something and in doing so making yourself miserable. Sometimes, Lily, I think you were more sensible when you were fifteen!'

'Yes, well, that was because I wasn't involved with bloody Guy Hamilton!'

Cassie glowered at her friend and stood up. She moved towards the door. Clutching the the handle, she said, 'Take it from one who knows, Lily, Guy adores you. Don't blow it tonight because

291

you'll be a darn' sight more miserable tomorrow if you do.' And with that she left.

Lily pouted, considered her words, then sank even lower in the bath.

On his way back to Cambridge Guy felt strangely elated. In fact, he couldn't believe how good he felt. A corner in his life had been well and truly turned and now he felt sure his relationship with Tom could only deepen and mature in the future because tonight his adopted father had shown him the sort of respect he'd always sought. How strange that he had his natural father to thank for that.

And now Lily. The initial anger he'd felt about her not mentioning the possibility that Seb was his father had almost gone. If anything, he realised, she'd been protecting him. He looked at his watch. It was eleven-thirty. Guy remembered his former longing for a night of passion. Well, it still wasn't too late. In fact, the excitement of the evening had heightened his craving for her. He drove round to the back of Lily's house and parked on the large patch of concrete next to her car. With a light step he hurried to the back door and knocked maybe a little too loudly. It was still several minutes before it was opened by Cassie. She blinked at him then smiled broadly. 'Guy, how nice to see you. Come in, come in.'

He did so and looked around the meticulously tidy kitchen. Obviously Daisy had been clearing up again. Lily had told him she couldn't bear to go to bed if there was so much as a crumb left on the floor. 'I'm really sorry it's so late. I'm afraid things didn't exactly go to plan tonight, Cassie.' Guy drew a deep breath and saw the concern in her eyes. For a second he was captivated by it and reflected that she really was the most extraordinary female. She made him so aware of her understanding, her complete acceptance of everything he did. He really and truly admired her but there just wasn't room in his life at the moment to develop a stronger relationship with Cassie.

'I thought as much. I told Lily you were most probably unavoidably detained.'

Guy chuckled. 'One way of putting it. She's not angry, is she? I mean, I know I should have rung, but I'll explain all that to her when I see her.'

292

Cassie's brow crinkled and she was about to tell him a little bit of the truth. Instead she said, 'No, Lily's not angry. But I think she may have gone to bed. Hang on and I'll get her. Go through to the sitting . . .' She stopped in mid-sentence, turned to look at him and said softly, 'Unless you'd like to go through to her bedroom?'

He gulped in embarrassment at the way she was looking at him and held up his hands. 'No, I'll let you do that.' Then he followed her out of the kitchen. 'I'll go through to the sitting room.'

It seemed quite a while before Lily came down. Wrapped in a towelling robe, with her hair still pinned on top of her head, she looked almost childlike and Guy was instantly reminded of their age difference. But the first thing he noticed was her cool manner. She didn't welcome him warmly, as he'd grown used to her doing, but came and perched on the sofa next to him as though he might contaminate her. Guy reached for her hand and it lay limply within his. 'You're angry, I can see you are.'

She withdrew her hand. 'What do you expect?'

'Well, yes, I can see your point. I'm sorry, truly sorry, but rather a lot has happened tonight or I would have been here ages ago.'

'So all this *rather a lot* . . . did it mean you were nowhere near a phone?'

He chortled, shaking his head. 'No, and I admit I could have phoned you, but if you hear me out you just might understand why I didn't. And, Lily, I am here now.'

She softened. Some of the tightness around her mouth eased a little. 'I'm being a cow, aren't I?' She moved towards him and he opened his arms to embrace her. 'I'm sorry, Guy, it's just that I've been so worried.' She looked at him. 'Please, don't ever do this to me again. I just can't bear it. And tonight of all nights! Ring me. Please, just take the time to ring me.'

He sighed and disentangled himself a little from her. 'At the very time I was about to pick up the phone to ring you, Lily, which was straight after *Top Speed*, I had a call from Seb and the news he passed on to me rather destroyed my former plans. 'He looked into her eyes. 'And, believe me, I did have plans for tonight.'

She was very interested now. 'Go on.'

'I think you probably know what Seb told me, because as I understand it you and he have already discussed our *likeness*.' There was a bite to his word now.

'Your likeness? You mean Seb and you?'

'Yes. Seb and me.'

Lily frowned. 'So what exactly did he say?'

'That he's my father.'

With that her face crumpled and her hand covered her mouth. 'Oh, Guy, I'm sorry. Of course. Now I realise what a cow I've been.'

'Why do you keep saying that? None of this is your fault. Seb assured me you didn't know.'

'No, I didn't. At least I didn't really – just kind of suspected.'

'But why didn't you tell me? All this time, Lily, you could at least have mentioned the likeness – given me some sort of warning. Why didn't you?'

She withered beneath his gaze. 'You're really angry with me, aren't you? Guy, I never meant to hurt you. Surely you know that?'

He took a deep breath. 'Yes, of course I do, but don't you see? I had to get over to my mother straight away and as you can imagine all sorts of thoughts were buzzing about in my head. If I'd have rung you at that point I'd most probably have said something I would later have regretted.'

'So how did your mother take it? Is she all right?'

'Yes, she's fine. Dad too. In fact, they were absolutely great about it all.' He leaned towards Lily, cupping her sad face in his hands. 'Including the fact that we're together.'

She brightened. 'Are we? I was beginning to wonder if you were having second thoughts.'

'Lily! It would take a lot more than this to make me have second thoughts about you.'

She put her head on his chest. 'Oh, Guy, I really am behaving like an idiot, but if you had any idea how I feel about you . . .'

He twisted slightly to look down at her and in doing so loosened her towelling robe so that it gaped, completely exposing her right breast. Immediately Guy's hand moved there and just as he'd cupped her face, so he cupped her breast. Lily caught her breath and drew back her head, their lips meeting. He groaned, 'I want you to come back with me, to my flat.'

After a night spent in purgatory, she rather wantonly ran her hand over his crotch, tracing her fingers around the bulge. 'I'd rather stay here.'

His reaction was sharp. He said quite firmly, 'Lily, I don't want to stay here, I thought you realised that?'

She raised her face to his. 'Why?'

'I've explained.' Fazed, he looked towards the door. 'It wouldn't be right.'

She took a deep breath. 'Cassie, you mean?'

It registered then that Lily was absolutely right. It was because of Cassie. How could he make love to Lily knowing that Cassie was probably listening to it all? Guy swallowed hard and decided to be truthful. 'Possibly, yes.'

Immediately she drew away from him and pulled her robe together over her breasts. 'Well, reticence didn't seem to stop you fucking her, did it?'

Guy's eyes widened and he could hardly believe his ears. Straight away Lily regretted her words. They sounded coarse and angry, as she'd intended them to, but somehow alien on her lips. 'She told you that, did she?' he asked angrily. Ashamed, Lily lowered her eyes. Guy insisted, 'Did Cassie tell you that.' Then he snorted. 'Well, she must have done, I suppose. How else could you know?'

Realising now that she'd blown the whole evening, Lily tried to make amends. 'But it wasn't quite like that. She didn't brag about it, if that's what you mean.'

He guffawed. 'Hah! I don't suppose she did! If I remember the occasion it wasn't exactly something to brag about.' All the same, he was surprised that Cassie had spoken of 'our secret' as she'd scrawled on that piece of paper left by his bedside. He would never have betrayed her.

Her pride in pieces, Lily stood up. Tightening the tie of her robe, she turned to Guy. 'Perhaps you should go. I'm sorry I've made such a hash of this evening.'

He stared at her. 'Is that what you want?'

Of course it wasn't what she wanted, but she was hardly in the mood to get dressed and go back to his flat to make love. Everything seemed to be conspiring against them, but maybe their worst enemy was her own insecurity. Trying to make light of it all, Lily quipped, 'Well, you don't want to make love to me here and I'm in no mood to come to your place.' Then she faced him and said a little too sarcastically, 'It works both ways, you know, Guy. This is my domain. Maybe I want to be loved here even if a former lover of yours happens to be on the other side of the wall.'

Angrily he stood up. 'Cassie is *not* a former lover!' He gripped Lily's arm and held it tightly, all the time aware of the age-gap between them. She was a child and acting like one. 'You're way out of order here, Lily. You've got a lot to learn.'

His words incensed her and her eyes flared indignantly. 'How dare you talk down to me!' She shrugged his hand away. 'Maybe it's you who has a lot to learn, Guy. Maybe if you climbed down off your high horse for just one moment you'd recognise the mess I've got myself into because of you.' She wanted to add that she wasn't experienced in lovemaking, she wasn't even experienced in relationships, apart from with her family and Cassie, but she was too proud.

Guy saw this as a criticism of his own behaviour. He was making her unhappy instead of happy. He lightly touched her face. 'This isn't working, Lily, and I'm sorry. It's best I go before we say anything else we might regret.' He didn't really mean it to sound as final as it did.

But his words certainly had the ring of The End to Lily. Explain, she thought, stop him while you can! Beg for forgiveness! Just don't let this man walk out of your life. But the Hamilton family pride overruled her better judgement and she stood aside as he walked from the room. She thought he would at least look back but he didn't. Likewise he thought she would stop him but Lily let him go out of the house. She waited, listening, until he revved his car and drove calmly away.

'Cassie! Oh, Cassie! I've done the stupidest of things.' Lily crawled across her best friend's bed, wakening her from a deep sleep, and slithered beneath the covers as though for protection. Cassie wrapped her arms around her. Lily sobbed, 'You were right, you've bloody well got me all sewn up, haven't you? I've blown it, Cassie. I've blown it with my own big mouth.'

Cassie turned then and put on the bedside light. She ran a hand across Lily's face, brushing aside the tendrils of hair straying into her eyes and mouth. 'You haven't got a big mouth, you're the kindest person I know.'

'I'm not! And you won't think I'm kind at all when you hear what I've just done.'

A nervous giggle escaped from Cassie's throat. 'My God, what is it?'

'It's because of you, damn it! It's because of you.'

Worry lines were etched across Cassie's face. 'Me? But what have I got to do with it?'

Lily rolled on to her back and covered her eyes with her arm. Tears rolled down on to the pillow and she shoved her fist into her mouth. 'I can't believe my own behaviour! I'm such an idiot, Cassie. Such a stupid, pathetic idiot.'

'You haven't fallen out, have you? You haven't sent him packing?'

Lily faced her friend. 'I didn't need to. He was only too keen to go.'

Cassie looked incredulous then shook her head. 'No, I don't believe that. And where do I come into it all?'

'You'll hate me when I tell you.'

Cassie leaned forward and kissed Lily's forehead. 'Don't talk rubbish. I'm telling you now, Lily, nothing you could do or say would ever make me hate you.'

'He wanted me to go back to his flat – to make love. We haven't, you see, we haven't done it yet, not even a whisper – well, apart from tonight when he touched my breast. But I want him, Cassie, I want him so much. Do you know how that feels?'

Cassie smiled ruefully. 'Yes. But, please, go on.'

'Anyway, I didn't want to go back there. I mean, look at me, I look a fright – the Bride of Frankenstein! And I'm in a right state. And anyway, when I suggested we did it here he flatly refused. He was bloody adamant! – And all because of you!'

Cassie's eyes widened before she nodded wisely. 'I can understand that. It's simple, Lily, it's just too embarrassing for him.'

Lily frowned. 'Embarrassing? But he can't want me very much if all he can think about is *you*!'

'But, Lily, it's my feelings he's thinking about. And yours. We're best friends, remember, and he knows damned well how I feel about him.' She snorted. 'And I'm sure you've left him in no doubt how *you* feel about our brief encounter?'

Got it in one. What a wise friend she had. Lily was consumed by regret. 'I know. Exactly. But he was *so* angry that I knew about it. It's as though he still cares for you, Cassie.' She searched her friend's face. 'He loves you too, you know, I'll bet my life on it.'

Calmly now, Cassie stroked her arm. 'Love has many faces, Lily. Guy and me . . . well, it's as though we crossed a barrier. I let him into a part of my life I'd let no one see before, and he put me out of my misery, thank God. The reason he was angry was because I asked for it to be kept secret and now I've reneged on that. A sort of mini-betrayal. But, you know, if he had any real lasting feelings for me he wouldn't have just walked out of my life the way he did.'

Well, he's just walked out of mine as well!'

'Oh, Lily, of course he hasn't! You're just as bloody stubborn as he is! Why don't you ring him? He'll be home by now. Just ring him!'

'And is that what you'd do?'

Cassie considered the question then nodded. 'Yes.'

'Well, why didn't you ring him all that time ago? Maybe if you had, he'd be *your* boyfriend now and I wouldn't be in the mess I'm in.'

'Lily stop it! You're turning this into something it's not!'

She sat up then and implored her friend with her eyes. 'But I do get these feelings, Cassie, that I don't quite fit the bill. I've had them for a long time now, *and* I have recurring dreams, and it's always you and Guy I see. In the dreams you're with him and quite often you're crying, but you are *with him*. It's not as if you're crying because he's going to leave you or anything like that. You're crying because you're with him and I'm not. Do you understand?'

Cassie frowned then looked blank. 'No. All I can say is it's insecurity. Nightmares, if you like. You're one screwed up chick, if you ask me.' She jabbed her forefinger into her friend's chest. 'You know what you should do. Get dressed, climb into that car of yours and get round there. Go fuck him! Go on, then you'll have some peace of mind.'

Lily slumped back on the bed. 'I can't. I'd probably make a mess of that as well, and then he'd really go off me.'

'He'll only go off you if you let him.'

'Oh, Cassie, it's not as simple as that. I'm not you. I'm me. I'm Lily Hamilton and everything I touch turns to stone.' She looked at her friend. 'You know, perhaps I'd be happier without him.'

'Oh, yeah? And perhaps you wouldn't. Look, if you won't take my advice, then calm down, get yourself together and give him a ring tomorrow. But I bet you he'll be ringing you before you get the chance.'

Lily shook her head. 'I don't think so somehow. I think I really hurt him. Wounded his pride.'

'Don't take it all on your shoulders, kid. Sleep on it. Tomorrow is another day. I promise you, it'll all seem better in the morning.'

Lily turned and hugged her friend. 'Oh, Cassie, I just don't know what I'd do without you. You realise you mother me, don't you?'

'And you mother me. And Daisy.' Cassie laughed. 'Well, we both mother her, but she needs as many mothers as she can get.'

Both girls giggled but Lily made no attempt to leave Cassie's bed. Together they settled down and eventually fell asleep.

Chapter Forty-One

Guy flew to Glasgow the following morning feeling ghastly. After his initial euphoria at finding both his natural father and moving on to a different level with Tom, he sank into depression. He hadn't rung Lily, he truly felt he couldn't. At least, not yet. They both needed time to sort out their feelings. As it was they were pulling in different directions, neither really understanding the other. And besides, if she really wanted him, she'd ring him. Wouldn't she?

At least for today he had to push her from his mind. Because of his chequered past he was able to do this, the only difficulty being reality always crashed home eventually. But he found himself tentatively looking forward to seeing Seb again. It did still niggle him that he'd only been given the position of presenter on *Top Speed* because of nepotism, but at the same time he knew that things would be different now. His approach to his natural father would be a family one rather than professional.

But Seb didn't put in an appearance at Glasgow. In fact it was over a week before Guy met up with him again and that was after the second screening of *Top Speed*, which drew an even larger audience than the first, much to everyone's delight. There had still been no contact with Lily, although several times Guy had picked up the phone to call her. But each time he put it down again. He wasn't quite sure why. Anyway, he was soon whisked off to Southend to try out the new Quanta 65 speedboat, with Electronic Diesel Control, minimum detectable vibration and a deep V hull for superb handling – with Julie this time. They were taking turns to put the boat through its paces, vying with each other to see who was the more daring with turns and the like, and Seb ostensibly paid *her* a visit, watching from the shoreline with a massive pair of binoculars. Actually, it was his son's animated face that interested him more than his girlfriend's ability.

At lunchtime they all piled into Fred's Discovery – cameramen, engineers, editors and assistants alike – which was parked on the beach, and aimed for the nearest pub. It was quite a while before anything was said between father and son then it was Guy who broached the subject first. 'I thought you might like to hear that my mother knows everything now.' His eyes searched Seb's.

The older man shifted in his seat, drawing closer to his son, not wishing anyone else to pick up on their conversation. 'Was she all right about it?'

'Not at first. But my father put things into perspective for her . . . and she's fine now.'

'Good, good. So what exactly did your . . .' Seb cleared his throat '. . . father say?'

Guy shrugged. It had originally been his intention to put Seb in his place so far as family was concerned, but now he decided otherwise. 'Just that he's very proud, and grateful.'

Seb nodded and smiled. 'So am I.' He faced Guy. 'You're not angry with me anymore? I never meant to hurt you, you know, or your mother.'

Guy pursed his lips then inhaled. 'No, I'm not angry.'

Seb touched his son's arm. 'And we can be friends?'

'We already are.'

'And that cousin of yours? Does she know about all this?'

Guy frowned. 'Lily? Yes. She knows.'

Seb tapped his arm. 'I tell you what, take her somewhere special – somewhere really special. Do it for me. Do it *on* me! There you are. Can't be fairer than that, can I?'

Laughing, Guy slowly shook his head. 'It's not as simple as that, Seb.'

'Why ever not? You know your trouble, son, you complicate things.'

Guy didn't reply. He needed time to think about this.

And Lily didn't fall to pieces as Cassie had feared she might. Apart from a constant nagging ache in her heart and a tug of guilt because she was too stubborn to ring Guy, Lily was in fact getting on with her life. Business was brisk, sometimes two parties on the same night, and she'd been forced to employ a part-time accounts clerk and a young girl assistant. Mrs Sniffnel had been kind enough to allow them to use the premises above the florist's shop. This was only a temporary arrangement as Lily was actually toying with the idea of moving to London where she seemed to spend a lot of her time. Cassie worried about her. Since her falling out with Guy, Cassie felt Lily was pushing herself in order not to think about him. She just wouldn't slow down. It was as though she was permanently on overdrive. 'And if you move to London, Lily, you'll be knackered all of the time instead of most of it, because I'm not moving with you and nor will Daisy!'

But Lily had a mind of her own and as most of their work was based there, it seemed logical to move. She reasoned that if Guy wasn't going to be in her life then it was best to start again away from Cambridge. Start afresh. At least that way she'd regain her confidence. Meanwhile, she expended her energy in organising and planning – and paying meticulous attention to the slightest detail. Always she aimed at improving the service they provided, making sure that any complaints, however minor, were sorted out. When Lily wasn't on the phone or charging about in her car, she was poring over magazines for new ideas. She didn't want to be the same as everyone else in the party planning business, she wanted to be different. To set the trends, not follow them. Most of the people they worked for came by word of mouth and had very definite ideas, some quite extreme, like the pink party where everything had to be pink: food – mainly prawns, lobster and salmon – flowers, glasses, cutlery, plates and linen. And clothes! It was Lily's intention always to give exactly what was wanted plus a little extra. She suddenly found life terrifically exciting, especially rubbing shoulders with so many famous people.

But Daisy had finally opted for a much quieter way of life. She stayed at the florist's in Cambridge and found herself practically running it now. She had her own assistant and actually managed very well. On the other hand, Cassie sometimes felt she should be split in two. She wanted to help Lily as much as possible – Lily thought her flair for flowers quite extraordinary – but she also hankered after a slightly less frenetic occupation. This was resolved by Cassie planning the flowers and Lily couriering them in and organising others to arrange them according to Cassie's designs.

*

Guy still didn't ring Lily but Seb did. In fact, he got in touch with her straight after his conversation with Guy in the pub at Southend. He rang saying he'd be throwing a party in the near future and could they meet for lunch? She jumped at the idea. Perhaps now she'd hear about Guy. Her mother seemed to know nothing, and Lily seldom saw her aunt and uncle to be able to ask them.

Lunch was at the Savoy, in the River Room, and there Seb showered Lily with attention. At first she wondered if he had an ulterior motive but the conversation soon became cosy rather than intimate and she realised that his intentions were strictly honourable.

Quite early on, he said, 'Tell me about that cousin of yours?'

She sighed. 'If you're talking about Guy, I'd have thought it should be you telling me. Sadly, I see nothing of him these days. Nothing at all.'

Seb shifted forward in his seat and put both elbows on the table. He said softly, 'But I thought you two had something going?'

She panicked slightly. 'Did he tell you that?'

'No, Guy gives nothing away. I suppose you could say I guessed, just as you guessed about me being his father. You did, didn't you?'

Lily lowered her eyes. 'Yes.'

He put his hand on top of hers. 'It's all right. Guy and his mother have been great about it.' Seb raised his eyes to the ceiling. 'Thank God.'

Lily sat back pulling her hand away from his. 'They adore him, you know. Uncle Tom, his father, certainly does.'

With a shrug and a sigh, Seb relaxed in his seat. 'What father wouldn't? A bit special is our Guy.'

Lily smiled warmly. 'And some of that is down to the Hamiltons. Pretty sane bunch, you know. Maybe a bit rough round the edges but still good Fen stock.'

Seb laughed. 'Do you know, Lily, my schooldays were some of the happiest of my life.' He saw the confusion in her face. 'That's when I met Lynda. I was at King's in Ely. We were teenage sweethearts. She was a cracking bit of stuff in those days.'

'Still is.'

'Is she really? I missed out then, didn't I? More fool me.'

Lily had to ask, 'How could you have done it, Seb? Didn't you ever wonder about your son?'

He looked suddenly old and drained. 'That was my punishment. Never a week went by when I didn't worry about him. Like I said, I was a fool. I don't deserve him in my life now, but I tell you one thing – I'll never let him down. I'll be there for that young man whatever happens.' Seb shifted forward and grabbed her hand. 'He loves you, you do realise that?'

She laughed hollowly. 'Well, he has a funny way of showing it sometimes.'

'But he's afraid of his own feelings, at least as far as you're concerned he is. But they're one hundred percent genuine, I'd bet my shirt on it!'

Lily swallowed hard. 'I think we're too entrenched in family politics.'

Seb looked surprised. 'What do you mean exactly?'

She bit on her lip. 'I can't explain, I wish I could.'

'You know, he does have a tendency to complicate things. Best not to get too heavy with Guy. He needs somebody who understands him, warts and all – somebody prepared to give him his head.' Seb grinned. 'And then he comes up trumps every time.'

Lily realised that she was being given a sound piece of advice but it unnerved her, not least because she knew it slotted into Cassie's way of thinking. But she wasn't sure she'd ever be able to adhere to it. 'How come you're so knowledgeable about someone you've only known for a few short months?'

Seb's smile widened. 'Am I not his own flesh and blood?'

She laughed then and reached forward to plant a kiss on his cheek. 'Thank you, Seb. I'm so glad I met you at that party.'

'And you'll remember what I said about Guy?'

'I'll remember, but it's not just up to me, you know.'

'But you're the one with the business brain, Lily.'

'Yes, but a business brain isn't much good when it comes to matters of the heart.'

He turned and called for the bill then looked at her once more. 'You know, if you ever need anywhere to stay in London, you're always welcome at my place.'

Her eyes widened. 'Where do you live?'

'In Fulham. Nice little house.' He reached into his pocket and withdrew a set of keys proceeding to release one from the fob ring. He handed it to her. 'Here, take this. I may not always be there, but that doesn't matter. And here's my address and phone number. Anytime you need a bed for the night, or even longer, please don't hesitate to use that key. I mean it, Lily. You really are welcome.'

'Oh, Seb, you don't know what this means to me. I really might take you up on it. There are so many times I'd love to crash in London. I'm even thinking of moving there, but it's rather difficult with Cassie . . . and Daisy. They prefer Cambridge, you see.'

Seb tapped her hand. 'Well, that solves it for you, doesn't it?' He beamed. 'I'm pleased you bumped into me too, Lily. It's because of you I have a family now, and I can't tell you what that means to me.'

As much as a couple of nights a week, Lily soon found herself staying in Seb's lovely extended Victorian terraced house in Fulham with its walled back garden that seemed to capture the late-evening sun. On occasion Seb wasn't there, but when he was he became a fatherlike figure to Lily. His girlfriend Julie often stayed over as well, and she and Lily became good friends. She knew the score, that Seb was looking after Lily for Guy, so there was no jealousy, and in the back of Lily's mind there was always the hope that she might bump into Guy – it had been six weeks now – but while at Seb's, she never did.

But she did bump into Keir.

'Hallo there.' He grabbed her arm and swung her round. They were at a party in Mayfair for a friend of Andy McVay's. Lily noticed he'd lost weight but she supposed he looked good in a rakish sort of way. In fact, she was right about the rakish bit. Keir was currently at a loose end and waiting for the next series of *Ace Driving* to get underway as all other offers of work he'd received had somehow or other fizzled out; Keir had slipped into *Ace Driving* like a dream, but other roles just didn't suit him and he was at a low ebb and consequently putting himself about at every opportunity. As his clothes became more and more expensive, and his tastes in food and wine and whisky more refined, his women became more numerous.

'Keir,' she said breathlessly. His eyes slithered up and down her body as he noted the short skirt and endless tanned legs. Her hair seemed to grace her gorgeous face then fall on to her shoulders. She looked divine. Keir, by now quite used to women easily surrendering to his charms, stroked her arm and pulled her closer. He was even tempted to move right in and kiss her. It wouldn't be the first time he'd approached a woman as directly at parties, but something held him back. Maybe the flash of annoyance in her eyes and the sudden backward step she took.

'Where have you been, Lily? I go to all these parties, which you've supposedly organised, and I never see you!'

She smiled. 'I can't be at them all, Keir. It was part of the deal tonight. Our esteemed host insisted I be here.'

'That's because a glimpse of you sets the seal on any occasion.' His eyes never left her face and again Lily noticed their slightly glazed look. 'So how's life treating you? No boyfriends or anything?' Guy still nagged at his thoughts. 'A lover or two, perhaps?'

'The only love I have is my work.' Lily moved to one side, ready to make a quick exit. 'Perhaps I'll see you later,' she added politely. 'I think I'm needed in the kitchen now.'

He grabbed her and held on quite firmly. 'No, you're not! Your job's out here, keeping the likes of me happy.' He turned towards the hostess of the party. 'I'm sure if you ask her she'll agree.' He tapped Lily's nose. 'So, no excuses, young lady, you can stay with me a while longer. Besides, I've got something very important to ask you.'

She looked surprised. 'Have you? What's that?'

He frowned and suddenly appeared childlike. 'To have dinner with me next week?' Immediately he saw the expression on her face. 'No, don't refuse me before you hear me out. I shall be in Cambridge next week – there are a lot of important people in Cambridge – and I've been invited to dine at Midsummer House with Andy and a few of his cronies. You know, backers. Bigtime wealth there, Lily, folk looking to spend their money. I thought you might like to join me?' He grabbed her arm again, sliding his fingers down to her hand. He squeezed it. 'Please, it's just dinner. No strings. There'll be about eight of us. Who knows what business you might drum up because of it? Do say yes?'

All her instincts told her to say no. She stared at him and mumbled, 'I don't think so.'

'Why not? It's business. Just business. And I promise I'll take good care of you.' He held up his hands. 'How could I not? It'll be good for me arriving with you, I'll be the envy of every man there, and it'll be good for you too. We'll both be doing each other an enormous favour. And I'd be flattered if you'd accompany me. Very flattered.'

She thought of Guy. He'd hate this. Probably never speak to her again. But for nearly two months now she'd heard absolutely nothing from him. In fact her anger at this had been instrumental in deadening some of the pain. She looked into Keir's forlorn face and made a swift decision. 'Okay. Give me a ring.'

He drew her into his arms and kissed her. She didn't pull back. There was no need, the kiss was over too quickly, but he did whisper in her ear, 'You won't regret this, Lily. I promise you won't.'

She was to remember those words.

Chapter Forty-Two

As soon as Guy walked into his flat the phone rang. Immediately his heart lifted. Even now, after so many weeks, he still hoped it would be Lily. He picked up the receiver.

'Doing anything tonight?'

He laughed. How could he resist this voice? He warmed to it immediately. 'Jane, how did you know I was here? I've just walked through the door.'

Pure chance, but she wasn't about to say that to him. 'Suffice it to say I have an extra sense where you're concerned, Guy Hamilton. Now, answer me, are you doing anything tonight, or are you too important to remember your old friend Jane?'

'Darling, I could never be so important as to forget you. You taught me all I know, for God's sake.'

'It's too early in the evening to start talking dirty, Guy. Are you doing anything tonight?'

He took a deep breath. He really had intended to call Lily. Visit her even. He just couldn't stop thinking about her. Time had made him realise that he should just swallow his pride and go back there, on bended knee if needs be. 'Nope. What had you in mind?'

'A simple dinner, at Midsummer House.' What she omitted to say was that she'd been let down. Ringing Guy had been pure speculation. Jane was like that. She just did things on a whim.

'Is this a tie job?'

'We're past all that, Guy. You can just have me on the back seat.'

He laughed and arranged to pick her up at eight-thirty.

Midsummer House, facing Midsummer Common and backing on to the river, is by many considered Cambridge's finest restaurant. A converted, rather intimate house, diners can find themselves on one of three floors, but the ground floor luxuriantly spilling out into a glazed Victorian-style conservatory is perhaps the most enchanting.

Lily had never eaten there before. When Keir picked her up promptly at seven-thirty she was looking forward to her evening. As the weather was warm, she'd opted to wear a simple cream silk fitted dress with a flouncy hemline and Keir looked smart but understated in a beige linen suit with white shirt and pale tie. He was gentlemanly in the extreme, only making polite conversation, and made no comment whatsoever about her appearance which actually set his pulses racing. As he normally fawned over her, she assumed he was on his best behaviour, wanting to impress his fellow diners. She'd go along with that. Lily wanted to impress them as well.

As they entered Midsummer House they were immediately shown to their table right in the middle of the conservatory overlooking a picturesque paved terrace. Everybody was there, Lily and Keir being the last to arrive. It crossed her mind that this had been deliberate and she noticed how gracious Keir was to the mainly male group of people. There were actually two other females, wives Lily later found out. Andy McVay had not brought along a partner but she noticed he automatically shuffled round, expecting Keir to sit next to him, which he did. Lily was seated on Keir's other side next to a much older man, Harry, who made a point of including her in his lively conversation.

And so the evening began smoothly. Lily noticed that Keir drank very little and was in fact good company. He seemed to come out with all the right anectodes, laugh loudly at any witticisms and be extremely charming into the bargain. It wasn't long before she relaxed.

It was a change in his expression that alerted her to the fact that something was not quite right. His eyes suddenly showed alarm and were fixed on the entrance to the restaurant. Lily's eyes followed his and she froze. Framed there, looking extremely handsome, was Guy, in the process of being shown to a table further back. With him was Jane Richardson. Lily's heart lurched. At first Guy didn't notice them, but when he did there were no smiles. His face blackened and his expression became thunderous.

'If looks could kill,' whispered Keir. 'I think if he gets the chance he'll thump me again. Maybe have a go at knocking all my teeth out this time!'

Lily didn't know what to say. Guy had deliberately averted his eyes without even acknowledging her. Was this how things were to become? She bristled and was tempted to cross the room just to make him say hallo.

'You know, he really hates me.' Keir grinned. 'Even more so because I'm with you.'

She noticed the glee in his eyes, but by this time the whole of their table was looking across at Guy. Harry asked, 'Isn't that the presenter on Nirvana's new production? The one who flies the helicopter . . . what's it called?' Somebody said *Top Speed*.

'Hmm,' mused Andy McVay, mouth twisting into a smirk. 'And I see his temperament hasn't improved. Watch it, you lot, he's likely to explode.'

This caused several joking comments and Lily was annoyed they all saw fit to poke fun when they hardly knew Guy. She spoke out. 'Actually, he's my cousin!'

There was a brief silence and everyone looked at her. In fact, it was as though the whole of the restaurant was looking at her, including Guy. She reddened and took a sip of wine.

'Is that right?' asked Andy.

Keir cut in, 'But only through adoption.'

Lily look angrily at him. 'Why did you say that?'

His perfect poise was slightly dented. 'It's the truth! Although I didn't mean to offend you, Lily.'

'I'm not offended, I just don't think it's a fair comment.'

'Too true!' added one of the wives. 'I'm adopted and I know how it feels.' She smiled at Lily.

Keir put in, 'But it's not Lily who's adopted, it's Guy.'

She took a deep breath and decided not to say anything else. Andy McVay spoke instead. 'So how do you get along with your *cousin*? He wasn't particularly friendly towards you when he walked in just now.'

She cringed. Thankfully Keir came to her rescue. 'Oh, that's because of me! I'm anathema to Guy Hamilton. You should know that, Andy.'

310

He smiled fondly at Keir then leaned across him to speak to Lily. 'But truthfully now, Lily, how do you get on with Guy?'

'Very well, actually.'

Andy pulled a face then sat back in his seat. It obviously wasn't the answer he'd hoped for. Lily's eyes stayed on his face and it flashed through her mind that maybe, just maybe, he was jealous of Seb for snapping up Guy. After all, his performance on *Top Speed* was proving to be extraordinarily good, like a breath of fresh air.

The evening wore on and she tried not to look at Guy. When she simply couldn't stop herself she noticed his eyes seemed glued to Jane and their conversation was intimate. Later she excused herself and walked across the restaurant floor to the stairs, heading for the ladies' room. Even though she didn't dare look in his direction, Lily felt sure his eyes were now following her. She went up the stairs quickly, found the ladies' and locked the door. She stared at her own reflection in the mirror and hated herself. If she'd known that tonight, of all nights, Guy would walk into this restaurant she'd never have accepted Keir's invitation. And then she reflected upon this. Why ever not? Guy didn't own her. Tonight he had barely acknowledged her even. She refreshed her lipstick then slowly made her way downstairs. It was as she alighted from the bottom step that she came face to face with him and this time he really did glare at her. 'Guy,' she said in a strained voice. 'Why are you looking at me like that?' He stepped to one side and put a foot on the stairs to pass her. '*Guy, please?*'

He pointed across the room. 'Because of *him*, Lily.'

'But this is business and . . .' She was actually close to tears. 'You could at least acknowledge me. I haven't heard from you in weeks – and it's not my fault if Keir is your enemy.'

He scowled at her. 'It's always business with you, isn't it, Lily?

'As far as he's concerned, yes, it is.'

'Well, go back to him then! It's obviously where you like to be.' Guy continued up the stairs, two at a time. Lily stood quite still, his words ringing in her ears. Finally she took a few paces forward, hesitated, and looked towards the restaurant door. She could make her escape now. When Guy returned he'd see she was gone. Then she looked across the room to her party and all of them, every single one of them, had their eyes on her. Trembling, she made her way back to them.

Keir stood up and squeezed her arm as she sat down. He sat down again and put his face close to hers. 'Are you all right? You look a bit shaken.' Outwardly he looked concerned but inside he was elated. He'd seen it all. Guy must have blown it now. The coast was clear for him to move in. There was no way this gorgeous female would stomach that sort of treatment.

'Cousin or no cousin, I think Guy Hamilton should be taught a few manners,' declared Andy. Nobody spoke so he continued, 'It's obvious the sort of person he is. I mean, reducing a member of his own family to . . . well,' he looked at Lily, 'I hate to say this, ducky, but a quivering mess. And in front of all these people! And just because he's jealous of the company you keep.'

Lily narrowed her eyes. Something inside her hardened. Next to Keir, Andy McVay was the man she disliked most in the world. She stood up decisively. 'Will you excuse me?' There was stunned silence as she slung her handbag over her shoulder and started to leave the room once more. Keir was beside her in a flash.

'Lily! Where are you going?'

She faced him. 'Home, Keir. I should never have come here with you in the first place.'

He looked astounded. 'But you can't go home. At least, not yet.'

Trying her hardest to fight back the tears, she added, 'Please, just go back to your friends and let me go home. I'm sorry if I've spoiled your evening but . . .' Her eyes fixed on Guy who'd returned and was moving back to his table. Fleetingly he glanced in her direction and she noticed the anger still in his eyes. She hated him then for treating her in such a way. 'I need to go home.'

Seething now, Keir looked towards Guy. 'How could you let him screw you up like this? He's not worth it, Lily.' Her eyes flashed at this, and once more she looked at Guy who was staring at them both, obviously aware that something was amiss. Lily was tempted to shout across the room, Yes, see what you've done? This is all your fault! Instead, she looked once more at Keir, then pushed past him to leave the room. He grabbed her arm. 'I'll take you.'

'No! I don't want you to. Please, Keir. Go back to your friends.' She tugged her arm free and made for the door. Still he followed. 'Just let me go! This was all a mistake.'

'The only mistake you're making is allowing that man to mess up your evening.'

She rounded on him. 'He hasn't! It's not him, it's me and you.' She looked back towards the room. 'And all this. It just isn't me, Keir. I don't belong here with you and your friends. Just let me go. I want to go.'

'Then let me take you.'

'No! I don't want you to.'

'Why? Am I so repugnant?'

'No, of course you're not.' Lily opened the front door of the restaurant and started to walk down the path to Midsummer Common. Still he pursued her.

'Lily! Please don't go like this. Please?'

But she didn't answer or look back, just gripped her handbag and quickened her pace until she was running across the Common, running and running, making her way towards Maids Causeway on the opposite side. She was aware that many eyes were on her as she ran but her feet were flying now across the grass and Keir knew he'd be a fool to follow. Finally, feeling a crashing idiot, he returned to his party. It crossed his mind that once again Guy Hamilton had scored a major point over him.

Chapter Forty-Three

When Guy dropped Jane home later, her parting words were, 'You broke that poor girl's heart this evening. Nobody runs off like that, in such a frantic way, for nothing. I really think you owe her an apology, Guy.'

He stared straight ahead, out of the car window, into the darkness. He didn't want to talk to Jane about his relationship with Lily, just needed to think about it; to analyse his own feelings and understand his continued anger at Keir. After all, he didn't need to be angry anymore. Guy was doing a job he loved and the bitterness and hurt of his marriage to Naomi and Keir's part in its ending had faded completely by now. But maybe it wasn't Keir he was angry with – maybe it was just Lily?

The following day he rang her. There was no reply but the answer machine gave another Cambridge number so he rang that. Cassie, in the office above the florist's shop, picked up the phone and when Guy asked to speak to Lily, recognised his voice immediately. 'She's not here, Guy. This is Cassie. Lily's taken a short break.'

'Oh, hallo, Cassie.' He came straight to the point. 'What do you mean, a short break?'

'A holiday. On the coast.'

'Which coast? Where?'

Cassie drew a deep breath. Knowing how bitterly upset Lily had been the previous evening over Guy's treatment of her in the restaurant, she wasn't sure whether her friend would want him to know where she was. Who was she trying to kid? Of course she would. 'Southwold. I believe you know it well?'

Guy pulled a face. 'Southwold? Lily's gone there?'

'Yes. Why not?'

Why not indeed? 'But aren't all the family there at this time of the year?'

Cassie hesitated. 'Maybe she needs some company. Maybe things are getting her down.'

Guy recognised he was being ticked off. 'Yes, I was pretty foul to her last night. I suppose she told you all about it?'

'Correct.'

'Not you as well, Cassie. I thought you of all people would understand how I feel about Keir?'

'Oh, Guy, don't give me that. Yes, I understand how you feel about him, I just wish I understood how you feel about Lily.'

'But that's ridiculous. You must know I'm . . . I'm in love with her.'

'Well, you sure have a funny way of showing it!'

'I know, I know. I behaved appallingly. Correction, I keep behaving appallingly! That's why I have to speak to her. To apologise. It's okay, I'll ring the house at Southwold.'

'Or, better still, you could get in that monster of a car of yours and zip down there to see her. Apologise to her face. Now *that* would be cool.'

He sighed. There was no reason, no reason whatsoever, why he couldn't do just that. He'd got three whole days with nothing to do. Three days. But the thought of spending them with various members of the Hamilton family at their house in Southwold, albeit situated in South Green overlooking the sea, did not appeal. 'Who's down there anyway?'

Cassie hesitated. 'My advice to you is – take a chance.'

'What do you mean, take a chance?'

'Just go, Guy. Go!'

'Okay, I might. Thanks, Cassie. Speak to you soon.'

She replaced the receiver and buried her face in her hands.

Guy didn't waste any time. He packed a few spare clothes, climbed into his car and set off at a cracking pace for Southwold on the Suffolk coast. It took little over an hour for him to get there and as he approached nostalgia gripped him in a way he hadn't expected. First the magnificent fifteenth-century church of St Edmund with its splendid flint decorations seemed to welcome him warmly. It was like dipping into the better part of his childhood. Then, as he drove further into the narrow streets where in bygone years only fishermen had lived, he reflected upon what an idyllic place Southwold really was with its spankingly clean cluster of red and yellow brick, flint or brightly washed houses topped with pantiled, slate and pegtiled roofs. Quite slowly now, he twisted and turned and made a point of driving along North Parade alongside the well-kept promenade with its neat row of gloriously painted beach-huts and wondered if *Tipsy Bill* was still there, or whether the family's bright yellow hut had been sold off. He'd heard they fetched a good price these days.

And now back into the town centre, past the Swan Hotel in Market Place and left towards South Green, one of the nine greens in Southwold, where he parked next to Lily's white Cavalier at the rear of the Hamiltons' two-storey, plus attic, nineteenth-century house. It was large, to say the least, with four enormous bedrooms – five with the attic – a light and airy kitchen, an equally enormous dining room and sitting room, with bay windows looking out on to the sea. Many a festive family Christmas had been spent here. The exterior walls of the house were painted brilliant white and all the woodwork a pale apple-green. Always had been for as long as he could remember. He noticed now that everywhere looked fresh, newly decorated in fact. He did admire his family for that, they certainly knew how to look after property.

As he walked towards the back door beneath a porch draped lavishly with wisteria he turned and considered the fact that there was only Lily's car outside. Perhaps the rest of them had gone out? He tried the door. In the past it had always been open, nobody ever locked it, there was simply no need. Different members of the family were always there. He turned the knob and much to his surprise found it locked. Guy stood back and surveyed the house, raising his eyes to the bedrooms above. Absolutely no sign of life whatsoever. He stepped further back, deciding to follow a narrow passageway between this property and the next, leading to the front of the house. Here he caught his breath at the sight of the well-established prolific garden meandering down to a small flint wall facing on to the promenade. His eye went even further out to the glistening sea and he wondered if in all his life he'd ever seen anything so glorious? This was quickly followed by the answer yes, because as he gazed at the blissful scenery he saw something much more glorious – beautiful, in fact – and his heart practically jumped into his mouth. He wanted to rush forward and sweep her into his arms. He was reminded of a similar occasion years ago in Ely's Hayward Theatre. She'd had the same effect on him then.

Lily, feeling refreshed after a lengthy amble along the beach, unlatched the gate and started to walk up the path to the house. Wearing a simple pair of white shorts and a skimpy black mid-riff t-shirt, carrying her sandals in one hand, she didn't notice Guy. He was actually moving towards her before she saw him. In surprise she dropped her sandals and bent quickly to pick them up. By the time she straightened herself he was standing so close she actually thought he was going to kiss her. He didn't, although he thought about it. 'Lily.' There was pain in his voice.

'Guy, what are you doing here?'

He took a deep breath. 'Can't you guess?' He ran his fingers through his hair. 'I came to apologise . . . for last night. I spoke to Cassie this morning and she said you were here, so to cut a long story short here I am.' He searched her face and in the sunlight her eyes looked distinctly green, and angry, until she moved. Then he wondered how he could have ever thought they were green, they were as blue as the ocean.

She moved away, walking towards the front door, withdrawing a key from her pocket. He followed, realising she wasn't going to forgive him as easily as that. 'Where's everybody?' he asked.

She turned towards him. 'Everybody?'

'The rest of them. The family.'

She put her key into the lock, twisted it, pushed on the apple-green door and stepped inside. Guy followed, recognising the familiar smell of beach and polish. He loved this smell, it meant *holidays* and sent a tingle of well-being through him. 'Nobody's here, Guy. That's why I came. I needed a break.'

Cassie's words came flooding back. *Take a chance.* 'Nobody? Nobody at all?'

'Nope. Not until next week.'

'That's unusual, isn't it?'

She looked at him. 'No. The house is often empty these days.' She threw her sandals on the stone-flagged floor and walked towards the kitchen. 'But as you're never around, I suppose we can't expect you to know that.'

317

'Well, it was never empty before. That's the one thing I remember about this place. It always teemed with family!'

She looked at him again reproachfully. 'Only during peak holiday times, Guy. And Christmas, of course.'

'Oh, I see. In that case I stand corrected.' He pushed his hands into his pockets and followed her through to the kitchen where she proceeded to put the kettle on.

'Do you fancy a cup of coffee?'

He grinned. 'A beer would be nicer.'

She shrugged. 'There isn't any. I'll go shopping later ... if you're staying, that is?'

He breathed in and looked at her. 'Do you mind? If I stay, I mean?'

She turned away from him so he couldn't see the overwhelming relief and happiness in her eyes or the rise and fall of her chest. Crisply she said, 'Suit yourself.'

'Well, I'd certainly like to. It'd give us a chance to talk. I need to talk to you, Lily. It's long overdue.'

She wanted to turn and throw herself into his arms. Instead she smiled secretly and knew that at long last she was going to catch up with Cassie. She'd make damn' sure of that.

They wandered down to the Red Lion. Neither of them was hungry, but Guy drank Adnam's beer and Lily a spritzer. She was still wearing her shorts and cut-off t-shirt and Guy had changed into shorts as well. For a while, it seemed safer to talk idly about this and that, not to mention the previous evening, then drift back into comfortable silence. But as the sun grew hotter and hotter Lily became anxious to move back to the cool of their own private garden. As they strolled back to the family home, Guy feared a major showdown but he was wrong. Lily went straight upstairs, changed into a bikini then stretched out on a sunbed beneath an enormous parasol in the garden. He did likewise, next to her, but while she appeared to sleep, he kept his eyes ahead, watching the passers-by on the promenade and the magnificent glittering grey North Sea. He was at peace with himself, but also desperately wanting to put things right with the young woman lying beside him. He looked at her, lying on her stomach, and noticed the curves of her body, her satin smooth skin the colour of toffee and the gloss of her hair. How could he have ever walked away? Her

318

face was hidden and he assumed she was sleeping. He wanted to touch her, to explain how he felt.

He started to speak, even though he thought she might not hear. 'You know, this house brings back so many memories – golden memories now. In fact it seems ridiculous to think how I've fought against the Hamilton family tie bit, but it was simply because I never got over the fact that I was the odd one out, the adopted one. There were so damned many of you and I always felt I didn't fully belong. That's why, as soon as I could, I escaped. To get peace of mind.' He snorted. 'But you know all this, Lily, don't you? You must be sick and tired of hearing about it. So I'll get to the point. That night, when we fell out, I wanted you so much and, like an idiot, I couldn't see that you had needs too.' Guy hesitated, considering his next words very carefully. 'And all this Keir business . . . I want to forget it. He doesn't matter anymore. I suppose one of my problems is, you're so much younger than me, Lily. 'He touched her hair. 'But if you're prepared to forgive me, I really would like to try again . . . Lily, are you awake? Are you listening?'

She raised her face and stroked the hair from her eyes. 'Yes, I'm listening.'

'Can we try again?'

She shifted, twisting so that she faced him. He noticed the rise of her breasts and wanted to touch them, kiss them. She interrupted his train of thought. 'Remember you said that when we made love, you wanted it to be somewhere private? Well, is this private enough for you?'

He smiled and glanced towards the promenade. 'Aren't you a bit worried about the passers-by?'

Playfully she dug him in the ribs. 'I'm game if you are.'

He moved off his sunbed and pulled her up next to him, wrapping his arms completely around her. 'I think we'll go indoors, if you don't mind.' He felt her breath caress his neck as she sighed and he lowered his face to kiss her.

She pulled away slightly. 'The thing is, I have no real experience of lovemaking, you know. You might be disappointed. Maybe that's why I sought the comfort of my own bedroom.'

He kissed her forehead and wondered what exactly no experience meant. 'You don't need experience, Lily. Real lovemaking isn't taught.'

319

She found herself being pulled back into his arms and drawn towards the house. Oh, Cassie, she thought, dear sweet Cassie. You were right all along.

Afterwards, when they lay in each other's arms, still stroking and gently kissing each other, it was as though each was very, very slowly building up to doing the same thing over again. During that long afternoon, Guy repeatedly told Lily he loved her, and repeatedly told her she must never again leave his side. And Lily, well, Lily just couldn't imagine ever being without him. She was awakened now and knew she'd never be able to get enough of him in the future.

During the following two days their cars remained behind the house and the lives of the two lovers slowed to a pace vastly different from anything they'd grown used to. Neither wanted to leave their paradise. They took long walks along the shingle beach, ate leisurely dinners at the Swan and the Crown, bought food from the local shops as they meandered around, and generally lazed within the Hamiltons' holiday home. Nobody rang and they rang nobody. It seemed as though a lifetime was slotted into three blissful days, but in reality it was over in a flash.

'It's incredible. Somehow or other within my busy schedule of filming I had three free days and you just happened to have the same ones. Considering how things have been, what an amazing stroke of luck.'

She smiled. 'And in some ways we have Keir to thank for getting us together again.'

As they lay side by side in the master bedroom overlooking the sea, Guy put his forefinger over Lily's mouth. 'Tell you what, let's not talk about him?'

She pouted. 'But he's nothing to us. Why turn him into something so important he can't be mentioned?'

Guy had to think about this. 'I suppose that's female logic, is it?'

'No, I just don't want anything in our relationship to be taboo.'

He laughed. 'True, Lily.' Then he feasted his eyes on her again. 'So, we'll have no taboos?'

'None.' Her eyes darkened. 'Can I ask you something?'

'Anything. Nothing's taboo, remember?'

'In that case . . . why did you make love to Cassie?'

Guy's brow puckered and immediately he looked uncomfortable. Lily watched him swallow and turn on to his back. 'Is this necessary, Lily? I don't intend to ask you about previous lovers.'

'I haven't had any.'

Narrowing his eyes, he looked at her. 'None? You were a virgin?'

She pouted. 'Not technically.'

He tweaked her cheek. 'What's that supposed to mean?'

Her face clouded over. 'I had a bad time with one of my teachers at school. At the time I thought . . . well, I really thought he cared. I let him get too close and he took advantage. I was a fool.'

Guy shifted closer, feeling cold with outrage at what she implied. He wanted to protect her. Gently he ran his hand over her face. 'He didn't—'

'Didn't what?' Lily saw the horror in his eyes and quickly shook her head. 'No, he didn't rape me. But he . . . I suppose he seduced me when he ought not to have done.'

'Oh, Lily.' Guy studied her face and reflected upon her beauty and their lovemaking. He wondered how anyone so pure could have let a schoolteacher get so close. Then he recalled the child of yesteryear dancing at their grandpa's birthday party. So ingenuous, so innocent in her approach. Men would always take advantage of that. Hadn't he himself over the last few days? In fact, it was half the thrill. And with each new day she was more exciting; it was like watching a flower unfurl. Softly he asked, 'And he only did it the once?'

'Yes. I never let him near me again.' She buried her face against him. 'After that, I stayed away from men. Then I got stuck on you, as Cassie would say.' She poked Guy's chest. 'So tell me, why did you and she get together like that?'

He braced himself, not wanting to talk about it. 'It just happened, Lily. Two people hungry for sex, if you like. That's all there is to say.' He kissed her forehead where the hair was still damp from their lovemaking.

'But she loves you.'

He was silent and thought about Cassie. He knew she loved him. He also knew she'd been a good friend to both of them and it didn't seem right to be discussing her this way. 'She's your best friend, Lily. Don't let's talk about her like this.'

She looked up at him. 'You love her too, don't you?'

He drew back and blinked. 'I care for her but it's nothing like the feeling I have for you.'

'Honestly? You won't dump me for her one day?'

He laughed softly. 'No. Oh, Lily, you've got a lot to learn about me. You're not by any chance jealous, are you?'

'Madly. It's such a contradiction. I love Cassie so much, and yet I'd kill her if she came anywhere near you now.'

'Well, you won't have to. She's quite safe. Because I'm never going to leave your side, for as long as you live. I promise.'

'So what'll we do now? I mean, you're off again tomorrow and so am I. Our lives are impossible. How do we maintain a relationship when we're both flying about all over the place?'

Guy sighed. 'Live together, I suppose. At least then we each go back to the same home. Would you consider that?'

She pondered a while. 'Yes.'

'Well, you don't look too sure?'

'Oh, I'm sure. It's just, well, I'm an old-fashioned girl from an old-fashioned family.'

He shifted back and studied her and considered the family implication. The last thing he wanted was to offend the Hamiltons. 'So what do you suggest?'

She looked so childlike. Her magical eyes switched from green to blue then back to their wicked green again. 'You could marry me?'

A familiar pain stabbed his chest. 'Oh, Lily. I'm not sure I'm ready for all that again. Really I'm not.'

'Why?'

He saw the flicker of hurt in her eyes. Hurriedly he tried to explain. 'Because last time was a disaster. I'm scared stiff of marriage. What we've got is brilliant. Why ruin something special? We don't need a piece of paper to unite us.'

'But I do. I've always liked weddings. Every girl does.'

He frowned and propped himself on one elbow. Weddings? 'When you say married, you surely don't mean the full works? Church, big white dress, the lot?'

'Well, don't look so surprised. Why ever not?'

'Because I can't! I'm divorced – and I'm not such a hypocrite.' Slowly he shook his head. 'No way, Lily.' He watched her freeze and pull away from him. Guy reached out and pulled her back.

322

'I'm sorry. I'll marry you if that's what you really want, but there's no way I'm going through all that wedding stuff again. It's a circus. I hated it. You must know I hate big parties?'

'No, I didn't.'

He rubbed his nose against her hers. 'Well, you do now. If we marry, it'll have to be quietly. No fuss. I'm sorry but that's the way I feel, and I'm not being pushed into something again that just doesn't feel right.'

This was the first time in nearly three days that he'd opposed anything she said. Lily stared at his resolute expression and realised that on this occasion she wasn't going to win. But she wanted him so much; wanted him to be hers and for the world to know. She shrugged. 'Okay. I'll settle for a register office do.'

He laughed out loud and pulled her even closer, cradling her as though she was precious. 'God, I love you, Lily. I'm so lucky to have found you.'

'You didn't find me,' she protested happily. 'I was born just for you.'

Chapter Forty-Four

'It's okay. I know what you're going to say.' Cassie moved swiftly across the office towards the window looking out on St Andrew's Street. Until she composed herself, she couldn't bear to see the bloom on her best friend's face. It meant satisfaction. Fulfilment. Everything she herself craved. Cassie braced herself and turned with a smile, holding out her arms, and Lily walked right into them. 'Didn't I tell you to hang on? Didn't I just say so?'

Lily looked into her friend's eyes, seeing the hurt there and the contrasting stoic resolve to accept the inevitable. 'Yes, you did.' She shook her head, unable to restrain the words of joy she wanted to share with Cassie. 'But I never expected it to be like this.'

'Pretty sensational, huh?'

'You could say that.'

Cassie squeezed her hand. 'I am pleased for you, Lily. Truly.'

She looked around the office, almost embarrassed to show her true feelings and grateful that nobody else was there. 'Things been busy, have they?'

'Yes. Took several more bookings.' She tapped Lily's arm. 'Got some catching up to do. Somebody wants a medieval party, and somebody else wants a blue one.'

'A blue one! How on earth am I going to organise blue food?'

Cassie grinned. 'I was joking about that one.'

'Oh, Cassie.' Lily squeezed her friend again. 'Where would I be without you?'

'I think you'd cope.' She laughed and moved away slightly. 'So, do I get to hear all the details?' She turned and caught Lily's eye. 'Or on this occasion will you keep them to yourself?'

Lily took a deep breath. She and Guy were now strictly private. 'He's wonderful, Cassie. It's as simple as that.'

Cassie smiled. Of course. She already knew as much.

They were saved from further conversation by Daisy clattering into the office. She wore her perennial pink gingham overall, which for some reason she loved. She had three, and every evening one was carefully handwashed and hung out to dry, then carefully ironed the following evening. Probably for the first time in her life Daisy was really happy. As well as being Cassie's vocation, flowers had turned out to be Daisy's too. 'I thought I heard you arrive back. Did you have a great time? How was Southwold?'

Lily's eyes moved from her best friend to her sister. In a flash she realised Daisy knew nothing about Guy being with her at the family's holiday home. 'It was fantastic, Daisy. I had a ball.'

Cassie giggled and the two friends raised their eyebrows at each other. 'And guess who was there?' put in Cassie.

Daisy looked blank. She didn't like having to guess. 'Who?'

Lily walked towards her sister and gave her an enormous hug. 'Guy. It was Guy.'

Daisy's face was immediately suffused with pleasure. 'Guy was? Just you and him?' Her hand flew to her mouth. 'Oooh, really?'

'Yes, really. I had a fantastic time, Daisy.' She looked at Cassie. 'And I think you should both know ... we're getting married, only please keep it quiet. At least for a while.'

Cassie stopped breathing and Daisy threw her arms around her sister. 'You're marrying Guy? Oh, Lily! You lucky, lucky thing! I wish *I* was marrying him.' She looked across at Cassie. 'Don't you? Don't you wish you were marrying Guy?'

Breathing more easily now, Cassie smiled. 'I sure do.' She folded her arms, ignoring the pain inside her.

'So, did you sleep with him?' asked Daisy, looking with great interest at her sister.

'Daisy!'

'Oh, go on. Tell me. *Please*.'

''Course she did, ninny! What would you do if you'd had three days on your own with Guy Hamilton?'

Daisy's eyes widened. 'Oh, I'd definitely sleep with him.' Then her face clouded over. 'Except he wouldn't want me, would he?'

325

She quickly went on, 'So did you like it, Lily? Was it good this time?'

She took her sister's arm and started to guide her out of the room. 'It was absolutely wonderful, Daisy, but also very private so let's keep it that way. Now why don't you show me the flowers downstairs? Have you got any new ones in?'

Delightedly, Daisy began to tell Lily about the flowers in the shop, their correct names slipping easily off her tongue.

Cassie followed them downstairs with a heavy heart.

Lily moved into Guy's flat in Cambridge. Because of their busy lifestyles they had little time to look at properties elsewhere. Both of them half-wanted to move to London, but they also wanted to stay in Cambridge. The priority in Lily's life at the moment was her forthcoming marriage which they'd slotted in for immediately after the end of *Top Speed*'s run. It was to be a quiet affair at Cambridge's Shire Hall Register Office, with just immediate family and Cassie and Fred in attendance. Afterwards they'd booked an equally quiet lunch at the Cambridge Lodge, off Huntingdon Road, five minutes from the Register Office. Lily took great delight in buying a stunning outfit which Guy knew nothing about.

A couple of weeks before the big day she was both surprised and excited to read about her relationship with Guy in one of the Sunday newspapers. Neither of them knew anything about it in advance but the writer seemed to know plenty about them, there being a large coloured picture of the two of them shopping together in Cambridge, which neither had been aware was being taken, and extensive coverage of Guy's enormous appeal on television. There was also a lot said about Lily's beauty and the success of Fare & Flair. She showed the article to Guy, who pulled a face. 'Aren't you pleased?' she asked. 'It can only be good for you. I mean, it does show how much the viewers have taken you to their hearts.'

He shrugged. 'So long as it stops there. I don't want to feel I can't go shopping in Cambridge without pictures being taken. Isn't that why we like living here?'

'Is it?' She scrutinised the picture again. 'Although I do find it rather exciting.' She lowered the paper and smiled, proud to be the one with him. 'It says in here that we're deliriously happy.'

He pulled her to him and kissed her. 'Well, we are, so at least they've got their facts right.'

'It also says we're getting married. D'you think there will be photographers at Shire Hall on the day?'

Guy groaned. 'More than likely. Another circus!'

She nudged him. 'No, it won't be. It'll be special, Guy. I'm really looking forward to it.' He took the article from her and quickly perused it. 'Well?' she insisted. 'Aren't you?'

He looked at her and winked. 'Of course I am.' He threw the paper to one side and drew her into his arms. 'Seb's tickled pink. But I had to explain to him why he wasn't invited. He was upset.'

Lily hugged him before saying, 'I think, under the circumstances, it just wouldn't be right. The whole thing is too intimate. He'll get used to the idea . . . he'll understand.'

'And we'll have a *Top Speed* party later on.'

Lily grinned. 'And then I'll be Mrs Hamilton.' She kissed his nose. 'Makes a change from Miss Hamilton, don't you think?'

'Just a bit, Lily. Just a little bit.'

But it wasn't a little thing to Lily. She couldn't wait to become Mrs Hamilton. On the day itself she showered and dried her hair naturally then applied her make-up in the usual way. In anticipation she walked through to one of the spare bedrooms and opened the wardrobe door. Her dress was ankle-length and the colour of ivory; the fabric Shantung. Wild silk, the woman in the shop had said, and the texture of the weave enhanced the simplicity of its style. The low neckline showed the swell of Lily's breasts; three-quarter-length sleeves and close-fitting bodice, quite tight into the waist, following the curve of her body like a dream. All the way down the back were pink pearl buttons. It wasn't really a wedding dress, but with the veiled pill-box hat and satin shoes she chose to wear, would certainly look like it. She slipped into it then put on the hat, pulling out the veil to cover her eyes. Her hair she just flicked into place around her shoulders. Lily scrutinised her appearance and smiled, hoping Guy would like her choice of wedding attire. She left the bedroom and walked back into theirs, where she knew he was dressing.

'Well?' she asked standing framed in the doorway.

At first he caught sight of her in the mirror and immediately stopped what he was doing. Guy was looking at a vision of such

327

beauty he couldn't speak. He turned and stared at her before whispering her name as he walked forward, arms outstretched. 'You look magnificent! My God, how I love you.'

She was in his arms and kissing him rapturously, ruining her glossy pink lipstick without a care. 'Do you really like it? Honestly?'

He pushed her away slightly, holding her at arm's length. 'I adore it. You couldn't look more lovely, Lily. The hat, the dress—'

'In that case, I want you to know I don't care about the big white wedding bit. In fact I'm pleased we're doing it this way. I like it, really like it, because all I want is to be your wife. I'm thrilled, Guy. I'm really thrilled!'

He realised then how much he wanted to marry her. 'So am I, Lily. It's all I've wanted for so long.'

The photographers were out in force. Fred, *Top Speed*'s roving cameraman and now Guy's good friend, had offered to drive them to Shire Hall then film them after he'd parked his Discovery, which he'd cleaned especially for the occasion. As he approached he saw the throng outside, and the enormous crowd of curious onlookers. All he could do was drop the happy couple and it was quite a scramble from his vehicle to the Hall. Bulbs flashed, people shoved, and everybody seemed to shout out. It could have been mayhem except for Guy's swift thinking as he guided Lily forward, not stopping once. She would have been only too happy to slow down and speak to everyone but instinct told Guy not to do that.

Both Lily's and Guy's parents were already inside, and Daisy and Cassie. All they had to do was wait for Fred who soon arrived, filming everyone as he did so.

Cassie, in a pale pink suit, stood before her friend. She inclined her head and sighed. 'Wow!'

'I look okay then?'

'I'll say.'

Lily bent forward and kissed her cheek. 'Thanks.' She added in a whisper, 'True friend.'

Cassie squeezed her hand. 'I'm really happy for you, Lily.'

Lily knew she meant it.

*

Everything seemed perfect. The dash afterwards to the Cambridge Lodge was mildly annoying with photographers following, but once they were there the staff banned all intruders from entry so the small group of people was able to enjoy their wedding lunch without interference. Fred made everyone laugh until their sides ached with his jokes and tales of Guy's adventures while filming *Top Speed*. Other diners in the restaurant that day were entranced; this would be a talking point for a long time to come.

But all good things come to an end and as the lunch drew to a close Guy and Lily prepared to go back to their apartment in Newnham where their things were packed ready for their honeymoon in Barbados. They were leaving very early in the morning. As they departed from the restaurant there were many hugs and tears and finally they all braved Huntingdon Road and the tireless photographers. Fred, on Guy's instructions, soon managed to lose them. After many twists and turns he safely dropped his precious passengers off in Newnham. Not a soul was about. They were relieved and quickly went inside.

As soon as they were in the apartment Guy grabbed Lily, spinning her round. 'Come here, Mrs Hamilton, there's something I want to say to you.' She smiled and willingly allowed herself to be pulled into his arms. 'I'm so proud of you. There simply isn't enough room in my heart for the love I feel for you. I'm bursting with it, Lily. I'm such lucky man.'

She wrapped her arms around him and whispered, 'I don't believe you.'

This was her game and he willingly entered into the spirit of it, first burying his face against her neck and drinking in the scent of her hair. 'Do you want me to show you?

She stretched against him, squeezing her hands together behind his neck. 'Now how can you do that?'

In one movement he picked her up and carried her right through the apartment until he kicked the bedroom door closed behind him.

'Can I drive? Please, Guy?' The dawn was just breaking, the sun sneaking through a mottled sky.

He looked at his watch. 'We can't afford to hang about, Lily. Perhaps I should—'

She put her hands on her hips. 'Since when have I hung about?'

He smiled. 'Yes, well, there's driving and there's driving.'

'How can you say that? I drive really well. I'll have you know I passed my test after only one week's tuition.'

He smiled again. 'Okay. You drive.' He chuckled and threw her the keys. 'I can see you're starting married life as you mean to go on. Calling the shots.'

She grabbed them. 'Certainly am.' Then prodded him in the chest. 'You, Guy Hamilton, are going to be one hen-pecked husband.'

'Am I really? Well, I shall look forward to it. I just hope you lay lots of golden eggs.'

She hesitated and grinned. 'Would you like that? Little Hamiltons? Shall we start straight away?'

He kissed her gently on the mouth. 'Let's just get to Barbados first, shall we?'

She turned and picked up her bag. Guy stopped her. 'No, I'll carry that. It's much too heavy for you.'

'Guy, I'm not helpless. Before you came along, I had to carry my own bags.'

'Well, I'm here now, so you carry the smaller ones. I'll take these two. Come on, or we'll be late.'

Feeling thoroughly spoiled and loving it, she did as she was told.

Chapter Forty-Five

'We'd better stop and fill up with petrol before we hit the M11. There's a garage on our right up here, Lily, so pull in, okay?'

She manoeuvred Guy's Porsche to the centre of the road on the outskirts of Cambridge and waited for an oncoming car. It was just before six in the morning and the roads were relatively quiet. She crossed over and drew to a halt beside the super-unleaded petrol pump. He jumped out and filled the car, then went off to pay. Lily sat behind the wheel, tapping her hands against it, excited as a young child to be going on another holiday with the man of her dreams. She watched him as he emerged from the kiosk, a bag of mints in his hand, and smiled to herself.

'Fancy a mint?' he asked as he reseated himself and pulled down his belt, snapping it into place.

'Yes, please.' She smiled. 'Just now, as you walked towards me, I thought, Am I ever going to get used to having Guy? I must be the luckiest woman alive, do you know that?'

He glanced in her direction and winked. 'I'm truly glad you think so.' Then touched her face with the knuckle of his forefinger. Lily started up the engine and coasted out to turn right. There was a slight twist in the road ahead. Her vision wasn't all that clear but there appeared to be no oncoming traffic. As Guy threw the mints on to the footwell, having taken two out of the packet, Lily pulled out to cross the road.

The motor-cyclist seemed to loom up dramatically from nowhere, his speed way above anything sensible on such a road. As Lily gently moved the car forward, he was round the bend in a flash, thundering towards them at such a rate that all Guy remembered afterwards was looking up and something intimidatingly black about to hit them, which it did with such force that the cyclist himself was thrown completely across the road. The colossal thud and shattering of glass, the crunch of metal against metal, filled Guy's head as the Porsche was shunted sideways along the road. Lily's side of the car just buckled and all the air-bags were inflated. Then an eerie silence hung over the scene.

Immediately Guy looked at her, slumped against him, her wondrous hair actually resting on his shoulder. 'Lily! Oh, Christ, *Lily!*' he cried. He bent forward, his hand resting on the now deflated air-bag, instinct telling him not to try and move her. He rapidly released his own seatbelt, opened his car door and staggered out before scrambling round to her side, dully aware of an agonising pain in the lower part of his right leg. When he saw the impact of the motorbike on the driver's side of the car he was filled with horror and unaware of his own heart-rending screams for help.

It was mayhem with people arriving from everywhere, the screeching tyres of vehicles coming to a standstill, then sirens, everywhere sirens. First police cars and an ambulance, then another ambulance. In all of this Guy sat once more in the passenger seat of his car and gently, so gently, began stroking his wife's hair, telling her to hold on, that help was coming. 'Don't die on me, Lily,' he implored over and over again. 'For pity's sake, don't you dare die on me.' But anger overwhelmed him as he looked across the road at the motorcyclist who was now sitting up with a dazed expression on his face. Obviously his helmet and the black leathers he wore had saved him from serious injury.

'She's not dead! She's got a pulse, I checked it! For Christ's sake, she's not going to die! Tell me she's not dying?'

A paramedic looked compassionately at Guy as another guided him out of the car and into the ambulance, but he didn't want to leave Lily's side. 'She is coming too? She is, isn't she?'

'Yes, sir. She'll be with you. We just need to release her from the car. It's best you get into the ambulance, sir. Come on now. She'll be with you as soon as possible.'

And so he allowed himself to be taken away from her, heart filled with rage and disbelief and such pain for the abject, totally unnecessary suffering of his beloved. Guy wanted to weep with despair. But he couldn't.

*

'*Cassie!*' Guy's strangled pitiful voice alarmed her as she picked up the phone.

Startled, she almost dropped it. Only seconds before she'd been poring over a picture in the Sunday newspaper of Guy and Lily arriving at the Register Office the day before. 'Guy? What's the matter? Where are you, for God's sake?'

'You've got to get here, Cassie. Straight away. Tell everybody. Tell them for me, will you? Please, Cassie, *I just can't.*'

As a strange panic gripped her, she struggled to stay calm. 'What's happened, Guy? Where are you?'

'Addenbrooke's. I'm in Addenbrooke's. Oh, Christ, Cassie, this is awful and you've got to get here. *Please.*'

'Whereabouts in Addenbrooke's?'

A silence. 'I don't know. Just get here . . . Casualty, I suppose. Please, I can't talk anymore. Just get everybody here . . . quickly.' He put down the phone.

For a few seconds Cassie held the receiver against her shoulder, thinking, thinking. What had happened? She looked at her watch. It was nearly eight. They should have been at the airport by now, getting ready to fly off to Barbados. Quickly she dialled Lily's parents, racking her brain to think what on earth she could say to them. Whatever she said would worry them sick. It must be serious. Guy had sounded desperate.

She spoke as calmly as she could. 'Hallo, Stephen, this is Cassie.' There was a pause and it was as though he recognised the fear in her voice immediately. 'Look . . . I'm so sorry to alarm you but Guy has rung me. Something dreadful must have happened, we all need to get to Addenbrooke's.' Stephen bombarded her with questions, none of which she could answer. Her own voice cracking now, she pleaded, 'Please, just get to the hospital as soon as possible.' Cassie rang off. There was nothing else she could do. She did the same thing with Guy's parents, and finally went through to the kitchen to tell Daisy.

By the time Cassie and Daisy arrived at the hospital and had been told by the staff about the accident, Guy had been sedated and appeared quite calm. Lying on a trolley-bed in a side-room in Casualty, waiting to be moved to X-ray for a suspected cracked fibula, he hardly raised his head as they walked in. Daisy, bewildered, just followed in the footsteps of Cassie who appeared to be in total control.

'Guy,' she said softly, putting a hand on his shoulder. 'We got here as quickly as we could.' She moved closer and carefully sat on the bed, placing a gentle hand on top of his. Daisy just stood behind her, noting that Guy hadn't acknowledged them in any way whatsoever. He looked grey and frightening and Daisy wondered if she was going to be able to stop herself from crying.

He raised his face, looking earnestly at Cassie. 'For Christ's sake, can you get me some cigarettes?' Her eyes widened and she turned to Daisy who nodded and wandered off, pleased in a way to be able to get out of the room. Guy shifted uncomfortably and Cassie noticed that the lower part of his right leg was badly bruised.

'They told me about the accident, Guy. I'm so sorry. And Lily . . . ?'

He looked at her then, his eyes, normally mesmerising, dark with horror. 'They're operating on her now. Christ, Cassie, if she dies, I just don't know what I'll do!'

She gripped his hand. 'She won't die, Guy. Of course she won't.'

Just briefly there was hope in his eyes, but it faded rapidly and he turned away. 'It was all too good to be true, I should have seen the signs . . . it was all too bloody good to be true.'

'Oh, Guy, of course it wasn't. Don't say that. Just hang on. It'll be okay, I promise. It'll be okay.'

'But you didn't see her, Cassie. *You didn't see her.*' For a few seconds she was speechless then Daisy returned with the cigarettes which Guy grabbed from her. Daisy bit her lip and fought back the tears. 'Matches? Did you get any matches?' He looked at her and in a flash recognised the terror on her wretched face. It frightened him even more and he rapidly turned away and looked at Cassie. 'I need some matches, Cassie, *please.*'

She grabbed her handbag and rummaged round inside, grateful she'd always made a habit of picking up complimentary packets of matches in restaurants. She passed one over to Guy who lit the cigarette with trembling hands. He sucked on it for dear life, inhaling and lolling his head against the pillows.

A porter arrived with a wheelchair. 'Are you ready, sir? For X-ray?' With the cigarette in his mouth Guy started to shift off the bed, wincing with pain, and the porter was beside him in no time. 'No pressure, sir. Charge-nurse said no pressure.' Guy hopped with one arm around the porter's shoulders to the wheelchair. He sat down heavily and drew once more on his cigarette. 'Can't have that, sir. You'll have to put it out.'

Cassie watched Guy, who for a split-second looked as though he might cry. He turned to her and handed over the cigarette. 'We'll stay here, shall we?' she asked.

The porter looked at her. 'You can come if you like. It's not far.' Then he studied Daisy and his face broke into a smile. 'Hey, don't I know you?' He was grinning now. 'Yes, I remember you, you broke your foot. I'm Harry, remember?'

For a brief second Daisy's face flushed with a mixture of gratitude and relief. Cassie watched as she gravitated towards the porter. 'Hallo, Harry. Yes, that's right. I'm Daisy.' Very sadly she looked down at Guy who held his head in his hands. She put a trembling forefinger to her mouth and whispered, 'It's my sister, Lily, she's been hurt in an accident.'

Harry nodded and squeezed her arm. 'She'll be all right. Follow me, Daisy, we're off now.' Then he proceeded on his way to X-ray. Cassie looked at Daisy, took a puff of the cigarette then turned and stubbed it out in the saucer of the cup of half-drunk tea beside the trolley-bed. She struggled to smile, grabbed Daisy's arm and together they followed.

After X-ray Guy was moved to a single room in an orthopaedic ward to await surgery on his leg. Cassie noticed the staff not only recognised him but were all taking immensely good care of him. Lily was still in surgery and it was as though the whole of Addenbrooke's was praying for her to pull through. On the desk in the reception area of the ward she noticed a newspaper showing Guy and Lily happily smiling at Shire Hall the day before. It was heartbreaking.

Stephen and Sarah, Tom and Lynda, arrived with grave faces. Daisy threw herself into her mother's arms and began to sob. With a miserable expression Guy watched for a while before turning away and lighting up another cigarette. All around were no smoking signs, but so far nobody had said anything to him.

Lynda moved to her son, putting her arms around him and

kissing his cheek. 'Guy,' was all anybody seemed to be able to say to him. Tom followed, then Stephen and Sarah.

He grabbed Sarah's hand. 'I'm so sorry. *I'm just so sorry.*'

Fighting back her own tears, she wisely said, 'Nobody's blaming you, Guy. Nobody.'

He squeezed his eyes shut. 'I shouldn't have let her drive. Why, oh why, did I let her drive?'

Stephen, worried sick because his pride and joy was now fighting for her life, looked across at him sympathetically. 'She has a will of her own, Guy, and that's why she'll pull through. Just you wait and see.'

Briefly the worry seemed to drop away from Guy's face. 'Will she? Do you really think that?'

There was a chorus of 'We all do' before the anguish returned to his face. He wasn't convinced.

After what seemed an eternity the surgeon entered the room. He looked at Guy and at the six other expectant and fearful faces. Normally he would have asked them to leave but not on this occasion. He moved towards Guy and with a practised air sat on his bed. For one moment, Cassie actually thought he was going to take Guy's hand. He didn't, of course. 'Mr Hamilton.' He paused before continuing. 'I'm so sorry. We did everything we could . . .' Guy's eyes widened in the most dreadful horror and the surgeon braced himself to continue. 'Because of the colossal impact, the pulmonary vein was torn. I'm afraid this caused massive bleeding. It was an impossible situation, just too much for her . . . we weren't able to save Lily.'

Still with a cigarette in one hand and his mouth agape, Guy raised clenched fists to his temples and started to shake his head. 'No! Dear God, *no!*'

Sarah and Stephen had to support each other and Daisy collapsed into Cassie's arms. The room was filled with agonising cries of grief. Only Guy didn't shout or scream or even look close to tears. He just sat there, staring at the surgeon, who very quietly continued to explain why Guy's wife had died on the operating table.

Chapter Forty-Six

When Keir turned on the radio in his car on Monday morning and heard the news of Lily Hamilton's tragic death, he changed direction immediately and instead of heading into London, headed out. Things hadn't been going too well for him lately, and his biggest, most ardent regret was parting company with Guy. He now realised that Guy's talent was far greater than even he'd imagined; and his own, well it could best be described as limited. The trouble was, he not only realised this himself but others around him were beginning to realise it too. Even Andy, who fancied the pants off him! And now this. Lily had died, and Keir was actually glad because it couldn't have happened at a better time. Guy would be devastated, at an all-time low – hadn't Keir seen it all before? If he was cunning enough he could slip in there, become his most supportive friend . . . which could lead to all sorts of opportunities in the future. All he needed to do was pile on the sympathy and he'd be away. He could clinch it. That was his gift. Seeing his chance and taking it.

'Have you seen them?' hissed Cassie to one of the nurses. 'They're like vultures! Why can't they just leave us in peace? The last thing Guy wants is to start giving interviews.' She raised her eyebrows at the sympathetic nurse and continued on her way to fetch more cigarettes for him. Stephen and Sarah had gone back to Ely after seeing their daughter in the Chapel of Rest and Tom and Lynda had returned with them. It was Lynda's intention to visit Guy in the afternoon. Daisy was back at the florist's. She preferred it that way. Guy didn't seem to want her around anyway. It was strange really because the person he leaned on most was

Cassie. He wasn't kind to her, not at all, he was quite brusque and rude in fact. But she would have laid down her life for him and in some ways wished she could, in place of Lily, because in the space of twenty-four hours Cassie couldn't believe her own hurt at the loss of her friend. It was worse than any other feeling she'd ever experienced. She just wanted her back, desperately, and couldn't believe she'd really gone.

As Cassie slipped down one flight of stairs, Keir alighted from the lift and shoved his way past a group of journalists and photographers who recognised him and took pictures. Carrying a bottle of malt whisky, he entered the ward and smiled at one of the nurses who also vaguely recognised him. 'Could you tell me where Guy Hamilton is, please?'

She frowned. 'Are you family? He's not seeing any visitors at all.'

Keir nodded. 'Yes, I'm a cousin. We're close. He'll see me.'

She pointed down the ward to the far end and the room on the right and Keir graciously smiled before striding towards it. The nurse watched him go.

He entered the room and was shocked by Guy's appearance. If he'd looked bad during his troubles with Naomi, it was as nothing to the devastation on his face now. His leg was in plaster from the knee down and he was lying on top of the bed, head lolling against the pillows. His face was grey and he neither moved nor showed any interest in who'd just entered the room. Tentatively Keir stepped forward and had actually placed the whisky on the locker beside the bed before Guy looked at him. Then he hitched himself up, anger welling within him.

'I know! I know!' said Keir, holding up his hands. 'I've got an almighty cheek coming here, but please, Guy, just hear me out. Please?'

Exhausted from misery and sedatives and anaesthetic and antibiotics, he slumped back against his pillows. He didn't care about anything anymore. So what if Keir was here? So what?

'I had to come. I had to tell you to your face how sorry I am.' Keir pulled up a chair and sat down, more confident now that his erstwhile friend was not going to throw him out. 'I can't imagine how you're feeling, but if there's anything, anything at all that I can do, *anything*, I will. I know you must hate me, Guy, but believe me, you don't hate me as much as I hate myself.'

Guy looked at him then and his mind went back to the last conversation he'd had with Lily about Keir. No taboos, she'd said. He looked straight ahead of himself and drew on a cigarette.

'D'you fancy a drink?' asked Keir.

Guy glanced at the whisky, thought about it and nodded. Keir broke the seal on the bottle and poured a healthy measure into two plastic beakers. He passed one to Guy who took it and knocked back the contents in one go.

'What can I say, Guy? What can I say?'

He rotated the beaker in his hand then tapped ash into it from his cigarette. 'Try . . . nothing, Keir. Nothing.'

He lowered his eyes and shook his head. 'I'd better go. How long are you in for?'

Mildly surprised, Guy looked up at him. 'Sorry?'

Keir pointed to his leg. 'How long before you can . . .' he hesitated '. . . what I mean is, before you can go home?'

Guy sucked on the cigarette and said flatly, 'Tomorrow.'

'Can I at least call and see you again? Please?'

Narrowing his eyes, Guy looked at him. 'Why? Why should you want to do that?'

Out of character, Keir thumped his fist on the bed. 'Because I care, damn you. Because I bloody care!'

Guy was surprised by his temper. Since the accident nobody had shown him anything other than kindness. In all this misery, Keir's anger helped. Only a tiny bit but it did help. He shrugged. 'Suit yourself.'

'Where are you going? What I mean is, you'll be needing help.'

'I shall go back to Ely for a while.'

'Fine. I'll come and see you there.' Keir touched his shoulder and turned to leave the room. At the door he paused and looked back. 'If I could turn back the clock for you, Guy, in more ways than one, I would. I really would.' He didn't wait for any reply, just left, but as he walked back down the ward there was smile on his face.

The funeral was planned for the following Monday and all the arrangements were being taken care of by Cassie. She called to see Guy at his parents' home every day, bringing cigarettes, and although her presence never raised a smile, she had a suspicion he actually looked forward to seeing her, though perhaps it was purely for the cigarettes. On the Friday she spotted a Jaguar sports in the drive and as she entered the kitchen noticed Lynda was making three cups of tea. Cassie knew that Tom was back at work and wondered who the extra person was. Seb had rung and sent a long, long letter, but had considerately stayed away. Perhaps it was Sarah. 'Who's the visitor?' she asked.

Lynda sighed. 'Actually it's Keir.'

Cassie was horrified. 'Keir? Keir's here? You're joking!'

Lynda shook her head. 'I'm not, Cassie. And please don't look like that. Guy needs all the friends he can get at the moment.'

'But Keir isn't a friend! He's a prime-time shit!'

Lynda looked horrified by her directness. 'I don't think he is! He seems so sorry for everything. They were good friends once, Cassie. How can *you* know anything about it?'

'I do know, Lynda. I know better than anyone!' Hadn't she seen him running his hand up Guy Hamilton's fiancée's skirt more than once, and what sort of friend did that? 'He's here to manipulate, Lynda, and he's not getting away with it!'

Lynda grabbed Cassie's arm as she moved through the house. 'You're not going to cause any trouble, are you? Please, we don't want anymore unhappiness.'

'Lynda, if we don't get rid of Keir bloody Doughty there'll be one helluva lot of trouble in the future!'

'But Guy seems to want him here.'

'Garbage! he doesn't know what he wants at the moment.' Cassie put a hand on Lynda's arm. 'Please, let me sort this out.'

Lynda couldn't help it, she just let the angry young woman have her head. Something about Cassie convinced Lynda that she had her son's best interests at heart.

'Keir.'

He turned, for some reason surprised to see Cassie Milbank standing there, and even more surprised by the overwhelming sensation of desire he still felt in her presence. Apart from the drawn look on her face, she looked gorgeous. 'Cassie.' He moved towards her with an outstretched hand. Cassie didn't even appear to notice, she just looked across the room at Guy. He sat in the same chair in front of the window, wearing the same blue jeans and grey sweatshirt he'd worn all week. His hair hadn't been washed and there was nearly a week's growth of beard on his face.

He looked awful and her heart went out to him. She crossed the room, aware of his mournful eyes on her face, and noticed just a tiny flicker of a smile. Cassie bent down and kissed his cheek. He smelt smoky, of too many cigarettes, and she wished so much he didn't smoke. All the same she handed over another packet of twenty. He didn't say thank you, just shoved them down the side of his chair. Only then did she turn again to Keir.

'My condolences, Cassie, my deepest condolences.'

She surprised him then and grabbed even Guy's attention. 'Cut the crap, Keir, for God's sake. We're not interested.'

He shrank back, eyes full of confusion. 'I–I'm sorry. I never meant to intrude.'

She walked towards him. 'Well, you are intruding, Mr Doughty. Well and truly. But you know the old saying: Fools rush in. I believe it goes on to say, Where angels . . . and all that! Well, it might interest you to know that there is an angel in this room. A real angel. And it might also interest you to know that *she doesn't want you here!* This place is for people who loved her, and people who love Guy. So to use another well-known saying – piss off!'

Guy sat with his mouth open, absolutely staggered by Cassie's vehemence. He'd never seen her so angry before. Keir retreated towards the door, mumbling something about her misunderstanding the whole situation. For one brief second Guy actually wanted to laugh. Then he remembered his agent's words. He'd predicted that one day Keir would dig himself such a hole that all they'd need to do was push him into it. Well, it was happening now, in front of his very eyes, except it was Cassie doing all the pushing. And, boy, was she pushing.

'You've got it all wrong, Cassie.' Keir looked at Guy for support. 'You understand, don't you, Guy? We were friends a long while before she came on the scene, you know we were.'

He drew on his cigarette and looked out of the window. His thoughts were elsewhere. Cassie had said there was an angel in the room and, yes, he could actually feel her presence. If he really stopped to think about it, he might be able to see her as well.

'Guy?' insisted Keir.

But Guy was having none of it and Cassie had driven Keir to the door, which she held open for him to go through. 'Goodbye. And don't come back.'

He scowled at her and helplessly looked once more towards

Guy. But he was trying his hardest to summon Lily once more, his angel. 'I'll be in touch, Guy,' Keir called out.

Guy turned then and waved his hand dismissively. 'Tell you what – don't bother.'

Cassie's eyes were on fire. 'You heard the man. *Now go.*'

Knowing he'd lost, Keir walked through the door and out of their lives.

The funeral was a simple affair, just a brief ceremony at Cambridge's Crematorium, but the press was out in force. Guy, looking smarter in a dark suit, insisted on carrying the coffin and so, with one crutch, he did, along with Stephen and Tom, Fred, Billy Hamilton Jnr, now sixteen, and Cassie's father. The small cortège that followed were hardly able to stem their weeping. It seemed that on that day it was only Guy who never shed a tear. Daisy was inconsolable.

There was an equally quiet affair back at Stephen and Sarah's bungalow in Ely, a total contrast to old Bill Hamilton's noisy wake. Cassie watched Guy through the long afternoon and seriously began to wonder if he was ever going to get over this. He was sullen, distant, unco-operative and, worse, quite rude to Daisy. Cassie couldn't understand it, and neither could Daisy.

After everybody had gone home, except for Cassie who was waiting to take Daisy back to Cambridge, something happened which was to deepen Cassie's misery for months and months to come. Guy sat in Bill Snr's old chair in the sitting room and Cassie watched Daisy gingerly walk towards him. She just wanted to comfort him, and maybe draw some comfort for herself. She knelt down and put her hand on his knee and propped her chin on the arm of the chair. 'Guy,' she said sweetly, 'I know how it hurts. I miss her so much. I never thought I had so many tears inside me.'

He looked at her, eyes dilating, before he shifted forward in his seat, the movement shoving Daisy aside. Guy struggled to find his crutches and when he did stood up. He hobbled across the room. Anxiously Daisy followed. 'Guy! Why won't you speak to me anymore?'

He turned and stared at her and his words crucified her. 'I'm sorry, Daisy, it's just I can't bear to look at your face. Don't you see? It reminds me too much of her.' Without further ado he made his way out of the bungalow and into the front garden. Cassie

342

watched a forlorn Daisy flop into the nearest chair and sob her heart out.

Foolishly perhaps she followed Guy, carefully closing the front door behind her. By this time he'd lit up yet another cigarette. Cassie bravely stood in front of him. 'What do you think you're doing, Guy? You can't talk to Daisy like that. You simply can't say those things to her.'

'Why? What difference does it make?'

She stuck her forefinger into his chest. 'She misses Lily every bit as much as you do, you idiot! Don't you realise what she's lost? Lily was the only person in this whole rotten world who really cared about her . . . and next to Lily she adores you!'

Briefly, Guy looked surprised. Then he turned away and flicked his cigarette across the lawn. 'Well, I'm sorry about that, but what I said to her is the truth.'

'It might well be the truth but you have to rise above it, Guy. For goodness' sake, take a look at yourself! Stop being such a pathetic loser and start being what Lily would have wanted you to be!'

He turned on her then and in his eyes she read outrage. 'How dare you speak to me like that? Who the hell do you think you are, Cassie Milbank? You're not even family! You come here and start throwing your weight about, ordering people around. Well, you're not ordering me around. And so, in your own words, if you don't like the way I behave, I suggest you piss off out of it along with Keir!'

His words stung, especially the coupling with Keir, but she wasn't going to back down and stood her ground. 'I can't piss off, Guy. It might interest you to know that I am needed around here whether I'm family or not – especially by Daisy. So my advice to you is, take a long hard look at yourself. And when you have, you should apologise to your sister-in-law!' She turned on her heel and went back into the house where she grabbed Daisy, said a hasty goodbye to everyone and left. It was exactly what Daisy needed. She was desperate to get away, to get back to Cambridge. She couldn't stand the misery in Ely any longer.

Out of the corner of his eye Guy watched them go and maybe felt a twinge of guilt along with the anger that consumed him. But quite honestly he didn't care. Not a jot. His life was finished. Over. Lily's death meant the end of everything.

Epilogue

Chapter Forty-Seven

But it wasn't really the end of everything for Guy because time
and love can ease the worst pain. Two years later he found himself
once again in the Hayward Theatre in Ely, only this time to
celebrate Billy Hamilton Jnr's eighteenth birthday. He watched
the young man with his pretty girlfriend dancing around the floor
and was instantly transported back in time to a vision of such
incredible beauty he now knew it would stay with him forever.
For a long while Guy sat reflecting upon Lily dancing with Billy
all those years ago, and although the pain still cut deep into his
heart, his long slow haul to recovery was now underway.

He watched the antics of family and friends around him, sitting
back in his seat and sipping his beer. His eyes shifted to and fro,
he was enjoying himself. Of all things – Guy actually enjoying a
Hamilton party! Well, life has a way of surprising you. Or maybe
people do. Like Sebastian Turner. He'd eventually dragged Guy
back to London and the thrills of television, and did his best to
ignore his son's death-wish antics in cars, boats and planes
because he knew it was a passing phase.

Continually now Guy looked towards the double doors of the
Hayward Theatre until they opened and Daisy walked in. He
sighed with delight because in her arms she carried the most
precious thing, a three-month-old baby boy. Daisy looked across
the room and her face lit into a wondrous smile. So did Guy's. She
pointed, saying, 'There's Daddy, Daniel. See, over there? There's
Daddy.' The cherubic child with his father's blond hair and his
mother's blue eyes held out his hand and cooed in delight. Daisy
walked towards Guy and carefully handed over his son.

He sat Daniel on his knee and ran his hand gently across his soft downy hair. 'What have you been doing then?' The child clutched his daddy as Guy rubbed his cheek against his hair. 'You should be in bed.' Then with one swift movement he held Daniel high in his arms and the baby gurgled with delight – his daddy often did this and he liked it. 'It's *way* past your bedtime.' Guy sat the child on his knee once more and looked quickly around. 'Where's Mummy? Where's she gone? Where's your mummy?' He nuzzled his son. 'Mummy's not here. She's gone again. Naughty Mummy. Doesn't she know we need her?' Daniel cooed in delight at the attention he was receiving and clapped his hands, then jiggled about until Guy stood him on his lap which was a much better position for grabbing a handful of hair. Guy winced at the child's sharp tug and turned to release his hair – and that was when he caught sight of her. He watched for a few seconds, noting the glow on her face. Suddenly a lump came into his throat. How poignant it all was. To be back here in the Hayward Theatre like this with his son – how terribly poignant. His mind drifted back to those black days, merely a year ago . . .

He knocked on the door. The girl who'd answered the phone had assured him Daisy and Cassie would be at home this evening. He knocked again, louder this time. It had taken a whole year for him to pluck up the courage to return to Cambridge and visit them. Seeing Cassie again didn't bother him but Daisy – she was different. He still didn't know if he could stand the pain of looking at her face. It reminded him so very, very much of Lily's. Finally the door was pulled back and Daisy stood before him.

'Guy!' She blinked in surprise and took a step backwards. She was hardly recognisable. Gone was the forlorn creature of Lily's funeral. She positively exuded happiness.

'Guy!' she said again, then called out, 'Cassie! It's Guy.' She gazed at him. 'I didn't know you were coming, Guy. I wouldn't have been going out if I'd known you were coming.'

He shuffled his feet in embarrassment. 'Well, that's all right, I don't intend to stay long, but can I come in for a moment?'

She moved back into the kitchen, welcoming him in. 'Of course, come in.' As soon as he stepped over the threshold she rushed her words. 'I've got a date, you see. With Harry. Do you remember Harry? He was the porter at . . .' Daisy's hand flew to her mouth. 'Oh, no, I shouldn't have said that. I'm sorry.' Dismayed, she looked around her. 'Oh, dear, where's Cassie?' Daisy flew across the kitchen and practically bumped into Cassie as she entered. Guy just stood there, bemused, watching the interaction between the two women, naggingly reminded of a time not so long ago when there used to be three. He felt a strong urge to turn tail and leave. This wasn't going to be easy. How could he ever have thought it would be?

Calmly Cassie advanced across the kitchen to him. In the back of his mind he noticed a change in her; the light had gone out of her eyes and she was thinner, much thinner. But all this didn't really register until much later because he was only concentrating on himself and getting over the next hurdle of apologising to Daisy for his appalling behaviour at Lily's funeral. Cassie stood up on tiptoes to kiss him on both cheeks. 'Guy,' she said softly. 'How lovely to see you.' He closed his eyes and inhaled her scent. She always smelled the same. Inviting. A bit like Lily really. She'd always smelled inviting.

'I should have come before . . .' His voice cracked. 'But I just couldn't.'

All three of them pricked up their ears at the sound of car tyres on the drive outside. Hardly able to keep the excitement out of her face, Daisy said delightedly, 'That'll be Harry.' She turned then and left the kitchen to fetch her coat and handbag. Cassie smiled at Guy.

'Daisy's in love. A porter at the hospital. Nice chap.' She chuckled. 'And, believe me, he's potty about her. She's happy, Guy. Lily would have been so pleased.'

Grief flashed across his face and Cassie wished she'd kept quiet. But then again, if they were ever to get through this, it was best to be open and honest. Daisy returned and looked from Cassie to Guy. 'You don't mind if I go, do you, Guy?'

He swallowed hard and moved towards her, kissing her cheek affectionately. 'Of course I don't. I'm so happy for you, Daisy. Lily . . . well, she would have loved to see you like this.' Daisy opened her mouth to say something but Guy stopped her by pressing two fingers over her lips. She noticed they smelled smoky. There was a knock on the door and he rushed on, 'I came to apologise, Daisy, for saying all those things to you at the funeral. I hurt you deeply and I can't forgive myself. I'm really sorry.'

'Oh, Guy, you don't need to apologise. I'd forgotten all about that now.'

Guy smiled, realising she most likely had. It crossed his mind that it was only fools who suffered regret for things it was impossible to change. He watched as Daisy opened the back door to Harry, and he leaned forward and waved to Cassie, and then both of them were gone, closing the door behind them.

'Daisy doesn't understand the importance of introductions, Guy, but she does mean well.'

'I know she does. I'm just so relieved to see her happy.'

Cassie smiled and Guy noticed the tight lines around her mouth. It registered then how drawn and tired she looked. 'Can I offer you a drink?' she asked. 'Or do you need to get on your way?'

It had been his intention to make this a fleeting visit, but suddenly he didn't want to rush away. Maybe it was the departure of Daisy – the sight of her still perturbed him – but perhaps it was more to do with the calming effect Cassie had on him and he wanted some of that right now. 'I'd love a drink.' Then he touched her arm. 'Better still, are you doing anything tonight? How about dinner? I haven't eaten all day. I could murder a Chinese.'

She was tempted to say 'Full circle' but didn't. 'No, I'm not doing anything. There's one down the road, it's not bad, and we could walk if you like?'

He nodded and smiled, the smile almost reaching his eyes for the first time that evening. 'Yes,' he said, 'I'd like that.'

Afterwards he asked if she minded if he smoked. Cassie shook her head. 'Go ahead.'

He lit up, blew out the smoke and looked at the cigarette between his fingers. 'I'm trying to give this up.' He attempted a smile. 'Not easy.'

Cassie reflected how different he was. Time without Lily had taken its toll. He no longer smiled so readily, but then again neither did she. She missed Lily more than she'd ever have believed possible. Strangely enough, Daisy had got over it all relatively easily, but perhaps that was something to do with Harry replacing Lily in her affections. 'Sometimes we need all the props we can get, Guy.'

His eyes sought hers. 'Is that what it is, a prop?'

'Maybe.'

'And you? Do you have any props?'

Cassie exhaled between her teeth, making a hissing noise, then shrugged. 'I think the shop is my prop. And Daisy of course. She's blossomed so much and is a joy to watch. We finally bought the shop off Mrs Sniffnel you know. The money from selling Lily's business paid for it. Daisy and I now own it fifty-fifty and it works very well.' Cassie lowered her eyes, 'But I never thought it would be Daisy I'd be so involved with, not Lily.'

Guy could see her heartache. It was easy when you knew what to look for. 'You miss her a lot, don't you?'

'All the time. She was a beacon of light in my life. Even though—'

Guy raised his eyebrows. 'Yes? Even though what?'

Tears sprang into Cassie's eyes and she looked up at the ceiling in an attempt to stop them spilling down her face. When she was sure they wouldn't, she looked at him and chuckled, 'Even though she had you. What I mean is, even though she had happiness with you and I didn't have happiness with anyone.'

Guy frowned. 'But you're beautiful. There must be loads of men in your life?'

Cassie tilted her head from side to side. 'One or two. No one I let get close, though.'

Concern filled his face. 'But you're okay now?'

She knew he was referring to her uncle's abuse of her as a child. 'Most of the time.' She grinned. 'I did get some counselling, you know. It really helped.'

'Good.' He snorted. 'Maybe that's what I need now.'

Cassie leaned her elbows on the table. 'But you looked great in the second series of *Top Speed*. As though you hadn't a care in the world?'

He guffawed. 'Yeah, well, you can lose yourself in speed. Hopefully forever.'

'Oh, Guy, don't say that. That's the last thing Lily would have wanted.'

He lowered his eyes, his whole face even, then raised it again and drew heavily on his cigarette. 'It just doesn't get any bloodier easier, Cassie. In fact it gets worse. I swear it gets worse.'

She sighed. 'You know, you didn't have to come back here

today, Guy. You didn't have to put yourself through all this. We did understand. We never blamed you for anything.'

'But I did, don't you see? What you said to me about Daisy suffering as much as me . . . well, I just added to her suffering, and however I looked at it I couldn't forgive myself. Still can't, even though I see now that she's perfectly all right. It just makes the whole thing worse because I behaved so bloody appallingly. To you too, Cassie, after you took so much care of me. I just threw it all back in your face. I mean, can you forgive that? Can you ever forgive me?'

She grabbed his hand and squeezed it. 'Nothing to forgive, Guy.'

For a second he held on to her hand and Cassie watched his fingers wrap around hers. She took a deep breath when he pulled his hand away because it was like losing him again. 'Are you ready?' Guy asked.

He meant to leave. Sadness overwhelmed her. He'd be gone in a while and she'd have nothing again. Her life was about having nothing – apart from flowers that is. And there's only so much pleasure you can get from looking at flowers. 'Ready when you are.'

Later, they approached her house, she asked, 'Are you staying in Cambridge tonight?'

'No, I think I'll get back to London. I live with Seb at the moment. Remember him?'

'Of course. Lily told me all about him.'

'He's been fantastic. Seems like I found him just at the right time. God knows where I'd be now without him. And it's better living in Fulham. Not so many memories.'

'It's funny because Lily always talked about living in London. But I'd hate it. I like Cambridge. Always have.'

They walked round to the back of the house and Cassie watched as Guy approached his car. 'Thank you, Guy, for this evening. I really have enjoyed it.'

He turned and put both hands on her shoulders. 'So have I, Cassie. You're good to talk to.'

She swallowed hard then braced herself. 'Would you like to come in? Horlicks, coffee, hot chocolate, brandy?'

He smiled, 'No. I'll pass if you don't mind.'

She moved towards him then and once again reached up to kiss his cheek. Inadvertently he moved and their lips brushed. It was like slow motion. Cassie held her lips against his and he made no attempt to stop her. Then she drew back. 'Bye, Guy. See you sometime.' She walked towards her back door, took a key from her pocket and went inside without so much as a backward glance.

Guy watched her, his insides churning and his head filled with strange thoughts. For the first time in over a year he'd felt the need to hold someone. And to be held. If Cassie had drawn him into her arms then, he'd never have let her go. And then he felt disloyal and climbed into his car and immediately revved up the engine.

He was about to reverse, but stopped. The feeling was simply too overpowering. Instead he climbed out again, zapped the lock with his key and walked up to the back door of the house, knocking once more. She was obviously just standing there, waiting for him to go because it opened in seconds. Framed in the doorway, Cassie looked at him but said nothing. Guy stepped over the threshold and into her arms.

It was like everything, with wisdom, he'd grown to hate, pounding himself into her. But she responded, damn her, and that made it all the more exciting.

For several minutes it was a monumental release of all his tension, all his misery and all his fears and even as he climaxed he wanted to keep hammering away at her. His technique, laboriously taught by Jane Richardson, went by the wayside, but he knew that Cassie derived as much satisfaction as he did. It was as though they were both taking out their anger at Lily's death on each other.

Exhausted, he slumped back on the pillow beside her and it was only then that intense guilt at such a betrayal of his young wife's memory came pouring into his senses. He turned and looked at the woman lying beside him and in that instant blamed her. Immediately he clambered off the bed, dressed and only then did he turn to speak. 'I'll be in touch,' was all he said, but Guy had no intention of being in touch.

Cassie didn't attempt to stop him. She just turned on her side, curled her spent body into the foetal position and wept.

Chapter Forty-Eight

Five months later and still Guy couldn't get Cassie out of his mind. Indeed, he felt he had something else to apologise for now. But no way could he go back because he feared the same thing might happen all over again. Surely the memory of Lily was worth more than that?

It was actually an invitation to Daisy's wedding that gave him the opportune moment to speak to Cassie without actually having to visit her. He could have picked up the phone, and did, many times, but always replaced it before he dialled the number. How can you apologise to someone over the phone for taking advantage of them?

It was a white wedding with the reception held in Ely's Lamb Hotel. Everybody was well wrapped up against a particularly cold snap in February and it was Guy's intention to leave as soon as he was able. His parents had begged him to stay the night with them, but he just wanted to get back to London. Daisy looked the picture of health and happiness, almost beautiful really, and he was able to watch her now without feeling too much pain. But it was Cassie who really caught his eye. She'd changed, put on weight, looked wonderful in fact. He couldn't stop staring at her in the church. She reminded him again of the young girl he'd first seen arranging flowers in Benson's Garage off the Hills Road, except Cassie was someone who would only improve with age. She looked gorgeous.

'Cassie,' he said, grabbing a spare seat next to her at the reception.

She faced him then and her violet eyes sparkled. 'Guy, how

nice you could come. Daisy's thrilled you're here. She's told everybody about her famous cousin.'

He reached into his pocket for his cigarettes. 'Do you mind?'

'Not at all.'

'I still need my prop, I'm afraid.' He looked at her as he spoke and caught the nuance in her eyes. 'Something's happened, hasn't it, Cassie? You've changed. You seem so happy somehow. Is there a man in your life?'

'No. No man. But you're right, I am happy.'

Guy sucked on his cigarette, wondering why he felt such a sense of relief at the lack of a man in Cassie's life. 'But you're not going to tell me why?'

She hesitated then lowered her eyes. 'I would if you took me somewhere private. Actually it's long overdue, Guy. Something you should know. Something you have a right to know.'

He looked totally confounded. 'About Lily?'

Cassie shook her head. 'Not this time. This is about me. And you.'

He hadn't a clue what she was talking about. 'Where's private?'

She stood up and waved her hand towards the door. 'I'll show you.' He followed, inhaling her scent as he did so.

It was a small sitting room at the front of the hotel. Guy sat down next to Cassie. He stubbed out his cigarette and sat back, allowing his eyes to rest on her face. 'First of all, before you tell me whatever it is you're going to tell me, I have something long overdue to say to you.'

Her face clouded over and she reached forward and covered his mouth with her hand. 'Don't, Guy! Please. If it's what I think you're going to say, you'd offend me beyond measure.'

Worry lines crinkled his drawn face. 'I don't understand? What is this, Cassie? Bloody hell, you're not pregnant, are you?'

She let out a laugh and he knew he was right. His mouth dropped open. It was like being hit with a sledge-hammer. He slumped back in his seat and just stared at her, and all the time she was smiling. 'Please, Guy, don't look like that. I want nothing from you. Nothing at all.'

'Cassie! How can you sit there and say that? For Christ's sake, this is my child you're talking about!'

She covered his mouth with her hand again and he was tempted to bite it, but no, he didn't want to bite it, he wanted to kiss it, so he did. He turned it over and held the palm against his mouth.

'Guy, don't speak so loudly. Nobody knows, I promise. Nobody.'

He lowered her hand. 'Not even Daisy?'

She shook her head. 'Not even Daisy. When I knew she was getting married, I hoped I'd see you. Believe it or not, I've only just started to put on weight.'

'I do believe it, and you look gorgeous. It suits you.'

She licked her lips. 'So you're not . . . angry?'

He sighed. 'How can I be angry? I seem to remember I'm responsible.' He squeezed her hand. 'In fact, I don't know what I feel. I need time to think about it. Why didn't you tell me before?'

'Because you would have hated it and I so want this baby, Guy.' She prodded her stomach. 'At the time this little babe was conceived you were in no fit state to take on something like this. But, don't you see, it was meant to be? I can't tell you how I prayed to be pregnant. I've got something in *my* life now. Something to live for. And I don't give a damn what anybody else thinks. It's my baby and nobody can take it away from me.'

Taking a deep breath, Guy kissed her hand again. 'I'm pleased, Cassie. It's funny, I have this wonderful feeling of calm enveloping me, as though this is right, just as you said. As though this was meant to happen. But it doesn't stop me wanting to apologise for the way the little babe, as you call him, was conceived. I shouldn't have just walked away, it was wrong of me.'

'It might be a her! And actually I think he or she was conceived rather wonderfully. You can think what you like, but you awakened something in me that night I didn't know existed. Guy, if I never have that again for as long as I live I won't be sad, because you made me complete and you gave me my baby.'

He pulled her to him then and kissed the top of her head then tilted her chin, raising her face to his. He kissed her lips gently. 'I can't marry you, Cassie, you do know that? Marriage and me just don't suit.'

She stroked his face. 'Guy, I don't want you to marry me. I just want you to be pleased for me.'

'But I do want to be a part of it. You will let me be part of it?'

'Guy, I'd love you to be part of it.'

*

356

And he was. He saw her as often as he could and was there at the birth of Daniel. In fact, when the midwife placed his baby son in his arms, tears came to his eyes. Cassie knew then that this was right. Surely Lily would understand.

They moved in together. Lynda and Tom, Stephen and Sarah, were all delighted. Nobody cast any shadow of doubt on the whole affair, not even the tiniest bit. Guy and Cassie found a lovely house on the outskirts of Cambridge, close to the M11, and he would shoot off to London or wherever, and Cassie would take Daniel to the shop with her. Sometimes Guy would linger as he left in the morning, turning to watch the woman he now loved holding his son, framed in the doorway. And then fear would seep into his bones. Fear of losing them. Would he ever rid himself of it? If only he could rid himself of it. Then perhaps he could marry Cassie.

Guy's thoughts were brought back to here and now and the Hayward Theatre. From behind arms went around his neck and the scent of her hair mingled with all the other delightful smells she always exuded. She kissed Guy's cheek, murmuring, 'You okay?' And when he nodded she tweaked Daniel's. 'Are you being a good boy then? Did Aunt Daisy take good care of you?'

Still firmly holding on to his precious son, Guy pulled Cassie round in front of him, drinking in her presence. She smiled in her special way and kissed his cheek again. 'Shall I take him?' she whispered.

Guy shook his head. 'Nope. He's fine where he is.' He looked up at her. 'Unless you'd like me to get you a drink?'

She laughed. 'I think I can manage that by myself.' And then she was gone, strolling across the floor towards the bar at the end of the hall, her luxuriant blonde hair swishing around her shoulders. Guy's eyes hardly left her retreating figure, not for a second, until she struck up a conversation with his mother and eventually became obscured from view.

'Have you seen Cassie?'

Guy looked up at Daisy then inclined his head towards the bar. 'She's over there. 'Daisy's eyes swept across the room. So similar to Lily's, yet really not at all the same. He could bear to look at her now, sometimes he'd even stare, and if Daisy turned quickly and caught him doing it, she'd smile and look sad all at the same time, knowing exactly what he was thinking. But tonight Daisy looked particularly radiant because she too was pregnant. Guy contemplated the lustre on her skin and the glow in her eyes, only too aware that it was she who would provide the much desired grandchildren for Stephen and Sarah – not his beloved Lily.

His eyes moved from Daisy to Cassie who was returning with a glass of white wine. She smiled first at him, then Daisy, and then at her son. Daisy grabbed her friend's arm. 'Cassie, when do you think Harry and I should make our announcement?'

'Later, Daisy, when everyone has eaten. And don't forget, this is Billy's birthday party.'

Daisy's eyes flicked across the room to Harry who was busy talking to his father-in-law. 'Oh, yes, I haven't forgotten that, but do we have to wait 'til then? I really want to tell everybody now.'

Cassie smiled. 'I think they already know, Daisy. I'm afraid your mum is more excited about it than you are!'

Daisy looked down at Daniel who was being jigged on Guy's knee and grabbed his hand. 'And then you'll have a playmate, won't you, Daniel?'

Cassie winked at Guy and they both watched as Daisy walked off towards the bar and her mother. 'She's so happy,' whispered Cassie.

Guy reached up for her hand. 'Sit down here with me for a while.' Cassie pulled up a chair and sat down, leaning towards him and all the while touching her son. 'You're happy too, aren't you?' Guy asked.

She faced him. 'Of course I am . . . aren't you?'

He sighed. 'More than I'd have believed possible.'

Cassie stroked Daniel's cheek. 'And Lily would have loved you, you little tinker. She would have thought you a bit of all right!'

Guy pushed his hand through Cassie's hair and looked into her eyes. 'And she would have thought you a bit of all right as well. She loved you too, Cassie. You do know that?'

Cassie's eyes clouded over. 'But would she have forgiven me?'

'For what?'

'Daring to try and step into her shoes?'

Guy chuckled. 'Oh, yes. I'm pretty sure about that. I think she would definitely have wanted *you* to walk in her shoes. No one else.'

Cassie bit her lip. 'I'm doing okay then? I'm not making too much of a hash of it?'

He pulled her closer and kissed her gently on the mouth. 'I love you. That says it all.'

Tears were in her eyes now. 'I still miss her. Like crazy. I know you must too.'

He swallowed hard. 'But I've got you now, Cassie.' He smiled, hugging his son more tightly and drawing the three of them closer. 'She's in our hearts, she always will be . . . but I've got you now.'

Love & Lies
Chrissa Mills

Who knows what secrets lie behind closed doors?

A newcomer to the village of Great Chessden, artist Justine Donaldson is fascinated by the old manor house, Tixover Grange, and its inhabitants, the hot-tempered Bettina Lamb and her wayward daughter Jacinth. She is also completely disarmed by Bettina's nephew Charles.

Justine's boyfriend George, the Lamb's gamekeeper, tells her of the bad blood between Bettina and Charles. But as Justine falls into Charles' confidence she finds herself torn between the two men.

Then, to Justine's secret chagrin, Charles appears as susceptible to his cousin Jacinth's charms as the next man. Has he been deceiving her all along or is there an ulterior motive behind this startling mismatch?

'Chrissa has a knack of getting...readers involved to the extent that we need need to know what happens next'

Cambridge Evening News

Matilda's Last Waltz
Tamara McKinley

An Australian epic novel in the tradition of *The Thornbirds*

Churinga sheep-station in the Australian Outback is a parting gift from Jenny's husband – a legacy she only learns about after his tragic death. With nowhere else to turn for comfort she makes her way there to find a harsh, unforgiving place but with its own quiet beauty.

It also has its secrets. Jenny's new neighbours seem reluctant to talk about Matilda Thomas, Churinga's former owner. But the longer Jenny spends on the farm, the more she is aware of her predecessor's lingering presence.

Then she discovers Matilda's diaries and finds herself drawn into a tale more shocking than she could possibly have imagined. And the deeper she delves into the past, the more Jenny wonders whether inheriting Churinga is a blessing or a curse...

'most noteworthy are its sympathetic heroine, and the account of life in the Australian Outback which is vivid and unsentimental'   Beryl Kingston

'A marvel of inventiveness, the characters throbbing with life...Australia is vividly portrayed. A terrific read.'
Anne Worboys

The very best of Piatkus fiction is now available in paperback as well as hardcover. Piatkus paperbacks, where *every* book is special.

☐ 0 7499 3145 0	Love & Lies	Chrissa Mills	£5.99
☐ 0 7499 3184 1	Matilda's Last Waltz	Tamara McKinley	£5.99
☐ 0 7499 3174 X	Kilkenny Bay	Avis Randall	£5.99
☐ 0 7499 3166 3	Moving to the Country	Anna Cheska	£6.99
☐ 0 7499 3172 8	Between Husbands & Friends	Nancy Thayer	£6.99
☐ 0 7499 3151 5	A Lazy Eye	Jacqueline Jacques	£5.99
☐ 0 7499 3162 0	Another Man's Child	June Francis	£5.99

The prices shown above were correct at the time of going to press. However, Piatkus Books reserve the right to show new retail prices on covers which may differ from those previously advertised in the text or elsewhere.

Piatkus Books will be available from your bookshop or newsagent, or can be ordered from the following address:

Piatkus Paperbacks, PO Box 11, Falmouth, TR10 9EN

Alternatively you can fax your order to this address on 01326 374 888 or e-mail us at books@barni.avel.co.uk

Payments can be made as follows: Sterling cheque, Eurocheque, postal order (payable to Piatkus Books) or by credit card, Visa/Mastercard. Do not send cash or currency. UK and B.F.P.O. customers should allow £1.00 postage and packing for the first book, 50p for the second and 30p for each additional book ordered to a maximum of £3.00 (7 books plus).

Overseas customers, including Eire, allow £2.00 for postage and packing for the first book, plus £1.00 for the second and 50p for each subsequent title ordered.

NAME (block letters)_____

ADDRESS _____

_____

I enclose my remittance for £_____

I wish to pay by Visa/Mastercard   Expiry Date _____
